Shadows On The Wall

Bonar Ash

Lutestring Press

Chapter 1

Unexplained laughter

The study door opened and Patrick called out, 'Nell, go and see what's going on, will you? Your mother wants to get the car out and some silly ass is blocking the drive.'

'Okay.'

Nelly felt the usual squiggle of pleasure at the sound of her stepfather's voice. She never minded doing things for him. She liked the way he never panicked, was always so chill. Except when a deadline was looming, he got a bit tetchy then, but anybody would. She wondered sometimes if that was what she liked most about him, the way he was always so cool. It was such a relief after the way Papa had been.

She felt a twinge of guilt: it was funny how you could love a person but be terrified of them all the same. You never had to worry that Patrick was going to fly into a rage and shout at you; he never lost his temper, never. The most she had ever seen him get was slightly rattled, and that was with her mother Sonia, needless to say.

It being Saturday, Patrick had come in from the shed for his elevenses, which he never did on weekdays; and he'd be around at lunchtime too, instead of taking his sandwiches into the shed as he usually did. Things were much perkier when Patrick was coming to the end of a book. When this last book had been brewing they'd hardly seen him at all and life at home had been boring in the extreme. Things had been so God-awful, what with her mother having depression all over the place and Patrick nowhere to be seen, she'd seriously considered leaving home.

She looked out of the window. The man was still there, sitting at the wheel of his car. He'd been there for ages. Perhaps he was dead? But people didn't die in parked cars in the middle of Roehampton, did they? It wasn't like home. If this was St. Colombe the chances of his being dead would be pretty high, actually. She felt the usual pang of homesickness. She could hear her mother muttering to herself upstairs on the landing. She wished she wouldn't jabber away to herself like that, panicking as usual, she sounded completely barmy. Patrick had talked her into going to pick up the new cook from Richmond station and she hadn't stopped moaning about it since.

Nelly wiped her hands on her jeans and sloped to the front door. She pulled back her shoulders as she passed the study door and glanced inside. ('Posture is what counts in a woman,' she'd once heard Patrick say. 'Size and shape are irrelevant.') Patrick was standing by the window, his dark head jutting forward to see better, his spectacles dangling from one hand. She liked the way he stood gracefully balanced on one hip as though there was all the time in the world, as though he was at the races or something.

Patrick peered through the window. 'Daft place to leave a car.'

Sonia came belting down the stairs into the hall, panicking as usual. 'I'm going to be late for this damned train. Where the devil are the car keys?'

Nelly opened the front door and sashayed slowly down the drive, self-conscious in her new blue jeans. If Patrick had still been at the window he'd have been able to admire her back view in her new peasant top and hopefully appreciate her small waist and sexy walk, but as it was, she could hear his voice in the hall, calming darling Sonia down. Attention-seeking as usual; her mother never stopped.

Still, the front door was open; he might possibly be watching. With what she hoped was a graceful movement she pulled a sprig from the rosemary bush as she passed and held it to her nose. She didn't know why she wanted her stepfather to approve of her so much. It wasn't as if she fancied him or anything, it was more that it was so important that he went on liking them, her and her brother Alain, and more importantly Sonia who sometimes seemed to be doing her best to drive him away. She and Patrick had only been married for two years, for God's sake. If she would only go back to being nice to him like she was when they first met, Nelly felt she might be able to relax, but since her mother had come home from the hospital she seemed to have stopped bothering. If she kept on behaving like this they'd be out on the street again before you could say jack knife, and then where would they be? It wasn't fair. What about Nelly and Alain? What about them?

The car, a new-looking black Saab, was parked right across the entrance to the drive. Through the tinted glass Nelly could see the shadowy figure of the man behind the wheel. She walked round to the driver's side and tapped on the glass. 'Excuse me.'

The window slid down so he must have heard, but he

ignored her and kept right on staring through the windscreen as though he couldn't have been less interested. Sinister, Nelly thought. And rude.

'Excuse me,' she said again, a good deal more loudly. 'My mother wants to get her car out and you're blocking our drive.' She'd intended to woo him with her sweetest tones on the principle that it wouldn't do Patrick any harm to see her making a hit with a strange man, but if this was how he was going to behave, he could forget it.

Her first impression of him was that he was pretty buff: late twenties maybe, with good features and clean-looking, light-brown hair, long, with sideburns. He turned his head slowly and looked at her and their eyes met. His were an unusual golden brown. Instantly the insane thought crossed her mind that he might think her thighs, on a level now with his nose, were too fat. Then something leapt out of his eyes and penetrated her soul, and she forgot about her thighs and felt terrified suddenly. She took a step backwards into the road.

'Careful.' He had a light, pleasant voice with an accent which sounded a bit French. Or Spanish. Not English, anyway. 'Might be a car coming.'

Her mother could be heard revving up in the garage. The electric door rose slowly.

Patrick came briskly down the drive. 'I do wish she'd wait till the door opens, I keep telling her.' He bent down and looked through the nearside window as though curious to see who it was causing all this fuss. 'Do move along, there's a good chap. My wife's got to go out and you're blocking her exit.'

The man turned his head to look at Patrick so that all Nelly could see now was the back of his head. There was a spatter of dandruff on the collar of his dark blue jacket. Nelly saw his shoulders begin to shake. She recoiled with a thrill of discomfiture. He was crying.

Patrick frowned and stood up suddenly. The man turned to face the front again and Nelly saw with a slight shock that he wasn't crying but laughing. His shoulders quivering helplessly, he leaned forward and switched on the engine. The car moved off. Patrick and Nelly gazed after it. An arm emerged from the window and he waved, familiarly, as though to friends.

'What a weirdo,' Nelly said in an awed voice.

Sonia's blue Renault shot backwards down the drive and set off in the same direction as the black Saab. Sonia didn't bother to wave; she didn't give them a backward glance. It was if she didn't belong to them.

Patrick was writing down the Saab's registration number in the notebook he always carried with him. He stopped writing and looked at Nelly. 'Did you see his eyes? There was something horribly unnerving about his eyes.' He put the notebook back in his jacket pocket. 'I'll use that. It might be just what I'm looking for at the moment.'

Nelly looked at him, hoping for reassurance. 'Perhaps he's escaped from the mental hospital?'

Patrick patted her shoulder. 'He didn't look that bad. Still,' — he turned back towards the house — 'he was odd, wasn't he?'

They walked back to the house together, Nelly for once hardly aware of Patrick walking beside her. She was too busy trying to remember where she had seen the man before.

. . .

CHARLOTTE, standing outside the entrance to Richmond station as instructed by her potential employer over the phone, listened to her train pulling out with a sense of bridges being burned.

For the umpteenth time that day the thought of her erstwhile husband Riley came into her head, accompanied by the usual feeling of vulnerability. She looked around, frowning. She was supposed to be being met, but she couldn't see anyone looking as though they might be on the lookout for her. It was rush hour on a warm May evening and judging by the traffic surging past through the fume-filled air, whoever was coming to meet her was going to be late.

The pavement was crowded and her two battered brown leather suitcases were, despite her best endeavours, getting in everybody's way. She did wish whoever was supposed to be meeting her would get a move on. Bending double, she hauled the cases back inside the station entrance and resigned herself to wait.

'Charlotte Barber?'

Charlotte turned. In front of her stood a tallish, slight woman with short, dark hair and a sad expression. The woman smiled but the smile somehow made her look sadder still. She had indigo shadows under her eyes and a sallow complexion but she was nevertheless, Charlotte thought, quite as stunning as when she had seen her at the interview.

'Sonia Carey,' the woman reminded her, holding out her hand. 'Nice to see you again.'

She had a slight accent, foreign, not immediately identifiable to Charlotte but intriguing and exotic. The hand she extended was cool and dry and pleasant to touch. There were gold bracelets around her wrist and a gold watch and two gold rings, one set with an amethyst. Her nails were unexpectedly imperfect, unvarnished and several of them bitten to the quick. She looked as if she might be in her early thirties.

'The car is over here.' She turned to lead the way.

Charlotte followed, her heavy cases banging painfully against her legs. Admiring the slim, khaki-clad thighs and small behind weaving its way through the crowd, she felt more and more intimidated. She'd look terrible in trousers like that, she'd look like the back view of a hippo. The trousers were topped by a pale, coffee-coloured short-sleeved top in some kind of silky material. Charlotte felt home-spun in her simple, pale-green cotton dress which she'd liked when she first left Marjorie's flat two hours before.

Since leaving Riley she had been staying with Marjorie in the Portobello Road. Marjorie, who taught at a comprehensive in Ladbrooke Grove and whom Charlotte had known since primary school, was convinced Charlotte's taking this job was a bad idea. 'It's a huge commitment, Lotty,' she'd remarked.

She'd started abbreviating Charlotte's name without encouragement or permission shortly after Charlotte's arrival in the flat, and the fact that she put up with this impertinence caused Charlotte to despise herself a good deal. She kept trying to pluck up the courage to object but the longer she left it the more impossible it became. She made a point of addressing Marjorie by her full name, hoping the penny would drop, but in vain. 'If you don't like it when you get there,' Marjorie said, 'then for heaven's sake, leave. Don't whatever you do put up with second best now you've only just got out of the last rotten set-up. You've escaped. This is your new life. For goodness' sake do something that makes you happy, don't just throw it away on the first thing that happens along.'

Of course she wouldn't; she wasn't a complete moron. In any case, although she didn't say so because she didn't know Marjorie well enough, she felt that she hadn't so much escaped as been dismissed; but now looking back it did seem a kind of escape in that it was certainly true that now she was her own mistress again, answerable to nobody, at least not until her job started officially tomorrow morning; and it was indeed a huge relief not to have to feel guilty all the time because her husband was dissatisfied with her.

She still couldn't believe the way Riley had rounded on her. 'I've given you enough warning, God knows,' he'd admonished her, cold as a judge. 'I've requested that you lose some weight. I've told you I don't like the way you do your hair. The way you dress is a joke. I'm ashamed to be seen out with you, if you really want to know.'

She had looked at him, appalled. Of course, after quite a short while she realised that the truth was that there was somebody else, had been for quite some time, and what Riley actually wanted was a divorce. She'd been dumbfounded. What an idiot, she reproached herself during the weeks that followed, feeling hurt and made a fool of. She got on with making arrangements for their separation, working out where she was going to live and what on, since she didn't feel like accepting any alimony payments, and Riley went on going on about her looks and her weight.

The weight had started to pile on after the loss of their baby, stillborn more than five years before, and she just hadn't been able to lose it again. She'd tried and tried, this diet and that. Weight Watchers was the only thing that did any good but as soon as she stopped going it crept back on again. She went to the doctor for slimming pills but they made her feel sick. What didn't help was that Riley so enjoyed his food; indeed he often used to say, she had supposed in fun, that her being such a marvellous cook had been the main reason he had married her in the first place. Crumbs, what fools we are when we're young, Charlotte thought, hurrying to catch up.

Mrs Carey was opening the boot of a sky-blue metallic Renault Clio. She indicated Charlotte's bags. 'These will go in here. Is that really all you've got?'

Charlotte nodded. 'I thought when Autumn comes, I'll buy a new winter coat; mine's getting a bit past it. That's if I'm still here, of course.' This sounded as though she was unreliable so she gave a little laugh and said, 'I mean if you still want me,' which sounded pathetic, so she stopped trying and climbed into the front passenger seat, feeling exhausted.

Mrs Carey, looking as though she hadn't been listening, got into the driver's seat and started the engine. Charlotte began to feel that Mrs Carey was not a very comfortable sort of person to be with and that conversation was going to be difficult. She soon realised however that Mrs Carey was one of those drivers who like to concentrate in silence. Deeply thankful, she used the respite from having to talk, to do some surreptitious deep breathing to calm herself down, and to marshal her thoughts.

The sound of gravel rasping under the wheels and the sudden swing to the right as the car turned into the Careys' driveway brought her to herself with a feeling of great surprise. She had no idea how they had got there. She'd been miles away in Caterham, sitting out on the lawn with Riley. They must have been more or less happy once? She spent quite a lot of time trying to remember when.

'Here we are. I have released the boot.' Mrs Carey

opened the car door, swung her legs round and stood up in one swift, graceful movement. Charlotte was presented with a slim back view and the sound of the car door slamming shut. She sat for a moment listening to Mrs Carey's retreating footsteps crunching on the gravel. Then there was silence.

Chapter 2

More than kisses, letters mingle souls

It seemed to Charlotte, climbing slowly out of the car and turning to take in her first sight of the house that was now to be her home, that the house looked lonely standing by itself, tall and white in the late spring evening, the shrubs and bushes surrounding it seeming to keep themselves at a distance like ladies drawing in their skirts in disdain.

Only a huge magnolia tree, its dark leaves rustling against the house's right-hand wall, its sinewy branches like up-curved arms carrying a load of creamy, lemon-scented blossoms, seemed in sympathy with the house and willing to acknowledge it. Even this tree, with its bent and twisted trunk, seemed to have an exhausted and resigned look as though it would really much rather sit down.

Narrow blue-and-white striped awnings sheltered the two tall downstairs windows on either side of the porticoed front door. The awning on the right had tilted forward and fallen open, giving the impression that the house, having waited patiently for her to arrive, was winking at her. Charlotte, her eyes lighting on the pale blue front door, fell instantly in love.

Remembering that her cases were still in the boot of the Renault she looked around for Mrs Carey, but she had vanished. It seemed rather bold to take matters into her own hands but since there was nothing else to be done she went round to the back of the car, opened the boot and hauled her suitcases out. She looked around again – still no sign of her employer. She slammed the boot shut and picked up her cases.

The front door flew open and she saw framed within the opening what looked from this distance like a rather attractive man. She liked the look of his lean but sturdy frame, his dark hair and the elegant way he stood, poised for an instant, looking intently down at her and holding the door open as though there was a draught somewhere and he was stopping it from slamming shut.

He heaved a metal door stop sideways with his foot to keep the door open and came bounding down the stone steps with both arms outstretched as though welcoming a friend after a long absence. His face, now she could see it more clearly, was kind, which was all Charlotte was looking for, and really quite good-looking, which was a bonus, and in his dark grey flares and a navy roll-neck sweater he certainly did look good enough to eat.

Oh, Charlotte, she told herself. Better watch out.

'Charlotte – Mrs Barber.' He arrived at her side and looked around. 'I heard the car. Where's Sonia?' He gestured at her suitcases. 'Goodness me, put those down at once.' He took hold of her arm as she lowered them obediently to the ground. 'You poor girl, what a welcome, you must think us so rude.' He looked round with a concerned expression in his kindly brown eyes. 'Good Lord.' A lock of dark hair fell forward over his forehead. He pushed it back impatiently. 'Did Sonia just—? You'll have to forgive us, she's not quite herself at the moment.' He glanced over his shoulder. 'And where's Nelly?' He shook his head as though he simply couldn't believe the appalling behaviour of his family.

Only of course Nelly wasn't his child, Charlotte reminded herself, she was Mrs Carey's.

The lock of hair fell forward again and again he pushed it back. Why did he wear it so long, then? She wondered if he left it long like that just so that he could do that? Then she felt sorry. She *was* feeling cross. I mean, what a way to behave, just leaving her like that. She looked perfectly normal, Mrs Carey, but that wasn't a normal thing to do, was it? And where were the children Charlotte had heard so much about? It wouldn't have been too much to ask for one of them to put in an appearance. At least they could have helped her with her cases. Nevertheless she felt mollified by Mr Carey's apparently sincere apology and warm welcome, in such contrast to the cold, uncaring attitude she had begun to anticipate, waiting at the station scanning the crowd in vain for Mrs Carey, a good hour before.

'I expect she was late – was she? Did you think nobody was coming? It did cross my mind that you mightn't wait.' He picked up her suitcases. 'If you had taken a taxi, I would have refunded your fare, of *course*. What fun, we've never had someone to cook for us before. I can't think where Sonia's got to, it's bad enough her being late in the first place. I was in the shed, you know, lost to the world. My writing shed. She said she wanted to help and I thought – well, you know – why not? It would be good for her, I thought. You do forgive us, don't you?'

He looked at her anxiously, apparently genuinely interested in her reply. Charlotte nodded and smiled. He was so charming; how could she resist?

He jerked his head down to peer more closely. Down came the hair again. 'Oh *good*. Well, come in and I'll show you to your room. You've no idea what a treat it is for us that you've come, it will make such a difference. Oh,' — he dropped the suitcases and held out his hand — 'Patrick Carey. You met my wife before today, didn't you, briefly? We thought a preview would be a good idea in case you hated each other on sight.'

'Yes, we have met.' Charlotte put her hand in his and smiled to show she knew he was joking. 'At the Brightman – the agency. We had lunch.'

'Did Sonia actually eat something? She hardly eats anything nowadays. Helen Brightman's a friend of ours of course.' Patrick dropped her hand and picked up the cases again. 'We knew we could trust her. If she said you would do, we knew you would.'

He set off for the front door steps and Charlotte followed, puffing slightly, her shoes crunching on the gravel. She was aware suddenly of being enormously tired. A reaction, probably; it had been a long day.

It was very quiet after the hurly burly of Richmond station. A blackbird warbled dreamily in the magnolia. As they neared the steps the texture changed underfoot and she noticed paving stones set in the gravel. The driveway was bordered by stone pots filled with greenery. The quiet air seemed full of scents and suddenly there was a tang of some herb – thyme or marjoram – underfoot and the scent of rosemary as her arm brushed against a large bush growing at the bottom of the steps.

Mounting the steps, Charlotte puffed harder and wished fervently that she wasn't so fat. It was warm for

April and her neck under her thick hair, held back by a ribbon at the nape but nevertheless hot and heavy, was perspiring freely. He sweats, you perspire, I glow, she reminded herself to give herself confidence, admiring the back of Patrick's long legs and his neat, strong-looking buttocks. She did like a man who could really move. Riley walked as though he had piles, but then he did have rather short legs, she thought, and then felt guilty for being mean.

She pursued Mr Carey across the enormous hall, her new cream stack-heeled clogs clattering on the black and white checked stone floor, then up a long flight of blue-carpeted stairs to a large, square landing. Was she supposed to keep this clean? She wasn't entirely sure what her job entailed, apart from cooking. Mrs Carey had been extraordinarily vague at the interview.

At the top Mr Carey turned. 'We have Mrs P. to do the cleaning.' (Psychic, too.) 'She comes in a couple of times a week. You'll like Mrs P., she's a lovely old thing. Very thorough. Polish. Can't pronounce her name but Mrs P. seems to do.'

Charlotte didn't know quite what to make of Patrick. He sounded as though he ought to be in a play by Noel Coward. Perhaps he was gay? Her heart gave a lurch. Idiot, he couldn't be, he had Sonia. But she had had a nervous breakdown. Perhaps that was why. It did happen; people made mistakes. Goodness, she was seeing life. Looking up as they climbed the stairs she saw a small figure standing in the shadows on the landing, but when they got there, there was nobody there.

Two archways opened off the landing into wide passages left and right. The walls were hung with grey and white striped paper and there were a lot of expensive-looking paintings, mostly in gold frames. Charlotte, despite the real warmth of her host's welcome, began to feel a little ill-at-ease. When she'd taken the position she hadn't imagined anything quite as grand as this. Patrick plunged down the right-hand passage with Charlotte skipping along behind him and stopped outside a door on the right-hand side. He put down one of the cases and flung the door open.

'This is where we've put you. I do hope you'll like it. I must say,' — he looked into the room then back at her — 'the colour scheme really suits you with that marvellous hair.'

Charlotte blushed.

'Sonia chose all the decorations, you know, she has a very good eye for colour.' He looked sad for a moment then gave a little laugh and nodded his head to encourage her to enter ahead of him.

He followed, depositing her cases side by side on the bed. 'You'll be able to unpack more easily if I put them here.'

Charlotte looked around. 'Oh, golly. This is lovely.'

'It is nice, isn't it? There's a rather pleasant view' — he walked over to the window — 'over the orchard. The house faces southwest at the back.' He looked out, leaning on the window-sill and narrowing his eyes against the evening sun which was beginning to flood the room.

'It's wonderful.' Charlotte looked around the room with a lilting heart. 'It's perfect. Thank you so much.'

'It should be quite quiet, this isn't a noisy street, it's all residential around here. People sometimes take a short-cut through to the park, but on the whole—'

'It couldn't be better.' She looked at him, glowing.

He smiled and looked pleased. 'Now, take your time unpacking.' He came away from the window and strolled towards the door. He indicated a radio sitting on a chest of drawers. 'That's for your use. Grundig. It should be okay. I expect you like music, the charts, etc.'

This remark made Charlotte feel wonderfully young. She couldn't remember the last time she'd listened to *Top of the Pops*. There was something so relaxed and laid-back about Mr Carey, she could practically feel her blood pressure going down.

'I expect Sonia will pop up to say hello as soon as she turns up. Don't know where she can have got to, perhaps she decided to go for a run, she does that quite a lot. See you later.' He gave a last smile and closed the door gently behind him.

Charlotte kicked off her clogs. What you do now, she told herself, nervous again now that he had gone, is unpack. You don't brood, you don't start feeling sorry for yourself. Look at this room, it's a delight.

It was. It was simpler in furnishing and style than the parts of the house Charlotte had seen so far which had struck her as unnecessarily pretentious and ornate. This room was different. It was as if whoever had planned its decoration and furnishings had known who was coming, so exactly did it reflect her own tastes and preferences.

The pale aquamarine wallpaper dotted with tiny pink and silver nosegays gave the room a gentle, under-water feel. The carpet, soft under her bare feet, was a darker tone of the same blue-green. The floor-length curtains framing the windows picked up the silver-pink detail in the wallpaper. Charlotte found herself pausing frequently in her unpacking to look about her with a curl of pure aesthetic delight.

The furniture was mostly Edwardian: a mahogany dressing table with a small triple mirror, two comfortable chairs upholstered in a soft blue stripe and to her great joy, a small mahogany writing table and a bookshelf mostly emptied of books to allow space for her own. She couldn't help pausing to look at the titles of some of the remaining ones and was amused to find *Seven Types of Ambiguity* cheek by jowl with the *I Hate to Cook Book*, and Sylvia Plath and Emily Dickinson flanked by *Wise Owl's Story* and *A Bullet in the Ballet*. She didn't dare linger any longer or take a book from the shelves, knowing that if she settled down to read the world would disappear and she would still be there at midnight. Not the way to impress your new employers.

The only incongruous note in the room was struck by the enormous Victorian wardrobe which reared up against one wall like the gateway to Narnia. Opening the mirrored central door, Charlotte found drawers and hanging space for jackets and blouses, while there was more hanging space on either side. Her things would take up about an eighth of it. She began to unpack, putting her few clothes away and every now and then pausing to walk around the room and examine her surroundings.

When her cases were empty she zipped them up again and tossed them on top of the wardrobe (she had to throw them as it was too high for her to reach and she didn't like to stand on a chair, just in case) and went over to the window. She opened it as wide as it would go and leaned out, breathing in the scents of the garden with its burgeoning leaves and blossom. At the far end of the garden she could see an orchard of what she thought were apple trees. Amazingly, she could hardly hear any traffic at all from here. Mr Carey was right; only the steady hum of the by-pass in the distance, and then only if she absolutely hung out of the window.

Her attention was caught by a flutter of white at the

bottom of the garden. Mr Carey was walking about under the apple trees, reading a letter. Charlotte could see the flash of white as he turned it over, apparently absorbed in its contents. He seemed to be reading it over and over again.

Somebody opened the window of the room next door. Charlotte quickly pulled in her head and shoulders, then paused, listening. With a shock of discomfort, she heard it again: someone was crying. How desolate it sounded, how lonely, that sobbing. She stood still, resisting the impulse to rush next door and find out what was going on. It was none of her business, she told herself firmly; not that that had ever stopped her before. But she'd better not, it wouldn't do to look as though she was prying.

She closed the window as silently as she could and went back to her unpacking. Could that be Mrs Carey next door? She was a strange one: temperamental. Riley's mother was a bit like that, in a world of her own half the time. Charlotte wondered sometimes if Mrs Riley put it on to get her own way. If she didn't want to do something she pretended not to get your drift.

She dabbed some power on her nose and tied back her hair with a red ribbon in honour of the occasion. Red ribbons brought back wistful memories ... Riley had said once, long ago, when she had been wearing one in her hair, that she reminded him of that girl in the Renoir painting, the one with the group of young people partying by the river. She'd never forgotten it – perhaps because it was one of the few compliments he'd ever paid her.

She'd better get a move on if she was supposed to be cooking dinner this evening. Patrick hadn't said, but he seemed rather a vague kind of person, sort of casual as though nothing mattered very much. Or perhaps that was just his manner, a kind of public-school insouciance. Charlotte was rather thrilled by this idea. She wasn't a snob – she had nothing to be snobbish about – but Patrick was certainly different from any of the men she had met so far.

She opened the bedroom door and peeped out, then ventured out into the passage, feeling like a new girl at school. She paused on the landing. No sound came from the room next door. A good half hour had gone by; if it had been Mrs C., perhaps she'd managed to pull herself together and gone downstairs.

After a moment or two she exhaled her pent-up breath, composed herself and forced herself to walk along the passage and down the stairs.

Chapter 3

An angry girl with cloudy hair

Charlotte took a few uncertain steps across the hall, her heels echoing on the stone floor. The front door stood wide open. Voices floated in on the still air – Patrick's, robust, and a woman's, so quiet it was almost inaudible.

Patrick called out, 'Mrs Barber. Charlotte. We're out here.'

'Oh ... how lovely!' Charlotte stepped out through the front door. She tried not to look surprised that her employers were choosing to relax out here on the front drive in full view of passers-by, should there be any. At the moment the street beyond the gate appeared to be deserted.

'I found Sonia,' Patrick went on. 'She had decided to go running, after all. I managed to forestall her. Come and have a drink. The first Pimm's of the year to celebrate your arrival.'

A tall, plump jug full of amber liquid afloat with mint leaves and several varieties of fruit sat on a silver tray balanced on one of the stone urns, accompanied by four glasses. She saw that Mr and Mrs Carey were not after all exactly relaxing; they stood close together as though preparing to be confronted, Patrick with his arm around his wife who was dressed in black leggings and a pale blue sweat-shirt, a bright red bandanna around her head. At least, if it had been her Charlotte had heard in the next door bedroom upstairs, she wasn't crying anymore.

'Oh!' Charlotte exclaimed, 'you haven't any shoes on!'

Mrs Carey looked bewildered, then looked down at her bare feet and back at Charlotte again. 'I prefer it.'

Charlotte shuddered, thinking of the chewing gum, broken bottles, piles of doggy-do, litres of spit and other unmentionables littering the pavements around Marjorie's flat. Perhaps Roehampton was different from the Portobello Road.

Patrick looked amused. 'She always runs like that.' He nudged his wife. 'Sonia ...'

'Oh – yes. Mrs Barber—' Sonia began.

'Charlotte, please.'

'I am so sorry I left you like that. I went to fetch Patrick—'

'It doesn't matter at all – honestly.'

'You see—'

'It's really okay.'

Mrs Carey looked up at her husband as though for guidance.

He beamed at Charlotte and squeezed his wife's shoulders as though he was pleased with her. She didn't respond but remained stiffly upright. She seemed awfully tense; there was a look on her face that Charlotte couldn't quite interpret.

'So we're all friends. Have some Pimm's.'

'I'd love some. Thank you.'

Nobody moved. Mrs Carey said to her husband in a low voice, 'Is there any news?'

'No. No news.'

His eyes smiled at Charlotte over Mrs Carey's head. Charlotte looked at the jug of Pimm's, wondering if she was supposed to start pouring the drinks.

Apparently getting the message, Mr Carey released his wife's shoulders and moved over to the tray. 'Here, have a drink, darling, this'll cheer you up.' He filled one of the glasses and handed it to his wife, who took it and stood holding it as though she didn't know what to do with it. Charlotte accepted her glass with a pleased smile and waited for Patrick to fill his own.

'Chin chin.' Patrick raised his glass.

Charlotte took a large gulp. 'That's good!'

'*Mon Dieu.*' Mrs Carey looked at Patrick.

'Darling, try not to worry.' Patrick turned to Charlotte. 'It's Alain, our – Mrs Carey's son. He seems to have gone missing. At least,' — he glanced at his wife's bowed head — 'we're no longer sure of his whereabouts. He's travelling around India. He's probably fine, but he hasn't been in touch for a while and as you can imagine, the uncertainty is a bit of a strain.'

'Goodness, it must be.' No wonder Mrs Carey looked so unhappy. If it was her son she'd be going spare. Charlotte looked at her drink. She longed to take another gulp but she didn't want to appear heartless. 'Where was he when he went missing?'

'He was somewhere in the south.' Mrs Carey looked at Patrick as though for permission to speak. 'But that's the last we've heard. If only we could get some news. I imagine him lying ill somewhere. He might even be dead.' She put her untouched drink back on the tray.

'Now darling, don't go getting all morbid again, it isn't good for you. Come on.' Patrick put his arm around her again, steering her towards the steps. 'Let's go in. He's young. He's fit. The odds are he's as right as rain, don't you agree, Charlotte?'

'Yes. Yes, of course.' Obviously she hadn't the faintest idea. She took another swig.

'We thought we'd have a take-away this evening,' Patrick said over his shoulder. 'Do you like Indian?'

Charlotte adored Indian. Then she wondered if they should, if it would be tactless because of Alain, but Mrs Carey didn't seem to have noticed and she'd started talking to Patrick again in a subdued monotone so they weren't listening anyway. Charlotte finished her drink and put her glass back. 'I'll bring the tray.' She picked it up and followed them up the steps and into the house.

Halfway up the steps she paused and looked up. A window closed noisily above their heads. An angry-looking girl with cloudy dark hair stood half-hidden by a curtain, looking down at them.

NELLY LOOKED DOWN on the scene below with her usual feelings of frustration. *Quelle barbe* ... why couldn't she have a mother like everybody else? Why did she always have to go on like that? She could see that Patrick was irritated even though he was doing a good job of pretending he wasn't. He had his arm around Sonia who was making a fuss as usual. Probably about Alain. Wasn't it always? Goodness knows what Thingummy must be thinking: it was so *embarrassing*.

Her mother had been in a funny mood all day. She had surfaced out of what was beginning to look to Nelly horribly like the return of her depression and had been chatty and keyed up like the horses at Rose Belle used to be before a thunderstorm, galloping around nervously tossing their heads. Nelly wondered if she could have been at the bottle again, but she'd managed to get close enough to have a good sniff and there wasn't anything. It was just nerves, she supposed, because this new cook person was coming.

'I hope your mother's all right,' Patrick had said when Sonia's car had finally disappeared down the avenue on its way to Richmond station that morning. 'She seems a bit het up today.'

Trying to forget the mottled red flush on her mother's neck, Nelly said she thought she was probably quite relieved somebody was coming to help.

Patrick had gone into his study then and closed the door, so that was that. Nelly was terrified that yet again it was because he was annoyed with her mother. He'd said earlier that he might take the morning off and she'd hoped they might have had elevenses together or something. Perhaps they could have talked. But once the study door was shut she didn't like to interrupt, even if he wasn't actually working. It probably meant he would be catching up with admin, making phone calls or paying bills or perhaps just sitting staring out of the window with his brain in neutral which was how, he'd told Nelly once, most of his best work was done.

'Writing is eighty per cent dreaming,' he'd said, 'to quote somebody or other. It's why I'd make such a good house-husband. I could dream while I was doing the washing up.'

Nelly collected her workbooks from the window seat and let herself out through the glass-topped loggia into the back garden. She liked the loggia because it reminded her a bit of the *glacis* running the length of the back of the house at Rose Belle. About a million times smaller, of course, but it had the same sort of feeling about it.

She drifted down the garden, tingling a little as she passed Patrick's shed even though he wasn't there, and when she reached the orchard she dropped her books and threw herself flat on her back in the long grass which she was pleased to discover was damp. Too bad if it gave her rheumatism or pneumonia or whatever. Maisie appeared from nowhere and climbed onto her stomach, purring.

Nelly needed these few peaceful moments to think. She was beginning to be seriously worried about her mother. She'd been worried about her for ages, of course, but she had really hoped that finally flipping her lid and having to go into hospital would have sorted her out once and for all; but it didn't look as though it had. She'd had some sort of breakdown, Nelly had been told, but nobody seemed able to explain exactly what that meant or why she'd had it.

She wished they would. What she hated was not understanding. They never seemed to realise that. They thought they were protecting her when what they were really doing was making everything worse.

She looked up through the apple boughs at the overcast sky and cast her mind back to an afternoon she would never forget. It was early one morning, their first summer in England. Her mother, walking along a fallen log in Richmond Park, her arms out to balance herself, had suddenly started to laugh: ripples of genuine, happy laughter, a sound which Nelly, as far as she could remember, was hearing for the first time in her life. The memory of it always, without fail, brought tears to her eyes.

If she decided to go on the stage and it was one of those moments when they say think of something sad because you're supposed to cry in this scene, and if you can't we'll have to go and get an onion or something, she wouldn't have the least trouble. All she'd have to do would be to remember the sound of her mother laughing.

She heard the sound of a car turning into the drive. In a moment she was on her feet, dislodging Maisie and running up the garden as though the devil was after her. She managed to persuade herself that some horrible hobgoblin from the Black Lagoon was at her heels and gaining on her fast, and so convincing was the picture she painted for herself that by the time she reached the loggia she was practically screaming with delightful, self-induced terror. She hurled herself through the kitchen, up the stairs and into her bedroom where she slammed the door, leaning against it and breathing hard, opening it again for Maisie who, hot on her heels, was miaowing disconsolately outside.

When she heard the car pull up she went to the window and opened it an inch. Her mother opened her door and got out of the car, then the passenger door opened.

'And who do you think got out, Sandy?' Nelly complained to her best friend the next morning at school. 'Mrs Wibbly Wobbly, that's who. My dear, she's ginormous! Like – really *fat*. She totters about like a giant jellybean on legs. It's frightful!'

Sandy pulled a sympathetic face. 'Gross.'

They were sitting on one of the tables in the chemistry lab. Sandy was smoking. According to Sandy this was by far the safest place to smoke because the pong in there was so awful nobody could possibly tell. Sandy was lean and small and clever, with straight, chin-length dark hair which she had to wash every day without fail because if she didn't, she said, it started positively dripping grease. Her slight sensitiveness over this cosmetic handicap did nothing to lessen her enjoyment of other people's follies or shortcomings.

'I couldn't walk about looking like that,' Nelly went on in a pained voice. 'I'd rather die.'

'Can't even imagine it.' Sandy tipped her head back and blew a perfect smoke ring. 'Although I must say I have sometimes rather envied girls with a proper bum. I mean, look at mine, it just doesn't exist.' She looked down disparagingly at her own lean flanks. Then she looked about her and sniffed. 'Man, have they been dissecting things in here? There's a horrible smell. Even more disgusting than usual, I mean.'

'She's got fab hair though.' Nelly wasn't listening. 'It's the most amazing colour, a really bright gold, kind of flaming.'

'Jeez, she must stand out like a lighthouse.'

'And she just *stood* there, *smiling*. I mean what else could she do, with Sonia going on like a cat trying to sick up a fur-ball? Attention-seeking as usual. I mean that was later. They were drinking *Pimm's*. Thingummy, poor cow, didn't know where to put herself. When she smiles her cheeks are so chubby she gets these huge dimples on either side.'

'Sounds rather fetching.'

'It isn't, it's gross, Sandy. I've got to *live* with her.'

'Oh well. She's come to be your cook, hasn't she? I suppose if you're a cook you're bound to get fat. I think you're damned lucky, who can afford a cook nowadays? One more, Nell, and then we'd better get lost, people are beginning to look in and Tigs and Blossom said to meet them before the bell goes. And by the way, Tigs says she's got a bone to pick with you.'

Nelly had to admit, the thought of proper meals did soften the blow rather. Since Sonia had come home from the hospital she seemed to have forgotten what a saucepan was for. Everything came out of packets. Even if it was Vesta, it simply wasn't the same as proper food.

Mrs P. didn't have time to cook because as well as coming in twice a week to clean for them she cleaned for Mr Dennison down the road and lots of other people as well. Patrick had had a go at cooking but he wasn't a natural cook. He was okay with pasta but they'd all got heartily sick of pasta. Nelly was sure Patrick must have got totally fed up with never having a proper meal, even though he never complained. Poor Patrick ... *quelle poire* ... sometimes she despised him for being so tolerant of Sonia all the time.

Patrick had told her that Thingummy was coming to give Sonia a hand and make life easier for her but Nelly reckoned that really he was dying for a good square meal and just couldn't stand it any longer.

But what if he decided he *really* couldn't stand it any longer and threw them out? They'd be on their own again, she and Alain (assuming he came home safe from India, which Nelly was perfectly sure he would) homeless and trying to cope with their impossible mother. It didn't bear thinking of.

Chapter 4

Like a knife in my heart

Sonia strode around the cream and gold bedroom holding the palms of her hands against her temples, looking as though she was afraid that if she took her hands away her brain would fall out.

'Why do we have to have somebody anyway? We're managing, aren't we? I mean I know I'm not much of a cook.'

Oh well. Patrick resigned himself to the inevitable argument. This was supposed to have been their bonding time with Mrs – with Charlotte – but apparently not. 'We've been through all this.' He leaned against the bedroom door watching his wife with what he hoped was a sympathetic expression.

'I know. I just didn't realise it would *feel* like this.' She stopped striding and stood still with her hands, clenched into fists, pressed against her midriff, looking down at the carpet.

'How does it feel?'

She turned her green eyes on him and his heart

bounced unexpectedly. 'Like ... as though it's all being taken away. As though I'm being made a fool of again.'

'Nobody's trying to make a fool of you. What do you mean, again?'

She looked at him reproachfully. 'Now you're cross with me. You're fed up. But you don't understand.'

He made an effort. 'What don't I understand?'

She stood still with her back to him in the middle of the carpet, twisting her fingers together. 'You don't think I'm capable of running the house and looking after you, that's what this is all about.' She turned to face him.

His eyes slid away from her anxious face. He heaved himself away from the door and took a few aimless steps, not looking at her. 'Of course you can look after us, darling, you look after us marvellously, but you haven't been well, you're supposed to be taking things easy. Can't you just enjoy the prospect of not having to worry about meals and the washing and all those things you say you hate anyway? I thought you'd be pleased; you hate all that domestic stuff.'

'I hate it when you say darling like that.'

'Like what?'

'Like you don't mean it. Why *say* it if you don't mean it?'

Patrick frowned. 'I wish I understood why you're so upset.'

She looked at him as though he was stupid. 'Because you think I'm useless. I do have some idea of how a house has to be run, you know. I haven't always had servants running around after me.'

'Of course, I know that; you managed perfectly before. It's just that you've been ill. We agreed it would be a good idea to have someone living in for a bit, to take the pressure off you. We discussed it. You agreed.'

'That was when I was in the hospital. It's different now I'm home.'

There was a short, intense silence. She had changed out of her running things into dark slacks and a sweater and had put on a pair of small gold slippers. She started to walk around in circles again, her feet making no sound on the soft carpet. He could hear the sound of her breathing, increasingly anguished.

'I'm not what you expected, am I, Patrick?' She turned towards him again and looked at him as she used to, her eyes aware and interested and as if she was really seeing him. She didn't often look at him like that now. Now it was as if she was locked up inside herself, as if she herself was a prison she couldn't escape from. 'You know, when you saw me at the wine bar, when we met. I was happy there. I was good at it. I could talk to people.'

'You didn't need to talk, you just looked.' He remembered that look, it was what had attracted him to her in the first place. She looked as if she couldn't give a damn.

'I should have stayed there.' She turned away and went and stood in front of the window with her back to him. 'I should have kept on working.'

As always, the sight of the tender back of her neck with her short dark hair upswept over the small hollow at her nape moved him so that he stepped towards her, wanting to take her into his arms. He stopped several feet away. Given half a chance, he loved it all, her small neat hands; her soft, round hips; her bitten nails; her full mouth with the droop like a disappointed child's; the brilliant smile. Although she seemed lately to have forgotten how to smile. He bit his lip, irritated, sad. At least she seemed to have calmed down, she'd stopped charging about wearing the carpet out.

'You thought I was just like the rest of them, didn't you,

Patrick? But I'm not. Why didn't you ask questions? Why didn't you wait to find out what I was like? You make up your mind to do something and you just do it. You don't think first.'

'I fell in love.'

'But who with? How can you fall in love with somebody if you don't know who they are?'

'I know who you are.'

'You think you do.'

'Oh, *Sonia.*'

'Now you're cross. You're angry with me.'

'Of course I'm not angry. I'm *sad.* I'm sad that I can't – that you're still so unhappy. But things are better now, aren't they? You're much better than you were.'

'Do you think so?' She put her head on one side, as if weighing up the situation.

'Don't you like her?' he asked, to distract her from her self-absorption.

'It isn't that.' She closed her eyes and opened them again. She walked over to the window and looked out. 'I hate to feel so useless. You forget that when I was younger than Nelly I was looking after my father. That I took care of my mother during her last illness. Oh look!' She smiled and tapped on the window glass. 'Maisie's up a tree! I hope she isn't after a bird. She's so cruel.'

'She doesn't think of it like that.' Pleased that Maisie had succeeded where he had failed, Patrick came to stand beside her, pretending not to notice the slight flinch she always gave if he came unexpectedly too close to her.

Maisie leapt out of the apple tree into the long grass and streaked towards the house.

'Hah! She's down. She knows it's spring. Look at her, she practically turned a somersault. You'd never think she was such an old lady; she thinks she's still a kitten.' Maisie disappeared through the open door into the loggia.

Sonia turned to look up at him and he marvelled again at the beauty and brilliance of her almond-shaped eyes with their fringe of black lashes and irises the colour of jade.

'I'm sorry, Patrick. I know you're only trying to help. I know I'm not much fun at the moment.'

You were never exactly fun, Patrick thought, but you were exciting; you were exactly what I wanted. All the same he kept his arms folded. There had been too many rebuffs.

She put her hands on his folded arms and lowered her eyelids. 'Perhaps ... if I were less exhausted.'

He assumed she was talking about her unwillingness to share his bed, a situation that had existed since her return from hospital. Who was she trying to kid? She didn't mean it, this wasn't new. Whatever her problem was, it wasn't exhaustion.

'That's the whole point of having Charlotte.' He knew the moment the words were out of his mouth that he'd made a mistake.

'What, so that I'll want to sleep with you again? Thanks a lot. Thanks very much, Patrick.' She removed her hands from his arms, her face flushing. 'I thought you said we were getting her to take the stress off, not make it worse.' She began walking around the room again, her arms crossed tightly across her chest.

Patrick frowned. He leaned his back against the window sill, watching her. Since when did making love have to be a source of stress? Unless of course you didn't want to be doing it and, in that case what the hell were you doing with that person anyway?

They'd only been married a couple of years, for God's sake. He refused to believe she didn't still have feelings for him. But there was a problem, there had been, right from the beginning. They'd made love often, but sometimes, afterwards, he would be woken by the sound of her smothered sobs. Or he would roll over and put out his hand and she would not be there.

At first he'd got up and gone to look for her, and he'd found her walking around the garden or sitting huddled by the Aga.

'Please leave me,' she would beg him, bending her head so that her hair hid her face from him. 'I'm all right. I just need to be alone. I'll come back to bed soon.'

Not knowing what else to do, he let her be. The children, woken sometimes by the racket she made moving about the kitchen or fighting the locks and bolts with claustrophobic desperation in her attempts to escape from the house, seemed to accept their mother's behaviour as a matter of course. When he tried to talk to them about her they either looked at him blankly or shrugged and looked the other way.

Sonia's bedroom was beginning to feel like a prison. At least the book's nearly done, he thought, the knot in his stomach relaxing. He could hear children's voices in the garden next door, light-hearted, laughing. He remembered the letter he'd stuffed into his jacket pocket that morning. It had come in that morning's post, which for once he'd glanced at on his way in from his walk.

He'd trained himself not to look at the post until he'd finished work for the day so as to avoid being distracted, but today for some reason, possibly because the end of the book was in sight and he was beginning to relax, he'd glanced down at the pile of letters and there, staring up at him from a plain white envelope, was Laura's instantly recognisable black, curly handwriting. He'd put the envelope in his jacket pocket and forgotten about it until he'd suddenly remembered it in the middle of showing Charlotte her room.

Now he remembered it again and felt a quiver of interest. He looked at Sonia's tense back. This whole situation was becoming such a bore; it had gone on too long. Then he noticed again the tender line of her neck, the gentle swell of her hips, and his heart melted. Oh hell, he thought: she's my wife, I love her. And I want to help her, I really do.

'And I hate these curtains.' Sonia batted at one of the floor-length gold brocade drapes framing the tall sash windows. 'I hate this room. It isn't our room, it's hers.'

'You never said before that you didn't like it.' Patrick made no attempt to hide his astonishment.

He realised to his dismay that she was crying. He went to her and put his arms around her. She tensed, then pushed her arms inside his jacket and held him, her face buried in his shirt front. He pulled a hanky out of his trouser pocket and tried to reach her face but it was hidden against his chest. She disengaged her left arm and took the hanky from him and began to scrub at her cheeks with a kind of hopelessness, like a child.

'Don't cry. I hate it when you cry.'

'But it hurts. If I say what I want it hurts. It's like a knife stabbing into my heart.'

He sighed, his chin resting on the top of her head. 'I don't understand. Talk to me, darling. Try to explain.'

'I can't explain.'

He held her and rocked her gently. She felt so small and slight in his arms; her softness brought a rush of longing so intense that he tightened his arms around her and bent his head to rest his cheek against her silky hair.

'You've been borrowing my shampoo again,' he said

tenderly.

'I like the smell ...'

He began to be afraid she would sense his growing frustration. 'Look. Let's give Charlotte a go, shall we? When things are back on track we'll think again.'

'She'll be so expensive.' She lifted her head from his chest. 'Oh Patrick, I do wish Elizabeth would write about Rose Belle. It's taking so long, do you think the sale will go through?' She began to pull away and his arms dropped to his sides. He felt a terrible sense of emptiness.

'There's no hurry about that. Look – Sonia.'

'Yes?' She wandered listlessly over to her dressing shelf and began putting things into one of the two fitted drawers: a silver hand mirror, a box of face powder, a comb. The oval looking-glass over the dressing shelf had bulbs all the way around it like a mirror in a theatrical dressing room.

She was like a discontented child. And yet it was her very childishness, her vivacity, that he had loved the summer they met. She had danced through the bracken in the park, edged precariously along fallen tree trunks and played football with the children in the long grass. She was like a person who'd just been let out of jail.

He'd first seen her leaning over the counter in Brahms and Liszt, the wine bar in Sheen, her head tilted in concentration as she strained to hear over the hubbub the order from a rather pushy man Patrick took an instant dislike to who had hovered around her all evening.

She and the children, Alain who was sixteen and Nelly, two years younger, were living in a horrible flat behind the railway line and she was in some sort of trouble, he'd realised almost at once. It wasn't just the lack of cash; there was something wrong with her, but he couldn't put his finger on what it was. There was something odd about

Alain and Nelly too; their manner was both incurious and watchful at the same time. He got along with them fine, although like their mother they curled back into their shells the moment he started trying to probe. He could see that whatever it was had touched them too.

He admired this exotic woman's courage and the fact that she never complained about how difficult life had become. Because it was obvious from her few but expensive clothes that she hadn't always lived in such straightened circumstances. He ignored the warning bells that rang from the beginning, and decided after a matter of weeks that if he didn't persuade her to marry him he'd never write another word.

'I fell in love with you the moment I saw you,' Patrick told her later. 'Love at first sight. Never believed in it before.'

He was fascinated by her mouth which, full at the centre under a short upper lip, drooped at the corners to form a perfect cupid's bow. In spite of her slimness she looked both fragile and voluptuous. She was averagely tall, about five-five; there was something uniquely strange about her jade-green eyes and slightly darkened skin, and when he heard her voice for the first time, that was it, he was hooked. She spoke with a slightly broken accent and her voice was husky but musical, its cadences thrillingly erotic to Patrick who took to dropping in at the wine bar most evenings at the end of his day's work and sitting over a glass of wine, concealing for many weeks his passionate interest, feeling like a school-boy and longing for her to speak.

'I just *hate* this dressing table.' Sonia's voice brought him with a jerk back to the present.

Patrick said to distract her, 'I was going to say something and I've forgotten what it was.' He couldn't bear the thought of her starting to cry again. 'I know, I've remembered. Look. I do realise how difficult you found it, you know, my shutting myself away all the time.'

'Well, it's nice of you to say so.' She shut the drawer slowly. 'It's true, I hate feeling so cut off from you when you're writing; you did warn me but it was such a change from before, I just didn't realise how bad I would feel.'

'Other men go to the office.'

'I know. I know. Perhaps I would have hated that too.' She paused. 'It's different though, isn't it?'

'Because I'm at home, you mean.'

'You're there but you're not there. And it's not as though you really have to work.'

Here we go. He'd wondered when that would come up. 'Yes, I do,' he said firmly. 'I'm far too young not to work. I know I'm lucky, we've got a few shares from Mother and the house and everything, but my writing is important to me, I love it, I'd wither up inside if I didn't do it.' He scratched his head, which had begun to itch. He hoped Nelly had remembered to flea Maisie. 'Anyway, it's a living. Or at least it helps. I know it isn't easy for you.'

She stood looking at him, chewing the corner of her lip. 'There was something else I've been meaning to say.'

'Oh?'

'I've not had a chance to apologise for ... well, for what happened to your manuscript.' She glanced at him then looked away.

'We don't need to talk about that.' Heat rose up his neck and into his head; his heart began to pound unpleasantly. He really didn't want her to bring that up now. He didn't want to have to think about it now – or ever, actually.

When he believed she had destroyed it, the manuscript of this latest book, the two copies and his typewriter which she'd smashed with a hammer, for a few moments he had felt capable of murder. She'd got horribly drunk, she said afterwards, in excuse; she hadn't known what she was doing. She was having a breakdown, the doctor said, intervening. What she needed was not furious rage and recrimination, but help.

She'd put the manuscript and one copy through the shredder, and then she'd found the second copy. After a couple of weeks during which Patrick, frantic, experienced emotions close to bereavement, she admitted that for some unaccountable reason she'd decided to bury this one, complete with its protective folder. (Patrick had never understood why. Perhaps some faint, remaining instinct of compassion had penetrated her sozzled brain and prompted this moment of mercy?) Finally, after another week, she was persuaded to divulge where in the garden she had hidden it.

They dug it up, just decipherable despite several pounds of garden soil and a solid week of rain, and Patrick, once he'd had it copied, twice, once he was quite sure it was safe, in his vast relief began to joke about it. 'Like the Moors murders. Myra Hindley refusing to tell where they've hidden the bodies.' Nobody at the hospital thought this the least bit funny.

It would have been pointless not to forgive her, and he had his manuscript back which was what mattered; but something had crept into their relationship which had not been there before: a watchfulness, a sense of menace emanating either from him or from her, he was not sure which. Was it that he was afraid that the incandescent rage he had felt would pollute his feelings for her forever? Or was it that he didn't trust her not to do it again?

Just in case, he made extra copies of his work as it progressed and kept them in a wall safe in his study which

Sonia didn't know about. Then he woke up in the night worrying that he might drop dead before the book was finished and that nobody would know about the safe: the work would be lost anyway. So he wrote an explanatory letter to his executors and lodged it at the bank.

Sonia stood with her hands clasped in front of her like a child. 'I wasn't myself. You do know I wasn't, don't you? Things kind of caught up with me. But I feel terrible about it. I realise now how you must have felt.'

Patrick clenched his fists. She didn't have a clue how he'd felt. But she was trying. 'As long as you don't do it again. You won't, will you?' He was only half-joking.

'Of course I won't.' She wrung her hands. Sonia's hands had a life of their own. She'd once told him that if she were forced to sit on them she wouldn't be able to talk at all.

She seemed to lose interest and turned away. 'I suppose we ought to think about supper,' she said listlessly.

'We're having a take-away, remember? I've ordered for eight o'clock, it'll give Charlotte a chance to settle in.' He turned towards the door. 'I'll go and see what Nelly's up to; she's supposed to be laying the table.'

'What's she doing? Mrs Thing – Charlotte?'

'Reading *The Times* in the drawing-room, Pimm's in hand. Strict instructions to relax, heaven knows it won't be for long.'

'I'll be down in a minute.'

Patrick ran two at a time down the stairs. She never called him darling. Never anything but Patrick.

He began thinking about Chandler again. His mind always escaped to Chandler when he felt hit by loneliness, something that seemed to be happening more and more often nowadays. Chandler was the uncouth, overweight but astute detective hero of his three, so far, reasonably successful crime novels and, it was beginning to dawn on Patrick more and more, his *alter ego.*

Is that really how I'd like to be? he asked himself sometimes, observing his hero's self-serving, manipulative behaviour as he blasted through the pages of the book, upsetting people, foul-mouthed, surly and un-cooperative.

At the thought of Chandler his heart began to beat faster. I think it's okay, he reassured himself. He couldn't wait to get back to work. He'd got to the stage where it was like reading something for the first time, only it was better because he had made it, it was his. If it was good he felt enormous relief, if it was bad he could still change it.

'Nelly!' he called. 'Nell!'

'Maisie's caught a mouse.' Nelly came out of the kitchen, her face red. 'A sweet little brown one with big black eyes. It's gone under the fridge and it won't come out. I've shut her in the larder. Please, Patrick, come and catch it. She's miaowing the place down.'

'I'm not killing it.'

'Of *course* not.'

'Well, what do you want me to do with it, then? What's this for?'

'It's a tumbler. You catch it in that and put the card over the top. Then you take it to the park and let it go. Or in the garden. Anywhere.'

'Oh God.' Patrick followed her into the kitchen. 'Go on then, where is it?'

'There it is. Can't you hear it squeaking? Quick before it dies of fright. I wonder what what's-her-name's like at catching mice.'

'It isn't part of her brief.' Patrick knelt down by the Aga. 'For heaven's sake don't tell her. She might leave.'

'Whacko.'

Chapter 5

Shadows of St. Colombe

Charlotte's habit was to come downstairs at around seven in the morning to make tea. None of the family seemed interested but personally she couldn't survive without her early morning cuppa. She loved the kitchen, especially in the mornings when she was alone and could sit sipping her tea, enjoying the warm, comfortable vibe of the room with its scrubbed pine table and sturdy Windsor chairs, the warm Aga and the old pine dresser which stretched almost the entire length of one wall, its shelves stacked with a complete Victorian dinner set of Blue Willow china.

One morning when she had been with the Careys for several weeks she opened the door into the kitchen as usual and found Sonia sitting in the dark at the kitchen table. Her feet were pushed into Patrick's old leather slippers and a pair of his maroon silk pyjamas hung ridiculously large on her size eight frame. She had not drawn the curtains nor put the kettle on, but at least the room was warm. The boiler came on at six.

'Sonia!' Charlotte felt her usual irritation at Sonia's idleness and self-absorption. She drew the curtains and noticed Sonia's flinch as the morning light, grey but glaring, flooded the room. She felt clumsy but repressed the instinctive apology; this was ridiculous; she had to draw the curtains; did Sonia have to be so sensitive? Then she thought, repenting, but I like to sit here in the early mornings, enjoying the peace and quiet, why shouldn't Sonia? She looked down at the table where Sonia was sitting; she'd made violent stabbing marks with a biro all over the shopping list Charlotte had left on the table the night before.

Sonia stirred and looked up at her. 'Hello.'

Charlotte loved the sound of Sonia's voice, which was faintly accented, and husky as though she smoked too many cigarettes. 'Good morning, Sonia. I hope you slept well?'

She smiled to herself as she bustled about making tea and putting coffee on to infuse for Sonia, recollecting failed attempts in front of the mirror in her bedroom to imitate the cadence and special intonation of Sonia's accent. She'd given up; it was hopeless.

The room held its usual homely fragrance of home-baked bread and Flash-wiped surfaces, with the additional faint exotic spiciness of last night's supper. Patrick had gone to a Neighbourhood Watch meeting (a couple of strange-looking men had been seen hanging about in the Avenue) and Nelly had gone to the cinema with Sandy to see *Walkabout,* so Sonia and Charlotte had shared a savoury spinach quiche with salad, followed by fruit and coffee. A women's meal: no bread-and-butter pudding, no potatoes. Charlotte had looked forward to the evening as an opportunity to get to know her employer better but Sonia had been in one of her wild-eyed, taciturn moods and the opportunity had gone by with nothing achieved, and this morning she still seemed to be in the surly mood she'd been in the evening before, as if a night's sleep had made no difference at all.

'Have some coffee.' Charlotte placed a steaming bowl of coffee in front of her. ('We drink our morning coffee in bowls,' Nelly had informed her loftily the first morning. '*A la français,* don't you know.') Nelly, as far as Charlotte could gather from their as yet limited acquaintance, chose to be sarcastic about absolutely everything, particularly her mother.

'A telegram came from Alain last night.'

'No. Really?' Charlotte sank onto a chair, her mug of tea in her hand.

'He sent it to Patrick.' Sonia's haunted eyes, which turned on her, were a startling, arresting green. 'It doesn't say where he is or anything. It's awful, he just says he's ill.'

'What's the matter with him?'

'Patrick didn't want me to see it but I needed some of those inhalant things for my cold,' Sonia whispered. 'He had them last so I looked in his dressing gown pocket and the telegram was there. Alain's got amoebic dysentery. Oh Charlotte, suppose he dies!'

'He won't die.' All the same, she thought: amoebic dysentery. Blimey.

'Very ill, he says. Not just ill. Very ill. He could be dead by now.'

What kind of child sent his parents that sort of telegram? However ill they were. 'They must have the right medication to treat him, this isn't the dark ages. If he's managed to send a telegram he's bound to be all right.'

'Do you think so? Do you really?'

Charlotte got up and put her arm around her. Sonia was trembling. Her backbone through the thin dressing gown felt like a row of pebbles sewn into the skin. Her shoulder blades were like two cuttlefish. 'You really mustn't worry. I'm sure he's all right, you'd have heard if he wasn't. Now drink your coffee. You haven't been here all night, have you?' She sat down again.

'I went for a run. I had a shower when I came in.'

'You went for a run with that cold?'

'Oh, it's all right.'

'You'll get pneumonia.' Charlotte leaned across and pushed aside a strand of silky dark hair trailing in Sonia's coffee.

'No, I won't. Anyway I don't care.'

She really did seem half off her head sometimes. 'Why don't you go back to bed for a bit? There's nothing special to get up for, is there? I'll bring you up a hot water bottle.'

Sonia suddenly seemed to revive. She stood up. 'I have to talk to Patrick. How can he possibly sleep like that, knowing how I'm feeling?'

Charlotte, watching Sonia head for the door still holding her coffee bowl, thought that actually Patrick didn't know how Sonia was feeling because he didn't know she had found the telegram. She wasn't going to wake him up, surely? 'Actually, Sonia,' she called after her, 'he worked really late last night. I heard him go out to the shed after supper.'

Sonia paused by the door. 'He's still got to get up. He's always up by now.'

'But it's Saturday.' Charlotte followed her into the hall.

'Patrick doesn't take any notice of Saturdays.' Tight-lipped, Sonia slammed her half-empty coffee bowl down on the hall table.

Charlotte winced. She hoped she hadn't cracked it; the bowls were Quimper. There were six in the set.

'He works just as much on Saturday as any other day,

haven't you noticed? Anyway I have to talk to him or I'll go mad. Patrick,' she called, climbing the stairs.

Bother, she would wake Nelly who would kill her. Nelly rarely surfaced before noon on a Saturday. Charlotte hurried after Sonia, tripped over the slippers which Sonia had discarded halfway up the stairs, and tried not to think resentfully that with a little less vigilance she could have broken her neck. She carried the slippers up to the landing and placed them neatly paired outside Sonia's bedroom door, then rummaged in the airing cupboard for a hot-water bottle.

Sonia's raised voice seeped through Patrick's door, punctuated by his placating, slightly plaintive rumble. Honestly, that man had the patience of a saint.

NELLY SAT cross-legged on her bed and looked at the wall opposite. Three of her bedroom walls were painted a deep, cerulean blue. The fourth was frescoed all over in brilliant poster colours with a scene born out of her terrible home-sickness: it was her commemoration of St. Colombe, the island in the Caribbean where she and Alain had been born.

Her mother's early life was a closed book to Nelly. She knew that Sonia had come to St. Colombe to marry her father Luis at an unbelievably young age, only fifteen, for God's sake. A year younger than Nelly was now. Sonia's mother Avril, Nelly's grandmother, had died of some illness, nobody had ever said what, and Sonia had met Luis, a distant and much older cousin, at her mother's funeral. She'd married him and come to live with him at Rose Belle, the coffee plantation in St Colombe where Alain and Nelly were born and where they lived until they came to England.

From what Nelly could gather, Sonia had loved Luis madly and he had been unkind to her. Four years ago he had been murdered – a violent death that her mother refused to talk about – and Sonia had bundled Nelly and Alain away in a great hurry from their beloved St Colombe without preparation, explanation or apology and brought them to this cold, grey country. To live in a grotty flat in Sheen.

The first year had been horrible. Nelly and Alain went to the local comp. and Sonia went to work in the wine bar, which meant she was always exhausted. There she met Patrick. Two years ago she'd married Patrick and they'd all come to live here.

Nelly had painted the wall the moment they moved into Patrick's house. She was too old for it now, of course; she told herself that she'd emulsion it over one of these days. But secretly she still liked it even though it might be a bit babyish; and more secretly still, in her heart of hearts she felt she could never bear to get rid of it – never.

Silhouetted against an ultramarine sea Rousseau-like palm trees reared at odd angles, their crowns laden with coconuts; banana trees curved, their burden of fruit in heavy bunches reaching almost to the ground. Macaws and parakeets, cardinals and bulbuls flew between fronded branches; monkeys sported, and under the trees a group of people in brilliantly coloured clothes walked about carrying baskets on their heads laden with fruit and vegetables, or sat cross-legged in the shade. Jaguars lurked in the foliage and bullfrogs crouched by a waterfall, so lifelike you could almost hear them bellow. Huge flowers glowed against dark green forest foliage, and on the ground a pair of cri-cri birds leapt about, wings spread in a frenzied dance.

Each of the people in the painting, immediately recognisable to Nelly if not to anybody else, represented someone she had left behind in St. Colombe. Every night she kissed each beloved face goodnight, repeating their names under her breath in a private roll-call: Lena, Amélie, Francine, Quasheba, Excelie, Cufée – Cufée who was dead. She was terrified of forgetting them. Because she despised herself rather for even having attempted the painting – because as she said to Sandy, you couldn't begin to show it as it really was – she had called the painting *Shadows of St. Colombe*. 'It's the smell that's missing, the indescribable smell.'

'You ought to have done a scratch 'n sniff.' Sandy brought her down to earth as usual. 'Like on that poster at the bus stop.'

Nelly got up, went over to her flowery, frilly dressing table (also grown out of, she'd much prefer something plain) and extracted from the top right-hand drawer a blue air letter addressed to herself in a strong, confident hand.

She threw herself on her stomach onto her bed and began, for perhaps the eleventh time, to read it through again.

Charlotte passed Nelly's door, hot-water bottle in hand. The door handle rattled. Charlotte paused. The door opened and Nelly's head stuck out. Her cat Maisie was draped around her neck, giving the momentary but pleasing impression that she was being strangled by a boa-constrictor.

'How's things in Bombay, then?' Nelly said cheerfully. 'Mumsie in a good old sweat about her darling son then, is she? Good.' She shut the door again.

Charlotte knocked. The door opened immediately and Nelly stood looking at her with a defiant expression.

'What makes you think he's in Bombay?'

Nelly looked at her for a moment then took her hand from behind her back and held out a blue air letter.

'Alain?'

Nelly put her finger to her lips and beckoned Charlotte into the room. She closed the door and leaned against it.

'How long have you had it?'

She shrugged. 'Dunno. About a week.'

'You've had that letter a whole week and you haven't said anything to your mother?'

'Don't look at me in that tone of voice, Barbar.' Nelly put her head on one side.

Charlotte's lips tightened. 'Don't call me that ridiculous name.'

'I think it's rather good. Quite descriptive.' She turned away with a dancing movement. Maisie wobbled precariously.

'I think it's rather rude, actually.'

Nelly turned and looked at her for a moment, bright-eyed. 'Do you? Oh, all right, Celeste then. She was the queen, wasn't she? Barbar was only the king.'

'The queen?' Charlotte fell straight into the trap.

'You know. Of the elephants. You remember – Barbar? Celeste?' Nelly outlined large, curvy elephant shapes with both hands, including the trunks.

The Lord preserve me from this aggravating girl, Charlotte thought. 'Why haven't you told your mother you've heard from your brother? She's going absolutely spare.'

Nelly shrugged. 'I dunno. Why should I? Let her sweat. She always makes such a drama out of everything. Means she can demand even more attention from poor Patrick. Anyway she never thinks about anything except what *she* feels, what *she's* going through. What about the rest of us?'

Maisie, sensing tension in the air and disturbed by Nelly's gesticulations, gave a yowl and leapt from her shoulders onto the bed.

'She has been ill. Give her a chance.'

'Oh fiddle, that's got nothing to do with it.' Nelly turned away again and said lightly, 'Anyway he's fine. He's *perfectly* okay.'

'She doesn't know that. She just knows he's ill.'

Nelly turned her head abruptly. 'What do you mean, he's ill?'

'Your father had a telegram.'

Nelly spun around. 'What? When?'

'Yesterday sometime. He says he's ill. And by the way, he's not in Bombay now, he's in Delhi.'

Nelly blinked. 'My, how the lad gets around.' She paused. 'What's the matter with him? Alain's never ill. In any case, they'll look after him. They always do, they love him, they think he's some kind of holy man.'

'Who do? What are you talking about?'

Nelly scooped Maisie up into her arms. 'You don't need to worry about Alain. Look. It's in the letter, yeah? He ran out of money so he went and sat cross-legged on the ground outside a village somewhere and after a while the villagers started to bring him offerings of flowers and food and things. They thought he was some kind of holy man.' She giggled, hugging Maisie. 'Typical Alain. Who else would have thought of that one? He's a genius. He'll never die.'

'He's a very sick genius. He's got amoebic dysentery now.'

Slight pause. 'Oh. Well, that'll teach him to drink the water, won't it?' She went over to the window and stood looking out. 'Look – he'll be okay. I wish everybody would stop fussing.'

'You haven't exactly helped.'

'I'll tell her in a little while.' She deposited Maisie on the window sill and went over to the painted wall which Charlotte had to admit she would have found an astonishing and moving artistic achievement even if it had not been done by a child of fourteen, and addressed one of the figures. '*Bon jour, Christophine.*' She turned around. 'She's always preferred Alain.'

Charlotte thought that if she had a daughter like Nelly she'd probably prefer Alain too.

Nelly moved back to the window and began stroking Maisie who had draped herself along the sill. 'He's the light of her eyes, you know?'

'She'd be just the same if it was you.'

Nelly shook her head. 'Look, could you possibly go now, do you think?'

Charlotte turned to the door. Behind her Nelly said, 'She's got no guts, that's what I can't stand about her. She's never had any guts.'

'What makes you say that?'

Nelly snorted. 'She never stood up to my father. She let him walk all over her. Nobody could do anything. My mother—' She stopped.

Smug cow, she thought, leaning her hot forehead against the cold window glass when Charlotte had gone. How could I even begin to explain to someone like that what my father was like? She's so innocent, so complacent, like a cream bun. It's like trying to explain Vlad the Impaler to Minnie Mouse. (What is that woman *doing* in our house? It's like putting a cart-horse in with a lot of polo ponies and expecting them to get on.)

She's like a bloody nurse. She's probably gone to fill that damned hot-water bottle again.

Chapter 6

St Colombe

Sonia was fourteen years old when her mother Avril died from the muscle-wasting disease that had claimed half her life. When she died, Sonia was stunned by a crushing sense of rejection and loss. She had expected to feel nothing but relief that her mother's long illness had at last come to an end, and there was relief but far more powerfully an overwhelming sense of being abandoned. Her mother had vanished into thin air, leaving her behind.

If she could have got her back she would have shouted at her, blamed her. She forgot how ill her mother had become and instead remembered only the adored, sweet, laughing mamma who had cherished and loved her and told her she was beautiful. And into the desolation of her bereavement Luis came.

When her mother died, the icy coldness of her body terrified Sonia. Her body had the chilliness of stone. She lay in her polished wooden coffin in a long white shroud made of some fine, silky stuff. Her expression was peaceful and remote and she looked as young as a child. It was hard to believe, looking at that beautiful, serene mask, that she was thirty-six years old.

There was a bib of the same material as the shroud covering her face so that Sonia had to steel herself to turn the bib back and lay it on her chest in order to gaze at the dead face below. Every time she did this she was terrified. Her imagination leapt ahead and tormented her with horrible visions of what she might find underneath.

She was permitted to look at her mother as often as she wanted throughout the morning of the day of the funeral, which was to be at 2 pm at the church of Our Lady of Mercy in Turrialba. Sonia couldn't leave her mother alone. She kept coming back to look, trying to persuade herself that this thing lying there was actually Avril, her mother. She couldn't believe it. The sixth or seventh time that she had crept over to the bier and mounted the steps to take yet another peek (because soon they would nail the lid of her coffin down and take Avril away and she would be gone forever and Sonia would never see her face again), there was a commotion at the other end of the room where people were gathered, talking in subdued voices, and Sonia turned her head and saw Luis. For years her memory of that moment would be connected in her mind with the silky feel of Avril's shroud between her fingers and the strong, sweet smell of the funeral flowers. Love and sex and death, all at once and all the same thing.

Luis came into the drawing room where the mourners were assembled and where Sonia's mother lay in her coffin at one end of the long room, a crucifix between her white hands which were folded together, the flesh already beginning to congeal in their position of prayer. There was a strong smell in the room of incense and candles and the sweet-smelling flowers piled around the coffin on the high dais. Luis held his hat in his hand and kept his eyes respectfully downcast. At the very sight of him Sonia's heartbeat quickened. She watched surreptitiously while this big man with the heavy good looks was made much of by the women. He put his arms around Sonia's father who was sobbing, seemingly unable to control his tears or contain his grief, and offered his condolences. He seemed to present the very picture of tender but strong young manhood, of virile youth comforting weak old age.

Although of course Felipe was not old, he was only forty-two, but grief had turned him into a quivering, sodden wreck; he seemed completely overcome by his wife's death, although it had not been unexpected, she had been ill for a long time before she died.

Luis comforted her father, which made Sonia admire him all the more. Her father's disintegration was adding to her terror. He stood there shaking, the tears soaking his face. Luis put his strong arm around his shoulders. His face remained concerned, tender and bland. He was careful at the beginning not to show his true feelings which at this time were a mixture of repugnance and disgust at his cousin's lack of self-control. He was feeling his way then, testing the ground.

Sonia thought Luis was the most elegant, sophisticated man she had ever seen. He paid great attention to her, treating her with respect and perfect seriousness. He was aroused by little girls and his admiration of her was genuine, but what she could not know was that his interest in her was entirely cold, entirely heartless.

In appearance Luis was not particularly tall but he was muscular and stocky with a proud carriage which made him appear taller than he was. He had big, dark eyes and full lips, his skin was swarthy and there were long black hairs on his arms and on his chest where they formed a thick mat. They fascinated Sonia, those hairs: her imagination would follow the open vee of his shirt and travel down the muscular chest to the flat stomach and belly button – and then stop. She was very young and at the beginning of their relationship, a virgin. She was a child. Beside Luis', her skin seemed to her so very white, her arms so frail; beside him she felt fragile and feminine. He could encircle her wrist with his finger and thumb. She began to feel he might be her saviour. With him there to protect her nothing could harm her. He was so knowledgeable, so street-wise; she was confident that nothing would surprise or disconcert him. He would never make a fool of himself, not like her father, who was innocence itself.

Luis stayed with the family for two weeks. When during that first visit Sonia began to feel momentary spasms of irritation at her father's unceasing displays of grief, Luis would subtly encourage her impatience, without of course seeming to do so. After a very short while he was playing his little cousin like a musical instrument, getting out of her exactly the response he wanted.

He had come to his cousin's funeral partly because he happened to be passing more or less through the area on his way home from a business trip to Columbia, and partly out of curiosity. He had heard via the grapevine that Felipe a while back had won the lottery, his win erroneously rumoured to have been the Big One. Luis believed Felipe to be a fabulously wealthy man. The fact that, as could be seen from the evidence of his own eyes, Felipe chose to live in the modest style that he had always preferred, was rumoured to be due to a natural modesty and a dislike of ostentation. The misunderstanding over Felipe's financial position came to light too late to prevent Sonia's marriage to

Luis which took place a year later, when Sonia was just fifteen and already pregnant with her first child, Alain.

On her arrival in St. Colombe Sonia found to her surprise that simply by marrying Luis she had raised her status, both financial and social, by several notches. She discovered that her husband was a rich man and that her new home was a plantation house on an estate called Rose Belle. Luis' income derived mainly from the growing of coffee and spices, which accounted for the marvellous smell, a combination of clove and nutmeg, coffee and flowers, which was inseparable from Rose Belle. She realised that from now on there would be servants to wait on her and more surprisingly bodyguards to follow at a discreet distance whenever she chose to leave the estate.

'But why?' she asked her husband, braver now that she had been on the island nearly four months. 'Why do I have to have those men following me around, those *sangliers* of yours? I don't like them, they frighten me. What are they afraid of? Nobody's going to hurt me.'

Luis laughed and cut a slice of paw-paw. They were having breakfast on the verandah; rain drummed on the roof, the sound sending shivers down Sonia's back, making her feel lustful and tender. Her stomach was beginning to swell visibly and she was frightened that Luis might not want her so much now that she was beginning to lose her slim shape.

'A great many people would like to hurt me. And they might try to get at me through you. Believe me, it's best that the lads are there to look after you. Try to forget about them; you'll soon get used to them and one day you may even have cause to be thankful.'

'Why would anybody want to hurt you?' Sonia's eyes filled with tears. She thought it must be the pregnancy making her cry so easily; tears would threaten as soon as she got the least bit upset. 'Why should they?'

'No tears.' Luis shot her a sharp glance from under his heavy eyebrows. 'You know I don't like it when you cry.'

'I'm sorry.' She got out her handkerchief and blew her nose. 'I just love you so much.'

She glanced at him from under her eyelashes and thought she caught on his face a fleeting sardonic smile, but when she looked again it wasn't there. She must have been mistaken. 'But I still can't think why anybody would want to hurt you; this isn't Haiti.'

He looked exasperated, spooning paw-paw into his mouth at top speed and smacking his lips greedily. She admitted to herself for the first time, with the cold, rational, other part of her mind, that his manners were not always very good and she even felt quite disgusted sometimes, like when he ate with his mouth open or had made a bad smell in the lavatory but didn't bother to open the window as she had been taught to do; or didn't wash his hands after going or before he ate; or was sometimes rough and careless with her during their love-making. If he hurt her and she cried out he would immediately stop and be full of solicitude, but her objections seemed to put him off. Often he would stop altogether and turn away from her, losing interest, which she couldn't bear and which hurt her more than any physical pain he might have been inflicting, so that she learned to keep silent for longer. She suspected the roughness was his instinctive behaviour and the solicitude and regret learned responses, the acting of a part rather than coming from the heart. Though inexperienced, Sonia was not a fool. But she put these thoughts aside.

Now he said, 'Look, it's just business, that's all. I have enemies, people who don't like my success. It's just jealousy. Don't worry about it. All the same it happens, so don't ignore it either.'

'If anything happened to you I'd die.'

'It won't, so stop worrying.'

'Oh, Luis!'

'What now?'

'The baby kicked!'

'Really?' His sombre face lightened. 'Let me feel.' He laid his big hand on her stomach with such tenderness that her eyes filled with tears again.

'Luis?'

'*Oui, p'tite?*'

'Couldn't we go back to bed for a bit?'

'What, now? Do you want to?'

'Yes, please.'

'Well, well!' He looked at her teasingly so that her insides melted with longing. 'You really love it, don't you? You're turning into a real little love bunny, aren't you? So what happens to little love bunnies, eh?' He got up, wiping his hands on a blue linen napkin, and moved to stand behind her, his hands on her shoulders. 'A big snake will come along and catch her by the throat!'

She giggled. He put his hands around her throat and gave a sharp, painful little squeeze, choking her.

She gave a cry. 'Oh! That hurt!' But he had taken his hands away already and now his forearms were under her armpits, lifting her body slightly, and his hands were fondling her breasts so that she forgot the pain in a rush of pleasurable sensations and arched her body against him in ecstasy. 'Oh, Luis, be careful! The servants will see!'

'So what?' His voice was rough and she could smell his

arousal. 'Where d'you think they think this came from?' He stroked her belly then his hand dropped to between her legs. 'Relax, sweetheart! They think nothing of a little jig-jig here; this is the Caribbean, it's natural. You'll soon lose those inhibitions of yours.'

'Luis! Not here! I couldn't do it here!'

'Well, come on upstairs then, baby, I haven't got all day.'

They made love incessantly during the first few months of their marriage. Knowing she pleased him gave Sonia a sense of security. She knew that sex was important to him and dreaded the call on his restraint that would inevitably follow the birth of their child. She didn't quite trust him and didn't want his attention wandering. He wasn't a reassuring kind of man, which ironically for her then was part of the attraction; she could never be quite sure what he was thinking or what he might do next.

Later, she came to believe that the misunderstanding over her inheritance and the blow to Luis' financial expectations were the soil in which the seeds of his dislike of her were sown and began to flourish, increasing over the years until life became unendurable for them both.

Chapter 7

Sleeping dogs

Storming into the kitchen on Sunday morning, Nelly, shining with anger, demanded to know what the hell Charlotte had done with her sneakers *this* time.

'I need them for gym tomorrow, can't you leave anything alone? Why do you have to keep interfering with everything? You've got no business moving my Vans. *T'es bête comme chou, non?*'

Charlotte, making toast for breakfast, felt her cheeks flush with resentment. She took a deep breath. 'I certainly don't interfere intentionally, as you put it. If you call tripping over them – twice – and moving them to where they aren't going to cause some other person to break their neck then I plead guilty. They're in the lobby where they're supposed to be.'

Put that in your pipe and smoke it, young Nelly, she thought, her lips tight, as Nelly strode out muttering black imprecations. Not a please or a thank you, and she did wish Nelly wouldn't keep bad-mouthing her in French so that Charlotte had no way of knowing how incredibly rude she was being: she really was the frozen limit. Maybe if you were brought up with servants pandering to your every whim you thought you were entitled to treat everybody like that. Sweet as pie when she wanted to be, of course, especially when Patrick was about.

'Right.' Nelly, still simmering, came back into the kitchen with her shoes in her hand. 'I've found them at last, no thanks to you, so at least I won't be late for school looking for them like I was on Friday. *Don't* let this happen again, yeah?' She mistimed this last remark so that unfortunately it coincided with Patrick coming in through the loggia hungry for his breakfast.

He came to an astonished halt. '*What* was that, Nelly?'

'And you can lay off and all. *Ve te faire cuire un oeuf!*' Scarlet-faced, she rushed out of the room.

Patrick stood there, looking shattered. 'What on earth was that about? Does she often speak to you like that?'

'Only on her bad days.' Charlotte put a dish of muesli on the table. 'Milk,' she reminded herself, going to the fridge.

Patrick pulled out a chair and sat down, looking appalled. 'I'm so sorry. I'll have a word with her; we can't have this sort of thing. We haven't actually been in this situation before, somebody from outside living in the house, I mean.' He helped himself to Shreddies. 'I thought you two were starting to get along. I can't think what's come over Nelly nowadays. She used to be quite reasonable for a teenager, now the slightest thing seems to set her off.'

'She's growing up.' Charlotte switched on the kettle. She was pretty sure that if she had a mother like Sonia the slightest thing would set her off, too.

She remembered her own mother: calm, practical and completely content, or so it seemed, with her settled and ordered life in the small Somerset village where she had lived in apparent tranquillity all her married life. Charlotte had grown up in an atmosphere of complete security and regularity.

She filled the cafetière from the kettle. She had to admit that Nelly and she were like chalk and cheese; there was a black anger inside that child, a burning rage and resentment. She took the cafetière to the table, longing to ask questions, but Patrick was deep in *The Sunday Times* and she didn't want to disturb him.

It was always so peaceful in the kitchen on Sunday mornings with just the two of them there. Sonia hardly ever got up for breakfast (although today for once she had accepted a cup of coffee early and gone out) and even on schooldays Nelly never came down until the last minute and had hers virtually on the wing. On Sundays it was extremely unusual for Nelly to appear at all.

NELLY WAS CONVINCED that her mother's present state of mind had something to do with the day the letter came from St. Colombe. Sonia had been home from the hospital a few weeks and things seemed to be looking up, and then the letter came.

The day it came, Patrick had got up early to write as usual and had gone off to the shed after his early morning walk which he took every day, rain or shine. Only for half an hour or so but at top speed. He said it was to counteract all that sitting. Alain, exhausted from end-of-term exams, was still asleep upstairs. Nelly, trying to be helpful, had brought the letters in from the chiffonier where Patrick had left them and brought them into the kitchen where Sonia was sitting at the breakfast table in her dressing gown, or rather, in Patrick's brown plaid one, which she'd taken to wearing, goodness knows why. Why she should suddenly take against her perfectly good kimono was anybody's guess. It was a good thing Patrick never wore his dressing gown himself.

There were two letters for Sonia, one from Harrods, obviously a bill, and the other a blue air letter addressed in handwriting Nelly didn't recognize. What alerted her was the St. Colombe stamp. Her mother put out her hand for the air letter and Nelly handed it over. With one eye on her mother she started to make toast for herself and coffee for her mother. Sonia began tearing the letter open.

'Use a knife, Mother.' Her mother was so impatient; she wouldn't wait for anything.

She put the toast in the toast rack and turned back to the table. She stopped dead. Her mother's face had gone so pale it was almost green: she looked like one of those creatures that live in the dark all the time. She looked as though she was going to faint. She was sitting with her head bowed, fingering the letter in her lap. Nelly put down the toast rack and hurried to her side. 'Mum?'

'*Mon dieu*. Luis.'

'Papa? What about him? Mamée, what is it?' She hadn't used her mother's pet name for years.

Sonia didn't seem to hear her. She went on muttering under her breath. Nelly shook her mother's shoulder. 'What is it? Who's it from?'

Sonia looked up at her with her eyes very wide, and crammed the letter into her pocket, crushing it up all anyhow. 'It's from Françoise Desmarchais, do you remember her? Her husband was the Commissioner of Police. They lived in that big white house in St Etienne, the one with the green shutters, do you remember? It's nothing,

nothing at all. Just some gossip from home. Nothing for you to worry about.'

'If it was nothing you wouldn't look like that.' She came close to her mother. 'Please tell me, Mamée. Please let me help.'

Sonia pushed her away and stood up as though suddenly revitalised, like one of those cartoon figures that inflate suddenly, full of life and air again after being squashed flat. Or as if she was advertising vitamin shots on TV.

'No. You mustn't know anything about it. Nothing at all. I mean that, Nelly, you must forget all about it. Now I have to go.' She looked around dazedly. 'I must find Alain.'

'Oh, here we go. It's always Alain. Why can't you tell *me*?'

Her mother didn't seem to hear. She turned to Nelly with a charming smile as though she'd just been introduced to her at a cocktail party. 'You remember the Desmarchais, don't you? Françoise and Pierre?' She started walking towards the door and paused by the Aga. She picked up a dish rag that had been left there in a damp heap and began absentmindedly wiping one of the hot plates. 'She was a good friend to me, Françoise. Almost my only friend, finally. I don't suppose you remember but towards the end we were like lepers in that house.'

Nelly thought in bewilderment, but it wasn't like that for me.

Her mother darted a sideways look at Nelly. 'People were afraid to come to the house because your father – well, you know he was drinking a lot. He didn't encourage visitors.'

'I don't understand. Please tell me what happened the day Papa died. Nobody's ever really explained. Why don't you trust me?' she wailed as her mother, seeming not to have heard her, put down the cloth and walked to the door. 'I'm sixteen! You can't just ignore me! I'm not a child anymore.' If her mother went through that door without saying anything then she was through with her, it would be the end of everything.

Sonia turned around with her hand on the door handle. 'Nelly, I mean it when I say you must forget all about this. It's just something I have to sort out. Believe me, it's better that you don't know anything.'

Nelly ran after her. 'Why can you talk about it to Alain? Why him and not me?'

She thought her mother was going to say something important but finally she said, 'I can't explain. You have to trust me.'

'You mean you won't. You can't be bothered.'

Her mother stood by the door with her head bowed. She looked up. 'You have to trust me.'

'Why should I? You won't trust me.' With an angry movement Nelly swept up the wet dish cloth and marched over to the sink. She wrung it out under the hot tap. Whatever she did, she mustn't cry.

A wave of longing for Lena came over her. She missed her so much. She missed all of them but Lena most of all. She turned the tap on harder. She didn't want to hear her mother leaving. She was always leaving. Leaving without explaining.

She pressed her lips together to stop herself from crying. If her mother would just come and put her arms around her and explain, she would never ask for anything else as long as she lived. But when she turned around again her mother had gone.

Nelly's lips set in a straight line. '*Je m'en fous*. I don't need you. *T'es une vielle bique.*' Her mother looked terrible in that blouse anyway, it was the wrong colour for her. She'd been going to tell her but now she wouldn't. Let her go around all day looking like a washed-out old dishrag, see if she cared.

Before lunch, Alain announced that he had decided to go to India and was leaving the following day.

Chapter 8

Poulet au Riz

Charlotte had expected to have to do a certain amount of tidying up, but every Tuesday and Friday morning Mrs P. came in for a couple of hours to clean and do the ironing, and as a consequence Charlotte found she had virtually none to do.

Mrs P. was the most self-effacing person Charlotte had ever met. Despite the gentle stream of incomprehensible commentary flowing from her lips as she dusted and mopped, wiped and polished, she was the most determined protector of her personal privacy Charlotte had ever encountered.

She was equally punctilious about not asking questions of other people, particularly those she looked upon as strangers. Charlotte found that this made for an odd partnership between them, amiable but impersonal, and she had given up trying to make conversation during the breaks Mrs P. allowed herself every hour or so, during which she would sit, for five minutes at the most, knees apart, large bosom resting comfortably on the edge of the kitchen table, drinking several mugs of the strong tea Charlotte provided.

Despite this apparently incessant thirst she seemed to find time to do most of the ironing as well, which left Charlotte more or less free to concentrate on cooking.

Quite often when Charlotte was cooking Patrick came into the kitchen near dinner time and walked about, lifting all the saucepan lids to see what they were having. Charlotte didn't normally object but one evening when her Hollandaise sauce was on the verge of curdling, she snapped, yelling at him to get out of the way.

'Oh, Patrick,' she said, her face burning with heat and mortification, once everything was safely in the hot drawer and things had got back into perspective. 'I am so sorry. I was worried about the sauce.'

'All my fault.' Patrick backed out of the room, not at all put-out. 'I am a thoughtless oaf. I will refrain from coming and bothering you in future.'

Charlotte panicked when Patrick said this. Suppose he stopped coming into the kitchen altogether! They had such cosy times over tea at the end of his working day, particularly if Sonia was out which she quite often was; she seemed to have developed a passion for visiting art galleries; and, in any case, she often went for her run about tea-time.

'I didn't mean to put you off. You're welcome in here any time, honestly.' It seemed a funny thing to be saying to somebody about their own kitchen. She wished he didn't have to see her like this so much of the time, up to her elbows in flour or with custard in her hair.

'Are you sure you don't mind? It's just it's so cosy in here. I love watching you cook, actually.'

'Do you?' Charlotte bent her head over the stove.

'It reminds me of coming home on the first day of the holidays when we lived in the old house in Kemerton – in Gloucestershire, you know – when I was a boy. I always did things in exactly the same order when I got home: first to the stables to see my friend Tom, then to the nursery to see Nanny, then to the kitchen regions to pester Cook.'

Cook. Charlotte felt a little chill: that didn't sound very glamorous.

Sonia wandered in at that point and sat down. Nelly followed her in and plonked herself onto a chair.

Sonia picked up her napkin. 'How was your day, Nelly?'

Nelly ignored her, her face deadpan as usual.

'Nell?' Patrick helped himself to a roll. 'Your mother just asked you a question.'

'Oh, sorry. I didn't realise she was expecting an answer. I know she isn't really interested in what sort of day I had.'

'Don't be so bloody rude. Of course she's interested.'

'Of course I am.' Sonia looked stunned. Her hand, stretched out towards the bread rolls, froze in mid-air.

'Oh, I see. I just assumed that if you were really interested you'd have come to the school play this afternoon like you said you were going to. You didn't come. I was the only person in my class with nobody there.'

Appalled, Sonia looked at Patrick for help, then back at Nelly's cold face. 'I'm so, so sorry. I didn't know it was today. You never said.'

'Yes, I did. I told you about it three weeks ago.'

'But – yes, you did, I remember now – but you mentioned it when I was rushing out of the front door in a hurry. I was late for that preview, do you remember? You knew I hadn't taken it in properly. Why didn't you remind me the next day, or put it in the diary?'

'Or mention it to me.' Patrick spooned broccoli onto his plate. 'What a bore, I loved your last school play.'

Nelly's mask slipped and she looked at him with something like coyness. 'That was ages ago. I didn't think you'd be interested.'

Sonia still looked horrified. 'You should have reminded me. I would have loved to have come.'

Nelly looked at her through narrowed eyes. 'But you're so busy. You have so many worthwhile projects taking up your valuable time.'

'Come off it, Nell.' Patrick picked up a dish of *courgettes au gratin*. 'Leave your mother alone and have some of these, they look wonderful. Charlotte, whatever did we do before you came?'

Patrick was not always tactful.

Nelly smirked. 'What indeed. How much time was it you spent in the kitchen, mother? Ten minutes a day? Five? No wonder you got fed up with it.'

'Oh, do stop it,' Charlotte said before she could stop herself. Honestly, it was like watching someone pull the wings off a butterfly. She blushed. Perhaps she'd gone too far. 'Your mother hasn't been well.' She blushed again, feeling that this sounded patronising.

'Yes, and don't we all know why.' Nelly looked coldly at her mother. 'Although nobody seems to want to talk about it.'

'Do have some of this.' Charlotte's serving spoon hovered over the *poulet au riz*. 'You said you were starving half an hour ago.'

Nelly shook her head and stood up. 'I've lost my appetite. It must be all the hypocrisy in the air, it gives me a stomach ache. I'm going upstairs.' She went out, slamming the door.

Sonia's eyes filled with tears. 'It's no use.'

Nelly put her head back around the door. 'I should go back and talk to your psychiatrist, mother. Doesn't he know about guilt complexes? I thought that was what they were there for. Tell him the truth this time, then you might start feeling better.'

'What truth, what are you talking about?' Tears rolled down Sonia's face. 'Why are you being like this, Nelly, what have I done?'

'That's the $64,000 dollar question, isn't it? For a start, if you ask me, you probably murdered my father.'

'TALK TO ME, SONIA,' Patrick said later in the day, walking around the bedroom picking bits of cat's hair off the carpet. 'Maisie's been moulting in here again. Must try to keep the door shut.'

'Sorry.'

'What's got into you? You've hardly said one word all evening.'

'There's nothing to say.'

Actually there was a great deal to at least discuss, Patrick thought, in view of Nelly's bombshell, but perhaps this was not the time. Of course Nelly had just been having a go, but still, that had been a tough one. Less a dart and more a Molotov cocktail. And Sonia's face – well, she'd looked gutted.

She was sitting in front of the dressing shelf brushing her hair. Behind her, Patrick shook the cat's fluffy hair from his fingers – it clung to them like thistledown – into the wastepaper basket, a padded, pink-satin-covered object that Sonia hated and complained about every time she threw something into it. He stood leaning against the door frame, his hands in his pockets, watching the hypnotic flick of her hairbrush, up and out, up and out, and admired, against his will because he was cross with her, her straight back, the fine bones of her wrist and the charming shape of her round, boyish head.

She was doing her hundred brushes a night, courtesy of that old Hollywood queen Quentin Mauser, an ancient copy of whose block-busting beauty handbook *Who's the Fairest of Them All?* Sonia had discovered in the bookcase while idling about following her release from the hospital. She had hardly put it down since; it had become her bible. She seemed to believe every word of Mauser's nonsense, from the concept of garlic as a romantic food to the efficacy of gymnastics for the eyes. Patrick found this childlike faith alternately touching and maddening. She seemed to think she had to obey every rule. One of the rules was that you had to brush your hair one hundred times a day. If you didn't, Patrick supposed, it would start falling out in handfuls.

The silence became curiously loaded. He'd felt her antagonism building up ever since she had come in from her run. Running was supposed to make you feel better, not worse. She'd hardly spoken through dinner. He'd felt embarrassed, wondering what on earth Charlotte must have thought. She'd gone to a lot of trouble cooking a complicated meal, some chicken dish with rice and a wonderful sort of lemony mousse thing for dessert. Sonia had picked at her food; he'd felt ashamed of her ungraciousness.

'That was a very good meal we had tonight.' He felt restless, his usual habit of patience depleted by tiredness. Increasingly by the end of the day he felt completely drained. He sat down on one of the twin beds. 'Charlotte certainly is a wonderful cook.'

In the mirror he saw her slant him a look of contempt.

'What's that for?'

'I know you think she's a wonderful cook.'

'Well, she is. Haven't eaten so well since Tony took me to Rules. Honestly, no kidding.'

Sonia looked mutinous. 'I really don't care about food.'

'Well, you could try to look a bit enthusiastic. There was no need to be quite so rude.'

Sonia stopped brushing, turned around and looked at him severely. 'What is wrong with you? Why are you so cross?' She started brushing again, watching his reflection in the mirror.

Patrick felt like snatching the brush out of her hand and bashing her over the head with it.

'You were rude to Charlotte.'

'I was not.'

'She'd been to a lot of trouble.'

'She's paid to go to a lot of trouble.'

'For heaven's sake! What's got into you this evening?'

Sonia put the brush down and turned to face him. She said in a choked voice, 'You expect me to trust you and believe in you, Patrick, but you're always fussing around other women. How do you think that makes me feel?'

'What other women? What are you talking about?'

'I saw you with her in the kitchen, making up to her, standing close to her. Saying things.' She turned back to the dressing table and bent her head. She let out a little sob. 'I know we haven't been very close lately. But even when we were it didn't make any difference, you were still looking at everybody else.'

'I was probably tasting something. You can't honestly think I'm interested in Charlotte in that way? The idea's laughable. Anyway, looking at somebody doesn't mean I want to jump into bed with them.'

'What's the difference?'

'There's an enormous difference.' He went to her and

put his hands on her shoulders. 'Darling idiot.' He bent and kissed the top of her head. 'You're talking nonsense, you know you are. I don't know what puts these ideas into your head.'

'Just don't tell me I'm imagining things.' From her voice he could tell she was actually gritting her teeth. 'Just don't tell me that.'

'I don't know what else to say. I enjoy looking at a pretty woman, of course I do. I looked at you, didn't I? I don't have a spark of interest in Charlotte; she's a nice person, but not like that. I can't think what makes you think I do.'

'*You* do.' She looked at him as though she wanted to hit him. Her shoulders under his hands were rigid with tension. 'It's hopeless.' She made as if to pull away from him. Still he held onto her firmly. She relaxed a little and sat still again. 'You don't understand. It isn't just her, it's lots of women. It's the way you look at them.' In a low voice she said, 'I just don't feel I can trust you.'

'Of course you can trust me, you're my wife.' He felt utterly confused by her complete misunderstanding of him. She seemed determined to erect a barrier between them he felt incapable of bridging.

'That doesn't mean anything.'

He held her shoulders, not knowing what to say. Her skin felt warm through the pink silk blouse she was wearing. He said on impulse, with a quiver of nervousness as the words left his mouth, 'If only you'd let me love you again. If we could only go back to how we used to be. You'd feel better then. You'd know then that I love you.'

She sat very still. There was a long silence in which Patrick weighed up his chances. It was quite possible he'd finally blown it with this remark and she was about to throw him out and instruct him never to darken her bedroom door again.

Sonia turned aside, moving out of his grasp, and then stood up, looking at her reflection in the mirror. She said quietly, 'I used to love it, you know.'

'What? What did you say?'

She looked down at her hands, held at waist level, her fingers loosely clasped. 'I do remember how lovely it was.'

'Darling.' He moved to stand behind her, joy and relief flooding through him. He put his arms around her waist from behind and caught hold of her clasped hands in both his own. He said in a low voice, pressing against her and looking at their combined reflection, 'I was never sure. You seemed to be enjoying it but sometimes I felt – that you were just trying to make it good for me. It seemed to upset you so much.'

'I didn't mean with you.'

Patrick couldn't believe she had said that.

'What did you say?'

'I meant with him, with Luis. When I was a girl. Before everything got spoiled. I loved it then; I wanted to make love all the time.'

He looked at her face reflected in the mirror. It was irradiated with a kind of bliss, her eyes dreamy; there was a little smile, he supposed of tender recollection, on her lips. It was a look he had never seen on her face before. He dropped his arms from around her and moved away. He felt dizzy. He clenched his fists and took a deep breath; he felt winded, as though she had turned around and smashed him in the face. Their eyes met in the mirror and her face changed as she saw on his face the shock and misery he was unable to conceal. She looked stunned, as though she were emerging from a dream.

'Patrick,' she said sorrowfully.

He felt that he had to get out of the room, preferably out of the house, as quickly as possible. He didn't trust himself. What he felt for her at that moment was the most intense emotion he had ever experienced. He could not have put it into words; it was more like a sound ringing through his head than a feeling. His entire body hurt.

This was how murderers felt.

At the door he turned. 'I think I'll go out for a while. Don't wait up.'

Why had he said that? She never waited up. They were still sleeping separately. He'd moved into the spare room when she was in hospital and the invitation to return had not yet been forthcoming. He closed the bedroom door and walked rapidly along the passage. There was a light under Nelly's door. Charlotte was in the kitchen clearing up. He would not be leaving Sonia alone in the house. He didn't know how she was feeling, if she was feeling anything at all except self-pity.

There was no hope for them. Utterly miserable, he ran down the stairs. He couldn't bear to stay in the house a minute longer. He went into the study for his jacket and car keys and let himself out into the darkness.

Chapter 9

Look at me, I'm Sandra Dee

Patrick phoned Laura from the call box at the end of the road. The box smelt of sweat, chewing gum and farts and he wrinkled up his nose fastidiously as he waited for her to pick up. The phone rang for so long he thought she must be out but finally there she was.

'Is that you, Patrick? Goodness, I am honoured. You don't usually ring me on a Sunday. Is Sonia away?'

'No. Can we meet? Are you free?'

'I might be. What's all this about?'

'Nothing special, just wanted to see you.'

'Oh.' Laura sounded delighted.

Patrick's courage faltered slightly. Ten years before, he and Laura had been engaged for two years. The relationship had ended when a former lover had come back into Laura's life and she had gone back to him. That relationship had ended and she and Patrick had met again last year when Laura, to his surprise and some pleasure, had appeared again, teaching in the geography department at Nelly's school. She had made it clear to Patrick that she was very ready to resume their relationship and appeared devastated to discover that he was now married and, he assured her, in love with his wife. So far, he had restricted the relationship to the occasional friendly meet for a drink.

She might read something into this break from routine, something that wasn't there; he could do without further complications.

Laura's voice sounded eager and breathless. 'Usual place? I'll be there in twenty minutes.'

Her red Ford Escort was the only car in the car park of the Moon and Sixpence. Through the rolled-up window he could see her fair hair shining in the reflected light from a solitary street lamp. His heartbeat quickened. It was very late.

He got out of his car and locked it, looking around as he did so. Before phoning her he had driven around for a long time, his emotions spinning through fearfulness, hurt and misery to a point of exhaustion where all he wanted was oblivion. Now that he had come to this point, made this decision, all he seemed capable of feeling was a craving for mindless sex. He felt hard-hearted and self-justifying. Damn Sonia. Damn her to hell.

Laura lowered the car window at his approach and smiled up at him. Looking down into her full, almost chubby face, as fresh and glowing as a child's, he remembered a moment during their engagement when lying underneath him in the rather twee, brass four-poster bed that she'd draped with white muslin like a baby's bassinet, she had looked up at him and said, 'Do I remind you of anybody, Patrick?'

'What, somebody I know?' Patrick stroked her hair with post-coital tenderness.

'No, silly. A film star. 1950s, sort of. I'm supposed to look exactly like her.'

Zsa Zsa Gabor? Grace Kelly? She didn't look a bit like either of those, or any of the other blondes he could think of. 'Marilyn Monroe?'

'Not *her!* Sandra Dee, silly. You know – Sandra *Dee*!'

And in the strange way that these things happen, a film with this previously by him unheard of screen goddess had come up on the television only the following week, when he'd been sitting around in the evening too tired to do any more work, waiting to be sleepy enough to go to bed so that the next morning would come quicker and he could start working again; and she did look quite astonishingly like Laura, chubby cheeks, bobbing blonde hair, pretty mouth and all.

'Hi.' Patrick leaned down to her window. 'Thanks for coming.'

'Why here?' Laura looked round at the deserted car park with some distaste. 'You could just as easily have come to the house.'

'I didn't feel like being indoors. Can I get in for a minute?'

'Of course.' She looked pleased and puzzled. She opened the passenger door for him and he heaved himself in, shut the door and sat looking straight ahead.

What was he doing here? There was still time to draw back.

'You sounded upset on the phone. Has something happened?'

He tried not to notice the eagerness in her voice. He remembered how, when they were together, before they had become engaged she had always probed, always pushed things on, hoping for new developments in their relationship. Once they had become engaged she had relaxed.

'Did I? No, not really. Just had a bit of a day, you know how it is.'

'No. I don't know how it is. Tell me.'

Patrick took a deep breath. He felt tempted to complain about Sonia. What she had said, or perhaps the fact that she had said it at all, to him, to his face, had so stunned him that he felt a longing to share his hurt, to discover whether his repelled reaction had been natural, to be expected, or if he was just being an over-sensitive fool.

Of course her relationship with Luis was all in the past. Over. It wasn't so much the statement that had upset him so, it was her absolute indifference to his feelings. Had she said it on purpose to hurt him? Or was she just completely insensitive? He didn't feel too enthusiastic about either alternative. He shook his head and shifted his weight around in the seat so that he was half-facing Laura. Mustn't tell, he thought. Mustn't be a complete bastard. 'I'd rather talk about you.' He took her soft, cold hand. 'What have you been doing since I saw you?'

'It's been three weeks. I thought you'd gone off me again. I wrote to you.'

'Yes. Thank you. It was a lovely letter. Of course I haven't gone off you. If you remember when we broke up all those years ago it was the other way around, or have you managed to reframe things in your usual bright and breezy way?'

He ought not to be here. He thought of Sonia, undressing for bed. Or in the bath. At any rate taking her clothes off, but not for him. Probably upset still. Perhaps she'd go down and talk to Charlotte.

'You look so sad.' Laura leaned forward and stroked his face. The touch of her cold fingers was like a small electric shock. She leaned towards him. She was wearing some soft, beige woolly thing under her loose black coat. He knew what her underwear was like. He knew what her legs were like and what they could do. He could smell her perfume. He'd been vacillating too long.

'Come here.' He folded her in his arms.

'Oh, darling, I thought you'd never ask,' she whispered. 'I'm so excited.' Her breath, smelling of toothpaste, was warm on his cheek. 'Come back home with me. I want you, Patrick. I want you so much.'

'I'm married.' He touched her breast. 'You know I can't give you anything. I'm no good for you, Laura.' But he kissed her again and her mouth opened wide under his. He felt an overpowering wave of lust.

'Yes, you are, you're perfect for me,' she whispered against his face. 'I love you, Patrick. I always have. Please, darling, please come home with me.'

'I must think.' Patrick's breath heaved, his inhibitions dissolving in his longing for physical relief and oblivion. He moulded her soft woman's shape with his hands, testing her, feeling like a boy again.

'Let's do it here. Please, Patrick, let's do it now.' She took his hand and pulled it down, pressing his fingers into the secret folds between her legs. She didn't seem to have any underwear on.

'Christ.'

She smiled against his face. 'French knickers.'

'Laura.' He felt himself slipping down the road to perdition.

'Come on, darling. On the back seat. I'll sit on your lap. Don't you remember, like on the beach at Hastings?' She had opened the door on her side and was looking back at him over her shoulder, laughing, deliberately enticing. She looked so pretty, like a naughty child. He put out his hand and caught hold of her sleeve to restrain her.

'Laura, wait. I can't do this. Not like this. I have to think.'

She was still for a moment and then she swung her legs back in, shut the door and leaned her head back against the headrest, her eyes closed. After a while, since Patrick did nothing but sit as if frozen, she took in a long breath. 'I think you'd better go. I feel a complete fool. I thought it was what you wanted but obviously I was wrong.'

'You weren't.' He shook his head. 'It's sweet and lovely of you.'

She gave a sort of snort.

'Laura.' He reached out for her but she stayed where she was. He dreaded that she might be crying.

She got out a handkerchief and blew her nose. She said quite calmly, 'I don't know what you want, Patrick, but you're going to have to make up your mind.'

She sounded not bitter but sad. Patrick felt immense gratitude that she seemed to have decided not to get emotional. He couldn't have coped with another scene.

'When you decide, I'll be waiting, but don't leave it too long. Now please go, it's past my bedtime.'

Driving home, Patrick alternately kicked himself for having turned down an opportunity many men would have given a month's salary for, and thanked his stars that he hadn't been a complete idiot. At least he would be able to face Sonia in the morning. He didn't know whether disappointment or relief was uppermost in his mind. He felt hardly able to think at all, he was so exhausted.

I'm getting past it, he thought, longing for his bed. The streets were dark and deserted; he felt dreadfully alone. As he turned the car into the avenue, he remembered that the book was nearly finished. The tension in his stomach eased. It wasn't all disaster. At least I've got Chandler, he thought, and felt a stab of relief that was almost happiness.

But he had to decide what to do about Laura. He couldn't go on letting things drag on like this, it wasn't fair on anybody. Putting the car away in the garage and feeling the oppression and the sense of failure close in on him again, he couldn't understand what had made him hesitate. He felt convinced that there was nothing for him here.

Next time, he told himself, there would be no holding back.

Chapter 10

Dance till you drop

Nelly sat cross-legged on Charlotte's bed watching Charlotte tidy up around her. 'Mum seemed to be on the mend until that letter came.' She gathered up Charlotte's cream-coloured pyjamas and folded them carefully. 'Do you always keep them in this bag thing? You're so organised.'

'That was my mother.' Charlotte took the pyjamas and tucked them into their sachet. 'I was brought up that way: a place for everything and everything in its place. What letter?'

'The one from St. Colombe, from Madame Desmarchais. I told you, it came about two months ago. She'd only been home from the hospital a little while. She's been a nervous wreck ever since it came. Well, even more of a nervous wreck.'

Charlotte must think her mother a terrible wimp, hiding up in her room and avoiding people the way she did. Except when she went running, she still did that. She'd started going up to town a bit more just recently too, which was something; to look at pictures, she said. Paintings in galleries. She would put on a blonde wig to go out and dark glasses as though she was afraid of being recognised. It was weird. Of course they were used to her being a bit eccentric but it must seem completely bonkers to a normal, cheerful sort of person like Charlotte.

'She's got a red one, too.'

'A red what?'

'Wig. And she jumps like hell whenever the phone goes.'

'She *has* had a nervous breakdown, Nelly.' Charlotte started pinning up her hair.

'Or anyway that's what they called it. Do you have to put it up?'

''Fraid so. Can't have it trailing in the *bouillabaisse*. What would you call it?' Charlotte looked in the dressing-table mirror at Nelly's reflection.

Nelly frowned, smoothing the cream silk nightgown case as though she were stroking a cat. 'I like all these lacey bits. I dunno. Dunno what's the matter with her except she seems scared stiff of something.'

Charlotte finished doing her hair and went back to straightening cushions and whisking things into drawers. She glanced at Nelly. 'You don't really think she had anything to do with your father's death, do you? I assumed you were just winding her up.'

At least she didn't say, *as usual*. Nobody had said a thing about Nelly's outburst, which made her feel worse somehow. At least Charlotte seemed prepared to talk about it.

Nelly didn't reply.

'Have you tried talking to her about it?' Charlotte put her brush and comb away in her dressing-table drawer. 'About what's bothering her, I mean?'

This was safer territory. 'You try. She's impossible. Anyway, what's the use of talk?' Nelly flung herself on her back and stared at the ceiling. 'Anyway, I *have* tried. She doesn't listen. It's like she's gone deaf or something. I wish Alain was here. She'd tell *him*.'

'Come on, Nelly. Off.'

'Ohhh ... can't I stay here?'

'No you can't. You've got school, anyway. You can help me make the bed, if you like.'

'Sonia just leaves hers.'

'I know. I end up making it. Come on. Move.'

'You're so cruel.' Nelly rolled off the bed and fell onto the floor. She lay there hardly breathing. Charlotte stepped over her and started to straighten the bottom sheet on her bed, tucking in the corners.

Nelly sat up. 'That's another funny thing. All this fuss about Alain going to India. She was the one who made him go.'

'Sorry?' Charlotte paused in the middle of plumping up the continental quilt. 'I do like these, they're so much easier than blankets.'

Nelly frowned. She wanted to talk about Alain, not continental quilts, however much she was enjoying her own. 'Well, not India especially. But she made him go away. It was her idea.'

'But she hates him not being here.'

'Tell me about it.' Nelly hauled herself to her feet.

'She'd hate you not being here just as much.'

'Oh *sure*. But why dismiss her darling boy?' She wandered over to the window and stood there biting her lower lip, remembering.

The day the letter came, after the row with her mother in the kitchen, she'd sulked for a bit, then curiosity had got the better of her and she'd wandered along to Alain's room. The door was ajar and standing outside in the passage she heard Alain say, 'Well, it might as well be Nepal. I've always wanted to stay in a Buddhist monastery.'

She'd walked into the room then and after a slight pause her mother said in a false voice, 'I mustn't forget to remind Patrick about the phone bill.'

'Don't look so worried, Nelly.' Charlotte put her hand gently on Nelly's arm. She looked nice. She was wearing a pale green, sleeveless blouse and a straight, natural-coloured linen skirt. It looked as though she'd got thinner but that might just be her clothes.

'Time for you to be off. You don't want to be late for school again. I must go down and put the wash on. See you downstairs.' She went out, leaving the door open.

Nelly sat on the bed and listened to her retreating footsteps. She hugged her arms around herself, wishing she could talk to Charlotte about St. Colombe, tell her how much she missed her father and Rose Belle and Pearl and Christophine. She had to admit, she was beginning to unbend towards Charlotte. She was the sort of person you just couldn't go on feeling angry with; she was so sort of well-meaning. You couldn't imagine her doing anything unkind. This warmed Nelly to her, albeit against her will. Maybe she had gone a bit over the top at the beginning, cheeking her all over the place.

She wasn't sure why Charlotte had got up her nose so badly at first. She discussed this with Sandy one afternoon. They were crouched in the ha-ha at the end of the playing fields having a quiet smoke after school before getting the bus home.

Sandy said, 'It's probably because she does the things you'd like Sonia to do and Sonia doesn't, like sort of taking care of you, that kind of thing. Your mum's not really into all that stuff, is she?'

'She doesn't seem to know how. We had servants in St. Colombe.' Because this sounded rather grand Nelly added hastily, 'I mean, everybody does over there, it's part of the culture. And Sonia's mother wasn't much of a mother either, I don't think. She got ill, you see. She died when my mum was fourteen.'

She had never known Avril, her maternal grandmother, but she distinctly remembered her father Luis saying to her mother, 'It was a bad day when your father married your mother. A more unsuitable pair it would be hard to imagine.'

Sonia was shocked. 'But my father loved her, so he was happy.'

'In a fool's paradise, a fool's paradise.'

Luis was good at pretending to care about things like that, her mother had told her once: like whether his wife's parents had been happy or not. He couldn't have cared less, actually, she said, but he put on a good show. Nelly hated it when her mother displayed these rare flashes of bitterness. She preferred to remember her father's good points: his strength, his good looks, his courage. The way he rode a horse as though he had been born in the saddle.

'There you are then. No role model. No wonder she's no good at it.' Sandy shifted her position on the ground. 'I'm getting grass stains on my skirt. We haven't all got Charlotte to do our washing for us.'

'I don't see the point of having kids if you can't be bothered to look after them.'

'I'm never going to have kids.'

'I say, Sandy. I was in Charlotte's room the other day – you know – talking—'

'I didn't know you talked!'

'We don't, not like this I mean. Obviously we have to communicate.' She didn't know why she held back from telling Sandy how much she was getting to like Charlotte. 'I'd gone in to get my skirt she was mending, the one I tore on my bike that time – you remember, it got caught in the wheel? Anyway, there was this photograph on her dressing table.'

'Yeah?' Sandy blew a smoke ring. 'What of?'

'This really gross-looking man. Too many teeth and yucky hair. Horrible leather jacket with the collar all crumpled. I mean really boge. Sandy, that's *Riley*.'

'Who's Riley?'

'He's Charlotte's *ex*! Would you believe it?'

'Jump back! I thought you said he was the love of her life.' Sandy tapped the ash off her cigarette.

'He *was*. She adored him. You know I told you she got divorced? She says he – Riley – went on and on at her, telling her she was too fat and she ought to cut her hair – that sort of thing – and all the time he looked like that! Can you believe the arrogance? Why do men think they're so wonderful and women always put themselves down? I'm not going to be like that, I can tell you.'

'They aren't all like that. Patrick isn't, is he?'

'Oh, Patrick isn't. But poor Charlotte. She deserves something better than that oaf.'

'Did you ask her about it?'

'About the divorce? Yeah I did, I asked her what happened and her face sort of wobbled and I thought, crumbs, she's going to start crying.'

'What did you do?'

'Suddenly remembered I had homework to do. I buzzed. Just couldn't face it.'

Nelly felt a bit bad about that. Perhaps Charlotte had really wanted to talk. She listened to Nelly often enough. Next time she'd be braver. Charlotte was okay.

After seeing Sandy onto her bus she ambled along to her own stop, a hundred yards further along. She thought about Riley, and about how different Patrick was. He'd never behave like Riley. And you could trust him, unless it was all just an act. I mean, you never knew, did you? Reliable Patrick, was how he seemed. He never flew into a rage or shouted at you, no matter how far you pushed him. Her father's rages had been terrible to behold. To be fair, they usually happened when he'd been drinking, so maybe it was the drink talking, as Excelie always said, but it didn't make him any less terrifying when he was drunk.

The bus shelter was empty, the 490 having just gone. Another one wasn't due for half an hour. She went into the shelter, her heart starting to pound. Into her mind came the image of her mother dancing, her beautiful white dress flying out around her like swirls of vanilla ice cream.

Oh God. However you hard you tried to suppress things you were desperate not to remember, they had a habit of popping up every now and again, like weeds through cement.

It was because she'd been thinking about her father. She sat down on the bench and leaned back, giving in to the inevitable. It was a bit like being sick, best got over quickly.

SHE HAD LEFT her bedroom because the music had woken her up. She was five years old. She knew that because it had been her birthday the day before.

She opened her bedroom door and peeped out. It was dark in the upstairs passage. There was a brown carpet running the length of it made of some hard-wearing material – sisal, Lena said it was – she could remember the roughness of it under her small, soft feet.

The servants had gone to bed hours ago and upstairs was in total darkness except for the light glowing at the end of the passage and the distant sound of music. Perhaps there was a party! Something was happening anyway, something exciting and delightful, involving music and laughter and fun!

She padded down the passage towards the open doors at the end, turned the corner and found herself in the gallery. Her ears were suddenly flooded with the wonderful, cheerful sound of music coming from the brilliantly-lit ballroom below. She crouched down and peeped through the balustrade.

Her eyes nearly popped out in amazement. What an incredible sight! All of the eight chandeliers were lit, blazing down the length of the vast room. She gazed open-mouthed, captivated by the millions of sparkling lights reflected over and over again in the huge gold-framed mirrors hanging on both sides and down the length of the room. To a little girl, it was fairyland.

Slowly, after the darkness of the passage, her eyes grew accustomed to the brilliance below her. She looked down and saw Papa. Dressed all in black, upright and commanding, he stood in the middle of one of the beautiful rugs, holding his long riding crop in his right hand. He looked wonderful, so strong and so handsome. Nelly's heart swelled with pride.

He was striking the palm of his left hand in time to the music which was coming from somewhere, Nelly couldn't see where.

POM pom pom, POM pom pom went the music in a

lovely lilting rhythm. He hit his hand with the stick on the first POM, accompanying the music like the conductor of an orchestra.

Then to Nelly's surprise and delight she saw her mother, dressed all in white, dancing. Round Papa she whirled and spun in time to the music, her white skirts flying.

After a long time, it seemed to Nelly, bursting with pleasure and joy at such a scene of happiness, her mother began to slow down; she staggered and almost fell. Nelly tensed, watching, but it was all right, her mother didn't fall.

She heard her mother say, 'I'm tired, Luis. Let me stop ... please let me stop now.'

'But I'm enjoying myself. You know how I like to see you dance.'

Yes! Nelly thought, agreeing wholeheartedly. Go on, Mamée, dance!

'No Luis ... please.' Her mother came and tried to lean against him.

He pushed her away. 'Dance!' This time his voice was not friendly but loud and commanding. Nelly blinked. Why was Papa angry? What had Mamée done?

He pushed Mamée so that she staggered. Again she nearly fell. This time Nelly cried out, but her little voice was lost in the loud music. Nobody could hear her. Mamée began to dance again.

Papa began to tap Mamée with the riding crop. At first he was gentle, and he was smiling, and Nelly laughed to see them, Mamée dancing and Papa tapping her in time to the music with his stick, POM pom pom, POM pom pom, as the music whirled round. But then he began to tap her harder, on her waist and on her back.

Mamée was holding her arms out to balance herself,

and at first Nelly thought she was having fun like Papa, but gradually she began to sense that something was wrong. Every time her mother tried to stop dancing, Papa hit her again so that it seemed to Nelly, watching in total incomprehension, that her mother had turned magically into one of Alain's spinning tops that if you hit it with a stick would go on whirling and spinning forever.

She heard Mamée cry out. '*Stop! Please stop!*' Her cries turned into screams which rose above the music, echoing round the silk-hung walls and bouncing off the surface of the mirrors and echoing now through Nelly's head as she crouched, shivering, on the bench in the bus shelter.

Occasionally Mamée would come down to breakfast in a blue, high-necked dress with long sleeves that covered her lovely arms. Nelly's father seemed to approve of this dress: he congratulated her on her appearance when she wore it, and when she looked back at him with her huge-eyed, wordless stare, Nelly wondered why she didn't look pleased. She ought to be pleased that Papa liked her dress when so often he disapproved. She blamed her mother for her ungraciousness.

Shivering in the bus stop, her arms hugged tight across her chest, Nelly thought that it was as if she was watching them through the wrong end of a telescope; they were so tiny and far away: her father all in black standing there so upright and handsome and commanding, her mother in her white dress, whirling and circling under the sparkling lights.

Chapter 11

Here come the girls

Nelly's best friends at school were Sandy, Blossom and Tigs. Creatures of habit, they spent every break, if it was fine, sunning themselves on the library steps in the weak early summer sunshine, doing their utmost to get their legs brown.

'Wish I didn't go this awful pink.' Tigs patted her pudgy thighs. 'I want to go brown like you, Nell.'

Tigs' very fair eyebrows and lashes had given her a distinctly albino look until one day, Sandy having pointed this out, she'd rushed off to Boots and bought a No.7 brown eyebrow pencil. She'd started having her eyelashes dyed, too, which the others thought was a tremendous improvement.

'You don't look quite so like a newborn guinea pig anymore, Tigs,' Blossom had commented kindly, seeing the result.

Now Blossom stretched out her legs. 'Jeepers, I'm glad I'm not white. You whiteys look terrible. You look as if you're about to expire. I love being black. Brown skin's much more attractive.'

'Absolute rubbish.' But secretly Nelly agreed with every word. Sometimes she could hardly bear to be near Blossom because her special scent, the sight of her smooth brown skin and radiant white teeth and the dense black knots of her hair made her feel quite ill with longing. 'Right, what's this bone you're on about then?' she said to Tigs. 'What am I supposed to have done?'

'What haven't you done, you mean? You took on a bet, remember? You said you could make Patrick fancy you. You haven't exactly done anything about it, have you?'

'That was ages ago. I've forgotten all about it.'

'If you ask me, you're chicken.'

'Well, you're wrong.'

'All right then, I dare you to get Patrick into bed by half-term. Shit, he's not even sleeping with her, is he? He must be desperate.'

'Oh, Tigs, don't be such a spaz.' Nelly reached into her bag for a tube of Coppertone and started dabbing her nose with it.

'Don't let Blossom hear you.' Sandy tipped her face up to the sun. 'She's put a temporary moratorium on sex.'

Tigs frowned. 'A what?'

'It's only because of that thing with Raymond.' Nelly started on her legs. 'She'll get over it.'

Blossom cleared her throat. 'I am here, you know.'

'Jeeps, these steps are hard.' Nelly shifted her bottom to more comfortable position. 'I need something to sit on.'

Tigs started drawing hearts on the back of her hand with a ball-point pen. 'Go on, Nell. Think of the pleasure you'd be giving to a lonely old man.'

'Have you actually *seen* Patrick?' Nelly stood up and pulled her jumper up over her head. 'He's not old. And he's the coolest cat you've ever seen.'

'Well, make a bit more of an effort then.' Tigs drew a penis with two enormous testicles attached. 'We can't wait around forever. We want to hear all the gory deets.'

'Speak for yourself.' Sandy yawned and stretched her arms up, 'Jeez, I'm knackered.'

Nelly spread her jumper on the step and sat down on it. 'Anyway, how do you know we haven't? I wouldn't tell you anyway.'

Tigs frowned. 'But we're mates. I tell you about Mum and her stupid BFs.'

'That's different, that's a laugh.'

'There goes the bell.' Sandy pushed herself to her feet.

Nelly rolled her eyes. 'Just when I'd got settled.'

'Let's have a look, Tigs.' Sandy peered down at Tigs' hand. 'Jeez, you're woeful.' She patted the top of Tigs' head. 'Don't be such a doofus, yeah? Well, gotta skitty, English next.'

Tigs watched Sandy fly down the steps. 'She's got the hots for Mr Bradley.'

'She has not.' Nelly stood up, unpeeled her jumper from the step and brushed it down. 'He's a good teacher, that's all. You've got sex on the brain, Tigs, what's the matter with you? Let's have a dekko.'

Tigs held out her hand.

'Oh, for goodness' sake.'

Tigs pulled her sleeve down over her hand. 'It's my mum's fault, she never thinks about anything but sex.'

'Well, rise above, dear.' Nelly pulled her jumper on over her head. 'Give it a rest.'

'You can talk.' Tigs put the top back on her biro.

'Oh, come on.' Nelly's head emerged through the vee-neck. 'You can't possibly compare Patrick with your mum's string of raunchy boyfriends. There's absolutely no comparison so you can just sit on it. Anyway, I'm off, I've got geog. next with pathetic old Laura.'

'What do you mean, pathetic?' Tigs hauled herself to her feet. 'Laura is totally bomb. I bet she's got hordes of men after her.'

'There you go again. Actually,' Nelly said with unusual venom, 'she's a complete wimp, with the sexual attractiveness of a fruit fly.'

'They're the worst of the lot.' Tigs followed her down the steps. 'We've been doing them in Biology. Do you know, the adult fruit fly reproduces every other day during its lifetime?'

'How completely sick-making. Now for goodness' sake go and take a cold shower or something. See you at lunch.'

Hurrying to the geography lab she felt obscurely ashamed. It felt disloyal to be making stupid jokes about fancying Patrick. She'd just got annoyed one day and let Tigs push her into admitting how much she liked him. Not in that way, of course, but straightaway Tigs had jumped to the wrong conclusion.

Nelly's solidarity with Blossom was absolute: men were pigs and that was all there was to it; but sometimes she felt a real hypocrite, assailed by almost overwhelming longings to jump into the sty. But not with Patrick! She wanted a dad she could rely on, not another disaster. Patrick was totally rad and sometimes she did fantasise a bit about what it would be like to be her mother and have a man like that crazy about you but that was just – well, a fantasy, not real. I mean what on earth would she do if he turned around one day and said, Righto then, Nelly my girl, I fancy you like anything: how about it? She would run like mad, wouldn't she?

Wouldn't she? Because if she didn't, she'd be as bad as Pearl.

SHE COULDN'T HAVE BEEN MORE than six or seven. She'd crept along the upstairs passage, feeling a sudden loneliness and a longing to smell Mamée's particular smell, the sweet, flowery smell which impregnated her clothes and her sheets; to press her face into her mother's bedclothes, her nightdress, her robe.

She squeezed through the swing doors and made her way along the passage. The door of her mother's room was slightly ajar. She pushed it open and looked in. The blinds were down and a soft silvery light fell in stripes onto the floor. She loved it when they were pulled down for siesta time and the rooms became mysterious and magical.

Something extraordinary was happening in her mother's four-poster bed. At first Nelly thought one of the dogs had got a mongoose, the noises coming from the bed were so strange: the bed was creaking and groaning like one of those pirate ships Alain told her stories about sometimes. As well as the noises the bed was making there were other sounds: out-of-breath sounds like when you try to talk at the same time as doing cartwheels, and grunting like the wild pigs made rooting around in the forest, and little screams like the rats made when the dogs got them ... sounds altogether so alarming that Nelly, terrified that someone was killing Mamée, took to her heels and fled.

She had to get help. She was running away at top speed and had almost reached the swing doors when somebody opened the door from the back stairs at the other end of the passage. Nelly stopped and turned to look and there was Mamée just stepping up onto the landing, dressed in her riding clothes and carrying her hat in her hand. Nelly stared at her, rigid with surprise. Her mother hadn't seen her. Following some inexplicable instinct Nelly began to run back along the passage to stop her but she was too late, her mother had her hand on the bedroom door handle, she was opening the door, she was inside.

Nelly turned and raced away, hurling herself through the swing doors, but not in time to avoid hearing her mother's horrified screams. She covered her ears with her hands and ran, but still the screams echoed and re-echoed inside her head. She ran out of the house and spent the rest of the day wandering in the plantation. Something terrible must have happened to make her mother scream like that.

In the evening she stumbled back to the house. Nobody had called her in for her lunch; nobody had even missed her. They had forgotten about her. Something terrible had happened and they had forgotten about her.

Pearl was sitting on the verandah on the swing hammock, a long, frosted drink in her hand. She swung the hammock gently back and forth with one foot resting on the floor, her other leg crossed elegantly over her knee. She had on pink high-heeled shoes and a pretty pink dress, short and swirly, completely different from the grey uniform she usually wore. The expression on her face was proud and cold but slightly uncertain, like the princess in Nelly's storybook standing on the balcony in the high tower waiting to be rescued.

Nelly was deeply shocked. 'Pearl. Whatever are you doing? Get up, my mother will come and scold you. Hurry up, before somebody sees!'

But Pearl snorted and laughed, throwing back her head and showing the pink inside of her mouth and her white, pointy teeth. 'For what you mammy she think she so big-up she can bad-mouth me, heh? You think you pappy he want to curse me off? For you pappy everything sweet, nuh!'

Pearl had obviously gone mad. Nelly went into the kitchen and found Excelie.

'Where's Mammy, Excelie?'

'You mammy she run off but she be back soon. But oh! chil',' Excelie burst out as though she just couldn't help herself, shelling peas at top speed into a bowl and hurling the pods into the sink. 'That pore woman she just naturally born for trouble, and that's the truth. Now don' you go worrying your head no more, dou-dou, she come back again soon, don't you 'fraid.'

'Where's Alain?' There was a feeling in the pit of Nelly's stomach worse than she'd ever had before.

'He somewhere 'bout.' Excelie's voice was falsely cheerful. 'You go fin' him, Miss Nelly. He just limin' aroun' somewhere.'

Alain was in the schoolroom, carving a little wooden boat with his sheath knife. He didn't know anything, he told Nelly. Everybody had gone mad, he didn't know where his father was, he didn't know where anybody was, and would Nelly please go away and leave him alone?

Mamée did come back. Not that night but the next afternoon they found her sitting on the verandah, her head bowed, the yellowing remains of bruising discolouring her face and arms, flies buzzing around the dried blood caking her upper lip. She looked like one of those women who sat on doorsteps in the town, begging. Alain and Nelly stood in front of her and stared at her. She looked like a mad woman.

Lena came running from the kitchen. 'Oh me Jesus, Miss Sonia.' She threw her apron over her head. 'Oh me God, trouble! What you gone done now?' She pulled her apron down again and came and put her arms around

Mamée, holding her like a child. 'Come – you let old Lena clean you up, make you all sweet-nice for the master. Come come, quickly now, Miss Sonia, before the master come!'

'Oh God, Lena.' Their mother's voice was cracked and dry like the river bed when it hasn't rained in a long time. 'Why doesn't somebody help me?

After supper the children descended nervously from the school room to say goodnight. Nelly was longing to see if Mamée was really there or if she had imagined it. Yes, there was their mother sitting in her usual place in the drawing room with Papa, as though nothing had happened. Her face was still bruised but she'd had a bath and put on fresh clothes. She looked almost like Mamée again.

When their father spoke Nelly didn't dare look at him. His voice was plummy and rich with satisfaction. 'Children, I want you to clearly understand something.' He paused for a moment, as though enjoying the drama of the situation.

He seemed, Nelly thought, completely baffled, to be trying not to laugh.

'Your mother took it into her fool head to leave you for a little while. Now she has returned. She knows that it is her duty to stay with you. I have warned her that if she ever leaves you again, I will take you away from her and she will never see you again.'

The children gazed solemnly at their mother, waiting to see what she would do. Nelly felt too over-awed to cry. Mamée bowed her head and stared at the floor and tears started to roll down her exhausted face.

'Come and kiss your father goodnight, children.' Their father didn't seem to have noticed Mamée's tears.

Nelly decided that either Mamée was ill or that she had done something so terrible, judging by the tone of their father's voice, that Nelly wasn't sure whether she ought to kiss her or not.

Cowardice made her turn away, but out of the corner of her eye she saw Alain touch his mother's arm and heard him say, 'Good-night, Mamée.'

Without looking at him, Mamée put out her hand to touch him, the tears still falling.

'Come on, Alain.' Nelly felt an obscure desire to hurt Mamée because she looked so strange and different, not like her mother at all. Anyway, Papa wouldn't say those things if they weren't true.

After that day Nelly felt that their mother was indeed not the same person. Somebody else was living inside the little house that was Mamée's head, looking out through the little windows that were her eyes. She hardly opened her mouth to speak, let alone to smile. It was as if something inside her had died. Nelly avoided her as much as possible. If she needed comfort she went to Lena. When her mother tried to approach her and put her arms around her she pulled away, stiffening. She found her terrifying.

Alain, two years older, was kinder. He put up with his mother's neediness, her occasional outbursts of emotion, with stoical endurance, though he was paler than usual and his mouth was often set in an unhappy curve.

They still had their lessons with Father André every day. Nelly longed to confide in him but he avoided her eyes, got on with the lesson and always seemed to be in a great hurry to leave when the lessons were over.

Chapter 12

Who killed Cock Robin?

Nelly took a grass stalk she'd been chewing out of her mouth. 'I think something awful happened that day.'

'Well of course it did, dumbo,' Sandy said. 'Somebody killed your dad.'

It was Sunday afternoon and they were lying in the long grass by the roadside in Richmond Park, not too far from Kingston Gate. Their bicycles lay abandoned on the verge, their helmets hooked over the handlebars. It was yet another beautiful Indian summer day, unusually warm for May.

Nelly sat up on her elbows. 'No, I mean something really awful.'

'What could be more awful than that?'

'It depends who killed him.'

Sandy turned her head, frowning. 'I thought you said that Cuffée person killed him. That's what it said in the paper, you showed me the cutting.'

'I know that's what it *said*.'

'Are you saying he didn't? It was his thingumabob – machète, or whatever they're called.'

'I know.' Nelly sat up and began pulling up handfuls of grass. 'But I knew Cufféе, Sandy. He *couldn't* have killed my father, even in self-defence. He was a peace-loving, harmless, gentle person. He couldn't even kill the *crapauds* – little frogs, you know – let alone being able to take a machète to another human being. He didn't believe in killing.'

'You never said this before?'

'I know.'

'Well, who did kill him then, if it wasn't him?'

Nelly looked at her doubtfully. 'My mother?'

'What, Sonia? Never!'

'Well, who else?'

Sandy rolled over onto her elbow. 'You're honestly telling me that you think your mother could do something like that? How? She wouldn't have been strong enough. I thought you said your dad was a big guy ... anyway, you said he had a gun. She couldn't have.'

'Well, if it wasn't her, who was it? There wasn't anybody else there, it was just the two of them and Cufféе.'

'So if it's between Cufféе and your mother, you'd rather believe your mother did it? You don't have much faith in her, do you?'

'It isn't a question of faith, it's a question of elimination. And it's the kind of thing people do when they're desperate.'

'Thanks, I'll avoid you in future when you're in one of your funny moods.'

Nelly didn't laugh. 'She was so frightened of him when he was drunk. And she was desperate to get us away from St. Colombe; she's told us that often enough.'

'Why?'

'Oh ...' Nelly shrugged. She began pulling grass out by

the roots. 'He was horrible to her. She doesn't talk about it but I remember a few things.' By mutual consent she and Alain never talked about it either. She couldn't explain, even to Sandy.

She lay down flat on her back and stared up at the blue, receding sky. Try as she might, she couldn't seem to prevent it from happening again. The past with its dark heat and pain insisted on intruding into this calm, bright, English afternoon. She closed her eyes and pretended to be asleep and in an instant she was back there; she was small and it was bedtime and her mother's hands were tucking the sheet in around her and arranging the mosquito net around her bed.

'MAMÉE,' Nelly sighed, reaching up and stroking a strand of Sonia's hair that had come down, 'I love Miss Bashie. I love her more than anybody else in the whole world.'

'I know you do, sweetheart.'

'I love you too,' Nelly said in a little voice.

'Oh darling, so do I. I love you so much.'

'I'm sad,' Nelly said.

'Why, darling?'

'I'm sad because my doll's tea set got broke.'

'Yes, that was very sad. I'm sorry, Nelly. I'm sure it must have been an accident. We'll try and find you a new one.'

'But it was my favourite. It had little flowers and – it was my favourite. It had little stripes.'

'I know, darling. I'm sorry we couldn't mend it but it really was smashed to smithereens.'

Nelly peeped at Sonia fiercely from under her pulled-together eyebrows. She was trying not to cry. She burst out, 'Why did you break it?'

'*What* did you say?' Immediately Mamée started to become agitated. 'I didn't break your tea set, Nelly. What on earth made you say a thing like that? I'd have come and told you if there had been an accident. I wouldn't just have left it for you to find. Don't be silly.'

'Don't be cross ...'

'But what on earth makes you think I broke it?'

'Papa said.'

'*Papa* said? What did he say?'

'He said you didn't want me to play with it anymore and that's why you broke it!' Bursting into a flood of outraged tears, Nelly buried her head in the pillow.

'That's crazy talk.' Mamée's voice trembled. 'Nelly. Listen to me. I would never, ever do a thing like that to you. I love you. How on earth can you imagine I would do something crazy like that?'

'Papa said you did.' Nelly's tears reduced to sniffs.

There was a long pause. 'Papa says things to tease sometimes.' Mamée's lips were snapped tight together and she had gone very pale. 'Sometimes he has a very peculiar sense of humour.' She made an impatient gesture and stood up abruptly. 'Look Nelly, all I can say is that it just isn't true. You have to believe me. I'll talk to Papa and ask him to come and tell you he was only teasing.'

All the next day Nelly waited for Papa to come and tell her he had only been teasing and that Mamée had not broken her tea set after all. But as it happened, Papa was particularly busy all that day and she didn't see him once. He wasn't even there at lunchtime. And in the evening Mamée didn't come up as usual to kiss her goodnight. Lena came instead.

'Your mammy, she got headache, she in she bed.'

'In *her* bed.' Nelly's voice was sullen. She loved Lena, but she didn't want her this time; she wanted her mother.

'In *her* bed,' Lena mimicked her, laughing. 'What for you put on that old screw-face, eh? All how you see you mammy in the morning. Aw ... don' you look so sad. You look like *nobody* child.'

'Lena, sit on my bed, move the 'squito net. There, sit there. Lena, do you know if it was my mammy who broke my tea set? Please tell me, Lena. Papa says it was, but Mamée says she never did.'

Lena said nothing for quite a while. She fiddled with the skirt of her dress and fingered one of her small gold earrings, and then she said, shifting her bottom on the edge of the

bed, 'Chil', listen to me. My mammy always told me, Lena, she said, don' you trust nobody in this life. Take what I'm telling you, trust only you own inside self and don' you listen to nobody. People gonna tell you all kinds of 'nancy stories they want you to hear. Now chil', you ask you own inside self why you mammy do something dotish like breaking that thing. What you think, heh? Ask you self, don' ask nobody else. You listening? You sleeping, Miss Nelly?'

Nelly's eyes flew open again. Lulled by Lena's sweet, sing-song voice she was almost too sleepy to care. 'Lena, sing me the bread-fruit song.'

'What, again, nuh? All the time you want for the bread-fruit song.'

'Ple..e..ase, Lena. Pretty please.'

'Close you eyes, then, Miss Nelly.'

'They're closed ...'

'And 'member you nothing to 'fraid.' And Lena began to sing in her sweet, high voice,

'Never let the bread-fruit fall,
For we love him the best of all.'

Sandy was sitting quietly, waiting. Nelly pulled herself back to the present. She turned over onto her front and lay with her head on her arms.

'Hey, I can hear a cuckoo!' Sandy's voice broke into her thoughts. 'Listen!'

Nelly lifted her head. There it was, the most English sound of all. Slowly she forced herself back to the present. Here was Sandy; there in the distance were the gold-green willows along the river bank; along the footpaths were people cycling, people walking. This was England.

'Was he really awful? Your dad I mean.'

Nelly pushed herself up on one elbow, supporting her head on her hand. 'When it's your dad, it's what he's like to you that counts. He was okay to me and Alain, most of the time. He drank, that was the real problem. He was drunk a lot of the time, and that's when he got nasty.'

What she couldn't say to Sandy but what she couldn't forgive was that her mother let her father go on treating her like dirt and messing with her head. Why hadn't she done something about it? Anything – fought back, left him, long before she did?

She lay flat again, her head resting on her arms. Her heart was pounding. There were other things she didn't want to remember. Remembering didn't seem to do anything to unravel the muddle of feelings she kept locked away somewhere, she wasn't sure where, sometimes it felt like in her head and sometimes in her stomach; in any case, hopefully safely contained like a packet of nuclear waste.

Better to remember the good things, the things she had loved. She closed her eyes and in a moment she was back there under her mosquito net, drifting off to sleep. It was night, her favourite time, and hot as hell, and raining as it usually did at night, the rain bouncing off the tin roof with a noise like horses' hooves, lulling and soporific. The sound of the interminable rain sent delicious shivers up her spine and she wished it would go on forever and ever ... or at least until she had fallen asleep.

She could practically hear the forest growing: the huge tree ferns, the *bois canot* and *immortelles*, the giant trees festooned with lianas on which in the daytime she swung, pretending to be Tarzan hollering for Cheetah and Jane ... and she knew that when the rain stopped the forest would give itself a shake like a dog climbing out of the river, and the sounds of the night would start up again, the stars would come out one by one, and soon the Milky Way would establish itself again, a powdery highway across the vast, tropical night sky.

Sandy flipped over onto her stomach. 'Listen, Nelly. Of course it's all been horrible, but it's no good torturing yourself, there's nothing you can do about it now. Have you found out everything you can about what happened? What about Alain? He must know, he was there, wasn't he?'

'I think he'd run off.' Nelly still couldn't pull herself back, not quite yet. She pushed herself up on her elbows again and looked around at the sweeping plain dotted with English trees, at the low skyline.

Sandy sat up. 'Changing the subject for a moment, isn't that your esteemed stepfather over there?' She pointed. 'Look. Walking near those trees. Who's that with him? That's not your mum, is it?'

'It can't be Patrick, he's playing squash with Tony.' Nelly sat up and looked where Sandy was pointing.

About a hundred yards away Patrick was strolling along

with his hands in his pockets, deep in conversation with a woman walking by his side. The woman was slim and smallish with honey-coloured hair. She was wearing blue jeans and a red Fairisle cardigan.

Nelly drew in a sharp breath. 'Hey, that's Laura.'

'Laura who?'

'School Laura ... keep your head down!'

They watched for a moment or two. Sandy shaded her eyes with her hand. 'It is Patrick, isn't it?'

'Seems to be.' Only what the hell was he doing walking in the park with Laura when he was supposed to be playing squash at the club with his agent?

'Well, what's he doing with lovely Laura?

'Good question. Probably nothing. Keep down. Don't want them to see us.'

'They're going in the other direction, it's okay.' She frowned. 'What's going on?'

'Dunno. He used to be engaged to her ... ages ago.'

'What? Really? You never said.'

'It was ages ago. Like, years.' Nelly knelt upright and wiped her hands on her jeans. 'It was before he met Sonia. I'm sure they're just friends now. They must have met up again now Laura's come back to teach at school.' She looked at Sandy who sat looking at her, eyebrows raised. Nelly shrugged. 'She's got problems. She gets involved with hopeless people who drink and that sort of thing and then expects Patrick to pick up the pieces.'

'She looks awfully interested in him for someone who's just a friend. Are you sure she isn't still hung up on him?'

'Positive. She must know he's married.'

'Why didn't you say, about them knowing each other before? You've never said anything.'

'I didn't think it was important, it was all over ages ago.'

But Nelly's heart was beating furiously. A pit of insecurity opened at her feet. *Merde*. Sandy was right. Laura was not behaving like someone who just wanted to be friends.

The couple were fast disappearing under the trees. Laura touched Patrick's arm briefly, then stopped and rummaged in her shoulder bag.

Sandy shaded her eyes. 'What's she doing now?'

'She's writing something down.'

'She's giving it to him. Maybe he wanted someone's address. Or phone number.'

'Not very likely. More likely she's giving him hers.'

Nelly sat back on her heels, thinking. He'd have her number already if they were seeing each other, so that was a good sign, wasn't it? Except it wasn't good because now he'd have it.

Or maybe they *were* seeing each other and he did have her old one but she'd changed it so she was giving him the new one. Or something.

Whatever, it didn't look good.

'Nelly, whatever are you doing?' Charlotte said, coming into the kitchen.

Nelly jumped and snatched her hand back from inside Patrick's jacket. 'He wants his keys. They aren't in there.' She barged out of the room, brushing against Charlotte as she left.

Patrick had breezed in, whistling, half an hour ago, hung his jacket over the back of a chair and gone upstairs to have a shower.

Charlotte sat down and put her mending basket on the floor beside her. She dumped a small heap of mending onto her lap and looked at it, frowning thoughtfully. Nelly's face had gone quite pink; she'd looked the picture of guilt. Best not to say anything though; she didn't want to rock the boat. She and Nelly seemed to be building up a surprising rapport, and sixteen-year-olds weren't the easiest people to get along with.

She picked up one of Patrick's socks and tucked the darning mushroom inside it, smiling to herself. Nelly was such a hoot. On Fridays, when they were allowed to wear their own clothes to school, she'd go off looking like something out of the Israeli army. She wore a long khaki overcoat (ex-army surplus) whatever the weather, Doc Martens and leggings with various layers on top, and to top it all, a black Stetson hat and dark glasses. She looked quite terrifying. You'd never guess there was such a neat little figure lurking underneath all that lot. But perhaps that was the general idea; Charlotte had been just as self-conscious at Nelly's age.

She was such a pretty girl, with her mass of cloudy dark hair, that babyish chubbiness still in her face and those bright hazel eyes. She had a sweet face, when it wasn't being pulled into some excruciating expression of quite marvellous disdain, which it usually was, especially if she was anywhere near Sonia. "Withering" would best describe her usual expression when in the vicinity of her mother.

Charlotte rummaged in her sewing basket for a skein of the right colour darning wool. What *was* it with those two? Nelly was such a sugar-puss to her nowadays, even more so when Sonia was around, and she was such a devil to Sonia.

Patrick came down, looking refreshed and wearing a tee shirt and jeans. 'Have you seen my shirt, Charlotte, the grey one?' He looked around as though she might have hidden it somewhere in the kitchen. 'Oh, by the way, did you have lunch? I hope it was okay to ask to have our main meal this evening for a change, it fitted in better with Sonia's plans.'

Charlotte felt a rush of gratitude, even if he did look rather as though his mind was elsewhere. 'Thanks, I did, and it's fine about dinner.'

'She's in town, you know. Something on at Tate Modern, I think. It's such a relief that she seems to have found something she's genuinely interested in.'

Charlotte didn't feel comfortable discussing Sonia. She set the sock aside and got up. 'Your shirt's in my room; I was sewing a button on the cuff. I'll just pop up and get it for you.'

'Angel woman, whatever did we do before you came? We're all being tidied up and sorted out; we don't know ourselves.'

He was teasing her but his smile was friendly. She smiled back. 'I like looking after people. Mother hen, that's me.'

She went and fetched the shirt and gave it to him. 'There. Clean and whole, as my mother used to say.' She sat down again.

'Thanks. That one of mine?' He indicated the sock Charlotte was darning. 'Aw, thanks, Charlotte.' He pulled off his tee shirt without a hint of self-consciousness and pulled on the shirt. He did it up, still a little distrait. He dumped the tee shirt on the chair, removed his jacket from where it was hanging over the back and started looking through the pockets. 'I was sure I'd put it in here.'

'Have you lost something? Oh, did you find your keys?'

'Keys?' He frowned. 'No it's a note, a phone number on it I needed to remember. A friend had to change their number ... being pestered by an ex. Not to worry, it doesn't matter.'

'Did you have a good game?'

'Sorry? Oh – the squash ... yes thanks, very good. Exhausting, though. I'm bushed.' He shrugged himself into his jacket. 'I'll leave you to your sewing. Might just pop out to the shed for a little while.' He nodded and went out into the hall.

Charlotte put the half-darned sock in her sewing bag. Time to get on with supper. Patrick would have worked up a good appetite with his game of squash. Charlotte hadn't met Tony, Patrick's agent, but according to Nelly he was extremely fit and gave Patrick a good run for his money.

She was planning on making something really tasty. *Crepes aux courgettes la Mère Poulard.* And perhaps a chocolate mousse for pud. That should fit the bill.

NELLY AND PATRICK did full justice to the crêpes but when they got to the pudding stage, Sonia, having picked at her food and sat in silence for most of the meal, suddenly burst out, 'I can't wait for the sale of Rose Belle to go through. It will give me some money of my own. Maybe I could buy a little house, a cottage perhaps.'

There was an astonished silence. Patrick, who had been tucking happily into his chocolate mousse, put his spoon down and said in a dismayed voice, 'But you have a home here.' He looked at her. 'Do you really hate this house so much?'

'I don't hate it – of course I don't—'

Nelly looked scornful. 'You're always saying you do.'

Sonia shook her head as though a fly was bothering her. 'I don't hate it but I might come to love somewhere different. Smaller ... like Mr Dennison's house. Mrs P. says it's going onto the market once his estate is settled.' She got up from the table and started to walk around the room, twisting her hands together. 'I might feel – good there, as though I was a different person.'

'I never knew this was something you wanted,' Patrick said, getting up and following her about. 'You never said.'

Sonia looked hunted. 'You never asked.'

Patrick returned to the table and sat down again.

Charlotte pushed her chair back. 'How about coffee?'

Sonia didn't seem to have heard. She was standing by the door looking at them without seeing them. 'That painting of Goya's, the one with the little dog's head looking as if it was decapitated ... I can't remember its name ... it's so sad, it expresses exactly the feeling I have about the loneliness of existence. It's agony to look at, that picture.'

Patrick looked annoyed. 'You don't have to be lonely. You have a choice.'

Nelly rolled her eyes. 'Can I go now? If you're going to start rowing. Again.'

'Nobody's rowing.' Charlotte looked at Patrick. 'Are you?'

Patrick shook his head but his expression was bleak.

'It's not a row,' Sonia said. 'Not a *row*. I was just thinking, that's all. That it might be nice. That was all.'

Chapter 13

Miss Bashie

Nelly was woken by the slam of the back door. She opened one eye and looked blearily at her alarm clock. Ten thirty, Saturday morning. Patrick coming in from the shed for his coffee break.

One more minute in bed. Yawning, she snuggled down under the duvet, wiping her damp cheeks on her pillow. She closed her eyes. Maisie, curled into the hollow of her legs, began to purr. Nelly slept.

Last night Nelly had dreamed her recurrent dream about her mother, and always after this dream she woke with her face wet with tears. In the dream her mother was the girl with the long hair and stricken eyes she remembered from her childhood walking barefoot along a passage holding a candle which cast deep shadows around her eyes.

In the dream she was a small child. Her mother was running away from her along the beach, her arms outstretched as if towards something she longed for above all else. Her hair streamed out behind her, a long, dark ribbon blowing in the wind. She ran through ankle-deep water, across slippery, seaweed-strewn rocks and patches of wet sand towards the wreck of an ancient galleon which clung to the reef like an old, brown moth, rearing up against the sky, paper-thin and slowly rotting away.

A strong wind was blowing in from the sea. Nelly's hair dragged across her face. Her small voice, screaming to her mother to come back, not to go so near to the dangerous reef beyond which surged the raging sea, was torn away by the wind as soon as it left her throat; she couldn't even hear it herself. The deafening wind blew her words away, the booming surf drowned her voice.

The dream compelled Nelly to listen to the small voice inside her head which said *this is your mother, and you are bound to her, like it or not, with cords too strong for you to break.*

Get a grip, she would tell herself each time, trying by force of will to calm the powerful thudding of her heart. She would dry the tears she discovered on her cheeks and shake the dream's resonance firmly from her mind. Sonia was not a person you could rely on for a minute. It would be a great mistake to start believing you could.

'Mamée,' Nelly said out loud and woke with a jerk. She flipped over onto her back, unsettling Maisie who squeaked reproachfully and resettled herself. 'I know, it's a dog's life, isn't it, Maisie Moo? Now do I or don't I get up and go down?'

She was desperate to talk to Patrick. She needed some reassurance from him that things weren't as bad as they looked between him and her mother, that they weren't on the verge of splitting up. There wouldn't be another chance for ages to get Patrick on his own. Charlotte had taken Sonia with her to buy vegetables in Kingston market, so Patrick and Nelly were alone in the house. But would he talk to her? Perhaps he would do his usual thing and crack jokes, deflecting any proper conversation.

She threw herself out of bed, pulled on jeans and a tee shirt and cleaned her teeth at the wash basin. She whizzed down two flights of stairs then outside the kitchen door she slowed down, took a deep breath to calm herself and strolled in. Patrick was standing by the sink looking out of the window, his coffee mug in his hand. Nelly examined his back view; he had lovely long, muscley legs and a cute bum. It was a pity she couldn't conjure up one iota of lust for him. It would really wind her mother up if he started fancying her. Do her good.

'Hi Patrick. Can we talk?' She picked up a milk carton Patrick had left on the table. It was empty so she threw it in the bin.

Patrick drained his mug and rinsed it under the tap. 'Don't you have school today?'

'It's Saturday.' Typical. Patrick never seemed to know what day of the week it was.

'I am rather in the middle of things.' Patrick upended the mug on the draining board.

You mean you can't be bothered to talk. 'Oh. Okay.' She turned to leave, her face heating.

Might as well go back to bed then. Didn't he care that the whole edifice of their lives seemed to be crumbling around their ears? She had half a mind to pay him back by taking Tigs up on her dare.

She turned back. 'Might have a drink myself.' She went to the sink, pretending she needed to wash her hands. She brushed against Patrick in passing, although she had to go slightly out of her way to achieve this. He moved a little to one side to let her pass.

She washed her hands. Inches away from her, Patrick

stood leaning his front against the draining board, looking out of the window, deep in thought. It didn't need three guesses to work out what was on his mind. Couldn't he stop thinking about his bloody book for five minutes? She pressed her elbows in to her sides to give herself more cleavage. Surely he'd be bound to notice how full they were? Much more interesting than Sonia's non-existent bumps.

Patrick glanced at her and took a hurried step backwards. 'Where's your mother?'

Bullseye. Nelly smiled to herself. 'Gone to Kingston market with the maid,' she said to annoy him.

He frowned. 'Charlotte is not the maid. You're not in St. Colombe now.'

'You don't need to remind me.' She turned around, her hands wet. Patrick had moved to the Aga and was leaning against the towel rail.

'Perhaps I do.' He turned around and pulled the hand towel off the rail. He held it out to her. 'What do you think of her, anyway? It's a help to your mother, having her here, don't you think?'

'She's all right.' Nelly sashayed towards him. She ignored the towel and stood looking into his eyes, drying her hands on her jeans by running her hands slowly down her thighs.

'Here, have this.' Patrick tossed the towel to her, backed away and made for the door.

She caught it awkwardly. 'Thanks,' she called after him. Well, that was a bust. Sometimes she couldn't be sure he wasn't laughing at her.

She dried her hands and draped the towel back over the Aga rail. What was the matter with him? He was a normal, full-blooded male, wasn't he?

She looked at herself in the hall mirror as she passed it

on her way back upstairs. She hated the hall mirror but all the same when she passed it she couldn't help turning her head to look at herself. It was an antique, and she couldn't stand antiques, which was unfortunate as the house was stuffed with them. Patrick's mother had obviously been besotted with them. The mirror was huge and imposing with gilt pillars on either side of it like something in a museum. It hung posily over the marble-topped chiffonier and in it, over her head, she could see reflected the vast portrait of Patrick's mother dressed in a kingfisher-blue evening dress, gazing off into the distance with a soulful expression, her head turned sideways so you could admire her wonderful complexion and cute little nose.

Nelly threw the painting a scornful look as she passed by. Bet her skin wasn't like that really; nobody's skin was like that. Patrick's mother must have thought an awful lot of herself; there had been photographs of her everywhere when they'd first come. Hardly any of Patrick, and he'd been her only child.

Of course you shouldn't speak ill of the dead, so Excelie always used to say. Only, although it was Patrick's house now so she ought to be grateful, it always felt as though it wasn't really. The presence of his mother lingered on so convincingly, like the smell of stale potpourri.

NELLY HAD to admit that Charlotte had been spot on when she'd suggested that doing something grounding like shopping in the market would be calming for someone as up in the air as Sonia often was. When they got back from the market an hour later Sonia was definitely mellower than she had been for a long time. While Charlotte made coffee and Sonia sat at the kitchen table doing the accounts, Nelly, at a loose end and as a penance for her half-hearted and in retrospect completely loony attempt to seduce Patrick, offered to help by putting the vegetables away in the storage racks in the larder.

They were rather beautiful, she supposed, when you really looked at them: the aubergines so smooth and shiny, the courgettes so very green. She ran her fingers over silky tomatoes, admiring the clear red of their skins and fingering the roughness of the dark, leggy tops that looked like spiders if you left them lying about. She lifted a tomato to her nose and inhaled its peppery aroma, and immediately a memory came of being lifted in her father's arms high, high up so that she could reach the tiny tomato she was clamouring for on its vine. She felt the hot beat of the sun and heard her own child voice saying, 'Gomato? Baby gomato?'

'That's right,' her father's deep voice said. 'There you go.'

Her heart contracted. Emotion flooded through her. *Merde.* Hastily she put the tomato down. She leaned her head against the larder wall and closed her eyes, her stomach curdling. Papa. Papa.

Had her father been good or had he been bad? She desperately wanted to know. The picture she had of him in her head was so confusing, the fatherly tenderness she remembered mixed in with other darker and more hidden memories, the difficult ones she only half understood. Like the time she couldn't find Miss Bashie.

Miss Bashie's full name was Miss Calabash and she was the love of Nelly's life. Miss Bashie was exquisite: she had a round, fudge-coloured face, a broad smile, big black eyes and a blue gingham ribbon in her mop of light brown hair.

She was Nelly's favourite doll and even though Nelly was six years old, everywhere Nelly went Miss Bashie went too.

One day, Miss Bashie simply disappeared. 'I lost her, she gone!' Nelly ran about, half off her head, looking everywhere she could think of.

'*She's* gone.' Alain went on kicking his football around the salon. 'Anyway, she can't have gone far, you had her just now.'

'That was yesterday!' Nelly rushed into the hall. 'Lena, Lena, Miss Bashie gone!'

'We'll find her, Miss Nelly.' Lena descended the stairs, holding the banister rail. She had problems with balance owing to a blow to one of her ears during a disagreement with one of Luis' bodyguards. 'Don't you go crying now. Master Lain, you-all take that ball outside the house now. Come now, chil', look at that old screw-face. Come along, Lena make you some nice *matété*.'

'But who's taken Miss Bashie?' Nelly's heart was bursting with an inexplicable fear. 'Where's my mammy?' she demanded.

'You mammy she gone Miss Sabrina get her hair done.'

'She's taken Miss Bashie!'

Lena stopped in her tracks and looked down at Nelly in disbelief. 'What nonsense I hearing? You-all goin' soft in you head? What for you mammy be so ex*tremely* int'rested to take along you old pic'n'y doll when she go to Miss Sabrina, heh?'

Nelly started crying. 'Papa said it was mammy tore my green dress and it was mammy tore up 'Lain's *William* book!'

Lena rolled her eyes. 'Look me trouble, the man crazy,' she said under her breath. 'Now, look you here, Miss Nelly.' She leaned down and took Nelly's hand in hers. 'I not sure what for you pappy play these damn-fool games with you. Just kindly remember things not always the way they seem. Don' you always go trustin' what's said to you.'

She let go of Nelly's hand and waddled off towards the kitchen. 'What for the master go get so big-up with he'self? Aie-aie-aie!' She shook her head. 'What for all this dotishness? Bring nothing but trouble to this house.'

Nelly waited impatiently for Mamée to come back from Port St. Luis. If she hadn't taken Miss Bashie with her then at least Nelly could tell her that Miss Bashie was missing. But when the car drew up in front of the house, Nelly, leaning out of the school-room window, saw that her mother had brought old Miss Ewing, Judge Ewing's sister, back with her. Perhaps Mamée had invited her to tea.

Nelly decided not to go down to say hello. She didn't like Miss Ewing. She smelt peculiar and had hairs growing out of her ears. When she got hungry she went down to the kitchen and begged some *macadams* and two glasses of lemonade off Excelie. She carried them carefully up to the schoolroom so that she and Alain could have a picnic.

The schoolroom overlooked the front drive so that Nelly was able to hear when an hour or so later Papa's car drew up in front of the wide curved steps leading to the front verandah. Janvier climbed out of the driver's seat and opened the door for Papa to get out. Nelly and Alain peered down.

'That will be bloody old Ma Ewing on her way then.' Alain drained his glass of lemonade. 'Pa can't stand the Ewings. He says Judge Ewing is out to get him.'

'He doesn't like anybody anymore.' Nelly wanted to say more but she was afraid to. Talking about her fears would make them real.

Alain turned away from the window. 'Anyway, he's usually all right to us – Pa I mean.'

'He isn't to Mamée. He's horrid to her. And you shouldn't say that bloody word. Father André says it's a sin to swear.'

'He has to say that, he's a priest. I can say what I like. Pa swears like anything.'

'He's a grown-up. You're only eight.'

'Anyway, you can talk, you're much too old to be making such a fuss about that stupid old doll. What a carry-on!'

'Miss Bashie isn't stupid!'

'Crumbs, Nell, don't start crying again! It's only a doll! Oh, all right, it isn't stupid. But shut up crying, can't you?'

'I want to talk to Mamée. When's that stupid old Ewing going to go?' Nelly hung out of the window. 'Oh look, there she is.'

'Come back in, they'll see you.' Alain came over and pulled her back roughly by the arm.

'Ow!'

He stood beside her at the window, peering cautiously down. 'Told you. Golly, Pa's looking like thunder. She's getting into the car. Janvier's going to take her home.'

'Why?'

'I dunno. P'raps he thinks she should have gone home in her own car.'

'Where is it?'

'*I* don't know, do I? P'raps Pa wants her off the premises now, so he's got to let Janvier take her. *I* don't know.'

'Don't be cross.'

'You ask such stupid questions.' Alain turned back into the room. 'Anyway I just wish they didn't row all the time. They're always rowing nowadays.'

'Who?'

'There you go again.' He knelt on one knee on his chair and leant over the table on his elbows, looking down at the map he'd been drawing before the interruption. He picked up his pen. 'Pa and Ma, of course. He gets awfully mad with her, haven't you noticed?'

Nelly screwed up her face. 'Excelie says it's the drink talking.'

'What difference does that make? He still gets mad at her. I wish he didn't, that's all.'

Nelly wished he didn't too. 'What will happen to us?'

Alain frowned at her. 'What d'you mean, what will happen to us? Nothing's going to happen.'

'I'm scared.'

'No, you're not. Don't be so stupid.'

'He says things.'

'What things? Anyway he doesn't mean it. It's the drink talking. Don't take any notice.'

Alain got off his chair and moved to the window again. Nelly followed him. The car was moving slowly away down the drive. Their mother, who had walked down the steps to wave Miss Ewing off, was slowly mounting them again. Her head was bent so that Nelly couldn't see the expression on her face. Papa was nowhere to be seen.

'I'm going down to see Mamée.' Nelly ran out of the room. She jumped two at a time down the three flights of the back stairs, then ran through the salon and into the dining room. There was no sign of her parents. She traversed the dining room, walked crabwise along the back verandah to make her progress more interesting, which took ages, then pushed through the heavy double doors into the entrance hall. The house sat in its usual sleepy afternoon torpor; silence lay heavy on the empty chairs and tables, on the immaculately polished floors, hung mysteriously behind closed doors.

She stopped. She could hear the angry murmur of voices coming from somewhere. She thought it might be coming from the library. She took a few steps towards the closed door.

Her mother's voice rose suddenly to a furious scream. '*No!* Let go of me!'

'Bitch!' She heard her father roar. 'Disobedient bitch!'

There was the sound of scuffling. Nelly's eyes grew enormous. She walked slowly to the door and opened it.

Mamée was standing with her back pressed against one of the book-lined walls. Her arms were pressed against her body, her right hand clutching the upper part of her left arm and her left hand supporting her head which was bent so that her face was hidden by long straggles of loose hair.

Papa was standing with his back to Mamée, his arms folded across his chest. Nelly's heart sank. She could see his face sideways. He had his angry face.

'Mamée?' Nelly's voice was tiny. Nobody seemed to hear.

Papa, ignoring Nelly, turned to face Mamée. 'Look, Nia,' he unfolded his arms and made a gesture of conciliation, 'it's your own fault, you shouldn't have provoked me, asking that Ewing woman to the house. And it's no use, you know, your making up stories about me to the children. They don't believe you; they know what you're like, that you do strange things. You're not very reliable, are you? And I am their father after all.'

Mamée raised her head to look at him. She opened her mouth but nothing came out.

'I'm sorry I had to hurt you. I lost my temper: you were extremely aggravating, you know. My mother was aggravating too, a bit like you. I must have watched my father beat her up a dozen times. He broke every bone in her body, blinded her in one eye; it was terrible.' He put his hand over his mouth, looking at the floor.

'Are you threatening me?' Mamée's voice was strange. It didn't sound like her at all.

He dropped his hand. 'Of course not; I'm trying to say how sorry I am. Oh, by the way.' He walked over to a black plastic shopping bag lying on a chair and lifted Miss Bashie out of the bag.

Nelly gave a cry of joy, but then she saw that Miss Bashie was covered with mud, one shoe and one arm missing, her mop of brown hair hanging by a thread. Her face was flattened, covered with a spider's web of tiny lines as though somebody had put the heel of their shoe onto her face and trodden on it, and where her beautiful black eyes had been there were two empty holes.

'I found Miss Bashie in the drive, Nelly.' Her father's voice was calm. 'She *has* been in the wars, hasn't she? Looks as though someone must have thrown her out of a car window. You'd better take her away and hospitalise her. Oh, and Nia.' He took something else out of the bag and held it out to Mamée. 'I found one of your bracelets underneath Miss Bashie on the drive. Weren't you wearing it this morning? Here you are.'

'I never wear that bracelet.' Mamée took it from him, looking as though she didn't want it.

Nelly looked in horrified disbelief from her father to her mother. 'You took Miss Bashie, Mammy.' She could hardly breathe. 'You stole her away and killed her.'

'Of course I didn't—'

Nelly burst into tears and rushed from the room.

'Dear, oh dear,' she heard Papa say.

. . .

In the larder Nelly brushed the memories aside like cobwebs and pushed herself away from the wall. She came out of the larder into the kitchen, shaking her head. 'All that from a tomato!'

'Sorry, what was that?' Charlotte came into the kitchen with her arms full of washing.

'Nothing. I was sniffing a tomato and having a chat with your courgettes.'

'You haven't done anything to them, have you?' Charlotte went out to the utility room.

'Of course not. Would I?'

'You tell me.' Charlotte dropped the washing on the floor.

'Is that my white shirt?' Nelly called through the door. 'I need that for tonight.'

'It's a fine day, it'll dry. Anyway it isn't the only white shirt you've got, is it?'

'It's special.'

'What's special about it?'

'It's my good luck shirt.'

Charlotte laughed. She tipped washing powder into the dispenser. 'You are a baby, Nelly.'

'Are you sure it'll be dry?'

'I'd stake my life on it. Going somewhere special?'

'Just having a drink with Sandy.' Nelly fiddled with the knobs on the washing machine. 'Where's Mum?' As if I care, her tone said.

'Gone to the Tate, I think. Actually, no, I think she said she had an interview.'

'An interview? Whatever for?'

'No idea. Perhaps she's trying to get a job.'

'A job? Sonia? Per–lease.'

'You haven't got much confidence in your mother, have you?' Charlotte started sorting the washing into heaps. 'She could be going to get a job?'

'Do us a favour.' Nelly bounced out of the room making noises of incredulity and refutation. All the way along the hall she could hear Charlotte giggling in the kitchen. One thing about Charlotte, she did have a good sense of humour.

She was also brilliant at mending things. Whenever she came across a dripping tap or a jammed lock or anything else that needed fixing she didn't just leave it, the way most people did, she did something about it. Nelly thoroughly approved of Charlotte's willingness to have a go even when she obviously didn't have the faintest idea how to go about it. Her only hope, she told Nelly, was the *Reader's Digest Repair Manual* which whenever she had to fix something, lay open by her side.

So when Nelly came back into the kitchen half an hour later and found Charlotte lying on her front on the floor by the door leading out into the lobby she was not unduly surprised. Charlotte was wearing a pair of vast blue dungarees in which she looked, Nelly thought, trying not to giggle, exactly like a baby elephant. The door stood wide open, balanced precariously on a pile of books.

Nelly squatted down beside her. 'Can I help?'

'Yes, you can,' Charlotte puffed. 'Just help me balance the door, will you? It weighs a ton. I've just got to get the bottom hinges back on.' She was holding a large screwdriver and manipulating several screws with her other hand. Her face was scarlet and streaked with dirt and her hair was coming down.

'What on earth are you doing?'

'It's – been sticking. I tried planing it but it really had to be re-hung. I've been putting it off for ages. That's got it. You can let go now.' She rolled over and lay on her back, heaving. 'This floor is extremely hard'— she sat up — 'even when you've got as much cushioning as I have. Thanks, Nelly, you arrived in the nick of time.'

'Where did all these tools come from? I haven't seen Patrick with a hammer in his hand all the time we've been living with him.'

'I found them in the broom cupboard. Perhaps they're your mother's.'

'Ha ha.'

Charlotte climbed awkwardly to her feet. ('For all the world, Sandy,' Nelly rehearsed, 'Like an elephant heaving itself out of the water-hole. I could practically hear the sucking noise.') She began tidying away an assortment of tools into a brown canvas hold-all. Nelly hadn't a clue what any of the tools were for apart from a pair of pliers, which she recognised, and the screwdriver.

'Well, I'm off out.' She was longing to tell Charlotte about the men she'd met in the pub on Thursday evening when she was having a drink with Sandy and the boys.

Charlotte filled the kettle at the sink, 'Did you have a good time on your night out?'

Perhaps Charlotte was psychic.

'Bangin', actually.'

'Found yourself a boyfriend yet?' Charlotte reached up for her favourite recipe book.

'What's for dinner?'

'You haven't had lunch yet. Are you by any chance changing the subject?'

'I like looking forward to meals.'

'Can I take that as a compliment? Are you in this evening?'

'That's a point, he might phone, in which case I'll be out.'

'Who might? I was thinking of a *pissaladiere* for lunch.' Charlotte leaned over the table, poring over her recipe book.

'A piss what?'

Charlotte giggled. 'It's a sort of pizza. Awfully good. And for supper ... duck!'

'Duck?'

'Duck!'

'*Duck?*'

'You know – duck! Quack quack quack!' Charlotte bounced around the room being a duck.

Nelly fell about laughing. She had to admit, she was getting awfully fond of Charlotte. 'Now, where's that recipe? Here we are. *Canard Roti à l'Ancienne Brasserie Flo*. That'll do nicely.'

Chapter 14

Talking to strangers

The Thursday before, Nelly, Sandy, Sandy's boyfriend Mark, and Piers, a friend of Mark's who was staying with him, had gone for a drink at the Dog and Duck in Hammersmith.

As they walked in, Piers draped an arm around Nelly's shoulders. Rather too familiar, in Nelly's opinion, since they'd never met before. Sandy was hanging onto Mark's arm, so Nelly guessed she was stuck with Piers. He wasn't bad-looking: he had a thin, rather ascetic face and dark hair cut unfashionably short in a fringed, tonsure-like style which enhanced (bet it's deliberate, Nelly thought scornfully) the monk-like impression. He was wearing flared jeans and a jacket over a dark blue sweatshirt with a Balliol College logo. Nelly as usual wished Patrick was here with her instead of these boys who were strangers to her and not nearly so interesting.

At the bar Sandy riffed with her fingernails on the counter and turned to go. 'We'll go and find a table, you bring the drinks. Mine's a shandy. Nelly?'

'I'll have a Pils. I'd like some crisps.' Nelly couldn't bring herself to say please.

Piers raised his eyebrows. 'Okay.'

'Don't you like him?' Sandy was looking drop-dead gorgeous in a short, coffee-coloured dress, fishnets, her new earth shoes and a lot of gold costume jewellery.

'Oh, he's all right, I suppose. You look nice.'

'Backatcha. I really like those flares. And your shirt.'

They found a low, round table with four comfortable chairs near an open fireplace in which a log fire burned. Sandy sat down and dropped her bag on the floor.

'It's just – he thinks I'm stupid.' Nelly plonked herself down in the chair next to Sandy's. 'I can tell by the way he talks down to me. Thinks he's so superior, just because he's at Oxford.'

'Balliol, no less.'

'Who cares?' Nelly thought longingly of Patrick sitting on the sofa with *The Times* at arms' length, breaking off his reading to make a comment, looking at her over the top of his spectacles.

'Anyway, he's probably just shy.' Sandy leaned back and looked around. 'It's nice in here.'

Nelly suddenly felt immensely lonely. This was no good, she wanted to go home. Just one drink and she'd make an excuse and leave. They'd be annoyed but too bad. 'Anyway, he's too young. I don't know how to talk to boys his age.'

Sandy hooted with laughter. 'I'll tell him you said that.'

Nelly grinned, cheering up. 'Don't you dare.'

'Tell who she said what?' Piers put their drinks down on the table. 'Crisps on the way, Mark's bringing them. Here, Nelly.'

Nelly took her drink. 'Thanks. Is that a real fire, d'you think?'

Piers sat down next to her. He looked at the fire. 'In what sense real? Are we talking idealism here? Are you a Berkley fan?'

Nelly gave him a look of deep scorn. 'I just thought it might be one of those gas ones. But it isn't, there's too much ash for a start.'

Piers seemed to decide to take her seriously. 'I don't think they make them that big.'

Mark arrived with four bags of crisps. He threw them on the table. 'Help yourselves.'

'How's term going, Mark?' Sandy asked.

Nelly looked around the room. She didn't know why she'd taken a dislike to Piers; He made her feel like a fool, perhaps that was it. It was the look in his eyes when he glanced at her.

She'd better make an effort. 'What are you studying?'

'I'm reading English.'

'That's his cover,' Mark said, pulling a pack of cigarettes out of his pocket. 'Actually he's writing a book.' He offered the pack around. Sandy took one.

Nelly perked up. 'Oh, really? My stepfather is a writer.'

Piers refused a cigarette. 'What's his name?'

'Patrick Carey.'

'I'm sure he's very good.' Piers took a long swig of beer.

'He is, actually. His last book was shortlisted for the Golden Dagger award.'

'Oh, he's a *crime* writer.'

Nelly rolled her eyes. What was wrong with crime? She made an effort. 'What's your book about?'

He thought for a bit. 'It's a bit Sartre-ean.'

Nelly said sweetly. 'So hard to be original, isn't it?'

Piers raised his eyebrows and took another swig. He'd practically drunk his pint and she hadn't even started her lager.

Piers turned to Mark, who had lit his own and Sandy's cigarettes. 'Have you seen anything of Tom Bradley?' Mark and Piers had been at St. Paul's together and their reunions often included detailed updates on mutual friends.

Nelly stopped listening again. She didn't know any of these people anyway. She took a long swig of lager. Her eyes travelled round the pub, idly scanning the other tables and their occupants, everybody except her having a good time. The noise level was rising as the pub filled up.

Suddenly she sat up. 'Oh!'

She'd almost said *shit*, an expletive Tigs used rather a lot and was catching, but restrained herself. Patrick hated her using that kind of language; he said it showed a depth of poverty of vocabulary that was heart-breaking.

The others stopped talking and looked at her.

'Sandy, look, see that dark guy over there with his back to us, talking to the fair guy? Look, him in the beigey jacket, he just turned his head sideways ... there! The blond guy's got a flowery shirt and a waistcoat. There – see?'

'What about him?' Sandy leaned forward and knocked the ash from her cigarette into the ash tray on the table. She turned her head.

'Don't let him see you looking! That's the guy who was sitting outside our house the other day, the one I told you about. That's him!'

Mark frowned. 'What guy?'

'He was sitting outside our house in his car the other morning, like he was watching the house or something. Well, that's him.' Nelly took a long pull from her glass.

Sandy looked dubious. 'How can it be, Nell? We're

miles away from home. How come he's picked this one pub out of all the millions of pubs in south London?'

'P'raps he knows his beer.' Piers lifted his glass up to the light. 'It is the best beer for miles around.'

Nelly drained her glass. 'Right, I'll go and ask him what he thought he was doing sitting outside our house. We thought he'd escaped from the loony bin.' She got up and began to edge past Piers. Her head felt a little fuzzy but hey, she was among friends.

Sandy leaned forward and grabbed her sleeve. 'Don't be a doofus. You said he was a weirdo. And you're walking all peculiar. You're blotto.'

'I am not. And I said he *looked* like a weirdo.'

'Mark, stop her.'

'Wait a minute, Nelly,' Mark said.

Pier put down his glass and started to get up. 'I'll go and ask him.'

Nelly wrinkled her nose at him, impressed in spite of herself. 'You wouldn't know which one he is.'

'Oh, right.' Piers sat back down and looked at Mark.

'Damn it, Jim, I don't need a nanny.' Nelly stepped over Mark's legs, grabbing one of his knees for support. 'I'll be fine. Now just wait here, children. If I need help, I'll whistle.' She looked down at Sandy. 'Do you know how to whistle? It's easy. You just put your lips together and blow.'

Sandy looked round at the others. 'Jeez Louise, she's wasted.'

Nelly moved off, slinking seductively, her hand at shoulder height holding an imaginary cigarette holder. She heard Sandy's snort of laughter behind her. Her legs did feel a little wobbly. She'd drunk that lager rather fast.

There was no mistaking the look of surprise on Weirdo's

face when he looked up and after a second or two of puzzlement, recognised her.

Nelly smiled down at him. 'Hi. Remember me?'

'Certainly do.' The guy got slowly to his feet. He stood holding the back of his chair, looking as though he wasn't sure what his next move was. His companion surveyed Nelly with interest.

Weirdo was wearing a light beige suit with a black polo shirt underneath it. He looked pretty groovy, Nelly acknowledged, trying to remember why she'd been so frightened the last time she'd seen him. He looked just like your average okay guy today. His fair-haired friend looked the bomb too in fawn leather flares, a flowered shirt and a fawn leather waistcoat.

Weirdo smiled. 'I believe I owe you an apology.'

His eyes looked perfectly normal; no devils jumping out of them today. He had pretty teeth, she decided: white and even and just the right size. Nelly was convinced her own teeth were too big despite Charlotte's assuring her that they weren't. This made her notice other people's teeth rather more than she might have otherwise.

'Do you?'

'I think I do.' He had a pronounced French accent. 'Michael. This is the young lady whose driveway I blocked the other day,'

His companion nodded. 'I heard about that.' His smile was polite but his eyes were wary. He had nice teeth too.

Nelly's eyes widened. 'You're French.'

'*Mais oui, bien sur,*' Weirdo said. 'How observant of you, *mademoiselle.*'

Nelly thought that his accent was so pronounced it would have been hard to miss.

'Let us introduce ourselves.' The man called Michael

put out his hand. 'My name is Michael Rayworth and this is Carl—'

'Dupont,' said Weirdo.

'Not *Dupont*?' Nelly said with exaggerated amazement. 'You mean – as in Monsieur Dupont who goes to the office every day while Madame Dupont stays at home and cares for Marie and Jean and Fifi the dog?' (Jeez, she must be drunk.)

Carl laughed. 'There's no Madame Dupont, at any rate.'

Nelly wondered hazily if she might have been rather rude.

Michael looked at Carl. 'You have to allow some Duponts. A bit like Smith I suppose. There are hundreds of Smiths in England.'

'Thousands,' Carl agreed.

'All right, you can have Dupont. I'm Nelly Jacquemet, by the way.'

'French?' Michael's eyebrows went up. 'You don't sound it.'

'It would take too long to explain.' She looked at Carl. 'Why were you sitting outside our house?'

'You're very direct. Have a drink with us.' Carl glanced at Michael who nodded. 'It's a bit of a long story.' He smiled at Nelly. He had a very attractive smile.

'Yes, do have a drink.' Michael got up. 'My shoot. What's it to be? Gin and tonic? Vodka? You look like a vodka person to me.'

'Do I really? Actually I'm with mates, thanks very much. I just came over to say hello and demand an apology.'

Carl smiled at her again. His eyes were an extraordinary colour, a kind of tawny gold, like the Somali cat belonging to a neighbour of Patrick's. The neighbour had moved, taking the cat with her, and Nelly had been heartbroken. Now of course she had Maisie.

Carl looked over to where the others were sitting. 'Would your friends mind if you stayed and had a drink with us?'

'It's not up to them.' Nelly looked around for somewhere to sit. Michael took hold of a chair and positioned it neatly between himself and Carl. Nelly sat down and looked up at him. 'I'll have a half of lager if you're really offering. It'll make up for the fright your friend gave me.'

Michael left to get her drink.

Carl put his hand in his jacket pocket and took out a gold cigarette case. 'Did I really give you a fright?'

'You damn well did. You have a very sinister laugh.'

'I'm a pussy-cat really.' He opened the case and offered Nelly a cigarette. She shook her head. He took a cigarette out and put the case away. 'I must have been nervous. I get nervous very easily.' He sat back and crossed his legs, winking at her so she couldn't be sure if he was being serious.

'Are you and ... Michael ... brothers?'

Carl felt in his jacket pocket for a lighter and lit up. She couldn't help admiring the cool way he handled the cigarette. 'Why, do we look like brothers?'

Nelly shrugged.

'We've known each other a few years. We share a house in Twickenham and run a little business together – electrical engineering. It's a small company but we're doing okay.'

'You speak awfully good English.' Nelly frowned and put her head on one side. 'Are you really French?'

He shook his head. '*Non. Pardon, mademoiselle.*'

'What?'

'*Non*. Sorry. I was winding you up. Too hard to resist,' he said in faultless English.

'Well, thanks a lot. I thought your accent had slipped a bit.' Nelly laughed but she felt like a fool. 'What about your name then? I suppose your name isn't Dupont either.'

'It isn't, I'm afraid.'

'Honestly!'

'I've never been very good at being honest. It just comes naturally to me to lie. I don't know why. It's more interesting, I suppose. Stops me dying of boredom.'

'Is the truth boring?'

'Well, that's a question.'

'What is?' Michael arrived back with the drinks.

'The truth. Is it boring?' Carl knocked the ash off his cigarette into the ashtray.

'Depends what angle you're looking at it from.' Michael put Nelly's drink in front of her. 'There you are. Has Carl been keeping you entertained?'

'He's an awful tease. He's just told me he isn't French after all.'

'Isn't he?' Michael sat down and took a packet of cigarettes out of his jacket pocket.

'It's no good, the game's up. Excuse me.' Carl leaned forward and tossed his lighter across. Michael caught it. 'Although to be fair I did live in France for a couple of years.'

'He does speak the lingo like a native.' Michael lit up and tossed his packet of cigarettes onto the table. Embassy Gold. Patrick's choice.

'What were you doing in France?'

'Building a *chateau*.'

'Go on.'

Michael nodded. 'It's true.'

'Well, technically, re-building a *chateau*. There was this friend of mine at college.' Carl took out a handkerchief and blew his nose. 'He was left this chateau in Normandy. It was pretty much a wreck so we decided to rebuild it ourselves. We didn't have any bread so it was just us doing it with the odd bit of labouring help here and there. It was going wonderfully well until one day it burned down. Razed to the ground.'

'But how terrible!'

'Some careless labouring man, *soul comme un Polonais* no doubt. That's drunk to you,' he said to Michael. 'He doesn't speak French,' he said to Nelly. 'Where was I? Ah yes, the chateau. Probably tossed away a match thinking he'd blown it out and – poof! The whole lot went up in smoke.'

'You're joking. That's awful.'

Carl smiled and drew on his cigarette. 'You're sweet. Isn't she sweet, Michael? Are you always this sympathetic?'

Nelly blushed. 'I suppose you got the insurance money?'

Carl shook his head slowly from side to side.

'No? It wasn't insured?'

'Nope. Rupe decided he couldn't afford the premiums. It didn't seem very likely anything quite so dramatic would happen to it while it was actually being built. We were going to insure it once it was habitable, of course.' He sighed. 'Idiotic, but still. We were going to run activity holidays there, walking, painting, cooking, that sort of thing. We thought it would work quite well with the right sort of people.'

'What a shame.'

'It's so easy to be wise after the event,' Carl said with immense seriousness.

Again Nelly had the feeling that he was laughing at her.

'Anyway, there we were with nothing to show for two years of hard labour but a pile of smouldering ruins.'

'That's terrible.'

'We came back to the U.K. with our tails between our legs and not a penny in the bank.'

'Then what happened?'

'All was not lost.' Michael lit another cigarette.

'Indeed.' Carl nodded. 'The next thing that happened was that my esteemed Papa, may he rest in peace, popped his clogs with a heart attack, leaving me as sole heir to his worldly possessions.

'To whit, one yacht,' Michael said.

'A year or so before his demise he had sold his house, his car and all his possessions and invested in an ocean-going catamaran in which he proposed to sail around the world. It had always been his dream, the thing he wanted to do most. Sadly, the heart attack got him only a week or so before he was due to set off. It was a real shame.'

'That's so sad. That's the saddest story I ever heard.'

'Shall I jazz it up for you a little? No. I won't. I like you too much. I'll stick to the truth this time. There I was, left with this fantastic boat. I know a bit about sailing but not half as much as my father did. I didn't feel confident enough of my abilities to go ahead and fulfil his dream for him, I'm afraid.'

'Did you sell it – her?'

'Nope. She's moored off the Isle of Wight, just come back from a charter voyage. I rent her out, basically.'

'What's her name?'

'We changed her name. Father called her the Flying Fulmar. I'd met Mike by then and he thought Temptation would be a better idea.' He grinned at Michael who was frowning down into his beer and seemed to be only half listening. 'That's enough about me. What about you? What did you say your surname was?'

'Jacquemet. My father's father was French. His mother was Columbian. I didn't know them, they died before I was born.'

'What about your mum?'

'She's half-English, half Costa Rican. We lived in St. Colombe, in the Caribbean.' Nelly blushed, conscious of giving away more information than had been asked for. 'I was born there. We only came over here recently – well, four years ago. My father's dead now, we live over here.'

'St. Colombe!' Carl glanced at Michael. 'How exotic! Don't you miss being there?'

'All the time.' Nelly looked away, biting the inside of her cheek hard. That usually worked.

'Why did you leave?'

'It's complicated.' She smiled, to show she wasn't too upset.

Carl lit another cigarette.

Nelly looked at Michael. 'So how did you two meet?'

'Where was it now?' Michael looked at Carl. 'At that thing of Maurice's, was it?'

'Mutual friends, I think.'

'You didn't go and sit outside *his* house.' She suddenly remembered the others. 'Oh, lumme, I forgot all about my friends.' She sat up. 'I ought to be getting back. Thank you for the drink. But before I go' — she hooked her bag onto her shoulder — 'that time you were outside our house. It's been bothering me ever since. Why did you laugh?'

Carl looked at Michael, then back at Nelly. 'Did I laugh?' He frowned. 'Ah yes, I remember. I feel bad about that. Actually it was that man.'

'What man?'

'The man who came out and asked me to move.'

'That was my stepfather, Patrick.'

'It was his voice.'

'His *voice*?'

'He sounded so posh. It was the way he said, "There's a good chap."' He looked at Michael and started to laugh.

Michael joined in. 'You'll be the death of me.' He shook his head at Carl. 'You really will. Can't take him anywhere,' he said to Nelly.

'Oh, do shut up.' Carl tipped his chair back and wiped his eyes with the back of his hand. 'I don't know what's got into you this evening, you're practically running a fever.'

'It's this child. It's the effect of her bright eyes. Isn't she gorgeous?'

Carl winked at Nelly. 'Gorgeous.'

'I do, I really do apologise for my ridiculous friend.' Michael drained his glass. 'Have another? Oh no, you have to go.' He looked away, as though suddenly bored.

'Is he ridiculous?' Nelly was mystified by the laughter and confused by Michael's sudden change in mood. Suddenly she didn't want him to be bored, she wanted him to like her. 'I really must go. Thanks for a lovely time.' She blushed. She sounded like a six-year-old.

'Do let us have your phone number.' Carl looked straight into her eyes. 'I do believe you're blushing. Look at that. You're sweet. Perhaps you might meet us for a drink one evening, if you'd care to?' He looked at Michael who nodded and gave a little shrug. 'You could bring a girlfriend. That girl over there, is she a friend of yours?'

'That's Sandy, I could bring her. Okay, that would be nice.' She started digging in her shoulder bag for something to write on.

'Here.' Carl passed her one of the cork beer mats and a gold ballpoint pen. She wrote the number solemnly on the beer mat, feeling very sophisticated, and gave it back to him. He put it in his pocket. 'Good.' He took the pen and put that in his pocket too.

'We'll be off too in a few minutes,' Michael said, leaning back and crossing his legs.

Nelly gave them a little wave goodbye. Carl was easier to talk to but she liked Michael best, She rather liked surly men. Also she sensed Michael was the one in charge. She wandered through to join the others who had moved to the snooker room. Sandy was leaning against the wall, smoking, watching the others play.

'You took your time.'

'Couldn't get away.'

She stood with Sandy, watching the snooker, her mind half on the game. They hadn't explained what Carl was doing outside their house. They kept changing the subject. Still, it didn't matter. The important thing was they liked her and they'd asked her out for a drink. She couldn't wait to tell Sandy.

Chapter 15

Secrets and lies

'That's what happened. More or less.' Nelly sat on the kitchen table swinging her legs while Charlotte, as promised, roasted the duck.

Michael had just phoned to suggest a meeting and in her excitement Nelly hadn't been able to resist telling Charlotte after all.

'Are you sure it's all right, Nelly?' Charlotte took her head out of the oven and closed the door. She laid down the basting spoon and started peeling onions at the sink. 'Oh dear, I'm going to cry now. There's something about putting a silver spoon between your teeth but it never seems to work with me. This Michael. You don't know anything about him, do you?'

'We're only going for a drink, we haven't even fixed a day yet. We can't come to any harm in a pub. He's nice. Honestly, Charlotte, you'd like him. Anyway, it's only a bit of fun. I don't really like him or anything.' She giggled. 'You should have seen Piers' face. He was terribly put out. Smug git.'

'Nelly, you mustn't call people smug gits.'

'Why not? He is one.'

'All the same, it isn't nice. Anyway, perhaps he really is keen on you.'

'Nah.' Nelly shook her head. 'His nose was put out of joint, that's all. He was getting ready to impress me and be the centre of attention and then along came Michael and Carl.' She smiled, remembering Carl's psyching her over the French thing. She jumped down from the table.

'Where's your mother? Is she okay?' Charlotte went into the larder with the colander.

'Oh, she's all right. Her usual cheerful little self.' Nelly bent her head. One of her Vans needed doing up again.

Charlotte carried the colander full of tomatoes back to the sink. She touched Nelly's head briefly in passing. 'Try not to worry.'

She always seemed to know what Nelly was feeling, however hard Nelly tried to hide it.

'I'll take her up a cup of coffee in a moment,' Charlotte said over her shoulder. 'Or would you like to?'

'No fear, we're avoiding each other.' Nelly stood up. 'Well, *j'vais me nipper alors,* must go and sort the gear out. Sandy will be all tarted up, you can bet your life.'

'Oh, is Sandy going too?'

'Probably.'

'Oh good.'

NELLY DISAPPEARED, whistling, into the hall. Charlotte smiled to herself. Nelly was definitely chirpier this morning, and if Sandy was going with her to meet these young men there'd be safety in numbers. One thing about Nelly, nobody could call her vain. She really seemed to have no idea she was so attractive.

She poured boiling water onto the tomatoes to soften the skins for peeling, and sliced the mushrooms. She chopped two cloves of garlic and put them in the mortar. She was about to start pounding them with the pestle when Patrick wandered in, a notebook in his hand.

'Any chance of a cup of tea? Honestly Charlotte, you wouldn't believe what I've just heard on the radio. Radio Four would you believe? I only put it on for the weather forecast. Do you know what he said?'

'Who?'

'Some M.P. or other. He was being interviewed about crime statistics. They're supposed to be educated, these people. It's because they don't give them a classical education anymore. It's a disaster.'

She'd never seen him so rattled. Reluctantly, because the recipe had just started to get interesting, she put down the pestle and mortar and went to fill the kettle at the sink. 'What did he say?'

Patrick pulled out a chair and sat down. 'He said – just listen to this, Charlotte – "This is an area prevalent with motor vehicle crime."'

'What should he have said?' Charlotte switched the kettle on, conscious that Patrick was looking at her expectantly.

'My dear girl, it's the *crimes* that are prevalent, not the area. It doesn't make sense. What he should have said is that motor vehicle crime is prevalent in the area.' He flipped over the pages of his notebook. 'Listen to this.'

Charlotte turned around from pouring the boiling water into the teapot. Patrick, notebook in hand, was looking at her over the top of his spectacles, waiting.

'Go on then.'

'This was from a university professor. You won't believe what he said.'

'Try me.' She did hope he wasn't going to burst a blood vessel. Perhaps a cup of tea would calm him down.

'He said, "I take umbrage with the word, 'explorer.' All these places have been invaded before."' Again he looked at her expectantly.

Charlotte wrinkled her forehead. Invaded? Umbrage? Explorer?

'He meant *issue*, Charlotte, *issue!*' Patrick snorted. 'Meaning he wanted to argue about it. I mean he could have said he took umbrage about something or other, but you can't take umbrage *with* something. The word he was looking for was issue. Well, why didn't he use it? Because he's not properly educated, that's why.'

'I'll take your word for it.' Charlotte poured him a cup of tea, put milk and two sugars into it and placed it in front of him.

'And is the word "might" ever heard nowadays? It's becoming as rare as the Mauritian Pink Pigeon. It might as well not exist, or as everyone seems to say nowadays, may as well. It positively sets my teeth on edge. Another one I heard this morning: "It's inherent upon us to do something about it." Inherent, I ask you. What the wretched man meant was "incumbent", if he's ever even heard of the word.' He looked at her pleadingly. 'Doesn't it bother you *at all*, this sort of monstrosity?'

Charlotte knew she was about to be a disappointment to him. 'Honestly?'

'Honestly.'

'I probably wouldn't even notice.'

'You wouldn't notice.'

'I know ... isn't it awful? But words aren't my business. Now if you were to try and sell me a tough leg of lamb—'

'Of course ... stupid of me, there's no earthly reason why grammatical errors should bother you in the slightest. I wouldn't know a tough joint, in its uncooked state, if you hit me with it.' He sighed. 'It's not that I think language shouldn't change: it should and it does; I don't want to stay stuck in the sixteenth century. What I do object to though is the *misuse* of language. Tell you another thing.'

'What?' Charlotte settled down companionably with her cup of tea.

'Have you never noticed,' — he paused and looked at her to make sure she was concentrating — 'the double is?'

Patrick sometimes made her feel as though she was in the fifth form. 'The double is?'

'The double is. People no longer say, "The problem is, you're too fat," they say, "The problem is, is you're too fat."'

Charlotte reddened. Patrick seemed not to notice.

He went on, 'Another example: "What you do is, is you put two teabags in the pot."'

'Are you *sure* people say that?'

'It's creeping in all over the place. On *The Today Programme*. Edward Heath says it. Everybody says it. Just listen out for it if you don't believe me.'

'How extraordinary. I've never noticed.'

'That's the thing you see. I can't help noticing it. I don't object; it's interesting, I've got used to it. It's an example of movement and change in the language. It shows that the language is well and truly alive.'

'Well, I never.'

'You're a great comfort,' Patrick leaned back in his chair and sipped his tea. 'What's for dinner?'

'Duck with a special sauce. That should cheer you up.'

'Oh Charlotte, yes it does. I feel better already. Bother, there's the phone.' He got up. 'Better go and answer it. It always seems to ring when one is having an interesting conversation.'

Charlotte rolled her eyes. 'It never stops.'

DRIVING to Laura's house Patrick thought, when I'm with Charlotte I feel grown-up and in charge, when I'm with Sonia I feel like a frustrated fool and when I'm with Laura I feel like a teenager.

Sometimes he found it almost impossible to believe that he and Laura were actually having an affair. When at the start of this school year Laura had re-joined the staff at Nelly's school, after an interval of several years, he had run into her quite by chance; at least he thought it had been by chance but sometimes he wondered. Laura was no fool; in the old days when they had been together she had run rings round him. If they had disagreed about something she had usually ended up getting her own way. But she had done it so charmingly that he'd never minded. In his darkest moments he told himself that she had bullied him into restarting their affair, and this was true to the extent that at last, fed up with his dithering, she had delivered an ultimatum. He told himself that he was lonely and that Sonia was to blame. He told himself that as long as Sonia never found out, no harm would come from deceiving her.

There was a time-warp feeling about his relationship with Laura which confused him, reminding him of the first time around when he had been younger and unattached, when he had been able to indulge himself without the guilt he was feeling now. He wasn't sure whether the anxiety attached to his present predicament added zest to the situation or more stress. He now had a duty to Laura as well as to his wife. He felt bad about Sonia, and about Nelly. In time, he knew, he would start to feel bad about Laura. It was a desperate situation. He had climbed onto a runaway train and had no idea where the brakes were.

He was worried by the possibility that Alain might have cottoned on to his reviving interest in Laura. There had been a couple of not terribly discreet meetings in Richmond Park, and once he had thought he'd glimpsed Alain with a group of his schoolmates when walking Laura back to her car after a stroll along the river at Hampton. There had been nothing going on then, it was all perfectly innocent; at the time he honestly had no thoughts of betrayal. Sonia was in hospital being sorted out and Laura had simply called on him in the spirit of friendship, for old time's sake. His work had been going like a dream: all he had really been interested in at the time was Chandler.

There was something wrong with him, Patrick thought, not for the first time and not without some sense of self-congratulation. He sometimes thought he wasn't quite human. He was as committed as the artist who draws his dying mother on her deathbed just to get that authentic dying look. He was almost convinced that the affair wouldn't have happened if the book hadn't been virtually finished. Perhaps the whole thing was the book's fault; he'd been about to lose his connection with Chandler again, and the loneliness he was feeling was due as much to that relationship coming to an end as it was to Sonia's worrying behaviour and her coldness.

He refused to think about Sonia. It was just as much her fault, all this. She had stuck a knife in his heart with that thing she'd said that he couldn't even bring himself to think about. And he couldn't be expected to go on forever doing without any comfort or delight.

This afternoon the opportunity to drop in to see Laura had arisen because Sonia had decided on the spur of the moment to go to a preview at one of the Cork Street galleries. Laura fortunately had happened to be in.

He trod on the brake and screamed to a halt as a seedy-looking old codger, muffled up to the ears, suddenly decided to switch direction and step sideways without warning onto the pedestrian crossing. The man hobbled smugly across the road inches in front of the car's bonnet. Stupid old fool ... Patrick's thundering heart felt twice its normal size. The bloody man had probably done it on purpose just to give himself a good laugh. He probably went around the Surrey streets playing fast and loose with pedestrian crossings and suing for compensation when he got clobbered. From the safety of the pavement the old man turned and glared at him.

'Don't feel you have to thank me for not hitting you,' Patrick said aloud, pushing the gear lever into first. He set off again, looking as grim as he knew how. He hoped the man was still watching. Surly old bugger.

He turned onto Laura's street. Looking for a parking space, the unwelcome picture came into his mind of Laura sitting by the phone night after night waiting for it to ring. Women did that. No. He dismissed the idea. He was an arrogant sod; she probably had a perfectly good life of her own. He just didn't want to know about it. He didn't want to get too emotionally involved; he needed to keep things light. Things were different now he was married, she had to understand that.

He hoped she would meet him at the door in her silk kimono with nothing on underneath. She sometimes did this just for the hell of it and two minutes later they would be on the sofa, on the floor, or sometimes, if they could wait that long, deep in the brass four-poster bed with its pale-blue satin sheets and goose down duvet.

'Saltfish stew is what I like, so doudou give me day and night,' he sang aloud. He had picked up the song, a Jamaican hit calypso, from Nelly, who used to walk around the house singing it at the top of her voice without the slightest idea of the possible nuances of meaning, he realised, somewhat startled. Ah, the irresistible charm of a woman's body. It was the smell of a woman that did it for him. The scent of the skin, the rousing, fishy odour of their secret places.

He felt irrepressibly light-hearted this evening. He was becoming accustomed to this double life, increasingly adept at crushing down his guilt, at rationalising his duplicitous behaviour, the lies that tripped all too easily off his tongue. Perhaps he was more like Chandler than he realised. He felt as randy as hell. He pushed away all thoughts of guilt and retribution, parked the car a discreet thirty yards down the road and leapt out, turning back to seize the box of Terry's Moonlight, Laura's favourite chocolates, from the front passenger seat.

WHEN PATRICK DESCRIBED to Laura what Sonia was going through over Alain's disappearance, he realised at once that Laura was jealous of his sympathy for Sonia and frightened by it.

She lay in the four-poster bed, sulking, while Patrick made tea in the kitchen. He trudged upstairs carrying their mugs on a vintage Coca-Cola tray and deposited the tray on the floor beside the bed. The small bedside table was crowded with objects: a Violet Winspear novel, a clock alarm, a jar of Pond's cold cream, a glass-shaded lamp with a pink bulb and two silver photograph frames with photos of Laura's mother, father and her Cockapoo, Mabel, pining for her at her parents' home in Bakewell.

Patrick sat down heavily on the edge of the bed and handed her one of the mugs.

'Come on, sit up and drink this before it gets cold.'

'You haven't brought the pot.'

'Couldn't find a milk jug. Mugs are easier.'

'It doesn't taste the same out of a mug.' She pushed herself up into a sitting position.

'Why do you have them then?'

'For the girls, I suppose. They seem to prefer them.'

He grinned at her. 'The generation gap showing?'

'Don't be horrid, Patrick.' She took the mug from him without thanking him.

'Darling, I'm only teasing.'

'Well, don't tease. I can't understand why you're refusing to come out to lunch with me on Thursday. It *is* my birthday. I would have thought you could have put me first for once; it's only one day in the whole year. It's a big day for me; I'm going to be thirty-two. I'm worried about it. Do you realise I'll be the same age as Sonia?'

It came as a shock to Patrick to hear her say Sonia's name. For a moment he felt a surge of indignation; it was as if in acknowledging out loud his other commitments, Laura had broken some unspoken agreement. Deeply curious about Sonia as the other woman in his life, she often made unsubtle attempts to bring her into the conversation, but Patrick, determined to keep his two lives separate, refused to rise to the bait.

But Laura looked so heavenly, her skin flushed and her

hair all tousled, and he felt so marvellous from the wonderful sense of release and well-being spreading through his whole body that he felt particularly tender towards her; he disregarded the allusion and let the nagging tone in her voice wash over him.

He heaved a pillow up against the headboard and settled himself beside her, carefully so as not to spill his tea. 'Darling, I've said I'm sorry. You know I'm not free in the daytime anyway. I have to work.'

'You must take time off sometimes.'

'Hardly ever. And never in the middle of the week. It's a principle with me.'

'Well, it's a stupid principle.'

'Anyway, it's too risky. We don't want to do anything to rock the boat, do we?'

'No ... I suppose not.'

'I've said I'll try and get away in the evening.'

'But I wanted to have lunch. And a long afternoon in bed. You know.'

He tried to think of something to say to comfort her. He felt bad about letting her down on her birthday; he had promised that they would try to do something special, and he had hoped that he would have delivered his manuscript by then. He was so deeply caught up in it now that he was superstitiously frightened of breaking the pace, of something happening to prevent his getting to the end.

Laura's hand curled itself around his upper arm. He had put on the dark-blue silk dressing gown that she had bought for him and kept in her wardrobe among her own clothes. He felt bad about the dressing gown. He wished she would not do these things which bound him to her too obviously. He had tried to pay for the dressing gown but she had been terribly offended and had wept, burying her face into its folds and soaking the rich, dark silk so that he had felt worse than ever.

He was sometimes afraid he might be playing with fire. She still had the intriguing ability, which he had forgotten about in the intervening years, to tease and charm him until he didn't know whether he was coming or going. She took tremendous pains with him, which he found flattering. Sometimes he felt in quite serious danger of falling in love with her.

At the same time he was wary of her. She was a good actress, and she was untruthful. He even wondered whether she might in fact not have bought the dressing gown for him at all; that it might actually have belonged to her previous lover, the one she had thrown out because of his drinking problem, with whom she had lived in this house for more than two years.

'Darling, I'm sorry.' Laura rubbed her face against his sleeve. 'It's just sometimes I feel so – marginalised. It's when it hits home that you always, always put your family first.'

Patrick thought, of course I do, you silly woman, what on earth do you expect? Then he felt brutal and shallow and that he was a sinner and in a mess.

He did not respond to what was obviously a hint demanding a reassuring response. He was still getting over the annoyance of discovering, from something she had let fall that evening, that their meeting again in the park when he was out walking early one morning had not happened accidentally but had as he had long suspected been carefully engineered by her. She had laughed about it to his face, congratulating herself on her cleverness, but he had been irritated by having his suspicions confirmed, and felt that he had been made a fool of. He didn't like to feel manipulated.

He sipped his tea, looking out of the window at the roof of the house opposite which had several tiles missing. It wasn't his roof and he didn't have to worry about it. This can't go on, he thought, as he did every time he saw her, wondering if this would be the last time but unable to bear the thought of ending it. He told himself that he did not love Laura but that she was necessary to his happiness and well-being. And sleeping with Laura helped him to be patient with Sonia, he rationalised. Being physically more relaxed meant he could take Sonia's histrionics and her coldness with some equanimity, which must surely be for everybody's good.

He suspected he might be kidding himself. He was afraid that he was fonder of Laura than he wanted to admit and what he was doing was running away from what was perhaps an insoluble problem.

'Patrick.' Laura nudged him. 'You haven't heard a word I've been saying. You're not thinking about that blasted book again, are you?'

'No – of course not. I'm just a bit tired. I could curl up right now and go to sleep with you for hours.' He leaned his head against her shoulder and pretended to be settling down to sleep.

'I'm afraid you can't.' Laura moved away from him, handed him her mug and kicked the quilt back. She looked over her shoulder at him, rather coolly, he remembered, thinking about it afterwards, and jumped out of bed. The pink silk teddy, its buttons all undone but the shoulder straps reinstated while she drank her tea, fell to the ground, leaving her naked. Patrick caught his breath, shocked by her beauty.

'I'm out this evening so I'm going to have to kick you out earlier than usual, I'm afraid. Sorry!' She yawned and stretched with a lack of modesty that was almost insulting. 'For once you won't have to drive too fast to get home in time for dinner.'

'Really? Oh well.' Patrick dragged his eyes from her body and leaned over to put the mugs back on the tray.

'Yes, really. So if you want the bathroom, you'd better get a move on and start running my bath for me, darling. Will you?' She picked up her hairbrush and started to brush her hair. 'It's rather a special date and I don't want to be late.'

In the bathroom Patrick turned on both bath taps and tipped a dollop of her extremely expensive foaming bath oil into the water. Feeling disconcerted and slightly lost, he watched the water turn pink. He wasn't used to being kicked out in a hurry like some guilty secret. He was used to being the one who left in his own time, leaving behind regret, he imagined, and a feeling of unfinished business.

Sometimes he wondered if she said these things as a ploy to show him he wasn't the only one, that she could have anyone she chose. Perhaps she was getting her own back because he had foolishly shown his sympathy for Sonia. Sonia was his wife, for God's sake. When Laura had started to brush her hair he had been uncomfortably reminded of her.

He cleaned his teeth vigorously with the toothbrush Laura kept for him in her smart white Allibert bathroom cabinet. Even if she were playing games, it had worked. He was hooked and jealous and there was no way there wasn't going to be a next time. Not unless, to quote Mrs Henny Penny, the sky fell in.

Chapter 16

You don't understand women at all

Patrick sneaked in at the front door, ran two at a time up the stairs and knocked warily on Sonia's bedroom door.

'Come in.'

He opened the door. Sonia was sitting cross-legged in the middle of her bed wearing a pair of rather fetching turquoise pyjamas.

'Mmm, cool pyjamas.'

Sonia had told him that nowadays she bought most of her clothes from second-hand dress shops, her favourite one so up-market it was actually in Sloane Square. Though slightly incredulous, once he had got used to the idea Patrick was pleased because it meant she could indulge her craving for designer labels without breaking the bank.

She looked at him gloomily. 'What, these old things?'

Patrick brightened since this remark seemed to indicate the possibility of humour. Then he saw that she was serious and his heart sank again.

'I got them at *Déjà Vu*, ages ago.'

'Love the colour.' Encountering a stone-walling expression in her eyes he said, 'Does the fact that you are wearing pyjamas at this hour of the day mean you're about to leap on top of me and have your way with me?'

Sonia blinked and looked at him as though he'd turned into a particularly unpleasant kind of insect.

'Obviously not. Well?' Spurred on by who knew what sense of irritation and euphoria, he lowered his head and shook it at her like a bull in a field. 'Are we never going to be allowed to mention sex in this house again?'

It must be the effect of Laura unhinging his brain; Sonia was looking at him as though she thought she would need the panic button any moment now. Still, she did seem to be keeping remarkably calm. Astonishing too that, seeing her again after what felt like a long emotional absence, he was experiencing the first flickers of forgiveness for the dreadful thing she had said to him; as if having revenged himself by fucking Laura he now felt able to be magnanimous and, if not quite forget, at least pardon her.

Sonia said slowly and carefully, 'How can you expect me to trust you when you're so completely unre–unre–'

'Pentant?' (Whoops. Or was it that subconsciously he wanted to tell her about Laura?)

Sonia looked at him, frowning. 'Have you got something to repent about?'

'Repent *of*. To repent of.'

She closed her eyes, then opened them again. 'Well, have you?' She peered at him as if seeing him through a thick fog.

He noticed then that her face had more colour than usual. He took a step closer; she leaned away from him like a sailboat before the wind. There was a definite whiff of whisky on her breath.

He retreated a few steps to reassess the situation.

She tried again. 'So completely unre–unre-liable.' She nodded, pleased with herself.

'Me? Unreliable?' He folded his arms. 'What are you talking about?'

Sonia leaned over and after a couple of attempts managed to extract a cigarette from a packet on the bedside table. She picked up the cute little silver and tortoiseshell lighter he'd given her last Valentine's Day and lit up, her hand shaking slightly. She put the lighter back too near the edge of the bed so that it teetered for a moment and then fell onto the carpet. She waved the hand holding the cigarette. 'Leave it. Actually you don't know a damn thing about women.' She inhaled deeply.

'Ah.'

'You think you're so clever.' She wagged her head and looked at him through wreaths of smoke. Sonia never normally smoked in her bedroom. Just to make sure, she wagged her head at him again. And again.

'I don't actually.' Patrick coughed. He panicked momentarily, wondering if she had found out about Laura. But she wouldn't be sitting cross-legged smoking a cigarette if she had, she'd probably be brandishing a knife. He was appalled by her inebriated state but at the same time, unworthily, relieved.

'You're always trying to make out you're the faithful type but the moment you get the chance you're all over some other woman like a rash.'

She *had* found out about Laura. 'I always think that a particularly unpleasant expression,' Patrick said, to give himself time.

'First there was that woman you met on the train. We'd only just met; you were supposed to be mad about me at the time but it didn't stop you chatting her up and making her like you.'

He hadn't the faintest idea what she was talking about.

Sonia began ticking points off on her fingers. 'Then there was that woman in the park out walking her dog. You picked her up too. And the one who went to live in King's Lynn.'

'She used to live next door.'

'And the woman we met in the bar at Richmond Theatre. You couldn't wait to go round to her house and get your feet under her table.'

'She said she wanted me to write a play for her. She's quite well known. Anyway that never came off.'

Sonia wagged her finger at him. 'That's how it always starts with you. You insinuate your way into people's lives. You're desperate to find out where they live, then you're round there having cups of tea, then they're on the phone all the time.'

'That's not my fault. Has someone been on the phone?'

'Then there was the woman who came round to sort out your income tax.'

'She's my accountant.' This was like being given some extraordinary sort of conundrum he was expected to solve. He hadn't the faintest idea what she was on about.

'You weren't treating her like an accountant. You were all over her like – like a rash.'

'You're repeating yourself.' What had got into her? It was the whisky talking. His wife was an alcoholic.

'You collect them like – like butterflies or something.' Sonia flailed her arms. Ash flew off her cigarette onto the bedspread. 'Why should I be expected to put up with that? I never heard of a man as fascinated by women as you.'

'They're just friends.' Patrick darted a glance at the

small pile of ash. He didn't want to be accused of fussing; on the other hand that was a perfectly good bedspread. There didn't seem to be any sign of smouldering. 'There's nothing wrong with having women friends.'

'Why don't you have *men* friends?' Sonia dashed the ash away, leaving a pronounced grey mark on the ivory bedspread. 'Why does it always have to be women? What's the matter with you?'

Patrick decided the moment had come to attack. 'Have you been drinking?' A frightful thought struck him and he made a move for the door. He'd better get out to the shed pronto and make sure his manuscript was still there.

'Stay where you are.' Sonia raised her hand like a policeman.

'You *have* been drinking.'

'So what if I have? How can I talk to you honelly and opestly about how I feel without a drink inside me?'

He tried very hard not to laugh. 'Is that what this is, openness and honesty? Anyway, why can't you? Am I so frightening?'

Sonia nodded gravely two or three times.

Patrick thought he'd better make quite sure she wasn't talking about Laura; his manuscript could wait a few minutes more. In any case he didn't honestly believe she would have done anything that stupid, not again, even in her condition.

'Go on about these women.' He took off his spectacles and dangled them from one leg. 'I had no idea I had so many women in my life.'

Sonia looked at him scornfully. 'You think you can just laugh this off. You think you can do whatever you like. You must be the vainest man that ever existed.'

*Who*ever existed, Patrick nearly remarked but thought

better of it. He felt more and more bewildered. 'I had absolutely no idea you felt like this.'

'Well, now you know.' She stubbed out her cigarette in a green onyx ashtray beside the bed. 'I hate this ashtray. How could your mother live with this ashtray?' She wiped her hands on her pyjama trousers. 'I don't know how you can call yourself a writer. Writers have to know about women. You don't know a thing about women.'

Hang on a minute here. 'My books aren't about women.'

'Well, it's just as well, they'd be a miserable failure if they were because you don't understand women at all. You think you do, ohhh yes.' She shook her head vigorously from side to side, like Yogi trying to dislodge a bee from his nose.

My God, she was drunk. Her voice was beginning to slur. 'No. It's no good my trying to rely on someone like you. I'll only get hurt. You'd have to have an ox as thick as a hide to be happy with someone like you.'

He suppressed a smile. 'But what is the problem? I'm not doing anything with these women.'

'You don't care who sees you putting your arm around them and gazing into their eyes and making them want you! You don't care a bit!' Her voice rose in a despairing wail. She began searching fruitlessly for her cigarettes.

'Here.' Patrick retrieved the packet of Players from the bedside cabinet and handed it to her. He bent down and picked up her lighter. 'Here you are.' He was beginning to feel sorry for her. 'Perhaps you'd like me to bring you up something on a tray. You don't look as if you could quite make it downstairs.'

'Run away, that's right.' She fell back slowly on the bed, her legs, still crossed, rising like the roots of a fallen tree. She lay immobile, gazing at the ceiling.

Outside the door Patrick paused to take stock. He felt

shaken to the core, partly by her accusations and partly by the horrible ease with which he seemed able to lie to her. He walked up and down the landing a few times. It was crazy. He didn't know what she was talking about. He didn't feel a thing for these women.

Sonia's voice droned on in the bedroom. He put his ear against the door.

'What's going on?' Nelly came out of her room. 'Whatever are you doing, Patrick?'

'Having a nervous breakdown.' Patrick suddenly remembered his manuscript. He took his ear away from the door and made for the stairs. 'If anybody wants me before supper, Nelly, I'll be in the shed. And after supper I'm going for a long, long walk.'

CHARLOTTE HAD TO ADMIT, as she chopped the shallots for the evening meal (tonight they were having *Poulet au Vinaigre le Petit Truc*) that she had been agreeably surprised by Nelly's reaction to seeing Riley's photograph. During the six years they were married, she'd never given a moment's thought to his appearance or indeed to how he might strike other people. Riley was just Riley and she'd loved him.

He had been a particularly dominating husband, she recognised now, sprinkling salt over the chicken pieces while they slowly turned a succulent golden brown in the skillet. When you thought how gentle Patrick was, how reasonable. She'd never known a man like Patrick before. Riley always tried to put her down, prove he was the boss.

It was obvious that Patrick liked women. He had a way with them; you could see he *liked* women and you couldn't help responding to his warmth and interest. It could be dangerous for Sonia if he didn't so obviously worship the ground she walked on. Mind you, if she were Sonia she'd make a lot more fuss of him. Only of course she wasn't, and that was the difference: Sonia was so beautiful she'd always have men falling at her feet.

She lifted the chicken pieces from the skillet and put them on a dish in the oven to keep warm. She tossed the shallots and tomatoes into the butter and slowly stirred the pan. She added chopped tarragon and the vinegar. She was slightly pushed for time because she had originally planned to give them *Poulet Mistral de Prieure* until she remembered that Nelly was going out and wouldn't want to be breathing garlic all over her friends. (Charlotte rather hoped that one might soon be able to substitute 'friend' for 'friends,' in which case there would be all the more reason for Nelly not to eat garlic just before.)

It was beginning to smell delicious. The family would be gathering any minute; it was nearly seven thirty.

She had arranged a nosegay of flowers in a little glass vase and set it on the table. Now she made sure the plates were warming, the table laid; they'd be coming in in a minute. She'd take the weight off her feet for a moment. She sat down with a sigh of pleasant exhaustion.

Patrick came in with a glass in his hand. 'Sherry for the cook.'

'Thanks, Patrick.' She took the glass and smiled up at him.

'Back in a minute.' He disappeared with a little wave.

The phone rang in the hall. Patrick spoke for a moment or two then put the receiver down. The front door opened and closed. Charlotte relaxed; waves of sherry-induced languor began to wash through her. She knew where he'd gone – he'd popped out to the pub to get Sonia's cigarettes. Sonia was lucky; he was so good to her. He was meeting his agent after dinner – something to do with his books, and with Nelly going out as well, dinner would be on time for once. She might even manage an early night.

AT AROUND ONE o'clock in the morning Charlotte woke with a start to find her bedside lamp on and Sonia sitting shivering on the edge of her bed wearing a pair of turquoise silk pyjamas and no dressing gown.

'Here, Sonia, put this around you.' She passed Sonia her bed jacket and struggled into a sitting position. Honestly, Sonia was like a child of three; what was she going to do if Sonia started making a habit of this? Why couldn't she come and chat in the daytime like a normal person?

Sonia's small, perky bosoms jutted against the silk of her pyjama top like a young girl's. Charlotte coveted Sonia's bosoms almost as much as her thighs. Or perhaps 'envied' would be a more appropriate word, she thought, bearing Patrick's strictures in mind. Sonia didn't need a bra. Charlotte's own bosoms, unfettered, flopped around all over the place.

Sonia seemed to have no idea how ravishing she was. If she had Sonia's beautiful face and slim figure, Charlotte wondered, would she bother to go around being so nice to everybody? Perhaps what she was doing was simply apologising to everybody for being fat. Did she really care if all those people fell down in the street, tried to lift bags that were too heavy for them, struggled with shop doors and sat crying alone in the park? Why did she always feel she had to rescue everybody? Why couldn't she mind her own business?

'Oh Charlotte, I'm so worried about Alain.' Sonia pulled the bed jacket close around her. 'I phoned the

Embassy again and nobody seems to know anything at all. I drank too much this evening and then I couldn't sleep. I said stupid things to Patrick. Now I have *le cafard* and I don't know where Patrick is.'

Charlotte, longing for sleep, let her ramble on. Sonia repeated horror stories she'd heard about deaths from amoebic dysentery and other dreadful fates befalling lone travellers in India, ranging from attacks by rabid dogs to poisoning by carbon monoxide in airless hotel rooms in Darjeeling. 'It's possible we will never see Alain again. And who knows where he is now?' She went on to list the places of interest Alain had said he might visit, including the houseboats on the Dal Lake in Kashmir, the Thar Desert in Rajasthan and Varanesi in Uttar Pradesh. 'He could be anywhere.'

Eventually she seemed to run out of steam and Charlotte suggested that she might feel like going back to bed.

Sonia uncurled herself and stretched. 'And Patrick's not come home yet. We had a row. I was rude to him. He was only going to the Yellow Hind for a drink with Tony – his agent, you know; that was hours ago. I can't think where he's got to.' She got off the bed and put out a hand to touch Charlotte's cheek. 'Thank you for listening to me, *cherie*. This has done me so much good.' She drifted off, closing the door with extreme, almost comical in the circumstances, quietness.

Charlotte heard Nelly's door open. 'What's going on?' she heard. 'Oh, it's you.'

'Oh, by the way,' Charlotte heard Sonia say quickly, since presumably Nelly was about to shut her door again, 'did Patrick say what his plans were for this evening? I thought he said he was going to have a drink in that pub down the road but I must have got it wrong. He wouldn't still be there at this hour.'

'What is the hour, Mother? Oh. Two a.m. No, you're dead right he wouldn't. Well, he's obviously having a night on the tiles, isn't he?'

Mumble mumble from Sonia.

Nelly made no attempt to keep her voice down. 'Well, I can make a good guess where he is. He's gone and met up with her after all.'

'Who?'

'That damned woman, that's who. Laura. Jeez. You'd better take care, Mother, if you don't want us out in the street again. If you ask me, you've got some serious competition.'

Her bedroom door slammed. Charlotte knew it was Nelly's door and not Sonia's. It had a very distinctive slam and heaven knows, she thought, I do know that slam rather well.

Charlotte's door opened again. Sonia put her head round. 'What girl? What is she talking about?'

Charlotte mimed complete ignorance.

Comprehension dawned. 'Ohhh, of course! *I* know who she means: that girl he used to be involved with. But she was just a child!'

She seemed as unconcerned as though she was talking about somebody else's husband. Charlotte wondered if Sonia was putting it on to convince herself she wasn't worried or if actually the lack of concern was real. Charlotte sometimes suspected that Sonia had a tendency to act out emotions she didn't feel but perhaps aspired to.

Sonia closed Charlotte's door again, not quite so quietly this time. Nelly's door opened again and Nelly said, 'Oh, and by the way. That pot plant's dead. The one I gave you for your wedding anniversary? You forgot to water it and it's dead.' She slammed her door again.

Charlotte shuddered.

There was a long pause. Sonia's bedroom door closed with the gloomy finality of a mortuary drawer.

Chapter 17

We live in a house on fire

When Sonia had started talking about the possibility of moving house, Patrick had wondered if she had been going to say she wanted to leave him. He allowed himself to take out and look at the fear that had been nagging him for some time, that perhaps in marrying him Sonia had simply been looking for security. Once the sale of the Rose Belle estate in St. Colombe was finalised, she would be quite a rich woman. His role as provider and protector would be superfluous.

He was foolish enough to voice these anxieties to Laura one afternoon in the carelessness of after love.

'This is so French,' Laura was exulting, sipping her tea cuddled up against his side. 'I mean, how many men nowadays manage to find the excuse to get out of the house to visit their mistress for *le cinq à sept* the way you do? You are clever, Patrick.'

Patrick handed her a plate with a piece of toast on it spread with homemade lemon curd. Knowing how much Laura liked it he had taken the trouble to look for the lemon curd in the Sue Ryder charity shop in town. They had simply marvellous homemade jams, Laura had told him. She was always extremely hungry after making love.

Patrick swallowed a mouthful of toast. The lemon curd was unexpectedly delicious. 'For a start, you're not my mistress.' He felt less guilty if he didn't have to think that she was his mistress. 'I don't keep you, you're an independent woman. And you're right, it's not at all easy to get away, especially working at home: I can't make the excuse that I've been delayed at the office.' He felt a heel saying this because he knew it would make Laura nervous. 'I'm becoming horribly good at lying.' He sighed. Actually he'd always been horribly good at lying but there was no need for Laura to know that. For some reason he was beginning to feel more and more guilty about being with her. He couldn't go on like this indefinitely, he was going to have to make a decision soon.

He felt sometimes that all the time he had known Sonia she had been living her life at a remove, her reactions so controlled that he'd wondered sometimes whether she might be in some kind of post-traumatic shock; at other times he wondered whether perhaps she was not actually capable of deep feeling. Then he would recall the wandering about at night, and the tears. It would be very easy, he thought, to be wrong about her. Now he wondered if their lack of communication might be partly his fault. Perhaps he hadn't tried hard enough to communicate with her; perhaps through laziness or fear he'd preferred to settle for the image she chose to present rather than make the effort to get to know the real woman underneath. Perhaps he was afraid of what he might find. Or maybe he put so much emotional effort into his fictional worlds that when it came to real people he simply wasn't able to make the effort required. Or perhaps it was a loss of control he feared: with real people, what you saw was what you got; you couldn't change them.

He knew himself well enough to admit that the role he preferred to apply to himself was that of the rescuer, the one who took charge; possibly he was not interested in having an equal relationship with a woman. Chandler was like that; Chandler had grown up in a family dominated by bossy women. He had sisters, two maiden aunts and a mother – all of whom he disliked and feared; no wonder he had turned out to be the misogynist, chauvinist pig which, Patrick had to admit, he was. Maybe Chandler had been trying to tell him something.

Perhaps it was time he took a long, hard look at himself. Maybe it wasn't possible to know the absolute truth about yourself, because there was never just one truth; but it ought to be possible to be reasonably honest with oneself about one's motives: he felt he might not be particularly proud of his. The fact was, he was emotionally lazy about everything else except his work. It was too important; perhaps there just wasn't enough left over for anyone else. Maybe he shouldn't have got married at all.

Then he thought, but I seem to have found time for Laura. Except that his relationship with Laura was such a light-hearted thing; it seemed to make very few emotional demands on him. If Laura were Gilbert and Sullivan, Sonia, he suspected, if one took the trouble to study her, might be grand opera.

'You know I told you about that money Sonia's going to inherit?' He licked lemon curd off his fingers. 'We talked about it again recently and she seems to fancy buying a house with it. Actually, I think she's longing for another house to live in.'

The moment he said it he realised his mistake.

'Really?' Laura's voice was laden with delighted misunderstanding.

He said quickly, 'I mean she'd like us to move into another kind of house. One that isn't my mother's.'

Laura recovered expertly. 'I thought you said things were pretty bad between you.' She put her empty plate back on the tray.

'Did I say that? Oh dear, I oughtn't to discuss my home life with you: I'm sorry.' He felt ashamed. He was getting too good at this.

'Oh, I don't mind. I'm glad. It makes me feel more as though I belong in your life.'

'I expect she'll decide against it in the end.' Another lie. He knew she would not. He had been astonished by Sonia's passionate feelings about the house. He sometimes thought he really didn't know her at all.

His thoughts escaped, as they so often did in moments of stress, to Chandler. Immediately his spirits lifted. My God, he thought, what the hell does that say about me?

Charlotte was relieved to note that Sonia was beginning to seem happier. Or at least more purposeful. She had appropriated one of the spare bedrooms and seemed content to spend hours up there by herself. She had taken to leaving *Art News* magazine lying around in the drawing room. Carrier bags decorated with Cornelissen's art logo had started mysteriously appearing in the bag drawer. Today she had gone to yet another exhibition at Tate Modern. Patrick, clearly delighted to see Sonia beginning to show an interest in something other than her own internal monologue, had broken his routine and come in from the shed to see her off.

Now it was half-past three in the afternoon and Charlotte was alone in the house apart from Maisie who was asleep curled up on Nelly's bed and Mrs P. who was upstairs, hoovering but about to come down for her mid-afternoon cup of tea.

Charlotte had just put the kettle on when Mrs P. jigged into the kitchen, chatting to herself under her breath. Charlotte watched her out of the corner of her eye. Mrs P. had the gait of somebody whose right leg walked faster than her left leg, so that every few steps her left leg gave a little hop to catch up. She looked as though she was dancing some gentle country polka whose music only she could hear.

'Hello, Mrs P.' Charlotte still felt a little shy with her. 'Ready for a cuppa?'

Mrs P. unloaded a neat pile of ironed clothes from her bosom onto the dresser. She put her hands on her hips and stretched her shoulders back as though to ease an ache. 'I think I get off home now.'

'This isn't your usual day, is it? I was sorry to hear that your Mr Dennison had passed on.' Charlotte didn't like to say 'died'. It sounded so final. Mrs P. needed time to get used to the idea.

'No, today is not usual day for me to come but Miss Sonia say okay. Now my Mr Dennison gone it not matter when I come. I rattle around in big old flat, drive myself crazy. So I come here and I go there and I work and I forget for a while.' She leaned heavily on one hand on the kitchen table, resting her hip against the table edge.

'You're tired, Mrs P. Sit down for a moment. You mustn't wear yourself out. I never knew such a hard worker.' Charlotte filled the kettle and switched it on. You never knew with tea, people tended to change their minds when they heard the kettle coming to the boil. 'You must miss him awfully.'

Mrs P.'s eyes were moist. 'He like a father to me. And then, you know, he make provision for me. So kind a man he was, so caring. Now I no longer have to work so hard.' Mrs P. put her head on one side. 'You know, Charlotte, Miss Sonia, sometimes she visit me when I cleaning Mr Dennison house. Always she love that house. One day she say to me, Mrs P., I think I live here in another life, a life I make big success, not big mess like this one. I remember I happy here. I know this house before I see it.'

'Really?' Charlotte poured boiling water into the teapot.

'Sometimes you hear this things. But I say to her, Miss Sonia, perhaps what you feeling is in the future, not in the past. One thing I know is, she prefer to live in different house.'

Charlotte reached into the fridge for the milk.

Mrs P. pulled out a chair and sat down. The chair creaked under her weight. She looked around the big kitchen as Charlotte tipped milk and spooned sugar into a mug of tea and pushed it across the table towards her. 'This is nice room, I like this room, but this house is dark house. Too much furniture and too – is too like old shop.'

'Antique shop?'

She nodded. 'Mr Dennison house full of sunshine. Big windows, let in much light. Nice furniture but simple, plain. Miss Sonia I think she need much light.' She drank her tea in one long draught.

'Another cup. Mrs P?'

When she had drained the second mug she set it down, put both hands on the table and stood up. 'Thanking you. Now I go put this ironings in airing, then I go home. Miss Nelly home from school soon.' She picked up the pile of clothes from the dresser, gave Charlotte a nod and jigged out of the room.

Charlotte turned on Radio Two, discovered that a programme of orchestral dance music was on and began swaying happily to a collection of lilting waltzes, a choice perfectly in keeping with her mood. She hummed as she started to chop the herbs for the *sauce vierge*.

On the kitchen table four large, rosy-fleshed salmon steaks, silver-skinned and ready for grilling, lay on a white plate. Charlotte lifted the plate, examined each steak thoroughly and put the plate back in the fridge. POM-ti-pom pom, POM-ti-pom pom went the music. Charlotte waltzed around the room, seized three tomatoes from the larder shelf in passing and threw them into a bowl. POM-pom-pom, POM-pom-pom went the music.

She poured boiling water over the tomatoes to skin them. Next she hurled three garlic cloves into the mortar standing ready on the kitchen table, aiming them one at a time from the chopping board by the sink. Only one got in on the first go but she rescued the other two and tried again. The second one went in. The third one took four more goes but the waltz had become so exciting that Charlotte, carried away by the music and whirling round and round between each attempt, wasn't aiming as carefully as she should have been.

She calmed herself down after this and tipped some chopped herbs into a bowl. It seemed to her that all her awareness of what it was to be alive had become heightened as though she were on some kind of drug. Everything she looked at seemed to be enhanced and glowing. The afternoon sunshine, dappling the room through the budding vine over the verandah and the swaying trees in the garden, danced on the table.

She was happy. For the first time in ages, she was happy.

She stroked the cool edge of the mixing bowl with the tip of her finger, admiring its soft biscuit colour and the tiny blue window reflected in the rim. It was beautiful. On the table lay the three orange-red tomatoes, a bottle of olive oil, the bowl of herbs and an earthenware pot full of parsley. This is heaven, Charlotte thought. I'm in heaven. She was so happy she almost burst into tears. The intoxicating strains of a Strauss waltz came on and she picked a piece of parsley and held it to her nose, inhaling deeply its wonderful aroma. She seized the sprig of parsley between her teeth and with her eyes closed began to waltz solemnly around the room.

Suddenly, with shattering force, the kitchen door flew open and banged against the wall. Sonia came in like a tornado. She flew at the radio and turned it off. 'I can't stand that music,' she said. Or rather, yelled, her voice echoing into the sudden silence as the music vanished.

Charlotte, who had ducked and just stopped herself from throwing herself flat on the floor in an instinctive attempt at self-preservation, stood there dumbfounded, looking at Sonia in amazement, the sprig of parsley dangling from her mouth. 'I'm sorry,' she said shakily, removing the parsley when she felt able to speak, 'it *was* on rather loud. I thought you were out. I'm terribly sorry.'

Sonia stood in her London clothes, supporting her bent head with her hands, her eyes staring at nothing, the skin of her face so taut that she seemed to have aged ten years in front of Charlotte's eyes. Tufts of short, silky dark hair stuck out between her clutching fingers. She opened her mouth to say something and then shut it again. She dropped her hands and darted a look at Charlotte and made a little noise, half cough, half laugh. 'It isn't that. I'm so sorry. It's just – not Strauss. Anything else, just – not Strauss. I'll go up and change.' She turned and left the room, shutting the door quietly behind her.

Charlotte thought she'd better not put on the radio again at all for a while. When she did, she turned the sound down low. That was a *major* trauma, she repeated to herself several times during *Waggoner's Walk,* finding it quite difficult to get over it. She tried to analyse the violent emotion that had come off Sonia like the smell of sweat, bouncing off the walls, off Charlotte, and presumably getting into the food, Charlotte thought disconsolately. She hoped her *sauce vierge* hadn't been ruined.

The front door slammed. That would be Sonia off for her run. She'd not had the chance to ask how her day in London had gone. Hopefully the effect hadn't been ruined by Strauss. What on earth could have brought that on? She went out into the hall, wondering whether she ought to dash after Sonia and make sure she was all right. She hurried down to the gate. A number of commuters were walking up the avenue from the station. Sonia was half way down the road, running through them, her feet bare, her dark hair flying. Charlotte watched as they moved out of her way, casting surprised, disapproving glances at her as she flew by.

When Sonia was out of sight Charlotte walked back up the drive. If only she would wear shoes, it wouldn't look so odd. After all, plenty of people went running. And what was the point of spending all that money on shoes and then going around barefoot half the time? It was only May still and not a particularly warm May at that.

Patrick put his head round the door. 'Hi Charlotte.

Have you seen Sonia since she got home? I was hoping she'd had a good time at that exhibition she went to.'

'She came in but she's gone out for a run, towards the park, I think.'

'Okay. Had a good day?'

'Very good. You?'

Patrick gave her a thumbs up and disappeared. Perhaps she ought to have told him about Sonia's outburst but on reflection it seemed too complicated to explain, when she really didn't understand what had happened herself.

Chapter 18

Monsieur Crapaud

Blossom threw her ciggy stub down and ground it out with her heel. 'I think I'd rather be gay.'

'Jump back!' Nelly inhaled and choked. She was doing her best to enjoy smoking but she still wasn't sure. Her eyes were smarting.

'I would. I don't like men much, they're such pigs. Most of them seem to really hate women.'

'No, they don't. You only think that because Raymond's such a phoney. They're not all like that. Here, have another fag.' Nelly offered her the half-empty packet of Embassy. 'But keep down. Laura walks home this way sometimes and she nearly clocked us the other day – Sandy and me.'

In fact, Nelly was almost sure Laura had seen them and the smoke curling up from their illicit fags but for some reason she'd kept right on walking. She's letting us off because of Patrick, Nelly had thought, paranoid. She'd nearly stood up and yelled, Hey, it's me, look over here, Laurapoo. But of course she hadn't. She blew out a long stream of smoke. 'You can't just choose. You either are or you aren't. You're not gay.'

'I dunno. How would I know?'

'Well, you don't fancy me, do you?'

'Don't be a bunny. Of course not.'

'There you are then. I'm a stellar chick. If you were gay, you would.'

A light drizzle had started to fall. 'Oh, great, I haven't got my mac.'

'Your bus is due soon. Does it let you off near your house?'

'Not far.'

'There you are then. All we have to do is get you to the bus stop before it really starts coming down.' She stood up and extended a hand. 'Come on then, darling sweetheart precious. Get a move on.'

'Piss off,' Blossom said amiably, standing up and dusting down her skirt. 'Look, don't say anything to the others, yeah?'

''Course not.' Nelly climbed out of the ha-ha, looking cautiously right and left. 'Coast's clear. You don't fancy Tigs, do you, Blossom? Nobody could fancy Tigs.'

'Don't be a goof.' Blossom climbed out after her.

Nelly turned around. 'Blimey, it's Sandy. You're in love with Sandy.'

Blossom narrowed her eyes. 'If you don't belt up I'll tell Tigs it was you who mucked up her chemistry experiment. I'll drop you right in it.'

'You wouldn't.'

'Watch me.'

Nelly set off again. 'It was only a joke; it went a bit wrong, that's all.'

'Tell that to Tigs; she didn't think it was funny, she got nought for that test. And it nearly took her eyebrows off.'

'Would have saved her a lot of trouble then, wouldn't it?' Nelly said, giggling.

Blossom chuckled.

Nelly started to run, her games bag flying. 'Race you to the bus stop. Last one's a rotten egg!'

NELLY CAME in from school and went straight up to her room. She didn't call out 'Hi, I'm home!' as she usually did, hoping there might be an answer from somewhere. She ran upstairs two at a time, went into her room and shut the door, threw her school bag onto the floor and flung herself onto her bed, landing with a wallop on her back. For once she didn't look at her mural: instead, her gaze fixed itself on the ceiling and stayed there. She stayed completely still, as though paralysed, and gradually a sort of paralysis did seem to creep through her limbs so that she couldn't have moved if she'd tried.

If Patrick really was hung up on Laura then everything was going to be ruined. It was obvious that they were seeing each other, but how serious was it? Could they really be having an actual ding-dong?

After everything she and Alain had been through, to have their life turned upside down again, just like that, it honestly was enough to make her want to top herself. But how would she do it? She could try some kind of poison ... or death by gas oven. Not hanging, she was far too squeamish. Not a paracetamol overdose, either: she'd seen quite enough of the consequences in *General Hospital* to be put off anything like that for life. Carbon monoxide poisoning?

She drifted off into a kind of doze, came to and started worrying about herself. Her heart was beating in a most peculiar way. She lay listening to it. Every so often she was sure it missed a few beats. Perhaps she was going to die anyway. She wouldn't be in the least surprised with all this stress. I mean, what was it that kept your heart going anyway? Why should it just keep on beating? It didn't make sense. She'd feel much more secure if it worked on a sort of pendulum mechanism, at least that would have some logic to it, but just to keep on and on beating, for no reason at all ... it was weird. Every so often it seemed to go boom-boom-boom very quickly instead of boom-boom: a kind of extra beat; it sort of fell over itself: it was terrifying. She'd have to go to the doctor. Only she hated the doctor, he looked at you as though he could see right into your inside to all the squelchy, smelly bits. It must be foul being a doctor, she didn't know how they could stand it.

From now on she would wear black. Black was slimming, anyway. All this beastly food was making her put on weight. What was Charlotte trying to do, turn them all into Roly-Polies like her?

Oh, Patrick ...Why did men always have to be after some damn woman? What was it about them? They made you sick. Why couldn't they leave women alone?

NELLY WAS eight when it began to dawn on her that while she had been looking away, Mamée had turned into someone quite different. Nelly began to watch her, anxiously waiting for what would happen next.

Whether her mother was happy or sad seemed to depend on how cross Papa was at the time. There was a little muscle at the corner of her mouth that jumped, tic-tic, tic-tic, when she was nervous, as if it had a life of its own. At the same time the eye on the same side of her face would blink, flick-flick, flick-flick, so that it looked to Nelly as though an invisible elastic was pulling her mouth and her eye towards a point in the middle of her cheek.

'Why are you staring?' Mamée would ask.

Her mother was comparatively tall, although slightly built, but beside Papa she looked small and thin like a young girl. She had always moved with a controlled grace and ease, but now Nelly thought she would really like to be moving much faster, perhaps even setting off at a run, but something was holding her back. Nelly worried a good deal about this.

She worried too because her mother didn't seem to be smiling much, or laughing. In fact, she didn't laugh at all. She walked with her head slightly bent, glancing anxiously to one side or the other with her beautiful green eyes.

'What are you looking for, Mamée?' Nelly asked her one day.

'Looking for? What a funny question! I'm not looking for anything!'

She began to walk more quickly. Oh good, Nelly thought. But then she saw that her mother was hurrying as though she was going to have to apologise for being late, rather than stepping out for the joy of being free, the way Nelly felt when she tore from one end of the lawn to the other for no reason at all. She wanted her mother to walk like that.

Her mother's neck was slim and long like a flower stalk and her head seemed weighed down by her astonishing dark hair which fell to her waist and which she piled up during the daytime and fastened to her head with tortoiseshell combs. Nelly thought that with her hair down her mother was the most beautiful thing she had ever seen. Far more beautiful than Pearl. Pearl was Couba's daughter and had recently joined the household as Sonia's maid. Everybody said she was beautiful, and as Alain told Nelly, she certainly thought she was. She looked down her nose at the children, who disliked her as a result.

Early one morning, Nelly, running to the bathroom, met her mother coming along the upstairs passage, barefoot, in her long white cotton nightdress, carrying a glass of water in her hand. Her hair hung down her back in a dark waterfall and she looked so angelic that Nelly's heart melted and she almost forgave her. Almost, but not quite. For Nelly was beginning to have confused feelings about her mother too. It was because of all the funny things Papa said she did.

Her father had begun to say things to her mother like, 'What kind of a mother are you anyway? Look at you. You'd rather spend time in the kitchen gossiping with the servants or lazing about the plantation on your own than looking after your children as you ought to be doing. You look quite daft wandering about like that, your head in the clouds. Don't you care about your children at all?'

Nelly thought, doesn't she care about us at all?

One Sunday they were sitting around the table in the salon having their coffee after lunch. At least, Mamée and Papa were drinking coffee, the rich, pungent-smelling aroma circling the table, Nelly fancied, like the ghosts summoned up by the obeah man. (Pearl liked to tell Nelly stories about the obeah man when Nelly would really rather have tried to get off to sleep on her own, especially as she suspected that Pearl rather enjoyed trying to frighten her.)

Alain and Nelly sat silent and thoughtful, enjoying the unusual peace brought on by them all having attended Mass together for once. Papa hardly ever joined them for

Mass, but he had this morning and the children had revelled in the unusual sensation of being a unit with their parents, instead of feeling as they usually did that Papa was the captain of an unruly ship and they were mutineers on the verge of getting their comeuppance. (The trouble was, it felt to Nelly as though Mamée was a mutineer too, if not the leader of the mutineers, and consequently bound to get into the most trouble when trouble came.)

Everyone seemed to be quite astonishingly happy and jolly until Papa suddenly said to Mamée, his irritation arising out of the blue as far as Nelly could see, 'Really, Nia, you spend far too much time in the kitchen with the servants. Why do you seem incapable of showing any interest in people of your own status?'

Mamée looked up in surprise from where she had been stirring her coffee, her head in a dream as usual. She blinked at Papa, struggling to hide the hurt expression Nelly saw wanting to come to life on her face.

Papa went on, 'Of all the half-baked things to do, refusing Sadie Rowntree's invitation for us to go back to take coffee with her and Senator Rowntree this morning – on the grounds that you had too much to do in the house, of all the idiotic excuses! Unfortunately I myself was caught by old Chambertin on the way out and didn't hear what was going on. I only found out what had happened from Senator Rowntree himself. Can you imagine how I felt, having him think I make a habit of letting my wife get away with making decisions about my social life without consulting me? And then I find you've been wasting your time hobnobbing with the servants as usual, all the rest of the morning. You can't seem to keep away from the servants. Why don't you make some proper friends of your own sort instead?'

Hobnobbing, Nelly thought, to distract herself. *What a gravalicious word. Hobnobbing.*

(Lena, Nelly's old nurse, said Nelly was gravalicious when she wanted another macadam when Lena thought she'd had enough; so she guessed it wasn't really anything very complimentary. But Nelly had decided that from the sound of it, it meant super-duper.)

'For heaven's sake, Luis.' Mamée's voice was tired, but at least she was standing up for herself for a change. Nelly saw Alain look up quickly.

Mamée pushed back a strand of hair that had fallen down. 'Most of the morning I was with you; perhaps you didn't notice. I've only been in the kitchen a little while. We're short-staffed; Excelie is sick, haven't you noticed? So I was helping Lena with the lunch. If you took more interest in their welfare, you'd have known that.'

Nelly didn't dare look up. She'd never heard Mamée answer Papa back like that before. She could feel Papa revving up like a chatty coming to the boil.

'And I do have friends, a few. Only, all the people I like, you seem to take a dislike to. Anyway, you only wanted me to talk to those people because you want to get in with them, it's not because you like them a bit really. I'm sick of it. Please, Luis,' she said, resting her head on her hand and leaning on her elbow as though she was very, very tired. 'Don't have any more to drink today, for my sake, please don't. You know what will happen. And we've had such a nice morning. Please.'

Nelly jumped as Papa exploded. He went up like a rocket. He grew about three feet in height (then Nelly realised he'd stood up out of his chair) and glared at Mamée, his back all hunched like the troll under the bridge in *The Three Billy Goats Gruff*. Nelly felt very frightened and she had the feeling that Mamée was frightened too. But Mamée sat quite still. She didn't run away and hide, the way Nelly would have done if Papa had looked at her like that.

'How dare you,' Papa shouted at Mamée. 'How dare you criticise me to my face in front of my children? Can't a man have a drink in his own house without some fool of a woman trying to stop him? Children,' he declared with a melodramatic sweep of his arm, 'pay attention. Note that your mother is objecting to my having a small, just a little, harmless, amounting-to-nothing drink.' He sat down again. 'What do you think of that, eh? And while you're about it, take a good look at her,' he said, with a sweep of his other arm so that, off-balance, he fell forward and hit his chin on the edge of the table.

Neither of the children felt a bit like laughing. Off he went again. 'Aren't you proud of her? I'll tell you something.' He sat up and rubbed his chin. 'She is the most useless woman I've ever come across. Honest to God, look at her, sitting there with her mouth open. What are you staring at, woman?'

'She isn't useless,' Nelly whispered, her head hanging down. She couldn't think where it had come from, the courage to defy her father like that: she was an awful scaredy-cat, everybody knew she was. She sat there, terrified.

'Eh? What did you say? Could you just repeat that, daughter, only louder this time so that I can believe my ears? No? Then would you be so good as to explain to me in what way your mother demonstrates her usefulness – to you, to me, or to anybody else?'

Nelly didn't understand one word of this. Indeed she was so frightened she hardly heard what her father was saying. She went on hanging her head, waiting for the sky to fall in.

'Does she take the trouble to mend your clothes? And goodness knows they need mending often enough, the way you are always up some tree or other or standing on your head like some little gypsy child, not like the well-behaved daughter of a man such as myself, such as you ought—' He began stumbling over his words and Nelly began to think that she could hear the drink talking and that it wasn't her father really shouting at her like that.

Her father recovered the thread of his diatribe. 'Who is it who mends your clothes? Your mother? No, Lena mends your clothes. Does your mother cook for you? No, Excelie cooks the food in this house. Does your mother clean the house – do the laundry—'

Mamée seemed almost to believe he was joking. 'But you employ people to do these things, Luis. If I were to do them, half the servants would be out of a job. And if you're so worried about your dignity, what's so dignified about having your wife doing these menial jobs? I didn't think that was at all what you had in mind.'

'What I'd like to know is why in hell I ever married you?' Luis roared at her suddenly, narrowing his eyes and thumping the table with his fist. 'I must have been crazy! A little sallow shrimp of a girl, all skin and bone, fifteen years old, with no dowry! And shall I tell you why I was obliged to marry her, children?'

Mamée snapped, 'That's enough, Luis. Stop right there.'

'Oh, I'm to stop right there, am I?' Luis wagged his large head from side to side, making a funny face.

Nelly giggled, mostly from nerves.

'You think that's funny, do you?'

Nelly hung her head.

'Oh, what do you know about it?' He threw himself back in his chair. 'You're just a pair of spoilt mother's brats and stupid with it.'

Alain looked up. 'I'm not stupid.'

He looked almost as though he were going to cry, only of course he never cried. Nelly peeped through her fringe at his eyes, but although Alain's face was red, his eyes stayed dry.

'Aren't you?' Luis peered at him hazily as though trying to work it out. 'Yes, you are. Stupid, lazy and spoilt. Just like your mother, the whole damn lot of you.' He put his hand inside his jacket and as if by magic pulled out a little flask, from which he poured a lot of tea-coloured liquid into his coffee cup. His hand was shaking and the cup chimed once or twice as the flask rattled against the edge of it.

Breathing heavily like Father Bear in Nelly's storybook, he thrust the flask clumsily back into its hiding place inside his jacket, then lifted the cup and tossed the drink down his throat in one easy movement, banging the cup down on the table when it was empty. He did a big belch. He bent down and spoke in a confidential tone to Nelly so that his strong-smelling breath washed over her. 'She doesn't care, you know. She doesn't giveadam. Heart of stone. Heart of stone.'

Nelly recoiled. Mamée didn't care. Heart of stone. She saw her mother's heart sitting inside her chest, a calcified grey lump incapable of loving Nelly. Her stomach sank in terror.

'Stop it, Luis. You're upsetting them.' Mamée leaned forward and looked into Nelly's face, her eyes burning. 'Don't listen to him. Of course I love you. I love you more than life itself. Don't take any notice. I don't know why he keeps saying these things.'

The children looked at their father for an answer. He began to shout, banging the table with his fist, words of abuse roaring from his angry mouth, his face red and his eyes bulging.

Nelly, terrified and peeping at him through her fingers every time he paused for breath to see if he had really stopped this time, thought he looked a bit like Monsieur Crapaud in her storybook. His eyes bulged too.

Chapter 19

It's fun to live dangerously

'Are you sure about this, Nell?' Sandy turned her face up and blew a smoke ring. 'You hardly know the guy.'

'I know enough,'

'I know you're upset about Patrick.'

'I'm not a bit upset. I couldn't care less.'

It was eight fifteen on Monday evening and they were sitting in the Dog and Duck waiting for Michael. Sandy wore a shiny red mini-dress with white, knee-length boots, Nelly a black, scoop-neck top and blue flares with her new earth shoes. She smelt strongly of her mother's *Grès Cabotine* scent.

The idea was that if Carl turned up with Michael, they'd make up a foursome. Sandy had twigged that Michael was the one Nelly really liked. If Michael came on his own then Sandy would after a decent interval make herself scarce, which seemed a pity, Nelly thought, considering how fab she looked.

Suddenly they were there. Nelly's insides clenched with nervousness. Carl looked older than she remembered.

He was wearing the same fawn flares, a blue flowered shirt and a dark blue jacket. I don't know this guy at all, she thought, and then she remembered that Patrick was keen on Laura and that at any minute now he might leave them. It felt like the end of the world. If everything was over then it didn't matter what she did or what happened to her. She couldn't seem to feel in the least concerned about Sonia; in fact, she blamed her for the mess they were in. It was all her fault.

She watched them approach. Carl, with his brown skin and dark hair, his ready smile and those remarkable yellow eyes, was better-looking than Michael who was more serious, dour even, and seemed preoccupied, as though there was something permanently on his mind. She didn't know why she liked him best. Perhaps it was because he presented more of a challenge.

'Hello.' The corner of Michael's mouth twitched as though he was tempted to smile. 'Glad you could make it.'

'Hi there.' Carl put out his hand to shake Sandy's. 'Is this Sandy? How do, Sandy? I'm Carl.'

'Hi Carl. Heard lots about you from Nelly.'

'All good, I hope.'

Sandy grinned at him. 'Well ... I wouldn't be too sure about that.'

Nelly felt a flutter of excitement as Michael pulled a chair round and sat down beside her.

Carl indicated a chair for Sandy beside Nelly and sat down on Sandy's other side. 'I'm glad you came.' He looked at Nelly and smiled and with a sudden shock she saw that his eyes were no longer golden but a deep, penetrating black, rimmed with yellow.

They couldn't be.

Nelly asked for a Pils again; Sandy was drinking vodka

and tonic. The men went to the bar to get their drinks.

Nelly touched Sandy's arm to attract her attention and spoke in an urgent whisper. 'Sandy. Did you see his eyes?'

'Whose eyes? What are you on about?'

'*Carl's*. Only it's not Carl, it can't be, you can't change the colour of your eyes. Maybe he's got a twin brother or something. What are we going to do?'

Sandy looked at her, disbelieving. 'Don't be daft, he's on something, that's all.'

'What, drugs you mean?"'

'Of course drugs. Coke or something. It makes your pupils dilate. Have another shufti when he comes back. I bet it's coke.'

'Good gosh. Should we book?'

'Don't be daft, he's not *dangerous,* Nell, he's just done a couple of lines, that's all. My parents do it all the time. Be cool.'

'They don't!'

'Yes they do. Lots of people do. Don't look so psyched, they're coming back. It's okay, honest.'

The men were both drinking beer. They sat down. Nelly thought, why do men always spread their knees like that? It looks stupid. She'd read somewhere that if men opened their knees wide people liked them more.

Carl sat back and crossed his legs. 'How've you been? Got rid of the bodyguard?'

Sandy gave him a coy look. 'Oh, Mark's okay.'

'Of course he is. It's nice to meet you, Sandy. What's Sandy short for, anyway? It must be short for something.'

'Cassandra.'

Carl laughed. 'Don't look so miserable about it.'

Michael looked at Sandy, his head on one side. 'It's a beautiful name. Old-fashioned. I like it.'

Nelly wanted Michael to look at her like that. 'I do too. I could call you Cassie. Or Cass.'

Sandy looked at her sceptically. 'Sandy'll do, thanks.'

'Do you like school?' Michael asked her.

'It's okay. Too many stupid rules.'

'Are you a rebel then? I bet you are, you've got a naughty face. Hasn't she?' Carl appealed to Nelly.

'I know what you mean.'

'What do you mean? I'm an absolute saint. Ask anybody.'

Nelly sipped her Pils. 'We don't do anything too terrible.'

'A bit of smoking behind the bike sheds, that's all.' Sandy blew a smoke ring.

Show-off, Nelly thought. Michael smiled and raised his eyebrows at Sandy. He never smiles at *me,* Nelly thought. She wanted Michael to like her. He seemed more mature than Carl, perhaps that was what she liked. Carl never seemed to take anything very seriously; perhaps that was the problem.

Michael reached into his pocket and pulled out a pack of cigarettes. He offered Sandy a cigarette. 'Do you work hard, Sandy?'

'No.' She took a cigarette and Michael got out his lighter and lit it for her.

Nelly frowned. 'She does really. She pretends not to, that's all.'

'Is she bright?' Michael offered Nelly a cigarette. She shook her head. He took one for himself, threw the pack on the table and lit up.

Sandy inhaled deeply. 'Oh, I'm brilliant. Anyway, what's with the inquisition? This is beginning to sound like a job interview.'

'Well, you never know your luck.' Carl looked at Michael.

'Come off it, Carl. She's way too young. They both are. Don't even think about it.'

'What for?' Nelly drained her glass. Oh shoot. She'd drunk it too fast. Again. She didn't want to feel wobbly and out of control like the time before. It flashed through her mind that she might have made a bit of a fool of herself last time.

Michael drew on his cigarette. 'It's just Carl getting carried away again. He's always getting these crap ideas. Don't take any notice of him.' He tapped ash from his cigarette into the ashtray.

Sandy looked at Carl. 'Could you really get us a job? What kind of job?'

Michael frowned and shook his head. 'No, we couldn't. I told you, forget it.'

'Well, there are possibilities.' Carl got out his cigarette case and took out a cigarette.

Michael tossed his lighter to Carl, who caught it and lit up. 'I won't be telling you again, Carl, just shut up about it, will you? We've got too much else on at the minute, anyway. Look, I'm having another drink. Who'll join me? Nelly?'

Sandy said she'd have another vodka and tonic. Nelly said what she'd really like was a tomato juice.

'Righto.' Michael got up, took his lighter from Carl's outstretched hand, dropped it in his jacket pocket and made his way to the bar.

Sandy said, 'Quick, give us the skinny. What's with this job then?'

'You'll get me into trouble.'

Sandy leaned forward. 'What kind of job is it?'

'I was thinking of the little side-line we run.' Carl

glanced over at Michael who was standing at the bar, his back turned. 'Look, some of our friends, business associates, find they're working so hard all the time they never get a chance to meet people or organise a proper social life. They're respectable people, nothing wrong with them, they're just too busy to find themselves a partner for the evening, for example. We know a lot of people, and we're always introducing people to each other, so one day Michael said, why don't we put this on a proper business footing and make some money out of it? So we did. It's just a side-line, it's not important.'

Sandy drew on her cigarette. 'Where do we come in?'

'It's a little difficult to explain.' Carl gave Nelly a long look. 'I wouldn't want you getting the wrong idea.'

'Why would we?' Nelly began to feel a bit worried.

'It sounds a bit off, but it isn't really.' Carl glanced over at Michael then leaned forward and lowered his voice. 'Look, it's like this. We have some friends who are really only interested in young girls – not silly girls if you know what I mean, but bright, intelligent, classy girls – like you, actually – who they find really hard to meet through the usual channels. People can be really stuffy about girls' age and things, which I personally feel is completely unreasonable. Everybody knows that kids grow up a great deal earlier nowadays. To pretend this doesn't happen is just stupid, in my view.'

Sandy nodded. 'Hear, hear!'

'These friends of ours get bored with the women they usually get lumbered with. What they want is intelligence and *youth*. They're prepared to pay generously for the privilege of meeting the right kind of girl. We keep our eyes open for girls who might fulfil the criteria and there's no doubt you two would be marvellous. But Michael's right, you're a bit on the young side, your parents would probably object if they found out. It's a pity because the money's terrific and you'd hardly have to do anything for it, just a bit of dancing, go out for a nice meal, that sort of thing.'

Nelly flinched as though she'd walked into a glass door. 'It's an escort agency.'

Carl looked dubious. 'You could call it that. But a high-class one. With the benefit of complete safety because of course we'd know where you were the whole time. Everything's organised beforehand, you see. You'd be quite safe.'

Sandy sat back and took a drag on her cigarette. 'Sounds okay to me.'

Nelly frowned. 'No it doesn't, you don't want some horrible fat old man pawing you all evening.'

'I dunno.' Sandy giggled. 'Depends on the moolah.'

Nelly looked at Carl. 'Do you know how old we are? It's probably illegal for people as young as us. Isn't it?'

Carl shrugged, his black eyes smiling at her over his cigarette. 'Age doesn't matter. It's how old you *look* that counts.'

His eyes worried her too. She felt prickles of alarm down her back.

Sandy giggled. 'I've never heard that one before.'

'It's rubbish,' Nelly said. 'What about school?'

'It would all be outside school hours. That's the beauty of it.' Carl had sincerity written all over his face. 'Sandy, you're looking quite interested. Are you, in theory?'

Nelly's lips tightened. 'No, she's not.'

'Yes I am. Think of all that lovely bread.'

Michael arrived with their drinks on a tray. Nelly helped unload. She bent down and leaned the empty tray against the side of her chair.

Michael looked at Carl who was smoking and looking at Sandy.

'What's going on? What are you talking about?'

There was a brief silence.

'You haven't. You haven't gone and said something? You idiot, Carl.'

'What's the problem? They understand, they're not children.'

Michael sat down. 'Pretty nearly. And you don't want them blabbing their mouths off all over the place. When will you learn to keep your mouth shut, Carl?'

Sandy looked indignant. 'We wouldn't. And too right we're not children. I, for one, am a woman of the world.' She drained her drink.

Nelly rolled her eyes. 'You're an idiot, Sandy. And you're drunk.'

Michael looked at her, his eyes cold. 'That's not a very nice thing to say to your friend.'

Nelly felt alienated from all three of them. It was as if all this talk about easy money had gone straight to Sandy's head and misplaced her brains.

Michael took a long swallow of his beer. He put down his glass. 'Can you dance, Sandy?'

He'd got over his objections pretty quickly. That was probably all a put-up job, hard cop, soft cop, like they did in police interviews, if you could believe what you saw on the telly.

'Dance?'

'I mean disco, that kind of thing.'

'I love dancing.'

'Well there you are. You could go dancing.'

'Only you mustn't say anything to anybody,' Carl interposed. 'Not a soul. Because you probably are a bit young, actually.'

Sandy grinned. 'Cross my heart and hope to die.'

Michael smiled at her. Again. 'Goodness, let's hope it won't come to that,'

Carl took a swig of his beer. 'We don't want to know how old you are. But I expect you are a bit young. People might object.' He put down his glass and sat back, looking relaxed. He crossed his legs.

Sandy stubbed out her cigarette. 'My parents are out of it most of the time, anyway.'

'Really?' Michael looked at her speculatively.

Nelly shook her head. 'Mine aren't.'

Carl, ignoring her, went on looking at Sandy. 'People get lonely, you see. They just want someone to have dinner or go dancing with. It's all perfectly above board. Come back with us to the flat and we'll fill you in on the details.'

'What, now?' Sandy smiled and sipped her vodka.

Michael shrugged. 'Why not? No time like the present.'

Nelly felt a pang of intense disappointment. Also fear. They were just a couple of *maquereaux*. Patrick had told her she was a hopeless judge of character. Was he right or what? If they thought she was going anywhere near their poxy flat, they must be crazy. Sandy was on her own with this one.

'Come to a party we're having,' Carl said suddenly. 'There'll be a lot of our friends there and you can meet them. Not tonight – next week.' He looked at Michael.

Michael looked doubtful.

Carl persisted. 'Why don't you both come? You'll enjoy it, I know you will.'

Sandy looked at Nelly. 'When's this party, then?'

He leaned sideways to put the lighter in his pocket.

'Next week. Friday. It'll be a great party. You'll meet lots of nice people.'

'Cool beans!' Sandy wagged her head and took another mouthful of vodka.

'Where is it?' Nelly said. She was really worried now. Why hadn't she stayed home and watched *Top of the Pops*?

Carl looked at her with revived interest. 'You on board, Nelly? Twickenham. That's where our flat is.' He got out his cigarette case.

'Well, give us the address, and we might bomb along.' Sandy accepted a cigarette from Carl with a little shrug.

'Don't look so disappointed,' Carl said, *sotto voce*. 'Were you hoping I would offer you something stronger?'

Sandy mimicked his tone. 'Are you offering?'

Michael frowned. 'Not in here. For heaven's sake, Carl, are you mad?'

'Just testing the water.'

'*Minute, papillon.*' Nelly reached out her hand and touched Sandy's arm.

'What's the prob?' Sandy turned unfocused eyes towards her.

Carl lit Sandy's cigarette. 'I can see you're our kind of girl.' There was a slight edge to his voice when he added to Nelly. 'I didn't realise you spoke French so well ... *elle est chouette, ta copine.*'

Nelly's face was hot. '*Elle est* nut-case.'

Michael drained his glass. 'You should come back with us now. Carl's right, you'd be more relaxed in the flat. I feel that now we've got this far perhaps we ought to discuss it properly.'

Nelly set her lips in a firm line. 'You can count me out.'

Sandy looked horrified. 'Nell, you're not going to be a party pooper?'

Nelly put her hands on the arms of her chair. 'I've just remembered, there's something I forgot to do.'

'What?' Sandy's face was flushed and her eyeliner had smudged.

'I promised to phone Sonia,' she improvised. Her heart was thumping. 'She wasn't feeling very well and everybody's out so I said I'd ring to make sure she was okay.'

'What's wrong with her?'

'Not sure, probably just depressed, as usual.'

'Probably wants to spoil your evening, you mean.'

'Why would she do that? She's not like that.'

Sandy tapped the ash off her cigarette and addressed the two men. 'Actually, she's a real neurotic cow.'

'She can't help not feeling well.' Nelly wished Sandy would stop ganging up on her with those two. 'I won't be a minute.'

'Well, don't you dare say anything. Michael and Carl wouldn't like that, would you?'

Michael looked hard at Nelly. 'Nelly understands that.'

Carl reached out and patted Nelly's arm. 'Of course she does.'

The phone was hanging on the wall near the entrance to the toilets. There was a clear plastic booth you put your head under to block out the pub noise. Nelly picked up the receiver with trembling hands. That last comment from Michael had sounded like a threat. Both mens' attitude had subtly changed, becoming more controlling, but Sandy was too wasted to pick this up.

Oh crumbs, make him be in.

'Patrick?' From the phone booth she could see the table where the others were sitting. Michael was standing up. Oh gosh, they were getting ready to leave ... but no. He was going to the bar, getting more drinks.

'Nelly? Are you okay?'

Nelly was so relieved she almost cried. 'Sort of. But could you come and get us? Now?'

'What's up? Where are you?'

'We're in the Dog and Duck in Hammersmith. We're okay, but I really need you to come and get us now.'

'I'm on my way. You're sure you're okay?' He spoke crisply. He hadn't asked what they were doing there, he was just going to come.

'Will you be long?'

'Twenty minutes, max. Probably quarter of an hour. That okay? Is Sandy with you?'

Nelly gritted her teeth. No, Sandy wasn't. She'd deserted. 'Sort of.'

'You're sure you're all right?' Patrick sounded reassuringly worried.

'We're fine. Only be quick.'

'I'm on my way.'

Where was the Ladies? That would kill five minutes. In the mirror in the Ladies her face looked flushed and her eyes large and frightened. She must calm down, they couldn't do anything actually in the pub. She just had to keep them talking. She didn't know why she was so scared. It was the way they went on, those two, there was something funny about them. And she felt so alone. If only Sandy hadn't decided to get bombed. She'd just get worse and worse now.

She dawdled as long as she could. If she and Sandy went back with the men to their flat they'd never be able to get away. She went into one of the cubicles and sat on the loo with the seat down. She pressed her hands over her eyes and, born out of her fear, the past came into focus and she was back again in the heat and dust of St. Colombe.

Chapter 20

Crunch time

She was nine. She was sitting on the verandah steps, blood running down her arms onto her knees; under her elbows she could feel her thighs slippery with blood. She heard her mother screaming for Lena but all she could feel was a great apathy and an irritation at the noise her mother was making when all she wanted was to be left in peace.

The sky came nearer with its searing blue and she smelt Cufféе's special smell: sweat and tobacco and a certain spice: nutmeg maybe. She was being lifted up in his arms. He held her close against his enormous chest. When she opened her eyes, she was in the clinic.

They say she tried to harm herself, somebody said. Would you believe it, a child of nine?

There was a blind flapping against the wall outside the window. The sunlight made bars across the floor. In the rectangle of her view, a palm frond dipped and swayed against a darkening sky. The wind was rising.

Big storm coming soon, Esther said, tucking her in. Esther looked after her in the clinic. She was young, with a sweet face. She had red lips and white teeth and she smiled all the time; it was as if her mouth could only be comfortable when she was smiling.

They closed the jalousies and it was dark. In the middle of the room which smelt of cloves, a hurricane lamp swung from a beam like a hanged man, giving out its soft light. She could hear the sea.

She doesn't ask for her parents, another nurse said. Nelly lay with her eyes shut. It's weird, the nurse said; she hasn't once asked for her mother.

She couldn't remember why, but she was angry with her father. She was hoping he would die in the storm. She hoped the wind would rise and lift off the roof of one of the shanty houses and cut his head off, like it cut off Sam Bequia's that time as he walked along the road.

Sam had gone out to look for his old pea-hen. 'I told him a hundred times,' his grandmother said afterwards. 'I said, "Don't go out, Sam, it's too dangerous. The wind will get you, or the sea. You'll be drowned in the flood."' But the old tin roof off Ambrose's house got him, skimming down the road just the right height from the ground to catch him clean like a discus so his legs carried his body one way and his head sailed on somewhere else and was found after the hurricane, wedged in a frangipani tree. All the other trees had been uprooted and, in the morning, there was just this tree remaining, upright in the stinking mud, having grown this strange and terrible fruit in the night.

When she leaned across Nelly in her white nurse's uniform to straighten her pillows, a warm, sweet aroma came from Esther's body, mysterious and inviting. Nelly's heart beat heavily, filled with strange longing. There was an atmosphere around Esther that drew Nelly to her and fascinated her. Only afterwards, years later, was she able to recognise this atmosphere for what it was: happiness.

She failed to recognise it because in their house happiness did not exist.

Slowly Nelly came back to the present. She took several deep breaths and came out of the cubicle and went to the basins. The face staring back at her from the mirror was the same face that had looked back at her before but she felt she had lived through a long time and was in a different place. She put on some more lipstick and pressed her lips together carefully on a tissue. Whatever you did you had to avoid getting lipstick on your teeth.

She ambled as slowly as she could back to the table. Now the bar with its red walls and gilt mirrors looked to her like a brothel in a Western. It was so hot in here. Perhaps she could ask for a glass of water.

'How's it hangin'?' Sandy's eyes were bright and amused. She was smoking again and she looked as though she was enjoying herself.

'Oh, all okay. I'd love another drink. A St. Clements or something. It's so hot.'

Sandy tapped her cigarette on the edge of the ashtray. 'Don't be so boring.'

'I'll get them to put some vodka in it.' Carl stood up. 'My turn, I think. You won't taste anything but it will relax you.'

'You're mighty hot on relaxation.' Sandy smiled up at him.

'No vodka, thanks.'

'Are you sure?'

'Positive. Actually, on second thoughts, I'll get it myself.' Nelly stood up.

'No need.' Carl put his hands up. 'Okay, no vodka. This is our treat.' He put his hand on her arm and held her back.

'I'd rather.'

'What's wrong?' Michael looked from Carl to Nelly, his face concerned.

'She doesn't trust me.' Carl was smiling at her, still holding onto her arm.

Sandy grabbed her other arm. 'Don't be so embarrassing, Nell. Sit down and stop being such a spoil-sport.'

'I'm not. Okay then.' She sat down.

Michael sat back. 'That's better.'

'What's the matter with you?' Sandy let her go.

'I don't like people buying me all these drinks. I don't want to feel obligated.'

'You're not, don't be silly.' Carl smiled down at her. 'It's different for us, we've got plenty of money. Don't worry about it.'

When he'd gone for the drinks Sandy laughed and took another mouthful of vodka. 'You know what they say. You don't have to feel you owe anything in return, just because some guy buys you dinner. That's for tarts.'

Michael's eyebrows twitched. He smiled. 'Spot on, Sandy.'

Nelly looked away. Why had she ever thought him nice. He was like the crocodile in the poem, welcoming little fishes in with gently smiling jaws. She just wanted to go home. Where was Patrick? It had to have been a good ten minutes since she'd spoken to him.

Sandy chatted with Michael. Nelly pretended to look for something in her bag.

Carl came back with the drinks.

Sandy said, with the deliberation of the rather drunk, 'I'm very tempted by the thought of all that bread. I want *things* and it takes bread to get them.'

Carl sat down. 'You'll get good money from us.' He pulled his chair a little nearer to Nelly's and handed her her drink. 'There. Enjoy. Positively no vodka, promise.'

Sandy drained her glass and plonked it down beside the full one. 'What's good money?'

Carl looked at Michael. 'Well, it depends. You'd make at least fifty an evening, then after that it's up to you. Some girls make as much as two hundred. It depends.'

'What on?' Sandy said.

Nelly's lips tightened. 'It's obvious what on. I don't believe this. Come on, Sandy, we're going.' She stood up.

'Sit down, for goodness' sake. I like the sound of this. Think of all that moolah.'

'Don't drink anymore – please, Sandy. You're smashed.'

'You're insulting her now,' Michael said roughly to Nelly. 'Do you think she isn't old enough to make up her own mind? What are you afraid of, anyway?'

'What do you think?' How did things ever get this far? she thought. And where the hell was Patrick?

Michael leaned forward. 'Come back to the flat. I insist, I really do. We can't have you thinking all these things.'

Sandy picked up her fresh drink and drank half straight off. 'I'm game.'

'Good girl.'

'Don't patronise her,' Nelly snapped.

Carl put his hand on Nelly's knee. 'You come too. We really do want you to come. You're a lovely girl. *T'es jolie comme un coeur, toi.* You have the most beautiful eyes. But they are much too sad.'

Suddenly Nelly felt like crying. She felt she would

really quite like to be nice to Carl and have him think she was lovely and do what he wanted.

Carl gave her knee a little squeeze. 'I'd love to see your eyes looking happy and not so terribly sad. Why are you sad, Nelly?'

'Because of types like you.'

Michael gave an appreciative chuckle. 'Carl likes you. He really does.'

Sandy put her hand on Nelly's other knee. 'Come on, Nell.'

Oh, why the hell not? Nelly thought. It can't be too bad. What does it matter anyway? It might be quite nice to relax and have a drink and do what they all wanted her to do, and make them all pleased with her instead of annoyed. Then she remembered she had asked Patrick to come and pick them up.

At that moment Patrick came into the bar. Nelly thought she'd never been so pleased to see anybody in her whole life.

She gave a fake start of surprise. 'There's Patrick!'

Carl took his hand off her knee. 'Who's Patrick?'

'Oh God, it's the cavalry.' Sandy downed the rest of her drink.

Nelly stood up. 'Come on, Sandy.'

'No way. I'm going with these two.'

Michael stood up. 'Sandy, I think you should go with your friend. Go on. Don't say anything to anybody, will you? It's our secret. Come on, Carl.'

Patrick was scanning the crowded bar. He hadn't seen them yet.

'We'll be off now. Don't forget our party. Friday night. Don't forget.' Michael nodded at them and disappeared into the throng.

Carl looked down at Nelly. 'I could come and pick you up. I could meet you at the end of your road, to avoid complications. Do come, Nelly, I want you to come. I'll call you.' He moved off after Michael.

He sounded so sincere. Perhaps she'd got them all wrong. Watching his tall figure disappearing into the crowd, for a tiny moment Nelly regretted phoning Patrick. Then she turned her head and it was like coming out from under a spell. All it took to snap her out of it was the sight of Patrick's anxious, familiar face and the sound of his voice, calling her name.

'Don't forget your bag, Sandy.' Nelly hooked the strap of her own bag over her shoulder and waved to Patrick who was still standing by the door. His face looked thunderous but Nelly was so overcome with relief at the sight of him that she didn't care.

Sandy bent to pick up her bag, staggering a little which she seemed to find hysterically funny. They forged their way through the crowd, Sandy giggling and holding onto the back of Nelly's shirt.

When they reached Patrick, Nelly's legs nearly gave way from sheer relief. 'Get us out of here, quick. Please, Patrick.' She just managed not to start crying at the sight of his dear, familiar face. 'Thank goodness you came.'

'Who were those men you were with? Good lord, Nelly, have you been drinking? I thought you said you never touched alcohol?'

Sandy giggled. 'Give us a break.'

'I only had a half of lager. And I don't, usually.' She nearly said, wanting someone to blame, that she hadn't felt she needed to drink until he'd started messing around with Laura.

'As for you,' Patrick said, looking closely at Sandy, 'what

on earth have you been doing? You look terrible. You're only sixteen, for God's sake. What do you think your mother will think about this?' he asked Nelly.

'Look, could we have the inquisition later?' Nelly implored. 'Let's go. Please.'

Patrick looked round the bar, his face set. 'I'm going to have a word with your friends. I suppose they are aware you're underage? They do realise they're breaking the law, buying you drinks?'

Nelly gave a huff of frustration. 'Probably not. Anyway you can't; they've gone. Now *please* can we just *go*?'

'How dare they fill a couple of children up with drink like this? Bastards. Nelly, I'm disappointed in you. I thought you had more sense.'

'I'm sorry. It was only a bit of fun. We didn't realise they were so—'

Sandy chimed in. 'What's the problem, Mr Carey? How did you know we were here?'

Patrick opened the front door and shooed them out into the dark car park, Nelly subdued, Sandy *chasséing* alongside. Nelly felt comforted. He really was angry. He strode ahead to open the car doors.

Sandy poked Nelly hard in the back. 'You rang him up.'

Nelly rounded on her. 'Of course I rang him up. You were a fat lot of help. God knows where we'd be if I hadn't.'

'I never knew you were such a scaredy-cat.' She began to spin around with her arms stretched out to either side. 'Oooh, everything's going round!'

Patrick took her arm in a firm grip. She smiled up at him. 'Hello, Patrick. Have you come to take me home?'

'Yes.' Patrick led her to the car. 'Now get in.'

She climbed into the back. '*Take me home, take me home ... to the place I belong,*' she sang.

Patrick said to Nelly, 'At least you had the sense to phone home. What on earth were you thinking, letting her drink as much as that? What sort of a friend are you, anyway?'

'I'm sorry.' Nelly climbed into the front passenger seat. He was being unfair but she felt too relieved and unlike herself to argue about it. 'Thank you for coming.'

'*West Virginia, mountain mama,*' Sandy sang.

'I'm terribly disappointed, Nelly. I really did think we could trust you to behave a bit better than this. Who were those men, anyway?'

'Michael and Carl,' Sandy said from the back of the car. 'Carl and Mike. Mike and Carl.'

'I think I've got that, Sandy.'

Nelly fished in her bag for a tissue and blew her nose. 'We met them the other day. They seemed okay then. They're just a bit—'

'Old,' Patrick said. 'From the two-second glance I got of them. What on earth were a couple of men like that doing involving themselves with a couple of kids like you? Did they offer you drugs?'

Sandy giggled. '*Here we go, here we go, here we go.*'

'Be quiet, Sandy. This isn't funny.'

Nelly wiped her nose and tucked the tissue away. 'Nothing happened, honestly, Patrick, we just had a few drinks. I'm really sorry, we won't see them again. I didn't like them much anyway; it was a mistake. I was curious, that's all.'

'Curious?'

'One of them was that man sitting in the car outside our house.'

'What, that chap blocking our drive? I don't believe you.'

'It was him, honestly. He seemed all right when I got to know him. At least at first he did. We met them when we were with Mark, you know, Sandy's boyfriend.'

'I know Mark, he's supposed to be quite sensible. Where was he tonight?'

'We didn't ask him to come with us, we just said we'd meet them for a drink. We thought it would be a laugh.'

'Well, you've had your laugh. For heaven's sake don't be such an idiot again. Do you think it's all right to drop Sandy off in this state? What on earth are her parents going to think?'

Sandy said languidly from behind them, 'They won't think anything, they're out. Yes, please, home James and don't spare the horses.'

Nelly almost giggled, but after stealing a glance at Patrick's stern profile she didn't. She couldn't help being pleased that he seemed genuinely upset.

'I should have thought with your mother in the state she's in you'd have given some thought to the effect on her if anything were to have happened to you. They could be anybody, those people.'

Nelly's lips tightened. So it was Sonia he was bothered about, not her. Then she felt glad that he cared enough about Sonia to be concerned about how she would feel. 'I've said I'm sorry. I'm not going to grovel. It was a mistake, that's all.'

'It could have been a disaster. Honestly, Nelly, I can't believe you could have been so stupid. I thought you were quite a sensible person.'

Nelly suddenly shouted at him, 'For God's sake, it was only a drink in a pub. Lay off, will you?'

'Suppose I'd been out.'

'Charlotte would have come.'

'What good would she have been?'

'Quite a lot, actually.' Nelly felt better for having let out a bit of her frustration and her fear. 'You'd be surprised what she gets up to. Did you know she can even mend doors?'

CHARLOTTE CAME out of the kitchen wiping her hands on a towel. Curiosity had won over her longing for an early night; woken by the phone ringing and the resulting commotion downstairs, Patrick getting the car out and rushing off, she'd thrown on her dressing gown and come downstairs.

The front door opened and Patrick came in, shepherding Nelly in front of him.

Sonia hadn't moved. She was still sitting on the stairs in her kimono, her feet bare, her face pale and pinched-looking.

Patrick greeted her coolly. 'I thought you said you were going back to bed.'

Sonia looked at Nelly, then at Patrick, then back at Nelly again. 'I couldn't sleep; I was worried sick about Nelly. What happened?'

Patrick turned to Charlotte. 'Could we possibly have some cocoa or something equally boring and middle-aged? Join us, we'll all have some.'

Charlotte nodded. Good idea, a hot drink might calm them all down.

'I thought it might be one of those mysterious phone calls you keep getting,' Sonia went on, 'where they hang up when I answer.'

Charlotte looked at Patrick in surprise. He looked definitely discomfited.

Sonia turned to Nelly. 'So, what's all this about? What happened?'

'Oh, hell, enough with the inquisition. Look, nothing *happened*. Sandy and I agreed to meet up with these blokes we met in the pub the other night, that's all. Just for a chat, nothing sinister. It got a bit heavy so I phoned Patrick to come and get us. That's all.'

'What blokes? What do you mean it got heavy?'

'I dunno what blokes. Just blokes. They're just two guys we met. It was meant to be just a bit of fun and they got a bit pushy, that's all. It was no big deal. Now I'm going to help Charlotte make the cocoa, then I'm taking mine up to bed. There's no problem. Could we all just stop worrying about it?'

In the kitchen she said to Charlotte, 'Fuss, fuss, fuss. You'd think we'd slept with them or something.'

'Parents always worry.' Charlotte handed her her drink. 'That's what they're for.'

'Oooh, my Miss World Protest mug. Cheers! Night, Charlotte.' Nelly disappeared out into the hall, carrying her cocoa.

Charlotte loaded a tray and took the drinks out to the others. Nelly had disappeared.

Patrick took the tray from her. 'Thanks, Charlotte, you're a lifesaver. Nelly's gone up. "Thank you," would not have come amiss.' He put the tray on the chiffonier and handed a mug to Sonia and one to Charlotte. 'Sonia, listen to me. I don't want to worry you but I think we should all be aware. One of the blokes Nelly was consorting with was the man we found sitting outside the house the other day, the one blocking our drive, do you remember?'

Sonia sipped her cocoa, her forehead ruffled. 'Of course I remember.'

'I don't want to worry you but I think something funny's going on. I think that chap was deliberately targeting Nelly. I think he may have been watching the house for some time. Do you—'

'My *God!*' Sonia's arm jerked so that some of her cocoa splashed onto the stair carpet. 'It's him! He's here!' She put her other hand over her mouth. 'I think I'm going to be sick.'

'Who?' Patrick put his mug back on the tray and hunkered down in front of her. 'Who is here? Sonia, we really do have to talk.'

Charlotte, hurrying to fetch paper towels, a dishrag and a bowl, thought how unpleasant sheer terror was for the onlooker. It aroused in you all the wrong emotions: exasperation instead of pity, disgust instead of compassion.

She wiped up the spilt cocoa, wishing she didn't feel so cross with Sonia. She didn't have a clue how exhausting her hysteria was for everyone else.

'You don't understand,' Sonia whispered, her eyes on Charlotte's hands as she wiped and wrung out.

'Well, of course I don't if you won't explain.' Patrick put both his hands on her knees as though to calm her and said more gently, 'What's going on? Don't shut me out. You've always shut me out.'

Charlotte stood up and began to edge away.

Patrick looked up at her. 'No. Please stay, Charlotte.'

'Yes, stay, Charlotte, I need you here, perhaps you can make him understand.' Sonia stared at Patrick as though willing him to hear what she was saying. 'Don't you see, they're trying to get at Nelly now? I thought it was Alain they would come after, or me, but not Nelly.'

'Who are? What are you *talking* about?'

'Oh, Patrick.' Her expression changed; she looked at him piteously. 'It had nothing to do with Nelly, she wasn't even there. I couldn't bear anything to happen to her.' She began to cry quietly, covering her face with both hands. Tears trickled between her fingers.

Despite herself a sympathetic lump formed in Charlotte's throat.

Patrick was having no such trouble. 'Look, I know you're upset.' He removed his hands from her knees and stood up. He dug his hands deep in his pockets.

'His name's Juan.' Sonia fished at hip-level for a handkerchief and then remembered she had her kimono on.

Charlotte handed her a piece of paper towel.

She took it and wiped her eyes. 'He's Luis' nephew. He's just got out of prison. Fran Desmarchais wrote from St. Colombe to warn me. She said Juan had been going around the island boasting that he was coming over here to kill Alain and me, in revenge for Luis' death. They're not like you over here. Revenge is a sacred duty to those people, a kind of law.'

'You're kidding me.' Patrick stood with his hands in his pockets looking down at her. He looked at Charlotte and then back at Sonia. 'Is this for real?'

'Do you think I would make something like this up? Listen, Patrick. Fran's husband Pierre is Chief of Police since the new lot took over, so he has his ear to the ground. Juan is a real thug, he's killed people already, it isn't just words with him. He means it.'

Charlotte couldn't help herself. 'But why? Why on earth would anyone want to kill Nelly?'

'Sonia?' Patrick was frowning, looking as though he still didn't know whether to believe her or not.

'One of those men must be Juan.' Sonia leaned forward, begging him to believe her. 'It all makes sense, his finding out where we live, his making contact with Nelly. He's probably intending to get all three of us, one after the other. He's a bad man, Patrick, even Luis didn't approve of him, and if *he* thought he was beyond the pale—' She shook her head. 'At least Alain is safe, at least he was the last we heard. That's why I made him go away. But if they're after Nelly too, we've got to warn her. They won't just kill her; they'll do unspeakable things to her.' She looked up at Patrick, her face grim.

She looked more present, more focused than Charlotte had ever seen her. But Charlotte still didn't understand. 'But Sonia, *why*? Why you? What's it got to do with you? And why send Alain away and not Nelly?'

Sonia looked piteously up at Patrick. 'I never wanted to have to tell you. I never wanted you to know. I thought you wouldn't accept him if I told you, that you'd get the wrong idea about him. He only did it to protect me.' She began to cry again. 'It was Alain who killed Luis. It was Alain.'

Chapter 21

Feed him to the sharks

The forest was unnaturally still. The night was cloudy with hardly any moonlight. Couba led the way with Nelly riding behind her. Then came Alain, then Sonia, with Cufffée taking up the rear.

It was dark in the forest. Sonia was filled with the kind of fear that almost stops you breathing; you know that at any moment the thing you most dread is going to happen. You can't stop it. It's the waiting that's so terrible: you almost want it to happen now, to get it over with.

She had known for months that she had to get away from Luis. Each incident of abuse was worse than the time before, the pain inflicted greater, his frustration more evident. Sonia knew instinctively that if she stayed much longer, he would kill her. He had told her many times that he would not allow her take the children away from him, that if she attempted to leave with them, he would kill her.

She had planned their escape for weeks, telling no one except the only two servants she knew she could trust, Cufffée and Couba. Couba detested Luis, whom she blamed for the death of her husband Josephus three years before.

The *Sangs Sangs* had murdered him, so the rumour went, for some supposed disloyalty. Gentle Cuffée, who was incapable of hating anybody, had come with Sonia from Costa Rica when she had married Luis. He was her oldest friend, her only contact with her childhood. She loved him and she would trust him with her life.

Rigid with tension, she gripped her horse's reins. Her gratitude to her friends knew no bounds. If they got out of this she would send for them, she would do something for them. Their chances, knowing Luis, were slim; his spies were everywhere.

The wind rustled the dark canopy of the trees overhead. The clink of bridle and stirrup, the faint rattle of stones under hooves and an occasional snort from one of the horses were the only sounds breaking the deep silence of the forest. As though infected with their riders' trepidation, the horses moved slowly and steadily along the uneven paths.

They came to the place near the edge of the forest where it had been arranged that they would leave the horses. Cuffée and Couba would collect them on the way back. In Blue Bay a boat was waiting to take Sonia, with Alain and Nelly, to Cuba.

Couba and Nelly dismounted first and vanished into the night. When Sonia's feet touched the ground her legs were so weak they could barely support her weight. I can't stand this, I'd rather be dead, she thought. Please God, don't let anything happen to the children. She was praying to a God she had long ago disowned. They trudged on foot for another half-mile. Couba and Nelly were out of sight and Sonia felt an increased sense of urgency. The trees were thinning, the sky was beginning to lighten: it was almost dawn.

In an instant everything changed. A shot rang out and

Cuffée, now leading the way, crumpled and fell. Luis, a rifle in his hands, stepped out from the trees a few yards ahead of them and stood barring their way. From what Sonia could see through the half-light he seemed to be smiling, and from the way he was lurching about from foot to foot he was also extremely drunk.

She stood ice-still from the shock. Everything seemed to be happening in slow motion. She looked down at Cuffée and all her fear left her. She put out her hand to Alain, standing behind her, absolutely still but apparently unharmed, then moved swiftly to Cuffée's side and sank onto her knees beside him, disregarding the stones which bit into her knees through her thin trousers. Blood was welling through a rent in his shirt front.

'Oh Cuffée, what's he done to you? Oh, my friend ... don't be frightened. Don't go to sleep, keep awake, stay with me.' Her heart was pounding. She tried to control herself. She bent forward and lifted Cuffée's head and shuffled forward, scraping the skin on her knees, so that she could cradle his head in her lap. His eyelids were flickering.

Somewhere, up in the canopy of the trees, a bird called. She had to stop this bleeding. She began to unbutton her shirtsleeves, then bent her head. He was trying to say something. His voice was so soft it was like a breath on her cheek. She bent her head nearer.

'Tell Master 'lain to go. Go with the others. Go after them.'

Sonia, looking back at Alain, realised that he was still rigid with shock. 'Alain! He says *go*! Go on! Cuffée's right! Run!'

Alain's voice cracked. 'I can't leave you here.' His face shone moony white in the half-light.

'You have to. We'll be all right. Do as you're told. Go *on*!'

'Hey!' Luis called out as Alain started to back slowly towards the trees, his eyes still on his mother. 'Come back here!'

She looked up. The barrel of the rifle swivelled uncertainly towards the crashing in the undergrowth as Alain disappeared into the trees.

'No matter.' Luis lowered the rifle. 'He won't get far.' He started to mumble, crashing about on the dry leaves underfoot, his words disconnected, his voice occasionally rising to an indistinguishable shout.

Sonia began to tear off her shirt, shifting her arms from under Cufée's head, first the right, then the left, as she wriggled out of the long sleeves. 'Cufée, can you hear me? Are you in pain?'

She heard Luis talking as though to himself. 'The boy will be lost in no time. Doesn't know the forest. I'll find him later.'

Sonia tried to staunch the blood coming from Cuffee's chest with her shirt. There was so much of it. In a moment the shirt was soaked through. 'We have to get a doctor,' she whispered.

He was speaking again, his voice a mere thread. She bent her head lower.

'Is no good, Mis Sonia.'

'Don't give up on me, Cufée. Stay with me, please.' She looked up distractedly and registered with hardly any emotion that Luis had raised his gun again and was pointing it at her.

She must try to get him to talk. If she could distract him then maybe Alain and Nelly would get away.

'Going for a walk, were you, *ma biche*?' Luis spoke as

though nothing had happened. As though he hadn't just shot Cufféе. 'Where's my daughter?'

She looked up. He had lowered the rifle again and was peering around. He began to lurch about, trampling the ground like a bull, staggering as though on the point of falling. For all her distress it flashed through Sonia's head that if Luis really did not know where Nelly was, there was still a chance that Nelly and Alain might get away.

She bent her head again and whispered, 'Cufféе, don't die ... don't leave me ... hang on till I can get some help.'

But there was nobody to help. She couldn't leave him there alone with Luis. Her heart thumped with dread. Cufféе's eyelids were flickering and his breathing was shallow and difficult. 'Can you hear me? Are you in pain?'

There was so much blood. Her shirt was soaked through and still she couldn't stop the blood coming. It was hopeless. She hugged him to her breast, willing him to stay alive. She looked up. She tried to sound calm. 'Luis, I know this was an accident. You must get help. Cufféе is dying. You don't want him to die, you know you don't. Please, Luis, go and get help.'

He didn't seem to hear. He trampled about, muttering to himself.

Sonia rocked Cufféе against her breast as if he was a child needing comfort. She closed her eyes and fleetingly the image came into her head of the man she had fallen in love with, the strong, handsome man she had believed she could lean on. She saw him come into the room where her mother lay in her coffin on the high dais. She smelled the sweet, sickly scent of the lilies piled around the coffin. She remembered her father. Grief pierced her so that she gave a little moan of distress. She looked down at Cufféе and saw with a jolt that his eyes were open and unmoving. His chest was still. She felt the side of his neck and began to stroke his face, her breath heaving as she tried to stem the panic threatening to overwhelm her. Her tears fell onto his face and she wiped them away.

'My dear friend ... I'm sorry. I'm so sorry!' Slowly, stiffly, she moved her knees back from underneath Cuffée's body and very gently laid his head down on the ground. She said inside her head, Oh God, if you're there, please take care of him. A terrible sense of loneliness came over her.

'Done for, isn't he?' Luis shambled about among the dead leaves. 'He's the first. I'll find out who was in it with you, you know. They're not very brave, these people.'

'Leave them alone.' She ought to be reasoning with him, but all she felt was an immense weariness. She made an effort. 'They didn't know anything, the servants. Don't hurt them. Only Cuffée knew.' She wondered whether the others had reached the shore yet, whether they were safe. She had no idea how much time had elapsed since Alain had gone.

What was Luis doing here, anyway, in the forest in the middle of the night? Had somebody given them away? Her mind worked furiously. She could trust Couba, couldn't she? Couba had Nelly with her. A new terror flooded her body; Luis surely heard the pounding of her heart.

It was as though he could read her thoughts. 'What have you done with Nelly? Is she wandering about in the forest too? Don't worry, I'll find her.'

She looked up. The gun was at his shoulder again and he was pointing it at her chest. His voice when he spoke was calm, conversational. 'You can't leave, you know.'

He was going to kill her. She felt a strange calm. She wanted to pray but she couldn't find the words. Still, she thought with a detachment that astonished her, it was appropriate that she was kneeling. *'Into Thy hands O Lord I commend my spirit.'* But save Nelly. Save Nelly.

The moon came out from behind the clouds and radiated by its light she saw Alain standing behind Luis, Cuffée's machète raised high in his hands. He brought it down and sideways with a terrific swipe just as Luis' gun exploded. Sonia felt a tearing pain in her shoulder and fell sideways into blackness.

When she came to, Alain was kneeling over her. His voice was thick with tears. 'Mamée, please don't die! Don't die, not now.' He was pressing a cloth to her shoulder. He appeared to be naked. Then she saw that he had torn off his shirt to use as a bandage.

'Mamée.' He smiled with relief as her eyes opened. 'I've stopped the bleeding, it's only your shoulder, I think it's only a graze, I'm not sure if there's anything still in there. Don't look over there,' he said as she tried to sit up, her head swimming. 'It's awful, please don't look. I had to do it, Mamée, he was going to kill you.'

'Alain ...'

'Try to stand up. We must find the others. The *gorilles* may come after us. They may have heard the shooting. He may have told them – he—' He couldn't bring himself to say the word 'father.' Alain was thirteen years old.

They left Couba standing on the beach as the boat left the shore in Blue Bay and made for the gap in the reef. Couba stood as proud as the Statue of Liberty, her right arm raised in salute. She hadn't wept at the news of Cuffée's death.

'Couba, we had to leave him there. Will you see to it that he is buried? A good burial ...'

'Men come. We bury him. The other one we throw in the sea.' Her lips stretched. 'Shark can have him.'

Chapter 22

The plot's afoot

Patrick stepped into the hall carrying his outdoor shoes in his hand. Sonia was standing beside the chiffonier holding a pile of letters. She was wearing his old brown dressing gown and she looked as though she wasn't at all sure what she was doing there. She looked at him and her mouth tried to smile without quite succeeding. Still, it's a start, Patrick thought.

'You're up early.' He glanced nervously at the pile of mail. 'After last night I didn't think you'd be up for ages.'

He hoped Laura hadn't taken it into her head to write to him again. She had a dangerous tendency to want to put things on paper. He'd tried to discourage her but it was next to impossible to stop Laura from doing anything she wanted to do; he'd forgotten how stubborn she could be. And she was behaving rather oddly at the moment.

'Doing my job for me.' He indicated the letters. 'I usually do that. You know, pick 'em up, put 'em there.' He looked at her more closely. 'Are you all right?'

'Sorry.' Sonia looked down at the letters in her hand as if wondering how they had got there.

'What for?'

She looked at him as though she couldn't think what to say. 'Lots of things. I borrowed your dressing gown. I felt cold.'

'It is horribly chilly for June.'

They stood for a moment or two in silence.

'Did you have a good walk?' She sounded shy.

'Great, it's a wonderful day, in spite of the cold. You ought to—'

She nodded. 'I'll go for my run later. Well ...' She looked uncertain. 'I won't stay chatting. I know you don't like talking before starting work.'

Quite right, he didn't: he made a deprecating gesture but she had turned away so it was wasted, and then he thought, for God's sake, she's trying to be friendly, can't you put yourself out just this once and encourage her?

He said quickly, 'I'm glad you told us about Alain.'

She turned around, her face flushing. She looked at him, her eyes bright. 'It's a big relief, such a burden off my shoulders. I thought you'd be angry because I hadn't told you before.' She paused. 'You seemed angry, last night.'

He took his time before replying. He needed to be very careful what he said next. 'I rather felt you should have told me before.'

'Before I said I would marry you, you mean? Did you feel I had deceived you, agreeing to marry you when you didn't know my son was a murderer?'

Her voice had frozen over again. His heart sank. For a few minutes she had seemed different, gentler, more like the Sonia he used to know, the one he had married.

She was right, that was exactly how he had felt for a short time, until he'd got over the shock and been able to look at the thing more rationally. On reflection he could see exactly why she hadn't told him. All the same he found the deception hurtful. It seemed to be just one more way in which she was determined to shut him out, not to trust him.

'Look. To be honest, at first I did feel that; I felt you should have trusted me.'

'Would you still have wanted to marry me, if I had told you?'

'Of course.'

'No, I mean really.'

He looked at her, frowning, feeling that he had spoken too quickly and that he owed her at least the dignity of an honest answer. 'I would have tried to persuade you to go to the authorities. After all, from what you said, Alain was only trying to protect you.'

'And if I had refused to go?'

'I suppose I would have had to accept your decision.'

She looked at him for a long time. 'You really believe that, don't you, Patrick?'

'What do you mean? I wouldn't say it if I didn't believe it.'

'No, I don't suppose you would. Look, Patrick. Alain saved my life. Luis was drunk. He had a gun. He'd already shot Cuffée. He took a shot at me and Alain hit him, to stop him. Just to stop him.'

'Surely he wasn't strong enough to tackle Luis all by himself?'

Sonia hesitated. 'He had a machète. It had fallen when Cuffée fell and Alain picked it up. He never planned it, he loved his father, both the children did ... at least when he was sober.' Her hands clenched convulsively. 'Well ... I'd better go and get dressed, leave you to your work.'

He put out a hand to stop her. 'Wait a minute, Sonia. I want to talk about this.'

She said quickly, 'Will you be warm enough out in the shed?'

Patrick looked at her in astonishment. She never expressed this kind of concern for his comfort. She hated the shed and everything to do with it. And for God's sake, didn't she want to know what he was going to do about the gunman who was supposed to be after her and whom she'd said she was terrified of? What was the matter with her? He frowned and nodded. 'It'll warm up soon.'

'Good.'

Patrick felt a surge of intense irritation. He thought, this is just why I don't like talking to people before I start work: this sort of thing happens and then how the hell am I supposed to concentrate? Might as well put my brain in a liquidiser and have done with it.

They stood in a fraught silence. Patrick felt he was glaring at her but she seemed not to notice. After a minute or two she put the letters on the chiffonier without looking at them – only of course she might have sifted through them already – and went and stood underneath his mother's portrait, looking up at it. Patrick thought, I am not going to start getting paranoid about Laura and letters. I am not going to even think about the post. His mind during his walk had been wrestling with exactly how to finish the book, the last sentence, the last line. Nothing he had come up with so far seemed exactly right.

Sonia looked from the portrait back to Patrick. 'She doesn't look at all like you.'

He came and stood beside her, trying to calm down. He looked up at his mother's averted face; rather significant that, he thought, wondering if the painter had chosen that pose deliberately. When he was a small boy his mother had always seemed to have her attention turned elsewhere: she'd had a very low boredom threshold.

'Was she a good mother to you?'

She had never wanted to know anything about that either. He thought for a moment. 'She was very critical.' He couldn't understand why she wanted to know.

'Critical?'

'She tried to be pleased with me but nothing I achieved ever came up to her expectations. When I come to think of it, her life must have been one long series of disappointments.'

'But you were successful, she can't have been disappointed in you.'

'She thought journalism was a bit of a naff occupation.' He moved restlessly and put his hands in his pockets. 'She was a bit more enthusiastic about the writing I suppose, but I was never going to win any prizes.'

He looked at his wife's interested face. It was as if he had come to life in front of her eyes. As though all this time he'd been an extension of her without an independent history of his own. It had always been *her* history, *her* problems. He looked down at her, genuinely curious. 'Why are you asking all these questions?'

She flushed and seemed to avoid his eyes. 'I suppose ... I think it's time I got to know you.'

'Sonia, we've been married two years! We've known each other longer than that.'

'I know. It's my fault. I feel I don't know you at all, and you don't know me.' She glanced up at him and then away again.

Patrick frowned.

'Patrick, can't you see I'm trying? I want to get to know

you, I want to be like other people. Otherwise Luis will have won. I want to stop being such a – selfish – cow.'

Patrick thought, what is this, does she mean it, could it possibly be that getting that business of Alain off her chest was all she had to do to sort herself out? He thought indignantly, she can't just turn around and decide to be nice and expect everything to be all right again, just like that. What about me?

What about Laura?

Laura. Was this some kind of plot? Had she found out about Laura? Was this some kind of strategy for getting the better of him in a war of nerves, a sort of softening-up process before the *coup de grace*?

Sonia seemed to sense his sudden hostility. 'Well, I'd better go now, I'll see you later.'

The expression in her eyes was sad again which annoyed him because it made him feel it was his fault she was looking like that.

'Don't forget your flask. Oh, and I haven't looked at the letters, I know you like doing that after you've finished writing so I left them for you. You must have some fun in your hard-working life.' She moved away, smiling at him over her shoulder.

'Hey, Nell!' Sandy, dangling a violin by its neck, poked her head around the string-room door. Percolating through a dozen neighbouring doors the varied sounds of cellos, clarinets and flutes mingled and clashed in a muffled cacophony.

'Yes?'

'Don't be like that. Come in here a min.'

'What do you expect me to be like after Monday night?'

All the same Nelly hesitated and did not pass by. In fact, she had come down to the music block hoping to come across Sandy who, she was well aware, had a practise period between three and four. She had cleared her throat with verve while passing the string room and sure enough, dere she be, Nelly thought. 'It would serve you right if I never spoke to you again.'

'Oh, don't be a pain, Nell.'

Nelly allowed herself to be pulled as if reluctantly into a small room which had nothing in it but a piano, two music stands, a small table and three wooden chairs pushed back against the wall.

'I got bombed, yeah? It isn't a capital offence.'

'It is if you drop me in it like that. What price sisterly solidarity? You were all set to embark us both on a career of mind-boggling sleaze.'

Sandy laughed. 'It would never have got that far. You know it wouldn't.'

'I know nothing of the sort. You were all set to go back to their flat!'

'Not really.'

'Yes *really*.'

'I was, wasn't I?' Sandy looked smug. 'Put it down to the demon drink.'

'Do you often get as wasted as that?'

'No, of course not; don't get the opportunity. It was quite fun though, wasn't it?'

'Well, no actually.' Nelly wasn't going to divulge even to Sandy how bleak her mood had been that evening.

If anything, things between Patrick and her mother seemed to have got worse. She had come looking for Sandy hoping to confide her fears about Patrick and Laura, but now she wasn't so sure. Sandy might laugh at her and she couldn't face that, not feeling the way she did at the moment.

'I wanted to tell you; Michael phoned.' Sandy laid her violin down on the top of the piano. 'About that party, Friday night? He phoned with the address.'

'Didn't realise you'd given him your number. Did you say we'd go?'

'Of course not. I was totally cool about it, of course. Didn't give anything away, just said we'd think about it. He says Carl's going to ring you and fix up where to pick you up, so watch out.'

'That won't go down too well with the folks.' Nelly picked up some manuscript sheets off the table and examined them. 'I told them I'm not going to see him again.'

'Well, you're not, are you?'

'Sorry?'

'You're not going to see them again.'

'What about the party?'

'You're not thinking of *going?*'

'I thought that was what this conversation was about.'

'No, you bunny, I just said Michael rang. I didn't say we were going, of course we're not going.'

'Who says? I haven't made up my mind yet.' Nelly picked up a manuscript sheet. 'Did you write this?'

'But you can't go!'

'Why not?'

'Blimey, you've changed your tune, you were the one who didn't want to have anything to do with them! Nell, you can't go. They may be white slavers for all you know.'

'There aren't any such things, that was a myth cultivated by our grandmothers to keep our mothers on the straight and narrow.'

'I bet there are too. Gimme that. Of course I didn't write it, that's Dvorak.'

'You're the one who's changed your tune; you were the one who kept egging them on.'

'How often do I have to say it to get it into your fat head? I was ratted, pie-eyed, Not Myself.'

'You can say that again.'

'I just have. Not clearly enough, you don't seem to be getting the message.'

'Yes I do, I just don't agree with it. I've changed my mind, I like Carl, he's nice. He likes me. I want to see him again.'

'I won't give you the address.'

'Don't need the address; he's picking me up.'

Sandy looked at her coldly. 'Don't be a prat, Nell.'

Nelly said after a mutinous pause, 'Hey, I haven't had a chance to tell you what's been happening back at the ranch, the next episode in the Patrick and Sonia show.'

'What's happened? Tell, tell! Park yourself.' Sandy patted a chair and jumped up onto the table where she sat with her legs swinging. 'But don't think you'll get anywhere by changing the subject. You're still not going.'

Nelly stuck her tongue out but her heart wasn't in it. She threw herself onto one of the wooden chairs. She was dying to tell Sandy about the awful situation at home. She was quite certain she would burst if she didn't tell somebody.

'When we got in the other night, they had a fearful row. They *keep* rowing. Patrick might decide to leave. You couldn't blame him. He's got Laura, you see.' To Nelly's horror a lump collected in her throat. She swallowed hard and turned it into a cough.

'Oh ... my ... gosh. Laura? Geog Laura? Was that really her with Patrick in the park?'

'That's the one.' Nelly stood up and made a business of tucking her shirt into the top of her navy skirt, then pulling her sweater down. She sat down again.

'But you said they were just friends. Have you been holding out on me? It's lucky you haven't really got a thing for Patrick, my dear, you'd be a bit narked if you had.'

Sandy wasn't looking at her but Nelly knew this was a hint, designed to give her a lead-in. She hesitated and was lost.

'Oh Sandy.' Tears welled up in her eyes. 'I think he's having an affair. I mean actually having an *affair!* It's *awful!* And I do mind, I mind terribly! I mean not the way stupid old Tigs thinks; it's just I so want us to be a proper family, but if he's really keen on Laura he'll leave ... or chuck us out or something. It's his house. I can't cope with Sonia on my own. What am I going to *do*? Sonia makes no effort whatsoever to keep him happy, it's a disaster.'

'Wait a minute, wait a minute. Calm down. Let's go back to the beginning. Tell me about Laura. Where does she come into it?'

'I told you, he knew her ages ago, long before we came on the scene. He was doing that visiting artist thing at school, you know, the thing Mr Newcombe's doing now. Patrick was doing creative writing. She was teaching the seniors. He met her then. They got engaged, they were going to be married. She left when they broke up and went and taught somewhere else and then this year she came back.'

'No!'

''Fraid so. Patrick told Sonia everything when he was trying to get her to marry him. Wiping the slate clean and all that stuff. I suppose she told him all about my father too.'

'Okay, Patrick was engaged to Laura; so why did they break up?'

'She broke it off.'

'*She* broke it off. Hmm, that's bad.'

'She broke if off and he was devastated.'

'Ooh, don't like that. Why did she break it off?'

'Dunno. Maybe because of this other guy. She took up with this other man and they lived together for a bit but he had a drink problem so she chucked him. So she decided she wanted Patrick back but by then he'd met Sonia and was mad about *her* so he wouldn't. He and Sonia got married and Laura wrote to them and congratulated them and seemed okay about it—'

'Wish I'd got a fag. Go on, I'm listening.'

'Only she's after Patrick again, I'm sure she is. And I'm so worried he may be wishing he'd gone back to her after all.'

'There could be some perfectly innocent explanation for his seeing her, couldn't there?'

'Like what? You saw them, Sandy.'

'Maybe she's always like that with guys. Some girls are.'

'But there's the phone calls. Somebody's been ringing up for weeks who hangs up if it isn't him who answers.'

'Hmn, that could be bad. People who phone people at home really want to be found out. It's kind of a threat. Could be she means business.'

'Do you really think so?'

'If you believe all those old black and whites. They're full of women ringing their married lovers, secretly longing for the wife to pick up the phone so they can divulge all.'

'But if Sonia picks up, she rings off.'

'Perhaps she isn't ready to divulge yet. Mark my words, it's only a question of time.'

'Oh Lordy, things are bad enough as they are.' Nelly hugged herself defensively. 'Sandy, I wanted to ask you something. Patrick says he's meeting Tony tomorrow evening, you know, his agent, but I don't think he is, I think he's meeting Laura.'

'What makes you think that?'

'He phoned her. She's changed her number and he was testing it. I picked up the extension upstairs. I put it down straight away of course.'

'Bet you didn't.'

'Yes I did.' But Nelly knew Sandy knew she was lying. She'd listened to every word of that conversation. 'Anyway, he's going over to her place tomorrow night. He was phoning to arrange a time.' She leaned forward and touched Sandy's arm. 'I've decided to follow them.'

'You what? *Follow* them? How? What are you planning to do, hop in a cab like Hercules Poirot and say "Follow zat car!"?'

'No, of course not, dumbo. I know where she lives. I've got her address.'

'Really? How did you get that?"

'I copied it off that card I found in his pocket, if you must know. It was one of those cards with the person's name and address across the top.'

'My mum has those.'

'So the thing is, I'm going there and I want you to come with me.'

'What? When? Tomorrow night? What about my dinner?'

'Blow your dinner. What about mine? I bet your mum's cooking isn't a patch on Charlotte's. She's just amazing.'

'Well, well, how times have changed. It's no time at all since you were cursing and groaning because this fat person was coming to live in your house.'

'I know. I feel awful whenever I think about it.'

'Well, blow me down.'

'She's awfully nice actually.'

'Oh, is she?'

'Yes, she is, actually.'

'Good, good. Well, for once you're going to have to do without little Miss Perfect's rice pud.'

'I must get her to do something boring tomorrow if I've got to miss it. I suppose that means it will be just her and Sonia. Poor Charlotte, it's hardly worth her bothering for Sonia, she hardly touches a mouthful. After all Charlotte's hard work too. Guess what? The other night—'

'*Nell!*'

'Hullo?'

'Will you please stop going on about food? The girl's bewitched! I don't want to hear another word about Goody Two Shoes' perfect pizzas, yeah?'

'Pizzas my foot. Duck *a la crème Florentine* more like.'

'There you go again.'

'Sorry. You can come to dinner if you like.'

'Really?'

'Absolutely. Charlotte welcomes all comers.'

'That's if Patrick will let me in the front door. So, when's rendezvous time? And where?'

'I'll meet you at the end of our road. No, at the bus stop. Six o'clock. Patrick's leaving at seven so that should give us plenty of time. It isn't far: East Sheen. I'll tell you the plan on the bus. Better go now, I can hear Randy Mac checking up on the folks next door: it'll be you next. Cheers. See you later. And Sandy.'

'Yes, oh foolish one?'

'Thanks.'

'*De nada.*' Sandy jumped down from the table and tucked her violin under her chin. 'Twiddle twiddle on the fiddle went Sir Lancelot.'

Chapter 23

The heart of Frieda Kahlo

'Have you talked to Sonia today?' Patrick came into the kitchen and threw himself into a chair.

It was five o'clock in the afternoon of the next day. Patrick looked shattered, pale and unkempt.

'Bad work day.' He shook his head. 'Thank God I've just about finished; I'd be going crazy otherwise. Where is she?'

'Out for her run. I tried to put her off going out until we knew what the police had to say, but she wouldn't be told. Did you get any sleep last night?' Charlotte put down her rolling pin. 'I shouldn't think you did, you look awful.'

'You don't look too hot yourself.'

'Thanks!' She screwed up her nose at him.

He gave a huge yawn without covering his mouth. 'Sorry.'

The phone rang. Patrick hauled himself out of his chair and went to answer it. Charlotte couldn't help wondering if this was one of those phone calls Sonia had been on about. Yawning, she went on rolling the pastry. She hadn't slept well either.

He came back. 'That was the police inspector I spoke to last night.' He sat down, frowning. 'You know I told him about the letter Sonia had from that Desmarchais person—'

'That woman in St. Colombe?'

He nodded. 'Her. Well, he's in contact with Interpol and they're going to find out what's going on. He'd heard about Luis' murder, which surprised me. He's taking it seriously but he's really more focused on what's happening this end.' He thought for a moment. 'He's interested in those friends of Nelly's. He says they're no more from St. Colombe than you or I are, and the police are watching them anyway. Have been for weeks, he says. I tried to find out why, but nothing doing. He likes wrapping everything up in a web of mystery, does our Inspector Nash.' He sat down again, reaching for his cigarettes. 'He says it's really important we don't do anything to alarm them. The best thing we can do, he says, is absolutely nothing. In other words, don't get in the way.'

'Don't you think you ought to say something to Nelly?'

'I most certainly do.' Patrick shook a cigarette out onto the table. 'It's all right, I'm not going to smoke this in here.' He sighed. 'I wish Sonia wasn't out there. I wonder if I ought to go and look for her.'

'So you think there still might be a problem?'

He took off his spectacles and rubbed the bridge of his nose. 'Well ... whatever the police here say, I can't see what reason that friend of Sonia's would have for making it up. I don't think Sonia should be going out on her own until this is sorted out. Still ... this is England, for God's sake.' He yawned again. 'Hell, I'm so tired.' He put his spectacles down, picked up the cigarette and fitted it back into the pack again. 'All the same I do wish she'd let me tell them about Alain. Get the whole thing out into the open. I can't believe she's been sitting on that all this time and never said anything. It's admirable really.'

Charlotte thought it showed a distinct lack of trust. 'She ought to have told you about it before.' She reached for her flan dish. 'No wonder she's been in such a state.' She buttered the dish energetically. 'I wouldn't like to feel someone was coming after *me* with a gun in his hand.'

Looking utterly dejected, Patrick put his spectacles on again.

Charlotte felt sorry for him. 'It isn't like you to be so down.'

'I know.' He sighed. 'I can't even get excited about Radio Four. Though somebody did get me going just now when they said the "gist" instead of the "crux" of the matter.' He smiled ruefully.

'Oh well. That's a start.'

'What are you making?'

'The *pâte brisée* for the upside-down pear tart.'

'Is that really what you're making?'

'What? Mind you don't get flour all over you.'

'An upside-down pear tart?'

'Yes.' She looked across at him enquiringly.

'How sweet. It sounds completely irresistible.' He was grinning at her now.

Charlotte looked at him, nonplussed. She couldn't understand why he quite often seemed to find her so amusing.

'You always manage to cheer me up.'

'Would you like a cup of tea?'

'I rather fancy a cup of coffee, actually. I'm afraid I'm disturbing you.' He looked at her hopefully over the top of his spectacles.

'Not if you don't mind my carrying on with this while

you talk; this is at a slightly delicate stage. You could make the coffee if you like.' That would occupy him for a couple of seconds.

She went on rolling the pastry while he spooned coffee grounds into the cafetière and switched the kettle on.

'I'm haunted by the feeling that she must have thought I wouldn't take her seriously.' He leaned his back against the sink and folded his arms. 'If she'd told me about that letter, I mean. I do take her seriously. I know she gets irritated when I try to jolly her up; it's just she's had such a lot of doom and gloom, enough for a lifetime. I can't see the point in dwelling on these things.' The kettle boiled. He unfolded his arms and filled the cafetière.

He went over to the fridge. 'You have yours black, don't you?' He took out a half-full bottle of milk.

'Maybe she needs to talk about her past.'

'She saw a counsellor when she was in the hospital.'

'But to you. Maybe she needs to talk to you.'

'Maybe. I'm not awfully good at that sort of thing. Anyway up until this morning, I would have said we were hardly speaking to each other at all. Now, who knows?'

He filled the mugs, poured milk into his and plonked Charlotte's down right in the middle of her pastry muddle. He sat down. Charlotte raised her eyebrows and put down her pastry knife. Oh well, it was only a quarter to five; there was plenty of time even though the pastry had to be made at least two hours ahead. Patrick looked as though he wanted to talk.

She pulled out a chair and sat down. Patrick picked up an off-cut of pastry and made it into a ball then rolled it about in the flour. Charlotte wondered for a mad moment if he might be about to confide in her about his phantom lover, if she existed outside Nelly's fevered imagination, and if he were to do so, how she would feel.

She looked encouragingly at him. 'Sonia's awfully wrought up, isn't she? Nelly seems quite worried about her.'

'Well, that's a first.' Patrick picked up the pastry knife and cut his pastry ball in half. 'Nelly's usually far too busy thinking up ways of cutting Sonia down to size. What she seems to think is her size. She's wrong, of course.' He sighed, putting the knife down. 'But Sonia's not in a good way. I really do hope she isn't cracking up again.'

'I think that's her now.'

Sonia came into the kitchen in her tracksuit. She was wearing a pair of running shoes. Charlotte, extremely pleased about the shoes, sipped her coffee and decided that this wasn't really the time to comment. Sonia went over to the sink and ran herself a glass of water.

'Where's Nelly?' She looked at her watch. 'Five to five. Shouldn't she be home from school by now?' She bent down and undid the laces on her running shoes. 'Did they ring, Patrick?'

'They did. They just repeated what they said last night, that those men have got nothing to do with St. Colombe or Luis. They want us to behave normally, not to spook them.'

'Not to – you mean they're still out there?' Sonia looked at him aghast.

'Yes, but did you hear what I said? They are not from St. Colombe. Sonia, whatever your friend told you, I'm sure the police know what they're doing.'

'That's easy for you to say. For God's sake, even if one of those men isn't Juan, that doesn't mean he isn't out there somewhere. Anyway, the police could be wrong.'

'I was going to say,' — Patrick closed his eyes and opened them again — 'that all the same, in view of what your friend told you, it might be as well for all of us to stick around the house for a while until all this is cleared up.'

'Why can't they just go and pick him up? He's threatened to kill me, for God's sake. What sort of justice is that?'

Patrick glanced at Charlotte. He was clearly making a real effort to be patient. 'But he hasn't shown himself, has he? If he *is* here they have no idea where he is. The inspector is talking to Interpol. Going to have a talk with your friend.'

'Françoise.'

Patrick nodded. 'Her. Yes. Get some facts instead of all this rumour and speculation. He *is* concerned, it's just that something else seems to be going on which is preoccupying them a bit.'

'Something *else*?' Sonia shook her head. 'They don't know these people. They may think they do but they have no idea what they're like. You and your police. There's no old-school tie and playing the game among those South American drug dealers. These men are animals. *Ils sont les salopards.*' She put her glass in the sink and made a gesture of contempt. '*Les salopards.*'

She pulled off her shoes one at a time and went out into the lobby. They heard the shoes thud to the ground. She came back, her feet bare.

'I'm going upstairs.' She went out into the hall. The phone started to ring. They heard Sonia speak and a moment later a loud shriek which sent Patrick flying out into the hall.

Charlotte held her breath. If only she could hear what was going on. Was it news about Alain? She couldn't tell if that had been a scream of horror or joy. Of course, it could be about something quite different. She heard the ting of the receiver going down and steeled herself for bad news.

Patrick came in. The relief on his face told her what she wanted to know. 'Alain?'

Patrick nodded, beaming. 'There's one happy bunny out there. She's gone upstairs to have a shower.' He sat down. 'That was Mr Rennie from the Embassy. Alain's found, he's fine.' He leaned back and picked up his mug.

'That'll be cold. I'll make you another.' Charlotte started to get up.

Patrick shook his head. 'This is okay. He recovered from the dysentery and went off again and was out of contact for a while. He says he sent another telegram home but apparently it never went, some local post office problem.' He shook his head. 'I've never seen her so happy.' He looked at Charlotte. 'I do hope this will help. She has been out of her mind with worry about him.'

'I'm terribly glad. As you say, it will be one thing off her mind.' Charlotte frowned. 'What was that Sonia said – about drug dealers? Who said anything about drugs?'

'Oh, Christ, I don't know.' Patrick put his hand over his eyes. 'I seem to have lost the plot somewhere.'

'Was her husband into drugs? Well, if she's right, I rather agree with her, they ought to be making more of an effort to find that Juan guy. Sonia isn't safe while he's around.'

'Oh, hell.' Patrick sat with his hand still shading his eyes.

Charlotte longed to go around to the other side of the table, put her arms around him and cuddle him to her breast. That was what he needed, a bit of comfort. Sonia was too self-obsessed. And too thin. 'Drink your coffee,' she said gently, then thinking it might help to change the subject, 'What does Sonia do up there all day, anyway?

There's a lot of interest and speculation in the servants' quarters. Mrs P. thinks she's "making bomb."'

He smiled at this. He took his hand away from his eyes and stirred his coffee. 'Goodness knows,' he said a little shakily. 'Making plasticine dolls and sticking pins into them, I expect.'

Charlotte thought it was as if today the real Patrick was showing through and she was seeing him for the first time as he really was, with the mask off.

As though reading her mind he burst out suddenly, 'You know, I really do love her.'

She looked at him in astonishment and saw that his eyes had filled with tears. He made a business of draining his mug, then pushed his chair back, stood up and took his mug to the sink.

He stood with his back to her. 'Sorry, Charlotte, how rude of me. You haven't finished.'

'That's all right, I'll drink mine while I carry on here.' She didn't want him to go, not while he was still upset. If only he would open up to her.

He came back to the table, drying his hands on the tea towel. 'At least the book's nearly done. I can't help wishing all this could have waited until I'd actually handed it over.' He looked shame-faced and said half-humorously, 'My God, what kind of a monster does that make me?'

Charlotte decided he'd chastised himself quite enough for one day. 'I loved *False Relations*.'

'That's kind of you. As Tony so frequently reminds me, crime sells. Ah well, no good wishing I was writing the grand literary novel instead of my sordid thrillers. I shall just quote Brecht to myself and soldier on.'

'Brecht?'

'"Grub first. Art later,"' Patrick quoted with a smile,

throwing down the tea towel. It landed on the *pâte brisée*. Charlotte restrained herself from springing to remove it instantly. It wouldn't do to look as if she were accusing him of lacking a proper understanding of hygiene.

Nelly came in, looking disgruntled. 'What's Sonia doing with that roll of stuff? She's got a huge roll of canvas she's lugging upstairs.' She dropped her school bag on the floor.

'Did you ask her?' Patrick said with interest. 'Does she need help?'

'She's done it now. She says she's making a tent. Why did I have to be born with a crazy mother? Why can't she do what other mothers do? Why does she need a tent for God's sake?'

Patrick picked up his cigarettes and stood up. 'Can't answer that. Perhaps she's decided to go and hide out in the park.'

Charlotte giggled. 'Goodness, do you think so?'

Nelly threw herself into a chair. 'Hide out from what?'

'Only kidding.' Patrick grinned at Charlotte. He went out into the hall.

He really did seem to have cheered up, she noted, pleased.

Nelly yawned, stretching her arms up in the air. 'Jeez, what a day.'

'Bad, was it?' Charlotte went into the larder and came out with a bulging brown paper bag.

'Probably because it was such an awful night. What's in there?'

'Pears. Pear tart for pud tonight.'

'Yummy! Mum was making such a row I couldn't get to sleep for ages. Is she okay? What on earth was all that about?'

Charlotte emptied the pears into the sink. 'It's okay

now. Try not to worry, Nelly. She did get a bit hysterical but as my mother used to say, better out than in.'

'I wish I could meet your mother. I wish things could be normal around here. I wish she could be happy. I feel so guilty that she's so miserable all the time.'

'She won't go on being miserable.' Charlotte hunted round for the peeler. 'And you could help, Nelly, you could be a bit nicer to her.' She glanced sideways at Nelly, who looked encouragingly crestfallen.

'I know. I am trying, honest. It's just I get so irritated. And she shuts me out, she always has. Actually, the only person she lets get near her is Alain.'

Hmmm ... Charlotte peeled rapidly. Why hadn't they sorted all this stuff out when Sonia was in the hospital? The counselling didn't seem to have helped at all. She remembered something. 'Nelly.'

'Yup?' Nelly came and stood beside her, yawning hugely. 'Can I help?' She turned and leaned against the sink.

'Thanks, you might help me lay later on. I was going to say something, now what was it?' She hadn't really forgotten but she suddenly felt rather shy. 'I know. Those chaps.'

'Oh per-lease.' Nelly moved away. 'Not more.'

'It's just, you weren't thinking of seeing them again, were you? You know, your parents really don't think it would be such a good idea.'

'Look.' Nelly came back and stood beside her. 'I probably won't be seeing them again, okay? It's not my scene, all that.'

All what? Charlotte thought.

'They're a bit weird. Not my type really.'

'That's good.' Charlotte quartered the peeled pears and

put them in a colander. 'Right, that's done.' She wiped her hands on her apron.

'What do we do now?'

'Beat up some butter and sugar and poach the pears.' She looked at Nelly who was gazing at the pears with what appeared to be genuine interest. 'If you like I'll show you how to cook. Would you like me to?'

'Is it difficult?' Nelly looked pleased.

'No, of course not, you just have to like food.'

'Would I get—' She stopped. She'd obviously been going to say, would I get fat? Charlotte took the pears over to the Aga, trying not to feel hurt.

'You'll never get fat. It's in the genes.'

'Actually, I'd hate you to get thin. You look nice like that.'

To her horror Charlotte felt tears of gratitude fill her eyes. 'Wow, thanks.'

Nelly came over and put her arm around her. Oh help, she mustn't cry.

Nelly gave her a hug. 'You're a super cook, too, I'm the envy of all my friends. I'd like to learn: give me a lesson sometime. Cooking is ace. If I'd had any sense, I'd have done Dom. Sci. at school. Right.' She let go of Charlotte and picked her bag up off the floor. 'Must be off. Homework calls.'

When she'd gone Charlotte wept unrestrainedly for a moment or two, wiped her eyes with her apron and started melting the butter for the pears. Oh dear; she mustn't let all this upset get to her; they needed her to be calm.

The phone rang in the hall. Patrick came out of his study and answered it. After a brief conversation he came into the kitchen. 'Charlotte, I'll be out to dinner tonight. Thought I'd better keep you informed.'

Charlotte looked up and nodded. 'Okay. Thanks for letting me know.'

He stood dangling his spectacles by one leg. 'Meeting Tony again. Things to discuss about the last book – sales and that sort of thing.'

'Going somewhere nice?' Charlotte said after a moment or two, as he still didn't seem to be leaving.

'Oh, just to the pub I expect, nothing exciting. Won't be half such a good meal as the others will be getting here.' He ran his hand through his hair. 'That smells good.' After a moment or two, he left.

Charlotte frowned. He'd looked like a small boy waiting to be told off by his headmaster. He actually shuffled his feet. What on earth was that about? Perhaps he thought she minded if he didn't turn up for a meal? She stood by the Aga stirring the pears while they gradually turned a rich golden brown. But she'd never objected, never, why should she? It was his house. It was his life. She'd better say something.

In the hall the telephone rang again. Patrick answered it almost immediately. He must have been walking past it when it rang.

'You're going out again.' Sonia bent her head back and stared through the apple boughs at the thinning blue sky.

'I'm meeting Tony.' He clenched his teeth together and turned away. If she'd guessed he was going to see Laura, she would say something now.

'You said.'

He turned back. 'He wants to talk about the book.'

'Of course. He is your agent.'

Patrick felt foolish. Sonia put her hand on the gnarled

old trunk of the apple tree, feeling the rough bark. He noticed how small and smooth her hands were and the sensuous way her fingers enjoyed and lingered in the rough, textured crevices as though she loved them.

'This tree must be very old. Did your mother plant these trees?'

'I think they were here when she bought the house.'

'They're so much nicer than apple trees are now. There aren't many apple orchards left in England, did you know that? Proper orchards, I mean, with trees like these. Mr Dennison told me that. He said that nowadays they're more like apple factories, they grow them very low and small so they can reach the apples. Don't you think that's terrible?'

'I suppose it is. I didn't know you knew Mr Dennison?'

'I used to go and see him sometimes. You know he died. He showed me photographs of old orchards somewhere in this country, the county of Kent, I think he said, huge trees with their branches bowed down with the weight of the fruit and sheep grazing in the long grass underneath. The trees were so beautiful. I'd love to see an orchard like that.'

'I expect we could find one.'

'Do you think so?' She ignored his coldness and looked at him, her face alive with what appeared to be genuine interest.

Patrick looked back at her suspiciously. She had never shown the slightest interest in apple trees before. Or indeed in nature in any of its guises. He had always viewed Sonia as essentially urban in her proclivities.

What was she playing at?

It was guilt. He was getting paranoid. Why on earth shouldn't she develop an interest in apple trees if she wanted to? She wasn't going to say anything about Laura. She didn't know anything. Anyway even if she thought she did she could only be guessing, she couldn't possibly have any proof unless she'd hired a private dick or something; but she wouldn't do that, she wouldn't know how to, anyway she had too much pride to do something like that.

It was him, he was imagining the whole thing, it was guilt because he felt so terrible about Laura. Christ, what was he going to do?

They walked back towards the house.

'You know, Luis had several Frieda Kahlo paintings. Do you know Frieda Kahlo? She was married to Diego Riviera, the painter ... South American,' Sonia said, since he looked entirely blank. 'She was injured in a car accident and she suffered terrible pain all her life, physical and mental too because he was unfaithful of course. Some of her paintings are about that, they are full of her suffering. In one of the ones Luis had, her body is being pierced all over with arrows.'

'How horrible.'

'Luis liked the paintings because he liked to see women suffer. He didn't get the point of them at all. He got it all wrong. He liked them because he hated women.'

'Sonia,' Patrick said but she was already walking ahead of him into the house.

Chapter 24

Stake out

Nelly and Sandy, dressed in black from head to foot – although Nelly, convinced that Patrick would instantly recognise it, had abandoned her Stetson – stood trying to look like two friends innocently chatting outside the front gate of a small, semi-detached Victorian villa in a road of identical properties in East Sheen. It was a quarter past seven in the evening. One of the gateposts between which they were lounging had a wooden post fixed to it with a large For Sale notice attached.

Sandy put her hand on the post. 'Are you sure this house is empty? We're going to feel a couple of right idiots if someone comes out and asks us what we're doing here.'

'Especially if Patrick turns up just then. My goodness, he'll kill us if he sees us. For Pete's sake, keep your back to the road.'

'Which one is it?'

'That one. Thirty-six. Don't stare at it, you idiot, she's probably looking out of the window.'

'I saw the curtain twitch.'

'No you didn't. Behave yourself, Sandy, I'm in a bad enough state already.'

'This was your idea, cherub.'

'Well, how else am I going to find out? I've got to know.'

'I wish he'd get a move on. He's late, dinner will be ruined. After all the trouble I've been to, too. Men are all the same.'

'Oh, do shut up, Sandy. Wait a minute, a car's coming. Blast, there's a parking space right outside this house. Suppose he decides to park here? What are we going to do?'

'Run for it?'

Nelly groaned. 'I bet he pulls in here.'

'You're spared, it isn't his car.'

'*Ciel*!'

'Well, make up your mind. Get a grip, Nell, for heaven's sake, if you go on like this you'll give birth. Calm down.'

'Sandy, this next car is him. It's the right colour and everything. Look at the *house*, Sandy. Don't look at the car, you wally, look at the house! It *is* him. I knew it!'

'It could still be— Wait a minute. Shut up. He's getting out.'

'He's got flowers, the absolute—'

'The bastard.'

'How *dare* he bring her flowers!'

'He's got to, she's giving him dinner, you have to take something. Flowers are better than wine. If he'd got a bottle of wine, it would imply he's looking forward to them getting drunk together. Flowers are good.'

'Oh, they're good, are they? Oh, I *really* don't want to be here!'

'Better than wine anyway. What's the matter, Nell? You've gone all red. It's okay, he's gone in.'

'Did you see her?'

'Yup. She greeted him at the door with nothing on but a fetching little frilly white apron and a frilly cap. *Oh là là!* Absolutely starkers otherwise.'

'Sandy!'

'We-ell. This is a bit hysterical, isn't it? So he's having dinner with her, so what?'

'So he shouldn't be, he's married to my mother! Mind you, Sonia goes on as if she couldn't care less. If I really thought she cared about him, at least I'd feel she deserved him.'

'How do you know she doesn't?'

'You mean she *does* care about him?'

'Well, it's possible. People have a funny way of showing it sometimes. And she has had problems, you said, like depression and things.'

'I know. You're right, of course you're right. Oh jeez!' Nelly sighed. 'What's happening now?'

'Nothing. All the curtains are drawn. Is it a flat or the whole house?'

'Not sure. He's still in there, isn't he?'

'Of course he's still in there, he's hardly had time to take his coat off yet. They're in the kitchen, putting the flowers in a vase and getting the wine out of the fridge. I can see it as clear as anything – she's in her fetching little black number—'

'Was it fetching?'

'She looked gorgeous from what I could see which was a two-second flash. Not a patch on your mum of course—'

'What do we do now? Wait till he comes out?'

'Not me.'

'What?'

'Can't stay later than half-eight. Didn't I tell you? I'm curfewed. Got to be in by nine-thirty at the latest.'

'Why? No, you didn't. Oh, Sandy. Was it because of the other evening?'

'You've got it.'

'But when Patrick asked, you said your parents were out!'

'I made that up.'

'But why?'

'Dunno. It seemed simpler at the time. Patrick was fussing about them – I do remember that much – and I wanted a lift home.'

'You devious so-and-so.'

'So here I am, forbidden to stay out later than nine-thirty. How long do you reckon to get home from here?'

'Better allow three-quarters of an hour. Do you mean to say you're leaving me to go through with this on my own?'

''Fraid so. That's life.'

'Hell.'

'You could always ring Bubbles. Perhaps she'll come and sit in the bushes with you on a freezing evening waiting for your fickle stepfather to come out of his mistress' home so you can murder him.'

'You don't mean that, Sandy.'

'What, that you're going to murder him?'

'No, that she's his mistress, idiot.'

'What's the difference? Mistress, lover, who cares?'

'Mistresses are more sort of settled. Paid for, aren't they?'

'That's a tart.'

'What's the difference?'

'You can have a relationship with a mistress. A mistress is allowed to have a personality, a tart isn't.'

'Some tarts do. High-class sort of tarts.'

'A tart is a tart is a tart.'

'Gemma Longfellow is a tart now, so somebody told me.'

'What, school Legs Longfellow? Who left last year?'

'Yup. She's got a suite at the Ritz or somewhere and she lets Sheiks and people come up there and – you know.'

'No! Really?' Sandy doubled up. 'Dirty old Legs!' She chortled. 'Well, good for her!'

'You don't mean that.'

'Yeah, I do. It's okay to be a tart as long as you know what you're doing. You've got to understand it's going to turn you off sex forever of course—'

'Why? I should have thought it would make you better at it. All that practise.'

'My poor innocent. It just does. Most of them are lezzies or else they can't do it without being paid for it.'

'How gross!'

'It's a risk. You might never meet anyone rich enough to keep on paying for it night after night.'

'Look, belt up, we're not here to have a discussion about tarts.'

'Well, what are we here for?'

'Evidence.'

'You've got it. He's in there living it up with lover-girl.'

'Perhaps he isn't intending to stay long. Perhaps it's a dinner party and other people are going to start arriving.'

'It's twenty past eight and I don't see anybody, do you?'

'Oh Sandy, what am I going to *do?*'

'You can't do anything. Grin and bear it.' Sandy bared her teeth, setting an example.

Suddenly Nelly realized she was at the end of her tether. 'Look, I guess there really isn't a lot of point in both of us sticking around. You get off home. Don't want you getting into any more trouble.'

'Will you be okay?'

'Gotta be, haven't I?'

'Give us a bell when you get home, yeah?'

'If it isn't too late. Cheers, Sandy.'

Left on her own, Nelly huddled against the stone gatepost and mourned. He was in there, less than fifty yards away. Their Patrick is in there with that stranger and what was happening was anybody's guess. He was probably kissing her right now. Perhaps they were even in bed.

Passers-by looked at her curiously. If anyone came too close she pretended to be studying a road map. By nine o'clock the street was deserted. Commuters had returned to their homes and anybody who was going out for the evening had gone.

A young lad whizzed by on roller skates, whistling. He did a whirl around the next lamp-post and sped on, nonchalant, brimming with self-confidence. Nelly stuck out her tongue at his back. It was still a man's world. Girls didn't look like that on roller skates. They looked as if they were expecting to fall down any minute.

By ten o'clock she'd almost made up her mind to go and ring the doorbell.

At ten-thirty a panda car appeared, cruising along the street. Nelly turned her back, dug into her shoulder bag for a scrap of paper and a pencil and tried to look as if she was copying details off the estate agent's board.

The car drew up alongside and before Nelly could pull herself together and construct a defence a voice behind her said, 'Excuse me, miss.'

She turned around. A large policeman and a small blonde policewoman were climbing out of the car. They approached her, adjusting their caps.

'Hello!' Nelly said brightly, trying to look as unthreatening as possible.

The policeman looked at his colleague and back at Nelly. 'Good evening, miss. Would you mind telling us what you're doing here?

Nelly's mind went blank. 'Well ... not a lot.'

'Some of the residents are a bit concerned. We've had several calls.'

'Why, do they think I'm a burglar?' Nelly laughed. 'I'm not, honestly. I'm just sort of – hanging out.'

'Is this your house, miss?' the policewoman asked.

'No way, I live in Roehampton.'

'Would you mind telling us what you are actually doing here?'

'Um – I'm – doing a survey for school. For psychology. You look at the way people pass each other in the street – you know, whether they go to the left or the right, if they're male or female, that sort of thing.'

The policeman looked down the deserted street. 'You'd do better on the high street, Saturday morning.'

The policewoman nodded. 'Or on a lunch hour.'

Nelly felt a blush coming. Jeez, this was embarrassing. 'It has gone a bit quiet. Perhaps I'll get off home now. I was getting a bit tired of it anyway.'

The policewoman nodded approval. 'Good idea, miss.'

'I'll go then.'

They exchanged glances and began walking back to the panda car.

Nelly felt like calling them back. She didn't want to leave Patrick alone in that house with Laura. What would they say if she asked them to go and bang on the door of number thirty-six and arrest Patrick for disloyalty?

The policewoman turned her head, her hand on the

handle of the car door. 'Just for interest, miss, and off the record, could you tell us what you're *really* doing here?'

'You wouldn't believe me.' She took a breath and said desperately, 'I've been sleuthing, actually. I wanted to see if I could follow someone without him seeing me. It's much more difficult than you'd think.' Hell, she sounded about six years old.

'You want to be careful, you know, miss. Where are they, then, this person you were following?' asked the policeman.

'I was just waiting for them to come out. Actually, they're being rather a long time.' Nelly's voice began to squeak. 'I think I'll get off home now.'

The officer looked at his colleague. 'We're going your way if you'd like a lift.'

'Are you really? That would be cool.' Nelly felt suddenly so exhausted she could almost have lain down on the pavement there and then.

'Hop in then. What did you say your name was?'

'Sonia!' Charlotte whispered, shaking Sonia's shoulder. 'Wake up! You're having a nightmare – it's all right, it's only a dream!'

Gasping for breath, Sonia struggled to sit up. Horror receded from her eyes as she looked around at the comforting glow of the lamp, her own familiar ivory bedspread and Charlotte's concerned face hovering over her.

'*Mon Dieu* ... Luis—'

'It's all right. It isn't real. You're safe now. Here, put your dressing gown around your shoulders ... Now how about I make you a hot drink to help you get back to sleep.'

'What's the time?' Sonia reached for her alarm clock.

'About two.' Charlotte tried unsuccessfully to suppress a bursting yawn.

Sonia tilted her head back against the headboard and rested it there. She closed her eyes briefly, then opened them again and gazed at Charlotte, mute.

Charlotte sniffed. 'There's a terrific smell of paint in here. It can't be awfully good for you, breathing that in all night. Have you been decorating?'

Sonia shook her head. 'It's my painting. I put it in the wardrobe. It's Nelly and Alain when they were small, playing in the garden at Rose Belle. Maybe that's why I had the bad dream. I was always so afraid for them, you see.'

'Were you? Why?'

No response, just a tightening of the lips.

'Cathartic, I suppose. The painting, I mean. Is that what you've been doing up here all this time, painting?'

'In the other room. My workroom. But I couldn't bear to be parted from this one, even for a night.'

'What are your clothes doing on the floor?'

Sonia looked at the clothes from her wardrobe piled in the middle of the floor. 'It was wet, I didn't want to get paint all over my clothes. Oh, *mon Dieu*! Nelly!' She started up.

'It's okay, she's fine, she's asleep.' Charlotte put out a calming hand.

'I know the police brought her home. I watched them through the bannisters. I was in my workroom when she got in. I knew I ought to come down but I thought it would only complicate things; I would have been bound to let it all out. I was terrified when it was the police. But then I saw that Nelly was with them and she was safe. I'd begun to worry because she hadn't come in.' She sank back onto the pillows. 'I ought to fuss her more, I suppose.' She closed her eyes.

'She's usually quite sensible.'

Sonia's eyes flew open again. 'Where's Patrick?'

'He's having dinner with his agent, remember? He's probably back by now.'

'Of course, I forgot.' Sonia frowned. 'Nelly said she was going round to Sandy's, you know. I wonder what happened. I mean, is it usual for the police to bring someone home in a police car at a quarter to eleven at night? That's not late, is it, nowadays? It's late for Nelly, but they weren't to know that.'

'Nelly told me she and Sandy were hanging around on a street corner playing some sort of game, and the police thought it was a bit late and offered to bring her home.'

'Maybe they've been keeping an eye on us too.'

'It would be nice to think so.' Charlotte slid off the bed. 'I'll make you some cocoa.'

'Why were they out on the street anyway?' Sonia said sleepily, but Charlotte was leaving and didn't reply.

Chapter 25

Showdown

Charlotte poured milk into a saucepan. She'd had no sleep at all so far. After the police had gone and Nelly had gone up to her room, she'd had her bath, keeping an ear open for Patrick's heavy tread coming up the stairs. Still he hadn't returned, and it was gone midnight by the time she'd collapsed wearily under her duvet with her favourite Agatha Christie and Radio Luxemburg on very low so as not to disturb anybody. Then she'd heard Sonia yelling.

She whisked Sonia's cocoa to a fine froth and was walking along the hall towards the stairs, mug in hand, when the key turned in the lock on the front door and Patrick came in.

'Hello, Charlotte, what are you doing up at this hour?' He threw a bunch of keys onto the hall table.

The grandfather clock at the foot of the stairs whirred, geared itself up and chimed sonorously three times.

'Patrick! You look dreadful. Has something happened?'

'Is it Sonia? Can't she sleep?' He looked at the mug in her hand.

'Nightmare.'

'Damn. Is she okay? God, I feel awful.'

'What's wrong? It isn't anything to do with that Juan business, is it?'

He shook his head.

'That's good. Is it the book?

'The book? Oh, the book!' He began to chuckle helplessly.

For a dreadful moment she thought he was going to burst into tears. 'What's the matter? Can I do anything to help?'

He took out his handkerchief and blew his nose. 'No, no! The book's fine.' He shoved his hanky into his trouser pocket, shook his head and looked down at the floor. 'No, there's nothing you can do, Charlotte. Good night.'

'Goodnight then.'

Sonia had fallen asleep sitting up. Charlotte eased her into a semi-recumbent position, pulled the quilt up under her chin and switched off the lamp. She took the mug of cooling cocoa back to the kitchen and found Patrick sitting slumped sideways in a chair, one elbow on the table, his tie askew and his hair ruffled.

'You look like the rake's progress. I can heat up this cocoa if you'd like it.'

'How can you be so calm?' Patrick exploded.

'Because I don't know what's happened. Is somebody dead?'

'Not yet.'

'Have you stolen anything?'

'Not exactly.'

'Well it can't be that bad then. At least, it's probably mendable.'

'I'm talking about *feelings,* Charlotte, *feelings.*' Patrick clasped his forehead as if he was afraid his brain might explode. 'God, I'm in trouble.'

'Tell me about it.' She pulled out a chair on the other side of the table and sat down. Perhaps he'd been arrested for drink-driving. His face was ghastly and his forehead beaded with perspiration.

'I'm afraid you'll be shocked; it will make you unhappy. Because you're such a good person – I'm afraid you'll be angry with me.'

Charlotte felt a brief flutter of fear, then she thought, no it can't be, he wouldn't.

'I've been having an affair.'

She put her hands over her ears when he said this but she could still hear what he said.

'I thought it was going to be a dalliance, but recently it became an affair.'

She heard this through the palms of her hands, which were trembling with shock.

'There, I shouldn't have told you, I knew I'd upset you.' He looked offended.

'No, no you haven't.' She lowered her hands. 'Is it that – er, Laura?' She felt humbled by disaster. She must help him. After all, it had nothing to do with her.

He looked taken aback. 'I suppose Nelly said something.'

'She did say she was afraid—'

'Yes. Well, she's right. It's Laura ... there are no excuses.' He watched her face.

'No, of course not.' She turned away, thinking that there were, in a way. She turned back.

Patrick sat with his head bent. 'She threw me out. I got up to come home because I suddenly couldn't bear what was happening and she said, if you go now I don't want you to come back. Don't bother, she said.' His voice came out muffled and miserable.

Charlotte visualised Patrick and Laura copulating on a wide French bed. There was incense burning, dimmed lighting and a patchwork bedspread kicked onto the floor. She felt a pang of jealousy so acute that tears smarted her eyes. 'I suppose she wants—'

'She says she doesn't want half a man anymore. She's had that, she says. She's been in a bad relationship, you see. He drank.' There was a long pause. 'She wants me to leave Sonia.'

'Are you going to?' She could hardly meet his eyes. She couldn't dismiss the image burned onto her inner eye of Patrick's strong, shapely buttocks moving up and down.

Patrick swung his legs sideways and sat hunched in his chair, gnawing the end of one of the legs of his spectacles. After a long silence he said, 'I don't know. I wish I could believe there was some hope for Sonia and me. And I don't know how deep my feelings for Laura really are. I know she means more to me than she should. We were engaged, after all. She's a simple soul, uncomplicated, the absolute opposite of Sonia, if the truth be told. I enjoy being with her, she's sweet and loving—'

'And there.' Charlotte spoke with uncharacteristic cynicism.

'How understanding you are.' Patrick looked a little upset.

No, I'm not, I'm not a bit understanding. You cheat, how could you? You're using everybody. At that moment she felt she hated him.

'How you must despise me.'

'Of course I don't. Of course not.'

'I feel such a fool. It's just – there's no warmth to be found here.'

'But Patrick.' She leaned forward. 'Hasn't Sonia always been the way she is now?'

Patrick thought for a bit. 'I knew she didn't love me, when I married her. I was fascinated by her; I still am. And she needed me, she turned to me, she – if you like, she permitted – and that seemed to be enough. You're right, I'm the one who's changed, not her. I always thought that would be enough. I'd had enough of easy conquests. But perhaps it's vanity that makes you long to have your love returned.'

'Of course it isn't vanity ... it's natural.'

'And I adored the children.' He turned back and leaned forward, his elbows on the table, his head in his hands. His voice when he spoke was muffled and hoarse. 'I'll never forget when I first saw them, a couple of little tangled waifs and strays. They were at the Penn Ponds in Richmond Park, chucking stones in. I showed Alain how to skim his, then Nelly wanted to be shown too. Seeing them with Sonia I knew I really had fallen in love with her.'

'I suppose things change.' Charlotte sighed, thinking of Riley.

'One's nerve ... one's endurance fails. God, I feel so wretched. What a heartless oaf I've been. That poor girl. She called me a bastard. She said I'd ruined her life.' He sat back and shook his head. 'What a disaster.'

'Patrick.' Charlotte plucked up her courage. 'Sonia needs you. She's always talking about you. She always wants to know where you are.'

He shook his head. 'She doesn't need me. I was an arrogant sod to think I could make her happy.' He got up and began to meander around the room. He paused beside the dresser and touched one of a pair of Italian cockerel jugs, tracing its jaunty rim with the tip of his finger. He walked on to the Aga and ran his hand along the drying rail, he stopped by the sink and fiddled with the cold tap, turning it on then off, then on again.

Charlotte sat still, watching him.

He turned back. 'I know so little about her past. She won't talk about it. But when she told us that horrible story about Alain ...' He stood still and stared at Charlotte. 'What they had to go through to get away from that maniac – my God, I realised then that I simply hadn't begun to understand.' He sat down again and looked across the table at Charlotte. 'It's impossible to imagine what that man must have put her through; it's a kind of parallel universe. The trouble is,' — he paused — 'really, Charlotte, I don't know if I can deal with this.' He shook his head as if baffled by his own stupidity. 'Here I am writing these books about hideous murder and mayhem, going to endless trouble to understand Chandler, loving him, caring about him. And here is my wife – *my wife* – whom I promised to love and care for, whom I persuaded to marry me almost against her will—'

'No.'

Patrick nodded. 'She didn't want to marry me at first. I persuaded her. And here she is, actually having *lived* all this stuff for real ... haven't you seen her, if anyone makes a sudden movement near her, haven't you seen the way she shrinks away? I have. Many times. And I can't deal with it. I don't know what to say to her.' He shook his head again. 'I'm too late, Charlotte. It's too late.'

'No it isn't, it's never too late.' She regretted this platitude the moment she'd said it, although she meant it.

'Sometimes it is.'

'I really don't think so. But it's no good running away, you've got to face things. You have to talk to her.'

'You know, I think she's half hoping that guy will finish her off. I think she's deliberately making herself a target.'

'Who – Juan?' Charlotte winced. 'You're not serious ... that's terrible!'

'I really think she might be. I think she's that desperate.' He shook his head again. 'And I haven't been helping. All this Laura business. I've let her down, of course I have, I've betrayed her in the worst way.'

'Perhaps if she doesn't find out.' If he would just stop feeling sorry for himself and make up his mind to stop seeing that woman, *now*, perhaps something might be saved. She was terrified, suddenly, that Sonia might find out. Somebody might have seen them somewhere and might tell her. Anything could happen.

'And now to cap it all she seems to have suddenly decided to start behaving as though she is interested in me – being pleasant and *warm*, for God's sake: it's terribly unnerving. I don't know if she means it or if she's putting it on. I mean if she lived with that monster all that time, she must have got pretty good at putting on an act. She couldn't let him see how she really felt, could she?'

'Perhaps she wants to change. I honestly think people can, if they make up their mind to do it. Look at people who have religious conversions.'

'It can't be as simple as that.'

'Can't it? And anyway, we all act all the time, don't we?'

He looked across at her. 'What am I going to do?'

She looked down at her hands, linked in her lap. He sat in front of her looking unnervingly humbled and chastened: she felt as though she was talking to a child. 'Look. You have to make up your mind what you want. I don't think you can go on – having your cake and eating it, so to speak.' (What the hell, she was human. Men. Honestly.) 'When you've made up your mind one way or the other, then if you do decide you want to continue with it, your marriage I mean, then when all this Juan thing is cleared up so she can stop worrying about that, and when she's got Alain home and knows he's all right so she can stop worrying about *that,* then maybe you'll be able to start again, from scratch. If Sonia could see – what she'd be throwing away—'

'But she can't change the way she is ... the damage is done.'

'No it isn't, it never is, there's always a chance. You just said yourself she's trying to be different. You've got to believe she can change, Patrick, or you'll have given up before you even start. She could have more counselling, talk to you about the past and her life with that man, get it off her chest. If you shared it, it might become a bond instead of a barrier.'

'Do you really think so?'

'Of course! It's worth a try, surely? Nobody's really tried anything so far, you've both been running as fast as you can away from each other.'

'Well, I have, I don't know about Sonia.'

'She's always running.'

Patrick said, his face lined with sorrow, 'I wish I knew what she wanted.'

'*Ask* her,' Charlotte banged the table with her fist. 'Make her talk to you. If she understood why she feels the way she does, it might at least be a beginning. The most important thing is, do you want to stay, Patrick?'

'Yes, do say,' Sonia said, coming in from the hall. The door was ajar and forgetting time and circumstance they had been speaking rather loud. 'I'd like to know the answer to that one too.'

. . .

SONIA STOOD VERY erect in the doorway in her blue silk kimono with the embroidered butterflies and flowers, staring at Patrick with a strange expression in her eyes, almost of detached curiosity, Charlotte thought. Her eyes were huge and dark in a face drained of colour.

'Oh God.' Patrick stood up and held onto the back of his chair as though for support. 'Look, I don't know what you heard, and I'm sorry you heard anything, but it isn't what you think.'

'How do you know what I think, Patrick?'

'Oh, come on, Sonia. Look. Okay then, if you want to know the truth ... I can't go on any longer with you freezing me out and refusing to – to—'

'Sleep with you?' Sonia said icily.

'I was going to say, talk to me. But since you raise the subject, yes, if you like. I am a *man,* Sonia. I need a wife, a partner—'

'Have you any idea how corny you sound?'

Patrick glared at her. 'If it's corny it's only corny because it's *true.* We're not supposed to be ... monks ... we're human, at least I am, I don't know about you, sometimes I honestly wonder about you.'

'Oh, do you?'

Charlotte thought, oh dear, do be careful.

'I'm sorry, I didn't mean that—'

'Yes, you did. You think I'm frigid. You've always thought so.'

'You've taken pains to make it clear to me you're not.' Patrick's voice was cold. 'Except perhaps with me.'

'I've apologised about that. I've said I'm sorry. What more do you want, Patrick?'

Patrick ran his fingers through his hair. 'A week ago I would have said ... oh, I don't know what I would have said.

Now ... I don't know. I'm sorry to be brutal but I honestly don't know. I just know I don't want to go on like this.'

'So you're leaving.'

'I didn't say that.'

'Who is she?'

'Who is who?'

'The person you're leaving me for. It's amazing. A little difficulty and already you're chasing after some other woman. It's pathetic.'

'A little difficulty! When have you *ever* given yourself to me willingly? There's not much point, my dear, in case you don't understand this, in making love to an unengaged recipient. No, don't go, Charlotte.'

Charlotte stood up. 'I really must. This has nothing to do with me.' She had feelings too, which they seemed to have forgotten. She didn't have to listen to this.

Patrick shook his head. 'It has everything to do with you. It's because you're here that all this has come out into the open. This is all your fault.'

'I beg your pardon?'

He said more calmly to Sonia, 'I'm sorry you had to find out. About Laura, I mean.'

'Oh *please*. Oh, it's *Laura,* is it? That girl you used to be engaged to? How sweet, I had no idea. All I actually overheard was Charlotte asking you if you wanted to leave. So, you see, you need never have told me about your mistress at all. I didn't realise things had gone as far as this. It's nice to be informed. So she's back on the scene, is she? It doesn't surprise me, she's always come running to you when she's made another mess.'

'At least she needs me.'

'Ah. I don't, of course.'

'It's different.'

'I need you too.' Tears began to trickle down Sonia's face. 'Damn her to hell. I need you. You're my husband, for God's sake.'

Patrick got up and moved towards her. She made a helpless gesture, lifting her arms and then dropping them to her sides.

Tears continued to pour down her face as though a dam had burst. 'I can't help how I am. You've got to be brave, Patrick. You must be patient. I can't help it.'

'I know ... I'm sorry ... I know.'

'Have you been sleeping with her?'

'Of course not. No.'

'Are you telling me the truth?'

'You want the truth?'

Oh help, Charlotte thought.

'Okay.' Patrick looked hunted. 'If you must know I only came home tonight because she threw me out. At least, I told her I was leaving and we got into a row. She says she doesn't want another relationship where all that's on offer is half a man – she wants all or nothing.'

'She wants you to leave me.'

Pause. 'Yes.'

'And will you?'

There was a long pause. Sonia was still standing with her chin up, tears rolling down her cheeks, looking at Patrick as though she were a queen, Charlotte thought, and he some grubby commoner who had just committed some appalling *lèse-Majesté*. Patrick just looked sulky.

Charlotte's legs were shaking. Patrick wasn't coming out of this very well. He was in the wrong but Sonia had driven him to it.

(Had she driven Riley to it?)

Patrick said at last, 'I'm sick of being on the outside. I used to enjoy your – your self-obsession—'

'My what? How can you *say* that?'

'All *right*. Your self-containment then. Whatever.' He started to walk about, looking at the floor. 'The way you walk around wrapped in your own little cocoon, as if nobody else exists, thinking you're the only person who's ever felt anything, as if nobody else could possibly understand how you've suffered.'

'That's not fair. That's not a bit how I feel. It's just there's so much going on in my head,' Sonia said. She looked stunned. Charlotte went over and gave her a tissue. Sonia wiped her eyes. 'Why haven't you said all this before?'

'I'm sure I have. You probably weren't listening.'

'But my problems are the only thing we ever seem to talk about. You like being the kind of person who rescues people. You're always collecting lame ducks: that boy who got into trouble at the university ... me ... now Laura ...you love it when people come and ask you for help. I think that's the sort of person you want me to be. But I want to move on.'

Patrick stood still and stared at her in amazement. 'I want you to be yourself, not some robot with me pulling the strings! I'm not Luis, Sonia, and the sooner you realise that the better.'

'Are you mad? Do you think I want you to be like Luis?'

'I don't know. Do you?'

'That's a terrible thing to say. How can you *say* that?'

'I don't *enjoy* saying it. I don't want to be unkind. But I don't seem to be giving you what you want, do I?'

'Don't try to put the responsibility for your behaviour on me. You're the one who's been having the affair.'

'I didn't say I was having an affair.'

'How can you possibly say that I want you to be like him? After all I suffered from him, all I went through to get away from him—'

'But you seem determined to stay the way you are, chained to your past. You don't seem to want to move forward, to take some positive action, to change.'

'Why do you think that? You assume these things. It isn't true. Haven't I just said I want to move on?'

Patrick started striding around the room again. 'I used to feel your self-absorption, your determination to suffer, gave me a sort of freedom, because it let me off the hook, I didn't have to try to understand, since you assumed it was impossible.'

'It gave you an excuse not to bother you mean. How dare you put all this onto me. Nothing's ever your fault.'

Patrick glared at her. 'You seem to think you exist on a different plane. You're just a woman, Sonia, like every other woman. You need the same things, there's nothing special about you. Okay, so you had a bad marriage, horrible things happened to you, but it's *over*, it's passed. You're dragging it around with you like a load of bricks, and whatever you say, you have no intention of letting go of it.'

'You are so unfair. There's nothing in the world I want more than to let go of it.'

'Well why don't you do something about it then? You wouldn't see that counsellor for more than a couple of sessions. You don't want to let go of it, that's the truth, isn't it? You enjoy being unhappy. It makes you special.'

'How can you be so cruel?' Sonia looked at him in consternation. 'How can you say that?'

'All right, prove it. You agree to go and get some help with all this fucking baggage you're carrying around with you and I'll believe you really want to be shot of it.'

'All right, I will. Why haven't you said any of this before? You don't really care, that's why. You're so wrapped up in your blasted writing you can't be bothered. Anyway, all you ever complain about is sex.'

'That's not true. Hasn't it ever occurred to you that I might have been afraid of putting more pressure on you by bringing up all this stuff?'

'It doesn't seem to be stopping you now.'

'Well, it's showtime, isn't it?' He approached her threateningly. Sonia backed away. Patrick threw his arms up in disgust. 'I'm not going to hit you, you silly woman. I love you, don't you realise that? And if there's to be any hope for us, from now on I'm going to share your life, not live on the fringes of it. I want you in my bed and I want you to go and get yourself sorted out and I want things to be normal around here.'

'What about me?' Sonia had backed away until she had her back against the door. 'Aren't I allowed to have any say in anything at all?'

'Not at the moment, no. If you ask me, we've all been listening to you for far too long. I'm fed up with listening to you.'

'Thanks a lot. That's wonderful. All of a sudden you're the masterful male taking charge of things. Well, I may have something to say too. You're *mad* to say I don't want to be happy. Of course I do. If you must know I think I have been beginning to get glimpses of what it might feel like to be happy.' She gave a sob. 'I *have* been trying to make things better. Just because I haven't talked to you about it. Perhaps there are reasons why I wanted to keep things to myself for a while. You don't give me any credit for anything. You think you're so perfect.'

'Of course I don't think I'm perfect. That's ridiculous. I

just happen to feel we could be happy together, if we made a bit of an effort. Maybe you're right, maybe I do like feeling I can help people, maybe it makes me feel good, *I* don't know. But it's different when you love somebody. I *loved* you.'

'Loved? Oh Patrick. Loved?'

'Oh darling, don't,' he said, starting to cry himself.

Charlotte watched as they took each other into their arms and her eyes began to fill. Bells, bluebirds and happy endings, she thought balefully, sliding out of the room. She trudged upstairs, wishing she'd made herself a hot-water bottle. She felt cold and shaken. She couldn't go back to the kitchen, not unless they came upstairs.

'Anyway, what did he mean, it was all my fault?' she said aloud, climbing into her cold bed.

Chapter 26

I like a man who can cry

There was an odd atmosphere in the house, Charlotte thought, washing up Nelly's breakfast things in the morning. It was like that limbo time between the death and the funeral service.

There'd been no sign of either Patrick or Sonia when she tiptoed downstairs in her dressing gown to make sure Nelly was having something to eat before going off to school. She'd tried very hard not to listen for tell-tale sounds indicating which bedrooms her employers were currently occupying, tempting though it might be, indeed undoubtedly was when crossing the landing.

In the kitchen she found Nelly jack-booting around eating a bowl of Ricicles.

'Hi.' Nelly stopped mid-stride.

Charlotte mimed sleepwalking and peered at her through half-shut eyes.

'Bad night?'

Charlotte pulled a face. 'Not good. All in a good cause though.' She stopped. Nelly knew nothing about the scene in the kitchen.

Nelly stuck another spoonful in her mouth. 'I heard Sonia having a nightmare. I'd have gone in if you hadn't. She hasn't had so many since you've been here. I suppose Patrick isn't in yet?'

'Why on earth should you suppose that? Of course he is. He did get in a bit late—'

'Oh, did he?' Nelly looked doleful suddenly.

Perhaps she had heard the row after all. Charlotte made no comment. Things were complicated enough already. Poor old Nelly caught in the middle of it all.

'Have you seen my sneakers?' Nelly put down her cereal bowl.

'They're in the cupboard under the stairs. No,' — she raised her hand as Nelly opened her mouth — 'not guilty. I neither put them in there nor did I move them from anywhere else: I thought possibly you might have put them there for some particular reason.' She started filling the kettle at the sink.

'I was only going to say ta. Well, I'm off. See ya later, alligator.'

'In a while ...' Charlotte flapped an approving hand at her. Nelly was trying so hard to put on a brave face. She had been utterly miserable when the police had brought her back, cold and defeated-looking, the night before. All Charlotte had wanted to do at that point was to take her in her arms and give her a good cuddle, but you simply couldn't do that sort of thing to a sixteen-year-old, especially a sixteen-year-old with that kind of expression on her face, so Nelly had trudged off to bed uncuddled and alone. She'd even refused Charlotte's offer of a hot drink.

At eleven the telephone rang. Someone answered it upstairs but rang off almost at once. I bet that's Laura, Charlotte thought. Wonder what I'd better do about lunch. And I need to start thinking about supper.

Sonia came down about noon and stood just inside the kitchen door. Her eyes were red and swollen and although she had dressed, in jeans and an old tee shirt, she hadn't bothered to put on her make-up.

Charlotte's heart sank. Oh crumbs, what next? Last night it had looked as if some huge reconciliation had happened. Obviously not.

She took care not to stare. She couldn't stand the kind of people who made a point of staring at you when you were obviously upset, when you were crying in the cinema for example. As if they got some kind of kick out of seeing you make an idiot of yourself. And it was obvious that Sonia was suffering; she could feel it right across the room.

'Coffee?' Charlotte turned pieces of lamb over and over to brown in the skillet.

Sonia approached and stood watching. On a dish beside the hot plate, pieces of marinaded lamb lay waiting their turn. She reached out a tentative hand.

'Be careful, that's hot.'

Sonia withdrew her hand instantly.

Oh dear, she'd sounded a bit sharp. 'It's just the pan that's hot. The dish is okay.'

'What are you making?' Sonia's voice was huskier than usual and ragged with crying.

'It's a sort of lamb stew. It has a red wine sauce. I hope you'll try some, it's really good.' She was dying to ask what had happened.

'It's no good, Charlotte.'

Charlotte's heart sank. She put down her spoon. 'Oh

Sonia. It looked as if you'd – well, come to some kind of understanding last night. I hoped that with your son being okay and both of you getting things off your chests—'

'We were both so upset. We even made love, for the first time for ages.'

Oh glory, too much information; she really didn't want to know. Charlotte picked up a skewer and pretended to test the meat.

'But it didn't mean anything – not really. Not to him, anyway. It was just the heat of the moment. Nothing has changed. And now he's taken the day off. It takes World War Three to make him do that. I'm sure he's gone to see her.' Sonia's voice choked up. 'I don't know if he'll come back. What can I do? What *can* I do?'

Charlotte pulled the skillet off the heat onto the side, propped her wooden spoon against the edge of the pan and took Sonia into her arms. 'It's all right.' She patted her gently. 'You're doing everything you can.'

'There's nothing I can do, that's the trouble.' Sonia sobbed into Charlotte's shoulder.

She was all skin and bone. It was like holding a bird. 'Yes, you have. You've shown him you care.' Charlotte detached herself and lowered Sonia into a chair. 'I'll make some coffee. You sit there and try to relax.'

When she'd made the coffee she handed Sonia a mug and sat down with her. Sonia sat hunched up, holding the mug between trembling hands. 'I've got a place at St Martin's. I only heard this morning. I thought he'd be pleased. But now it's all gone wrong.'

'Sonia, that's *wonderful!*' Charlotte looked at her in genuine amazement. 'Have you told him? Art college! And you never said a word.'

'I wanted it to be a surprise.'

'So that's what you've been doing all this time.'

'I thought it was what I wanted most in the whole world. But I want Patrick more. I need him.' Tears started to run down her face again.

'Of course you do.'

'I couldn't bear it if he left. I've been such a selfish beast.'

'He does love you, you know.'

'Do you think so?'

'I know he does.'

'I would try.' She sipped her coffee. 'I really would try. I saw this book about cognitive behaviour therapy in the health food shop. I think it would help. I wouldn't mind doing that. If it isn't too late.'

'I'm sure it isn't too late.' (They could be halfway to France by now.)

'If he only comes back.'

'He will. Of course he will.'

'He didn't say he would. He wouldn't say ...' Sonia gave an exhausted sigh and blew her nose. 'I've got through three boxes of tissues.'

'Try to find something to do, to take your mind off it.'

'I was going to go up to town this afternoon, to celebrate having got in. And it would be a distraction. I suppose I could still go.' She looked uncertainly at Charlotte. 'I can't go out when I don't know if he's ever going to come back.'

'He'll come back.' He could hardly do anything too drastic without coming back at least to pack some clothes. This didn't seem to have occurred to Sonia. 'I'm not sure if you ought to go out, though, until they've found out what's going on. I mean about that man, that Juan guy.' She looked at Sonia warily. No hysterics today.

'Patrick did say he would talk to that police inspector again today.'

'It would do you good to get out of the house.' But was it safe? However bad things were she was pretty sure Patrick would prefer Sonia to stick around.

'I could have lunch at the Academy. There's something on in the Sackler Gallery I want to see and the show I was going to is in Cork Street, just around the corner. I suppose it would be all right to go.'

'I can't stop you. I can't say I'm happy about it though.'

'I'll go mad if I stay here.'

Charlotte looked at her doubtfully. This wasn't some kind of a gesture on Sonia's part, was it? Sort of tit for tat? *If you're going to go off after your girlfriend then I'm going to show you I don't care by going off up to town.* In her limited experience those kinds of games did more harm than good. 'When he comes back do you want me to tell him where you've gone?'

'Would you? You don't think it looks as if I don't care? You will explain?'

Sonia's remorse did seem genuine enough. 'Of course I will. And he won't think that, he'll just be worried about you.'

Sonia heaved a long sigh, her breath shuddering. 'I'll go mad if I sit around here all day waiting for him to come home. Perhaps I will go. I do wish they'd pick Juan up, though. I can't help feeling this trouble with Patrick is all Juan's fault. I know that's silly, it's just that everything got so much worse after Françoise wrote. I've been so frightened.' She stood up and went to the door. 'I'll go up and get changed.'

Charlotte went back to preparing the evening meal. If only Patrick would come home. She felt responsible. If anything happened to Sonia it would be her fault for not stopping her going. On the other hand the break really would do her good, and who knew if Patrick would come back at all?

Sonia called from the hall, 'Bye then, Charlotte. I'll be back about seven.'

NELLY CAME in from school and put her head around the kitchen door. 'Where's everybody?'

'Out. Tea?'

'Not just now thanks. See you in a min.'

She ran up the stairs three at a time, head down, pretending to be in the S.A.S. On the landing she stopped and listened. Silence. She tiptoed along the passage to Patrick's bedroom door and turned the handle.

Once inside she looked around. The room had a deserted, masculine feel. It smelt of Patrick's *Essence de Brut* aftershave. His maroon silk pyjamas, neatly folded, lay on the pillow of one of the single beds. He had the habit of keeping his pyjamas on top instead of under his pillow because he said it was more hygienic. He was a great one for hygiene. He never used a face flannel either; some loony housemaster at his boarding school had convinced him they bred germs.

She went to the dressing table, picked up his hairbrush and sniffed it. It smelt of him and her heart lurched. Oh hell, she thought. He's going to leave, just when I was beginning to feel we could be a proper family at last.

She went out, closed the door quietly behind her and went next door into her mother's room. She went to the wardrobe where Sonia kept her clothes and opened the door.

. . .

AT HALF-PAST five the front door slammed. Charlotte heard Patrick's firm tread in the hall. She stood by the Aga, so relieved he was back that she felt quite sick. She stirred the stew which was bubbling deliciously. She felt a little embarrassed at the prospect of seeing him after the row, but they couldn't avoid each other forever. She'd just go on as though nothing had happened. He was bound to be feeling as bad as she was about it: worse probably. He had admitted being unfaithful and then, for goodness' sake, he had cried.

She did like a man who could cry.

The footsteps came up to the kitchen door, stopped and after a brief pause, withdrew. Charlotte, feeling chastened, went on stirring the stew. She was desperate to know if he'd been with Laura and what kind of decision he'd made, if any. Also if he'd talked to the police again about Juan and whether there was any news. If only he'd come in so they could have a proper talk.

Maybe he felt as embarrassed as she did about last night's revelations.

Or perhaps he just wanted to go to the loo or something first and he'd be in any minute. She did hope so.

NELLY STOOD in front of the cheval glass in Sonia's room and admired her reflection. She had on her mother's orchid-pink Bruce Oldfield evening dress and matching pink high-heeled shoes. The dress was figure-hugging and left one of Nelly's shoulders seductively bare: she had to admit that the effect was pretty stunning. The dress clung in all the right places; she'd been amazed it fitted her.

After teetering around for a while in the shoes she

kicked them off and rummaged in the shoe rack for a black pair. There were all sorts: Ferragamo, Hoofs, Bruno Magli, Gucci. Did Sonia go in for shoes or what? Nelly marvelled, on her knees. She found a pair of black evening shoes (Valentino) with large zircons in the middle of black bows on the toes: tarty but tasty.

She ripped off the dress and threw it on the bed. Black, she wanted black. She found a short Jean Varon dress with a scoop neck and tiny cap sleeves and wriggled into it; it was a bit tight and came to just above the knee. She felt even better in this dress. She caught sight of a hatbox on a high shelf and hauled it down. Inside was a tiny black pillbox hat with a veil. She pinned up her hair with some kirby-grips out of her mother's drawer and put it on. Lipstick next. She painted on Revlon's Scarlet Fever out of a pochette bulging with discarded make-up she'd found in a drawer, then powdered her nose vigorously with Rose Rachèle. Her face gleamed pale and sultry-looking through the black mesh of the veil.

Nelly's eyes widened when she saw her reflection in the mirror. After she was thirty-five she would wear a veil all the time in the daytime and keep the lights down low at night. She didn't want ever to get disgusting and old.

The hat needed a longer dress. She undid the zip with a bit of wriggling and stretching and let the dress fall to the ground. She kicked it away and then in a fit of conscience picked it up and flung it on the bed where it lay huddled up to the Oldfield model.

She heard Maisie head-butting the door and went to let her in, taking a good look up and down the landing to make sure the coast was still clear.

Well into trying-on fever she started pulling dresses off hangers and leaving them on the floor where they fell. She found another black dress of the length she wanted, halfway down the shin. This one was made of heavy black crepe and the shoulder straps glittered when you moved. She slid into it and zipped it up with slightly more difficulty. It was a very close fit.

This is IT, she thought. The shoes, hat and dress all suited each other, although she couldn't possibly wear any of them to the party; they were far too smart. She would wear her short bronze silk skirt and her Suzie Wong blouse. She might borrow a pair of shoes: Sonia would never notice. Her pale round arms gleamed against the black stuff and her legs looked nice in high heels. She turned around and examined her back view. Hmm, okay. A bit curvy but she could live with that.

Maisie lay on the bed in her seventh heaven, kneading silks and chiffons with her claws and dribbling, her eyes half shut and a besotted expression on her face.

NELLY TURNED BACK to the mirror, adjusted the hat and struck a pose. She felt like one of those forties film stars, Claudette Colbert or Joan Fontaine. She went right up close to the glass and peered at herself. It would have been great to have been born then: everything so settled and secure, with the war and everything. Everybody knew what they had to do, and everybody stuck together, not like now when we seem to have turned into savages; we'd eat each other if we were allowed, Sandy said.

The door opened behind her and Patrick came in. He stopped when he saw her. 'I didn't realise you were back.'

Nelly stood completely still.

'You're so beautiful.' His voice cracked. 'I love you.

She's nothing, nobody in comparison to you. You do know that, don't you?'

For a perfectly insane moment Nelly imagined he might be addressing her. He came up behind her and reached out his arms to surround her with his embrace.

'I'm sorry, I'm so sorry, darling.'

Nelly turned around to face him, her eyebrows raised in sardonic amusement. She laughed when she saw the expression on his face as he realised his mistake and backed rapidly away.

She felt tears coming and turned away. 'How touching. What a pity Sonia wasn't here to listen to that little speech. I know about *her* you know. About Laura. You bastard.' She turned back. 'If you think I'm so beautiful, will I do for a change? You don't seem to be particularly choosy.'

Patrick's face flushed. He held up his hands in a warding-off gesture. 'I thought – you look so like your mother.'

'Don't look so horrified.' Nelly tore off the hat and flung it onto the bed. 'I'm not serious. You're such a spaz, Patrick, honestly.' She started wildly unzipping her dress.

'Hang on a minute, give me a chance to get out of here.' He shielded his eyes and backed towards the door.

'You don't have to. I'll do a striptease for you if you like.'

The door closed.

'Bastard. Bastard.' She sat on the edge of the bed and crossed her arms tight around herself. A pang of acute nostalgia for St. Colombe, for her father, hit her with frightening force. She rocked to and fro. 'Oh, Papa ... Papa.'

She wept freely for a little while, then stood up, scrubbed her face with a ball of tissues from a box on the dressing table and pulled the pins out of her hair so that it tumbled around her shoulders again. She unzipped the dress and stepped out of it. It lay in a crumpled heap around her ankles.

Back in her school uniform, she was picking dresses up with trembling hands and draping them inexpertly onto their hangers when there was a knock at the door and Patrick put his head around.

'What do you want?'

'I just wanted to say something, Nell.' He came inside and closed the door. 'Listen to me for a minute. You did look lovely just now, absolutely beautiful. You should be flattered that I mistook you for your mother.' He came nearer and stood awkwardly with his hand resting on the bedpost.

Nelly turned her back and went on putting things away.

'I just wanted to say ... I don't think I've ever told you that – well – when I married your mother, to find myself with a daughter – as funny and feisty and lovely as you, has been the most wonderful joy and privilege. You're very precious to me, Nelly. I love you very much. I'm nothing special as a person, in fact at the moment I'm not proud of myself at all. I don't know you very well, not as well as I know your mother—'

'And *her*.'

'I think that's probably over.' Patrick sighed. 'It was a stupid mistake. I'm terribly sorry about it. I feel dreadful.'

'Poor old you.'

He gave a little vexed shrug. 'Yes, yes, say what you like, I probably deserve it. But haven't you ever done anything stupid, something you regretted the moment you had done it?'

Nelly turned and looked at him. 'But you went on doing it. Over and over again.'

'It hasn't been going on very long, you know. It was clever of you to guess.'

Nelly gave him a look of contempt. All the same she didn't think she'd admit to spying on him. 'A child of three could have guessed. *T'as le demon de midi, toi, non?* Poor old Patrick panting after sexy Laura. It's pathetic.'

Patrick winced. 'It wasn't quite like that.'

'All right then. Sorry. But it makes me sick. And don't give me all that *you'll understand one day* stuff. I understand right now, thanks very much, I understand perfectly. Sex matters more than we do. It's perfectly clear.'

'I said it's probably finished.'

'*You* said. She won't give up.' She picked up a Ferragamo shoe and looked around for its pair.

'No, but it's up to me, Nell. It takes two. Here.' He picked up the other shoe and handed it to her.

She took it. 'I know, I'm not stupid.'

'I shouldn't dream of implying that you were.'

'What will happen if Sonia finds out?'

'She knows. I told her.'

'What?' She looked at him in consternation. 'You *fool!* What did she say?'

He shrugged. 'She was very upset.'

'No!' Nelly gave him a withering look. 'Where is she, anyway?'

'Charlotte says she went up to town. To an exhibition.'

'What? She *didn't*. Holy cow.'

'She told Charlotte she'd be back for dinner.'

She turned away. 'Why did you have to tell her?'

Patrick shrugged as though he couldn't think why he had either. 'I suppose I thought it was time.'

Nelly picked up a chiffon scarf. How could her mother go swanning off to a show as though nothing had happened when she'd just been told her husband was involved with another woman and was actually thinking of leaving? It was unbelievable.

She just didn't care, did she?

Prickles of worry started up in her stomach. If her mother really didn't care, she wouldn't try to make Patrick stay and then it would be all over anyway.

Patrick turned to the door. 'I'm going for a walk around the block. See you at dinner.'

Nelly looked at him.

He looked back. 'Around the block, I said. You're going to have to start trusting me, Nell. Dinner's at eight. Charlotte says we're waiting for Sonia to get back.'

'Dunno why she bothers.' Nelly hung up the Gina Fratini dress. 'You could give Sonia chopped Kellogg's Cornflakes packets and she wouldn't know the difference. I do wish Alain would come home.'

Patrick left, leaving the door open. She listened to his footsteps descending the stairs. She couldn't wait to tell Sandy about this, she'd laugh herself sick.

Chapter 27

Towards zero

Charlotte was chopping garlic, peppers, chillies and ham to add to the *Poulet Basquaise* for tomorrow evening when the telephone rang in the hall. After the fifth ring she laid down the chopping board and knife, pushed her saucepan sideways off the hot ring and hurried to answer it.

Sonia stepped in through the front door, dressed in her London clothes. Charlotte handed her the receiver.

'Yes?' Sonia threw her shoulder bag onto the chiffonier. 'Who? Oh, Mr Rennie.' She listened intently for a moment or two. 'That's wonderful! Could you repeat the flight number, please?' Her hands, holding the phone, were shaking. 'Right, I've got that. Nine-thirty, Terminal Three, Heathrow. Thank you so much for letting us know. Yes, somebody will be meeting him.'

She put the phone down and looked at Charlotte with a dazed expression. 'It's Alain, he's on his way home. Oh, Charlotte.' She put her hand over her mouth. 'I think I might – be sick.'

'You're not going to be sick. It's the shock. Come and sit

down. It's wonderful news!' Charlotte quelled her instinct to wrap Sonia in a sisterly hug. She looked as though if you touched her she might collapse. 'Where's he been all this time, did they say? Is he okay?'

'Mr Rennie just said he's fine and he's on his way home. Oh, Charlotte, I can't believe it, I've been so worried about him, even after they rang to say he'd been found. Juan still might have managed to track him down over there. Oh!' She stopped. 'Patrick will be pleased.' She looked uncertain. 'Won't he?'

'Of *course* he will. You must tell him. He came in a little while ago; Nelly said he went for a walk around the block. Oh, my goodness, my sauce!' Charlotte set off at a trot towards the kitchen. In all the excitement she couldn't remember if she'd moved the pan off the heat.

Sonia hurried after her. 'How is he? Did he say anything?'

'We didn't speak,' Charlotte shrieked, rushing to the Aga. Thank heavens, no damage done. 'Sorry. It's just, burnt sauce is the last thing we need at the moment.' She moved the saucepan back onto the heat and began stirring gently, calming down. Sonia couldn't possibly be expected to appreciate the finer nuances of sauce Basquaise. 'I thought I heard him come in and go into the study.'

'Oh.' Sonia stood nervously pleating the front of her suit jacket between her fingers.

'Go and tell him, go on,' Charlotte urged her, bashing out incipient lumps against the side of the pan. It really didn't do to desert a sauce at such a crucial moment.

'Couldn't you?'

'Sonia!'

'He won't want to talk to me. I don't know how things are ... I'm embarrassed.'

Charlotte stifled her growing exasperation. Perhaps Sonia was afraid Patrick might tell her something she didn't want to hear. 'Look. Whatever else is on his mind, he's going to be thrilled about Alain coming home. Just focus on Alain and it will be all right. I think you should tell him, honestly. I don't think it's my place.'

Sonia hesitated. 'He's in the study, you said.'

Charlotte nodded. 'Go on!' She listened as Sonia's heels clacked across the black and white tiled floor.

It would be strange having Alain in the house. Everything was going to change. Even if Patrick decided to stay, things would change.

She heard footsteps in the hall. Sonia put her head around the door. 'He isn't there.'

'Isn't he? Perhaps he went upstairs.'

'He isn't upstairs, either. I've just been up to look. Do you think he's gone out again?'

'I wasn't aware of the front door, but I've had the radio on.' Perhaps he'd made up his mind, walking round the block, and had only come back in again to collect his things, and now he'd gone. Finally gone. There was a coldness in the pit of Charlotte's stomach. She followed Sonia out into the hall, her wooden spoon in her hand.

Nelly called from upstairs, 'Who was that on the phone?'

'Mr Rennie from the Embassy,' Sonia called back. 'Alain's on his way home.'

'Boo-*yah!* Jinkies, that's ace!' Nelly came leaping down the stairs in her underclothes. 'Is he okay?'

'I think he must be.' Sonia bit her bottom lip. 'It's such a relief. I can't tell you what a relief.' She noticed Nelly's state of undress. 'Are you going out?'

'Having supper with Sandy. Oh.' Nelly put her hand

over her mouth. 'Sorry, Charlotte. Forgot to say. I realise it's a bit last minute. Ohhh ... I'll miss your lamb.' She put her head on one side. 'Can you save some for me?' She grinned, turned and headed off up the stairs again.

Charlotte frowned. Nelly was a bit dressed up, wasn't she, for a girl who was going to have supper with a friend she saw every day at school? She had on a pale blue camisole and a suspender belt and stockings. Just as well Patrick wasn't about; Nelly really oughtn't to cavort about like that in front of him with next to nothing on. She looked at her watch. It was seven already and supper wasn't ready yet.

Sonia followed her into the kitchen. 'I can't believe it. Alain coming home. I've been so frantic.'

'It's *wonderful* news.'

'It's just, I wish I knew where Patrick was. I'll go for my run, that always clears my head. I think I'll leave him a note on his desk about Alain. I'd like him to know as quickly as possible; he's been worried too. I think I'll just do that and then go up and change.'

Oh damn, Charlotte thought, where is he? I haven't the first idea if it's okay for Sonia to go out again or not. Oh, *Patrick!* Don't you care? Where are you?

She heard Sonia go into the study. She came out again a few minutes later and Charlotte heard her trudging upstairs. If Nelly was going out there would only be three of them in for the evening meal. They could eat the chicken tonight; but it wasn't ready yet, it would make them even later, and the *sauce basquaise* would improve with keeping. No, they'd have the lamb tonight. She stood stirring the onion and tomato mixture, simmering sweetly on the stove. The pans were beginning to give out a wonderful combined aroma.

The front door slammed. She stopped stirring and stood listening. Was that Patrick? The study door closed and after a few moments, opened again. It *was* Patrick, she recognised his tread. The knot in her stomach dissolved in relief; she hadn't realised how tense she was feeling.

The door opened and he came in. He looked pale and baggy-eyed, almost plain. He hadn't washed his hair, which he normally did under the shower every day, and it clung unattractively to his skull, making him look older. He also looked extremely unhappy. He came and stood beside her.

She glanced at him and went on stirring the two pans alternately. 'Hi. Sonia's been looking for you.'

'Ah.'

Charlotte went on stirring. She waited for him to say more but he didn't. 'You got her note then? She went up to change for her run. It's very good news about Alain, isn't it?'

'It's tremendous. Really great. It will be wonderful for Sonia having him home again.'

'She thought a run would clear her head. She left you the note so that you'd get the news as quickly as possible. She wanted to tell you herself but you'd – she didn't know if you'd be back before she went out for her run.' She hoped this didn't sound accusing.

'I'll go up in a moment. It is, it's wonderful news.' He sounded horribly detached, as though it no longer had anything to do with him. There was a tense silence. Charlotte concentrated determinedly on the sauce.

'Oh, by the way, I spoke to Inspector Nash again. It's all okay. They spoke to the police in St. Colombe and apparently Juan is dead, he was killed in a prison riot several weeks ago. Monsieur Desmarchais, that's the husband of Sonia's friend, says his wife wrote to Sonia again telling her she could stop worrying, but obviously she can't have got the letter. All this hysteria was completely unnecessary, most of it's been in Sonia's head.' He sounded almost impatient, as though everything that had happened was Sonia's fault.

Charlotte turned right around and looked at him in complete disbelief. 'How long have you known this, Patrick?'

'He rang this morning.' He began to look a little discomfited. 'I would have said something sooner but it's all been a bit fraught.'

'A bit fraught! You didn't think to tell Sonia and put her out of her misery?'

'That's putting it a bit strongly, isn't it?'

'No. It isn't. She's been absolutely terrified. So have I.'

'Well, I'm sorry. To be fair, Sonia's been out all day. We haven't really spoken. Sorry, Charlotte. I didn't think.'

Charlotte turned back to the stove, her lips tight.

Patrick fiddled with the drying-up cloth hanging on the chrome drying bar. 'I've made a pretty good mess of things, haven't I?'

Oh blimey, what was the point in being furious with him? 'Not a complete mess, yet. Here, have a taste.' She held the wooden spoon up to his mouth. Olive branch.

He baulked slightly. 'Is it all right to do this?'

''Course it is. Your germs will all be assassinated by the heat.'

'Hmm.' He tasted, gingerly. His face cleared. 'That's good.'

'It's the sauce for the chicken for tomorrow. Lamb tonight.' Charlotte took the spoon over to the sink and rinsed it.

'Just like a woman.' Patrick almost smiled. Then he looked sad again.

Charlotte went back to the Aga. 'For what it's worth and I know it isn't any of my business, Sonia is devastated. She desperately wants you to stay, you know.'

There was a long pause during which Patrick took both drying-up cloths off the bar, folded them up as small as they would go, so that now they'd never get dry, and hung them up again.

'I know ... I know.' She thought he might be relieved – pleased – something, but he looked completely dejected.

He drummed his fingers on the Aga, finished off with a little flourish and put his hands in his pockets. 'I don't think I'm as good at being responsible for people as I thought I was.' He glanced at her and Charlotte was shaken by the bleakness in his eyes.

He began to prowl about with his head bowed, lost in thought. After a pause he said, 'I notice you didn't say "she loves you."'

She looked at him in dismay and he raised his eyebrows at her and turned away. He walked over to the window and looked out. 'To be honest with you, Charlotte, at the moment I feel like throwing in the towel.'

He'd admitted it. This was the end. Charlotte closed her eyes briefly and opened them again. 'I didn't say it, because it's none of my business.' She stirred vigorously. Too vigorously. She slowed down and turned the heat down under the saucepan. No point in ruining a perfectly good sauce just because the world was coming to an end. 'But I'll say it if you like, because I know it's true.'

'You make it sound so simple. I wish I could believe you.'

'Would it make such a difference, to be sure that she loved you?' Charlotte went to the sink and started running water into the washing-up bowl.

'Of course it would.'

'Well, it is simple. She does love you. She told me so.'

'Recently?'

Charlotte went into the scullery and returned with the colander full of vegetables. 'This morning.' She tipped onions, a head of celery and a bunch of carrots into the sink.

'Are you sure? She never says it to me.' He wandered into the middle of the room and stood with his hands in his pockets, fingering his keys.

Could you blame her when she knew Patrick had been two-timing her? He should give her credit for some self-respect at least. But perhaps he meant before she knew about Laura?

She shook her head. She hadn't realised things were still so bad between them. Perhaps Sonia hadn't got over the shock of finding out about Laura.

'Penny for them,' Patrick said. 'Oh, and by the way, I forgot to say, it isn't only Nelly who's deserting us this evening, Sonia doesn't want anything either. Too excited about Alain to eat, she says in her note. So it's just you and me.'

Charlotte went into the larder and came back with a bag of new potatoes which she dumped on the draining board. She said with her back turned, 'I don't think it's any use your looking for the usual kind of response from someone like Sonia. She isn't your run-of-the-mill kind of person. The important thing is, do you love her? I mean, do you love the real her, not the idealized version? That's what matters. If you do, then no matter what, it's worth doing everything you can to make things right.' She looked at the taps, her eyes brimming with tears. 'That's what I think, anyway.'

She heard his footsteps behind her and felt his hand on

her shoulder. 'Charlotte.' He squeezed her shoulder. 'Thanks.' He let her go.

She half-turned her head, trying to conceal the fact that she was holding back tears.

A moment or two after he'd left the room the study door slammed. Charlotte turned off the taps. Just Patrick and her for supper then. She wasn't quite sure how she felt about that idea. Thoroughly confused, she wiped away her tears.

Nelly called goodbye from the hall.

'Hey Nelly!' she called back.

'Where is everybody?' Nelly put her head around the door.

'Your Dad's here, he's in the study. Your Mum's upstairs, didn't you see her? She's just off for her run.'

Nelly pulled a face. 'Oh well. Catch her later.'

'But Nelly—'

'Say bye for me.'

'Wait – can't you pop back up and see her?'

'I'm late already, sorry. Must get a move on.'

'Are you going to be late home?'

Nelly dangled her front door key from one finger. 'Maybe.' She grinned.

'Where are you going? Let's have a look at you then.'

'We won't really be that late. Late-ish.'

'Have you squared it with your parents?'

'Yup.'

'Well, come on then, give us a twirl.'

Nelly dropped her coat on the floor and pirouetted a few times.

Charlotte whistled. 'You look terrific.'

'Will I do? Seriously, do I look okay?'

'You look wonderful.'

Nelly's excited face shone over a mandarin-collared,

sleeveless, embroidered cream brocade blouse. Under a short tan skirt, her legs looked impossibly long.

'Where are you going?'

'Nowhere special.' Nelly gathered up her coat and thrust her arms into the sleeves. 'You know what Sandy's like, any excuse to glam up. Well, charrah then, catch you on the flip – well, actually, not too early, it's Saturday tomorrow. I'm going to lie in till lunch.'

'What about Alain? And have you said goodbye to your father?'

Too late; she'd gone. The front door slammed.

Charlotte shook her head. None of them knew how to shut a door. She frowned. Nelly couldn't have forgotten that her brother was coming home? No, she'd been over the moon about it earlier, and after all, he'd still be here in the morning.

'Oh, has Nelly gone?' Sonia came in from the hall in her tracksuit and running shoes. 'See Charlotte? Shoes.'

Charlotte smiled to show she was pleased about the shoes. Sonia looked fractionally more cheerful. 'She seemed in a tearing hurry.'

'Did she say where she was going?'

'Just out with Sandy somewhere. She was worried about being late.' She felt a vague disquiet.

'I hope she hasn't forgotten Alain's coming home tonight.'

'I'm sure she hasn't. Are you sure you don't want something to eat before you go to the airport? You could have some early.'

'I am too upset to eat. Did Patrick say anything, Charlotte?'

'Hasn't he spoken to you?'

'What do you mean?'

'Where is he?'

'He's shut himself up in the study again.'

'And you haven't talked? Not at all? Why don't you pop in and see him for a moment before you go out.'

Sonia shook her head.

For God's sake, why hadn't he told her Juan was dead and the danger was over? Perhaps he was enjoying torturing her. Maybe he wasn't going to tell her he was leaving her, either, until he absolutely had to.

'He doesn't want to talk to me. If I go for my run at least I can forget about it for a little while.'

Charlotte sighed. Blast the man. Should she tell her about Juan herself? Would it be interfering? 'I really think you should sit down together and have a proper talk.'

'I don't want to talk to him. Not until he's in a better mood. Maybe when I get back from my run.' Sonia patted her tracksuit pocket in a preoccupied manner. 'Hanky, keys. Alain will be hungry when he gets back. Maybe I'll feel like eating then, too.'

'Well, it will heat up, luckily.' Charlotte tried to keep the barbs out of her tone: suppose it had been something that wouldn't. Still, she wished she could be that uninterested in food; she might get to look like Sonia.

Sonia pulled a doubled-over sweatband off her wrist and arranged it on her forehead. 'Perhaps I could persuade Patrick to come running with me sometime. I've been reading a book called *How to Improve your Marriage*. You're supposed to do things together instead of apart all the time.'

Charlotte shook her head in despair. Let him back in your bed for a start, would be one answer. Then she smiled: there was something disarmingly childlike about Sonia. Though her expression was sad, she had never seemed so approachable.

Sonia came nearer and lowered her voice. 'How is he, do you think? He hasn't said anything to me at all, he just looks—'

Sad, Charlotte thought. He just looks sad.

Patrick came in from the hall. If only he wouldn't wear those rubber-soled shoes, you could never hear him coming. Beside her, Sonia tensed. Surely he'd say something now? But neither of them seemed capable of speech.

Charlotte felt like banging their heads together. She turned her back, picked up an onion and her knife and started unpeeling the skin. 'Do you want me to do anything about getting Alain's room ready? Sheets and things? Mrs P. won't be here again till Tuesday and of course this morning we didn't know he was coming home. And should I make up the other bed?'

'Don't bother,' she heard Patrick say. 'I'll sleep in the study for the time being. I've got a camp bed stowed away in there somewhere. It'll do.' There was a pause. She heard him move towards the door. 'Have a good run.' The door banged shut.

Charlotte rolled her eyes. She put down her knife and turned round. The bloody man *still* hadn't told Sonia what the police had said. She would tell her herself.

'*Pour l'amour de Dieu.*' Sonia's eyes were full of tears.

Charlotte forgot everything in her pity for her. She put her arms around her and hugged her. 'Oh, my dear. Go for your run. It'll do you good. Forget about everything for half an hour. Things will work out. You'll see.'

Sonia nodded. She pulled a hanky out of her sleeve and blew her nose.

Charlotte turned back to the sink to give her time to compose herself. She started chopping the onion. Suddenly she remembered. She turned. 'Oh – Sonia—'

But Sonia had gone, slamming the door behind her. Drat. Charlotte's lips tightened. She chopped the onion and started on the celery.

The phone rang in the hall. Patrick came out of the study and picked up. 'Hello?'

Charlotte paused to listen. Not Laura again? She must be watching the house.

'Who?'

Not Laura then.

'I'm afraid Nelly's out. Hang on a minute, isn't she supposed to be with you? What? Calm down, Sandy, I can't hear a word you're saying. Nelly's where?'

Charlotte dried her hands and went out into the hall.

'She *what?*' Patrick looked at Charlotte, his face grim. 'Well, give me the address this minute.' He fished his notebook out of his pocket and opened it against his front. He scribbled for a moment or two with the receiver tucked under his chin. 'When? Who? Why on earth didn't you tell us all this before? Yes, well, goodbye. *Thanks.*' It sounded like a swear word.

He slammed the phone down. 'I don't believe it. Nelly's gone to meet that chap she met in the pub. Sandy says they were both supposed to be going somewhere with him but Sandy cried off. He was meeting her at the end of our road.' He looked at his watch. 'Fifteen minutes ago. I'm phoning the police.'

Chapter 28

Crash

In the passenger seat of Carl's black Saab, Nelly sat back, enjoying the sensation of sitting beside an attractive man being driven she didn't know where; nor did she care, it was just great to be out, to be going to a party, to be away from home. She looked out of the window at the tall trees lining the road, at pavements strewn with fallen leaves. A strong wind had arisen during the night.

They reached the high street, busy with late-night shoppers and commuters walking home from the station. Carl slowed at the pedestrian crossing; the lights changed as he reached it and he stopped.

Nelly looked out of the window at the small crowd of people waiting to cross.

'Holy cow, it's Sonia.'

'Who?'

'My mother.'

'Where?'

She pointed. 'There!'

The lights changed and Carl stepped on the accelerator. The car shot forward.

'There! No! Carl – *stop!'*

There was a loud bang as Sonia flung herself with all her strength onto the bonnet of the Saab. The sound of the impact was like a door slamming. Sonia slid down the front of the Saab into the road.

'Mamée!' Nelly screamed, falling out of the car and sinking to her knees in the road by Sonia's side. Her tights ripped on the tarmac. 'It's my mother,' she said frantically to a man who had leapt out of the car following theirs and was kneeling by her mother's side.

The man was already unzipping Sonia's tracksuit top. 'My name's Andy. Police.' He wasn't wearing a uniform but was dressed in jeans and a checked shirt. 'Lucky we were just behind you.'

Nelly opened her mouth to speak and shut it again. The man put his arm under Sonia's shoulders and raised her a little. 'What's her name?'

Nelly told him.

'Mrs Carey, my name's Andy Barnes. Everything's all right, you're quite safe.'

Nelly couldn't understand what was happening.

'Can you hear me, Mrs Carey?'

'Nelly,' Sonia murmured.

'I'm here, Mamée, I'm here. Are you okay? Does it hurt?' She grabbed the man's sleeve. '*Do* something. Help her. Look – there's blood. Is she going to be all right?'

'Ambulance is on its way.' A second man hunkered down beside Nelly.

Andy looked up. 'This is Mrs Carey's daughter.'

The man nodded to Nelly. 'I'm a colleague of Andy's. Greg Carnadine. Christ, Andy, what a balls-up.'

'Ladies present. Deal with him, Greg, will you?' Andy said in a low voice. 'Don't spook him, whatever you do.'

The man Andy had addressed as Greg stood up and went to Carl who had climbed out of the car and was hovering nearby, looking pale and shocked. Carl approached uncertainly with Nelly's bag in his hand. 'I'm more sorry than I can say. There was nothing I could do. I'm so sorry.'

Nelly stood up, her eyes still on her mother's face. 'It's not your fault. I don't know what she was thinking of.'

'Could she have tripped?'

Greg shrugged. 'It's possible. It must have given you quite a shock. How are you feeling?'

'I'm okay. I just wish I'd been able to stop—'

Greg nodded in sympathy. 'Of course, but there's nothing you could have done. There are plenty of witnesses, they're taking statements now.'

'Do you want one from me?'

'Tell you what. How about we leave it now and ask you to pop into Kingston later? Tomorrow will do. There's no point in holding up the traffic any longer, there's a hell of a jam building up already. You be on your way now, sir. We'll speak again in the morning.'

'Are you sure?' Carl looked uncertain. He gave Nelly her bag and put his hand on her shoulder. 'Would you like me to come with you to the hospital? I feel terrible about this.'

'Best get along now, sir. You can ring the young lady later, see how things are going. We'll be contacting the family straight away so your friend won't be alone for long. The most helpful thing would be if you could move your car, if that's okay with you, miss?' he said to Nelly.

'Yes, you go on, Carl, Michael will be wondering where you are. You can't miss your party. It wasn't your fault, it was Mum. I can't think what on earth she thought she was doing.'

'We saw what happened,' Greg said again. He started to move away. 'Perhaps if you come over here, sir, I can take your name and address in case we need to contact you. Then the most helpful thing would be if you were to move your car – it's blocking the whole of the one-way system.'

'Don't you need to see my license?'

'If you've got it handy that would save time, sir. Thank you very much.'

'I'll get it now. My God, what a thing to happen.'

Nelly crouched down again beside her mother. She heard the car door open and then slam shut. They were talking again, Carl's voice anxious, Greg's reassuring. 'If you back away slowly, you can move into the other lane, then the other cars can follow. I'll guide you out.'

She tugged Andy's sleeve. 'She can't breathe, you have to do something.'

The car engine started and the car began to back away. Suddenly there was more light, more space around her mother. Sonia moved her head a fraction. 'Don't try to talk, Mrs Carey,' Andy said. 'The ambulance is on its way. These fumes won't be helping. Where the hell is it?' he said to Greg, who had joined them again. 'Is someone dealing with the traffic?'

'Kingston have turned up, things are more or less under control.' Greg squatted down beside Andy. 'He's on his way.'

'She keeps trying to sit up.' Nelly wiped some blood from Sonia's mouth with her hand. Andy put his arm more securely around Sonia's shoulders and lifted her into a sitting position.

'It hurts,' Sonia whispered. Her breathing was rapid and difficult.

Nelly tried very hard not to panic. 'There's a funny noise when she breathes.'

Andy glanced at her. 'Stay cool, there's a good girl.' He said to Sonia, 'I'm just going to have a look at you ... there we are, does that hurt? And that?'

'I can't ... breathe.'

'Is it better sitting up?'

She nodded. Her skin had a bluish tinge.

A uniformed policeman came up and thrust a first-aid box into Greg's hands.

'At last. And get hold of a blanket or something, will you?' Greg opened the box and took out some gauze pads which he handed to Andy.

Nelly heard the scream of an ambulance approaching, its siren blaring.

'There they are now,' Greg said. 'They'll make you more comfortable.'

Sonia's voice was a thread of sound. 'Is he – that man—'

Andy nodded. 'It's all right, Mrs Carey. Your daughter's quite safe, I promise you. Everything's under control. Nothing to worry about.'

Sonia seemed to relax against Andy's side.

Nelly bent closer. 'I'm all right, Mamée. I'm fine. You're the one we're worried about.'

She looked at Greg. 'I still don't understand. Who are you?'

'All in good time.' He smiled at her. 'Let's get your mother seen to. Then we can talk about what's been going on,'

Nelly stood up, her knees wobbling. Suddenly she felt very pale and uncertain. Greg put his arm around her to steady her. 'There's the ambulance now. Can you hear the siren? Well done. We'll leave it to the paramedics now.'

'I have to go to the hospital with her.'

Greg nodded. 'Of course.' He looked down at her. 'Okay now? Don't need me to shove your head down or anything?'

'Here they are ... oh, thank goodness. Please help her,' she said to one of the paramedics approaching with a stretcher, 'she's my mother, she can't breathe properly.'

A crowd was gathering on the pavement. Greg gave Nelly's shoulders a squeeze. 'It's okay, sweetheart. Let them help her now.' He took his arm away. 'We'll get out of their way for a minute. You can go with her when they're ready, they just need to make her comfortable now.' He moved away, nodding at her to follow.

She watched her mother being lifted onto a stretcher. 'Mamée, I'm sorry. I'm so sorry.' She stood back, twisting her hands together.

Greg was speaking into a radio transmitter. 'He's gone on. You've told them about the delay? Don't let them cock it up, make sure they don't go in too early, we want to be sure.'

They had got Sonia onto the stretcher and were carrying her to the ambulance. 'You leave her to us now, miss, we'll take good care of her,' one of the paramedics said to Nelly.

'I want to go with her.'

'That's right, ducks, you go with them. Don't you let them tell you what to do, you 'op in there with your mum,' a woman's voice said behind her. She felt a hand at her back. 'She's going with 'er mum,' the woman addressed the small gathering of onlookers standing silently on the pavement, watching. 'Don't you worry, love, it'll all turn out all right, you'll see.'

Nelly turned towards this source of comfort, a fat, motherly-looking person carrying a bulging Sainsbury's shopping bag. She had thick, dark eyebrows although her hair, in a tidy bun, was grey. A sprig of white heather was pinned to her front. She pursed her lips and nodded. 'Most likely slipped, ducks. Them kerbs is diabolical.' She seemed somehow to have evaded the uniformed policeman who was attempting to keep the crowd at bay. Two panda cars were parked nearby, one of them on the pavement. An officer was talking to Greg and Andy who seemed to be taking notes.

Nelly began to shake. She saw her mother being lifted into the ambulance. She was propelled forward by kindly hands. She climbed in.

Chapter 29

Today is a good day

It was ten-fifteen in the evening and the policeman on duty near the arrivals gate at Terminal 3, Heathrow, was beginning to relax a little, looking forward to going home.

A young man came striding across the concourse towards him. He had just walked through the door disgorging passengers from the Air India Boeing 747 which had touched down three-quarters of an hour before. He had short dark hair, a composed manner, a lean, attractive face and steady brown eyes under level eyebrows. He was deeply sunburned and dressed in a loose white shirt and grey cotton trousers. He was carrying a backpack.

The young man stopped when he saw the policeman. 'Good evening, officer. I'm Alain Jacquemet. There's something I want to report. A murder. Well – manslaughter really. At least I think you could call it manslaughter. It happened some time ago.'

The policeman looked at him. He didn't look drunk or like one of those nutcases, but you never could tell. He might be an attention-seeker, of course, the sort who go around confessing to crimes they've seen on *Police 5* and wasting police time. However there was something about the brisk matter-of-factness of this one's manner that commanded attention.

He looked the young man over for a moment or two and made up his mind. 'You'd better come along with me, sir.'

The young man walked by his side. 'You could describe it as mother-defence. I don't know if there is such a plea but if there is I'm making it. I suppose I'll need a solicitor. Honestly, this isn't a wind-up,' he said as the policeman paused and looked down at him as though on the verge of changing his mind and sending him on his way. 'I wish to goodness it was. Please don't argue about it. I'm exhausted. It's been a long, hot flight. Could I have a cup of coffee, do you think? Then I want to talk to someone in charge. And I'd like you to ring my mother, if you would, and tell her my plane has landed safely: she's a bit of a worrier. The embassy did say they would let her know I was on my way home. I was a little surprised she wasn't here to meet me but she didn't get much notice. Maybe she was doing something else this evening.'

'I expect that was it, sir.' Who *was* this? He'd better go on being polite in case this was one of those tests they sprang on you from time to time or the guy was a minor royal travelling incognito. The way he was going on you'd think he was Lawrence of Arabia.

'Perhaps they'll let me phone home myself. My sister will probably be at home even if the others are out. I can't wait to see them all again. I suppose this will come as a bit of a blow to my mother but I made up my mind on the plane. No more running away and being scared somebody might find out. I never wanted that anyway. It was my mother; she couldn't face the consequences ... I should never have agreed to go to India, either. We'll all be much better off when this is out in the open.'

'I'm sure you're right, sir.' The policeman started pulling the hair at the nape of his neck, a habit he had when under stress.

'It doesn't do to let these things fester away, ruining your life; I've always believed in facing up to things. That's why it's been so hard going along with all this pretence. Honesty is always so much simpler in the end.'

Charlotte looked at Alain across the kitchen table and smiled. Painfully thin, conker-brown from the sun and a replica of his mother, he was tucking into Charlotte's lamb casserole as though his life depended on it.

'I haven't eaten like this for weeks.' He looked up and grinned at her disarmingly. 'Not weeks – months – actually, I don't think I've ever eaten like this. Are you a permanent fixture? Please say you are.'

She smiled. He was a charmer. But how thin he was. It must be the dysentery. She'd forgotten he hadn't been well. He had exquisite table manners, he ate neatly and with restraint despite his obvious hunger and the speed with which he was despatching most of the family's share of the food.

'I couldn't eat a thing on the plane, I was so scared. I'd made up my mind, you see. I don't know how much you know about what's been going on, past history and everything.'

'Quite a lot,' Charlotte said cautiously.

'That's a relief. I won't have to start at the beginning and explain. Now I've told the cops about it I feel like shouting it from the rooftops, it's such a relief – Luis, I mean, that awful business with Luis. I can't call him my father. I can't believe I actually killed my own father. I wonder if this is how all murderers feel. It wasn't like that at the time, I mean it didn't feel like murder, it was more like shooting a rabid dog that was biting people, or a buffalo that's suddenly gone out of control. He shot my mother, you know.'

'I know.'

He shook his head. 'He wasn't in his right mind. He wasn't always like that. I know he drank too much and he used to bash Mum about and treat her foully, but that day he really was mad. I know Mum thinks she did it for the best, making me keep quiet about it, but it meant I couldn't ever talk about how I was feeling. I was the one who killed him after all, not her. I've been feeling worse and worse until I thought I was going to go off my head.'

He shovelled another mouthful in and chewed thoughtfully, then swallowed. 'Now maybe I'll be able to talk to Mum about him and – and tell her I'm sorry. Of course I'm not sorry for stopping him from killing her, but if there had been any other way – only there wasn't. It was all I had, that machète. He was a big chap, much stronger than me.'

He put down his knife and fork. He laid them down slantways, the American way. His hands were shaking and his eyes were bright. Charlotte realised that the composure was all on the surface and that he was very near losing control.

'That wasn't the only reason I agreed to go away. It wasn't because I was scared that guy Juan was coming for me. I found out Patrick was having an affair. Can you believe that? With that nympho Laura. She wouldn't leave him alone. I couldn't stand it, knowing and thinking Mum was going to find out any minute. She's so insecure anyway I thought it would just about finish her off.'

Charlotte got up and went around the table. She put her arm around him. 'Everything will come out all right, I promise you. You were thirteen years old, for goodness' sake. You had to do what you did to protect your mother. It was incredibly brave and you've got nothing to blame yourself for. Your mother knows about Laura now, it's all out in the open and they're working it out. You've absolutely nothing to worry about anymore.'

'Do you really believe that? I wish I did. I hope she won't think I've let her down ... only I just couldn't stand it any longer.' Suddenly he pushed his chair back, buried his head in her shoulder and began to sob.

'Just you wait till Nelly comes home.' Charlotte fished in her apron pocket for a clean handkerchief. 'She's done nothing but talk about you the whole time you've been away.' She put her other arm around him and began to rock him gently, patting his back rhythmically. 'Everything's going to be all right.'

Mind you, they'd have to have a take-away if they were hungry when they got home; but too bad, let them suffer for once, it was worth giving Alain his head just to see him enjoying his food like that. So what if they had to make do with a pizza for once? It wouldn't kill them.

She looked down at the overgrown child she was holding in her arms. Bless him, she thought tenderly; then as the weight on her shoulder grew suddenly leaden, well, look at that, he's gone to sleep.

'*Je t'aime*.' Patrick said.

'Do you though?' Sonia winced. 'Ooh, that hurts.'

'Don't you know I do?'

She laughed, a tiny wisp of a laugh. 'Something seems to have gone to my head.'

Nelly gripped her mother's hand. 'Perhaps it's all that extra oxygen they gave you.'

It was eleven p.m. and the casualty department in Kingston Hospital looked and sounded like the departure lounge at Heathrow during a strike. Bells rang, teams of paramedics came and went and the triage nurse moved among the crowd like St. Peter at the gates of heaven. People sat around, bleeding and demoralised.

'This is just like *General Hospital.*' Nelly had revived after the trauma of the accident and was euphoric with relief that her mother, although injured, was apparently going to survive.

Patrick had arrived, delivered to the door, he told Nelly later, in a police car with its siren ringing and blue light flashing. He had been satisfactorily overwhelmed by the sight of his wife lying in a side-ward with a tube stuck in her chest. In fact he'd looked as though he was about to throw up or burst into tears or something. White-faced, he'd rushed to Sonia's side and seized hold of her hand, looking at her adoringly, and he hadn't let go of it since. Nelly wondered how she could ever have been such a fool as to imagine he'd stopped loving her.

Patrick sat stroking Sonia's hand. 'How long have you been here?'

'About two hours,' Nelly answered for her. 'I just phoned Sandy, by the way. She's coming over.'

'Are you sure it won't be too much for your mother?'

'She doesn't have to come in. We'll go and have a coffee or something. Leave you two together.' She'd been going to say lovebirds, but that would have been going a bit far.

They weren't lovebirds yet, but at least they were holding hands.

Sonia, propped up on pillows, opened her eyes and looked dreamily at Patrick. 'Is that ... really you, Patrick?'

'It was the last time I looked.'

'It wasn't him at all, you know. That Juan person.'

'I know, darling. Don't think about all that now. Just relax.'

'I saw Nelly ... with that man in the black car ...' She was finding it hard to talk. Patrick started to say, don't talk now, it'll wait, but she was so obviously desperate to explain. 'I thought it was Juan. I had to stop them ... and then there I was, lying in the road. I couldn't think ... how I had got there.'

'You could have been killed.' Patrick's hand shook as he pushed back Sonia's dirt-grimed hair from her forehead. 'It was incredibly brave of you.'

'I didn't want ... him ... to hurt Nelly.'

'She's broken three ribs. One of them went into her lung.' Nelly started shaking again. 'It's a pneumo-something. They had to give her oxygen. And this tube thing. And it's all my fault.' Suddenly she felt very upset.

'It's all right, Nelly,' Patrick said. 'If it's anybody's fault it's mine.'

To her surprise Nelly began to cry.

'It's the shock.' Patrick put out his arm across Sonia's body. 'I can't reach you. Come here. Mind you don't knock the tube. It goes down into this thing here.'

Digging in her jeans pocket for a hanky, Nelly edged around to his side of the bed.

He put his arm around her. 'There. You're all safe now.'

'I don't care about anything,' Nelly sniffed, 'as long as Mum is okay. I do wish Charlotte was here.' She began to cry again. Patrick hugged her gently. Sonia started to cry too.

'For heaven's sake. You'll get me chucked out.'

Nelly started to giggle. She blew her nose. Patrick dried Sonia's eyes with his hanky. He looked totally shame-faced. He said to her mother, 'This is all my fault. If I hadn't been so proud and so stubborn, if I'd told you as soon as I knew that Juan was out of the picture, you wouldn't have thought that man was him. I'm so sorry. I was angry. If I had, this wouldn't have happened. I feel terrible about it.'

Nelly looked from Patrick to her mother. 'What are you talking about? What business?'

Patrick said, 'We've got something to tell you. Perhaps we should have told you before but Sonia didn't want you to worry unnecessarily and we didn't think you were in danger; it was Alain they were supposed to be gunning for.'

'What? Why? What's so special about Alain?'

Patrick looked at Sonia. She gave the smallest possible nod. 'I think I'd better start at the beginning,' he said. 'Nelly, this may come as a bit of a shock. You have to understand that Alain had no choice. He did it to save your mother's life.'

CHARLOTTE PRESSED the receiver to her ear. Nelly's words were falling over each other in her excitement. Which was rather wonderful. And sweet of her to take the trouble to ring.

'Where are you phoning from?'

'There's a booth outside the refectory. Has Alain eaten all our dinner? I bet he has. I can't wait to see him. I'm meeting Sandy here in a minute. I do wish you were here, Charlotte, I can't tell you what it's been like, Mum nearly getting killed and the police and everything and what Alain did, and now Mum and Patrick are all over each other like honeymooners. I don't know where to put myself, it's so embarrassing.'

'But that's good, isn't it?'

'Yes, but the whole accident thing was my fault. She thought that Juan nutcase had got hold of me so she hurled herself onto the bonnet of Carl's car to stop him. Wasn't it brave of her? I could never have done that, not in a million years.'

'Shows she cares, doesn't it?'

'Yeah yeah.' Her off-handedness was belied by the happiness in her voice. 'And d'you know what? Patrick's going to buy Mr Dennison's house. We're all going to move there. Mum is over the moon, you should have seen her face. Apparently she's loved the house for ages. Well, I knew she wasn't that keen on Patrick's. I tried not to look too chuffed. I didn't want to hurt his feelings. We're going to build him another shed to write in. Oh Charlotte, it's going to be ace. The only thing is, all this is my fault and I feel just awful about that.'

Charlotte nearly said, but it's just as much Patrick's. If he had told your mother that Juan was dead, none of this would have happened. It was just like Nelly not to let herself off the hook by putting the blame on him. But it really was time they sat down as a family and pooled every bit of information they'd got. Like that letter Alain had written to Nelly which she'd never told Sonia about. Nelly was probably feeling bad about that too. Getting everything out in the open was the only way things were ever going to get properly tidied up around here.

Charlotte went back to her cooking. She'd been so

preoccupied with feeding Alain that she hadn't had time to put the finishing touches to her sauce.

Perhaps they'd better get Laura to sit in on it too, she thought sardonically, adding an extra sliver of chilli to the *Poulet Basquaise*.

SANDY UNWRAPPED her third KitKat bar. 'Good grief, Nell, you're winding me up,'

'Honest injun.' Nelly and Sandy were sitting on two hard wooden chairs in the hospital canteen, their feet propped up on each other's chair-rungs. 'And then he put his arms around her – and she would have put her arms around him if she could, only she can't move about much at the moment – and they both cried.'

'Strewth. I'm exhausted just listening to this.'

'And guess what?'

'What?'

'*She's* here.'

'Who?'

'Laura.'

'She can't be.'

'She is. I saw her in reception a few minutes ago.'

'What – ill? Visiting? What?'

'Just waiting around. Not ill, she looked the picture of health to me.'

'You don't think she'll try anything, do you?'

'What kind of thing?' Nelly sipped her coffee.

'I dunno – inject air into your mum's drip, that kind of thing.'

'For goodness' sake, Sandy, of course she won't.'

'I dunno. It happens.' Sandy popped her last piece of Kitkat into her mouth.

'Only on cop shows. Laura's not like that, she's a wimp. Anyway, she's not on a drip.'

Sandy chewed and swallowed. 'But what's Laura doing here?'

'Can't wait to find out if my mum's pegged it, I expect. Somebody probably heard about the accident and told her.'

Sandy screwed the silver paper wrapper into a ball and dropped it on the table. 'Jeez, she must be keen. Perhaps she really loves him.'

'She's got no business loving him, he's got a wife already.'

'You're awful hard, Nell, you know that? Maybe it isn't all her fault, maybe he led her on.'

'She looks well able to take care of herself to me.'

'Do you think we ought to tell Patrick she's here?'

'No! Hang on, we won't have to – there she is. Help, Sandy, she's coming this way.'

'Where?'

'There, over there. She's just come in.'

'D'you think she's seen us?'

'She's going to the counter.'

'Let's go.'

'I'm not going anywhere. I haven't finished my coffee.'

'Oh God, she's seen us. She's coming over.'

'She'll lose her place in the queue. Hello, Miss, what a surprise to see you here.'

'Hello, you two.' Laura stood beside the table, smiling nervously and fiddling with her car keys. 'I've been visiting a friend.'

Nelly frowned. No, she hadn't. Visiting was over hours ago.

Laura looked as good as she always did, blast her. She had on tight blue flares and a white tee shirt, a low-slung belt with a silver buckle and over that a slim-fitting, grey woollen jacket that showed off her tiny little waist.

Nelly didn't want Patrick to see her looking like this. Which was nonsense, of course, he knew exactly how Laura looked, it was just – tonight, Nelly didn't want him seeing her looking like this tonight.

Laura fiddled with the clasp of her grey shoulder bag. 'I heard something about an accident; is that why you're here?' She glanced from Nelly to Sandy and back again. 'Has someone been hurt?'

Nelly's lips tightened. Laura knew perfectly well about the accident. She was fishing.

'I heard them talking at the desk. I was worried—'

Perhaps she wasn't lying, perhaps she had been visiting a friend. 'It's my mother. Sonia Carey? You did know Patrick had got married?'

'Yes – oh yes, of course.' Laura was apparently finding it difficult to breathe. 'Can I sit down for a moment, do you mind?' She sank into a chair and leant her elbow on their table. She stared down at the table, her face drawn and white.

Sandy frowned. 'Can we get you something? A drink or something to eat?'

Nelly scowled at her but Sandy made a What? face with big eyes, and shrugged.

Laura took a breath. 'I'd like some water. Could you, Sandra? Thanks.'

Sandy got up and left. Nelly said, 'My mother's badly hurt. I expect you're pleased to hear that.'

'Nelly! Of course I'm not pleased, that's a terrible thing to say.' She'd gone red now. 'I was worried about Patrick because of course I know him, we were engaged once, you know, of course I was worried.' She closed her eyes then opened them again. 'But I'm horrified to hear your mother – that's terrible. How bad is it? I imagine – if you're in here – perhaps—'

'She's not dying, if that's what you mean.'

'Oh, that's – oh good, Patrick must be—'

'He's devastated. He adores her, you know.'

Sandy came back, holding a glass of water. Laura took it from her with a nod of thanks and drank. 'Thanks, Sandra. It was just—'

'I know. The shock.' Sandy sat down again.

'I must go.' Laura fished in her shoulder bag for a handkerchief and blew her nose. She put it away and looked at Nelly. 'Nelly. I never meant—'

Nelly looked away.

'Oh well.' Laura stood up. 'Please tell – please give your parents my good wishes.' She said awkwardly, 'I do hope your mother will be better soon. Well, I must go. Bye then.'

Sandy gave a sort of grunt. Nelly said nothing. Laura looked from Nelly to Sandy and turned away, looking as though she was about to cry.

Nelly lowered her head. 'And good riddance.'

Sandy winced. 'You look like a bull about to charge. Calm down, Nell. She did look awfully upset. P'raps she really loves him.'

'Well, she can't. What about Mum?'

'I know. Of course. Hey Nelly, did you see her boots? Western boots, sort of sparkly ... whatever else she is, you can't deny she's a cool dresser. Oh, don't let's waste time worrying about boring old Laura, this is supposed to be a celebration, yeah? This is a good day.'

'Yeah: my mum nearly got herself killed in a road accident—'

'And Patrick and her have made it up and your bro's

home – bless his cotton socks – can't wait to see him again ...'

'Oh, Sandy – Alain! You'll never believe ...' Nelly stopped. This wasn't the time. She would tell Sandy the rest of the story when she'd had time to absorb it herself. She needed to think through the implications, what the truth coming out would mean for Alain, for the whole family. She changed tack. 'You like Alain, don't you?'

Sandy bent and picked up her silver paper ball which had fallen on the floor. When she came up again her face was pink. 'Of course I like him. Why?'

'No reason. This is a good day, that's all. I'll go with that.'

Chapter 30

The art of ending

'I need you to explain about Carl,' Nelly said to Patrick.

They had left the car in the car park at Kingston Gate and were walking slowly up the hill through the trees. They were on their way to visit Sonia who was still in hospital, but first, Patrick had said, there were one or two things they needed to straighten out. A walk in Richmond Park had seemed the right way to go about it.

It was half-past ten on Saturday morning, a beautiful summer day, the cloudless sky serene and blue. They had left the track so as to avoid the people beginning to fill the pathways. Nelly, trying not to skip, thought how much she loved this time of year, the trees full, their leaves darkening, the windless air warm on her skin. For the first time in a long time she felt at ease, almost, she hesitated to admit, *happy*.

'How did the police know he wasn't Juan, for a start?' Nelly couldn't believe all the drama that had been going on completely without her knowledge. She didn't know which she was feeling most: irritation over the fact that they had once again been treating her like a six-year-old or relief that after all, her mother was going to be all right. She still felt shaky inside when she remembered the accident.

It was a bit thick, nobody telling her they'd thought Carl was this Juan person. Suppose he had been? She could have been halfway back to St. Colombe by now with a knife at her throat. Or at the bottom of the river with her feet in a block of cement. Her mother and Patrick didn't seem to have thought about that. 'He could have been. He could have done anything. Nobody seems to have cared.'

Patrick looked convincingly appalled. 'Of *course* we cared. Why do you think we got on to the police in the first place?'

'Why didn't you tell me? *I* was the person he'd made contact with.'

'Sonia thought first of Alain because—'

'Because she always thinks first of Alain.' Nelly picked up a stick lying on a hummock of grass, probably abandoned by some exhausted dog owner, and started beating angrily at the tall grass.

'*No*. Because he was the one who actually – who—'

'Who killed my father.'

'His father too.' Patrick stopped and faced her so that she had to stop and face him too. 'You do know what happened, don't you? You do know Alain had to do it, that he saved your mother's life? Your father had already shot her once; remember her shoulder?'

'I thought she'd hurt it in a fall. That's what she said when we met up afterwards.' Nelly scowled. 'I suppose Alain's known all this time. He never told me.'

'Your father would have killed her if Alain hadn't stopped him.'

Nelly could feel her face twisting itself into a horrible sneering expression. She couldn't stop it, she didn't quite know who the sneer was for, it was just that she wasn't going to give in that easily, not for anybody, even Patrick. She turned away. 'I haven't had a chance to talk to Alain about it. Not properly. Not with the accident and him being half dead with jet lag and things. I'll get him when he wakes up, make him tell me everything.'

'He *wants* to tell you. He's dreadfully unhappy about it.'

'He wasn't too tired to talk to you, then.' She could feel Patrick glancing sideways at her mutinous face. She knew she ought to lighten up a bit, that she was spoiling everything, but she just couldn't. I hate them, she thought, clenching her fists, the whole lot of them.

Patrick sighed. 'It wasn't planned. He came down to get a drink of water. I was in the kitchen and we had about three minutes' conversation. He told me he'd made a statement to the police and said how badly he felt about everything, and then he went back to bed.'

Nelly looked away. 'Did you talk about *her*?'

'Who? Oh – Laura.'

'Yes. Her.' She gave him a look of deepest disapproval.

Patrick shoved his hands deep in his trouser pockets. 'It wasn't relevant. That has nothing to do with Alain.'

Good, he was starting to get annoyed.

'I don't think he even knows about it yet. It's none of his business.'

None of yours, either, she could hear him thinking. Nelly strode ahead. 'It is our business if it's going to mess up our family.'

Oh jeez. What if all that lovey-dovey stuff in the hospital was just relief because Sonia wasn't going to die? What if he didn't mean it? Maybe he'd gone on like that because he felt sorry for her. He wouldn't necessarily stop loving her completely, even if he left her to go to Laura. So what he was feeling could have been real, just not enough. Not enough.

Behind her Patrick said, 'Nelly.'

'Yup?' She slowed down again.

'Look,' he said.

Her stomach tightened. He was going to tell her he was going to leave Sonia. She turned to face him, her eyebrows raised. 'Yup?'

'Things aren't that simple.' He had gone quite red, for him; he was usually rather pale. There was sweat on his forehead. His hair had grown rather long and it looked a mess, as though he'd washed it in the shower and hadn't had time to dry it properly so it stuck out in all the wrong places. Whatever she did she mustn't feel sorry for him.

'Yes, they are.' She turned away. 'I don't want to talk about it anymore.' She caught sight of his hand, hanging by his side, useless suddenly. It hung down, the fingers slightly curled. The sight of it made her want to cry. It was the hand which had cuddled Laura, which had betrayed her mother.

'Nelly,' Patrick said gently, exactly as if he knew what she was thinking.

Don't speak my name. Don't look at me. She wanted to be away from there, a hundred miles away from him, out of reach. Only it wasn't her or her mother he was reaching for; it was Laura.

She made a huge effort to pull herself together. 'It's okay,' she said grudgingly. She swished her stick around as though nothing mattered very much. 'Don't let's talk about it anymore.' If he wanted to go, there was nothing they could do to stop him. She would never understand. She walked on slowly. 'I should never have agreed to go to that party. It was my fault she got hurt.'

Patrick ambled by her side, his hands in his pockets again, looking at the ground. 'You didn't know. We didn't tell you because we didn't want to frighten you, and we really did think you'd decided not to see those chaps again. I should have realised you didn't mean it.' She could tell by his voice that he was smiling.

'I did at the time.' It was because of him and Laura she'd changed her mind; it was because she was hurt, because she was jealous.

'I know. Look, it was an accident, nobody's fault, right?'

'Okay.' She pulled a grass stalk and began to chew it. 'I really liked Carl,' she said nonchalantly, looking ahead.

'I'm sorry.' She could feel him looking at her.

'I can't believe he's a crook. Michael maybe – but Carl? Are you sure they haven't made a mistake? He's nice, Patrick, he's funny.'

'Sweetheart, I'm sorry.' He touched her arm gently. 'I'm afraid the criminal instinct is no respecter of persons.'

'But he's so sort of well-spoken, and he was so – kind of – charming.'

'Beware of charm, it's a very dangerous thing. Crippen had it in spades, I believe.'

Nelly's eyebrows went up. If that was true then it was a good thing Patrick didn't have criminal tendencies, there'd be no hope for any of them.

'Why are you looking like that?' Patrick said, but she had moved ahead to fondle the ears of a golden retriever who had lolloped up and was gambolling around her, taking absolutely no notice of a furious-sounding lady in a headscarf who was trying to call him to heel. Nelly took a look at his name tag.

Patrick smiled. 'Better let him go, his owner's about to have a heart attack.'

'Off you go then, Benjie.' Nelly watched with regret as the dog bounded away. She wondered how Maisie would cope if she had a dog. Would they let her?

She joined Patrick again and they walked on. 'So it was a drugs bust they were planning, was it? At Carl's party? I still don't see why he was sitting outside our house. Carl, I mean. That's what started all this. If I hadn't recognised him in the pub and gone to talk to him, none of this would have happened.' She bent her head and scuffed the turf with the heel of her boot.

'They did explain about that.' Patrick stood jingling the car keys in his pocket, gazing into the middle distance. After a moment or two he glanced at his watch. 'Perhaps we'd better be getting back.'

Nelly stood waiting for him to make up his mind.

'I was just thinking about *Bullet*. That inspector chap has given me some excellent ideas for Jimmy Bains. His couldn't-care-less manner, and his accent, he's got just the right accent. Must make a note of that.'

'Who's Jimmy Bains?'

'Who's – Oh, didn't I tell you? I thought Chandler needed somebody new to pit his wits against, someone younger: Lincoln Clerihew is too old really, not subtle enough, a bit of a plod.'

'Patrick.'

'Yes?'

'What are you talking about?'

'Sorry. Come on, let's turn around. What was it you asked me?'

'I was asking,' Nelly said bitterly, 'as if you cared about anything except your blasted book, what Carl was doing at our house.'

'I really am so sorry, Nelly. I know I can't possibly

expect you to understand.' (Now he was patronising her.) 'It's just such a relief to be able to think about Chandler again: you know, after all the distractions.'

He actually managed to sound penitent. Distractions. He called his wife nearly getting killed a *distraction*. He was absolutely hopeless.

'It wasn't our house he was watching; it was a house up the road. He didn't want to look conspicuous so he decided to park further down the road and by sheer chance happened to end up outside our house.'

'What was he doing watching their house anyway?'

Patrick shrugged. 'I really don't know anything about it. It was something to do with their drugs operation, that's all. Take it from me, it was probably something incredibly boring they'd been told to do by their superiors. They're really very small beer, your friends. I'm afraid they'll be going down for a good stretch before too long.'

It was blindingly obvious that he didn't want her to be dazzled. 'Really? Come on, it's only drugs.'

'Nelly!'

'We-ell. It seems such a fuss about nothing.'

'About – Nelly, you and I have got to have a long talk. Have you *any idea*—'

'I'm only *kidding*, Patrick, God, take a chill pill, will you?' But it wasn't just drugs, was it? They'd tried to lure her and Sandy into escorting revolting old guys for money. And worse. She'd have to say something to the parents eventually. But not now. Not today. 'Go on about Jimmy Bains.' She threw the stick up into the air and caught it again.

'I'm serious, Nelly.'

'I know.' She was beginning to feel better again. After all, Sonia was going to be okay which was the really important thing; and there was always Charlotte to have a moan to. And Sandy.

'Oh!'

'What's the matter?' Patrick stopped again.

'She *can* stay? Charlotte, I mean. Can't she? She won't have to go, once Mum's better, will she?' Nelly couldn't imagine life without Charlotte.

Patrick considered. 'If your mother's off to art college I guess we'll need her more than ever.'

'If Mum's *what?*' Nelly's eyes widened. Her mouth fell open.

He gave her a mischievous look. 'She only told me last night.'

'What is she *like?* Why didn't she *tell* me?' Nelly's face reddened with indignation.

Patrick put his hands up, mock defensive. 'She says she didn't want people to be disappointed if she didn't get in.'

'Well that is ace. It really is ace. So *that*'s what all that canvas was for; she said she was making a tent. How dare she take the mick like that?'

Patrick grinned suddenly. 'D'you think she'll get all arty and start wearing striped leggings and things?'

'Or dying her hair pink.' She set off again, surprised by a prick of jealousy. Hell, she rather fancied going to art college herself.

Patrick grinned. 'I rather like the idea of your mother with pink hair.'

They were nearing the car park. Patrick jingled the car keys in his pocket. He always got ready too early for things. If he was travelling by train he'd get his ticket out long before he got to the barrier. It was quite sweet actually.

Nearing the car park he stiffened and his pace slowed. She sensed the change in him and looked at him in surprise.

He'd gone alert and rigid, the way Maisie did when she spotted a bird within pouncing distance.

'What's the matter?'

Someone was walking towards them. She was wearing her blue jeans and the Fairisle cardigan over a white tee shirt. And the boots. She stopped in front of them. 'Hello Patrick.'

He had tensed all over as though he was suddenly cold. 'Hello Laura.'

Nelly turned aside. 'I'll get lost for a bit.'

Patrick put out his hand and grasped her arm. 'Don't go. Laura and I have nothing to say to each other that you can't hear.'

A look of bewilderment came into Laura's face. A flush rose up her neck. Nelly cringed inside at his cruelty. Laura had asked for it, she'd known about Sonia, but why did they have to do this? Why did men always have to get into this mess and hurt everybody? She could feel Laura's hurt and humiliation. To her dismay she felt a rush of real pity for her.

Laura said, and Nelly couldn't help thinking it was brave of her in the circumstances, 'I was terribly sorry to hear about your wife. I did actually come to the hospital to see if there was anything I could do. A friend phoned, who happened to be passing and saw. It was on the news, about the accident and everything. Is she all right?'

'She's going to be fine. Just fine.'

Nelly's heart was thumping.

'Oh, I'm glad. That's very good news.' Laura looked at Nelly. 'Do you think I could talk to your father alone for a few minutes? Just two minutes, that's all.'

Patrick said brusquely, 'I haven't any secrets from Nell. If you have something to say, you can say it in front of her.'

Laura recoiled as though he'd punched her in the face. 'Why have you changed?' She glanced at Nelly as if hoping for an explanation. 'You haven't rung. You said you would and I've been waiting ... waiting ...' Her voice broke. 'What have they done to you? Please, Patrick, come back. I'm begging you; I didn't mean what I said. Just come back. I won't ask for anything. Only I must be with you.'

Cringing inside, Nelly examined her feet.

'I'm sorry,' Patrick said, still in that cold, cruel voice. 'It's over, finished. I'm not going to see you again. Please don't phone or write, or make any attempt to contact me. I shan't read your letters or answer your calls. I don't want to see you again.'

'But I love you! What will I do, how will I live without you?' Tears were running down her babyish face, twisted now with grief. 'Don't do this, Patrick. You don't mean it. You can't mean it.'

'Look ... you'll manage. You've managed before and you will again. You're young and attractive ... you've got your whole life in front of you.'

'I don't want my life if I can't have you.'

'That's stupid talk,' Patrick said roughly. 'I'm sorry to be brutal, Laura, but this is the only way I can do this. My wife is fragile and hurt and she needs help, and I love her. I love her, Laura. I don't love you.'

Laura pulled a hanky out of her pocket and blew her nose. She turned aside for a moment, sobbing, trying to regain control. Nelly thought, how will I ever be able to look at her in class again?

Laura turned back to face Patrick again. 'You've changed your tune!' She turned to Nelly, dabbing frantically at her wet cheeks. 'For weeks and weeks he's been saying he loved me, he needed me. What is all this?'

'I'm sorry if I've been unfair.' His voice wavered slightly. He said more strongly, 'I expect this is all my fault. If you feel like hating me then go ahead, I don't care how badly you think of me. It would probably be the best thing in the circumstances. But you've got to leave me, and my family, alone.'

Laura had been listening to this with an expression of incredulity which hardened now into one of anger and disgust. 'You *bastard.*' She turned and walked away from them, stumbling over the tussocks of grass.

Nelly glanced sideways at Patrick. He had relaxed his icy demeanour and was trembling. There were tears in his eyes. He turned off the path and sat down on a rock. He seemed to be having difficulty breathing. 'Give her a minute. Wait till her car's gone.' He covered his face with his hands.

Nelly didn't dare speak.

After a minute or two he took his hands away from his face. 'How are we doing?'

'She's gone,' Nelly said, very gently. She put out her hand and helped him to his feet.

~

I hope you enjoyed reading ***Shadows on the Wall.***
Would you mind leaving a rating or short review?

Your feedback would be very much appreciated.

Also by Bonar Ash

Now I Can See the Moon

Seventeen-year-old Milly is adored by (almost) everyone at Half Moon House, the sprawling family home in the Surrey countryside she shares with an eclectic mix of family and friends.

Milly's life appears idyllic, but her mother's violent death casts a dark shadow over her life. Her days are filled with torment at the hands of of Pascale, her mother's childhood nurse. When night falls, she is plagued by mysterious and terrifying nightmares. Has Milly done something unforgivable, something she cannot remember?

When a charismatic older man arrives to fulfil a family obligation, a dark secret from his past is revealed, testing Milly's trust to the limit.

Can she escape the ghosts of her past and find true happiness?

Discover more

Please visit **Bonarash.com** to learn more about me, my writing life, and my forthcoming novels.

Printed in Great Britain
by Amazon